THE OM MALA
MEANINGS OF THE MYSTIC SOUND

The OM Mala

Meanings of the Mystic Sound

Nityānanda Miśra

BLOOMSBURY

NEW DELHI • LONDON • OXFORD • NEW YORK • SYDNEY

BLOOMSBURY INDIA
Bloomsbury Publishing India Pvt. Ltd
Second Floor, LSC Building No. 4
DDA Complex, Pocket C – 6 & 7
Vasant Kunj, New Delhi 110070

BLOOMSBURY, BLOOMSBURY INDIA and the Diana logo are trademarks of Bloomsbury Publishing Plc

First published in India 2018
This edition published 2018

ISBN: PB: 978-93-87471-84-9; eBook: 978-93-87471-85-6

2 4 6 8 10 9 7 5 3 1

Printed and bound in India by Replika Press Pvt Ltd

To my mother

"I wish I never get *moksha*
but am born again and again,
each time as your beloved child
your godly love may I attain."

Note to the reader

As I expect this book to be read by laypersons as well as scholars, I follow some practices for better readability—

1) A simple Roman transliteration scheme without diacritics is used. Exceptions are the second line of the section headings, the etymologies, and the full derivation of the word OM in the last section where IAST diacritics are used for clarity.

2) Devanagari is used in section headings and at some places in the explanations to distinguish between words with the same Roman transliterations.

3) The book has no footnotes or endnotes. Instead, the notes are separately published as a PDF under my Academia page at `http://independent.academia.edu/MisraNityanand`.

4) Each section in the book is typeset completely on a single page or on a spread (facing verso and recto pages).

5) The *Bhagavad Gita* is referred to as simply *Gita*.

6) The *Srimadbhagavata Purana* is referred to as *Bhagavata Purana*, while the *Devi Bhagavata Purana* is referred to as *Devi Bhagavata*.

7) The *Brihad Yogi Yajnavalkya Smriti* is referred to as simply *Yogi Yajnavalkya Smriti*.

8) 'Veda-s' and 'Vedic texts' refer to the *Samhita*-s, the *Brahmana*-s, the *Aranyaka*-s, and the Upanishad-s.

Preface

This is a special book, for it is written to explain just one word—OM. And yet, this book is not even the tip of the iceberg. I have spent hardly a few months on this book, whereas even a lifetime is not sufficient to understand OM. The *Madhyandina Samhita* of the Shukla Yajur Veda ends by proclaiming that OM is the Brahman, the sky. The metaphor is apt, for there is no limit to the infinite sky and likewise there is no limit to the meanings of OM. OM is the topic of deliberation in many Upanishad-s, the crest-jewels of Indian philosophy. OM is described vividly in the Smriti-s, which follow the meaning of the Veda-s—as Kalidasa states in the *Raghuvamsha*. OM is praised in the *Ramayana* and the *Mahabharata*, the two unparalleled epics of India. OM is described in many ways in the Purana-s, the bedrock of Hinduism and Indian culture. OM is extolled in the philosophy of Yoga, the gift of India to mankind. OM is celebrated in Tantra, the esoteric and mystical spiritual path. OM is the object of devotion in Vaishnavism, Shaivism, and Shaktism—traditions enlivened by *bhakti*. OM is a part of chants in Jainism and Buddhism and is also prominent as the one word, or *Ik Onkar*, in Sikhism. OM commands the reverence of all major sects of Hinduism and all major religions of India. No book, therefore, can even remotely present a complete picture of this mystic sound which yogi-s "always meditate upon", as a popular verse says.

Preface

So what is this book about then? OM is known by countless names in Sanskrit texts, and most of these names can be interpreted in several ways. This book presents eighty-four names of OM and their meanings in accordance with multiple Sanskrit texts including not only Hindu scriptures but also secular texts like dictionaries, poems, plays, and treatises on music, grammar, and Ayurveda. While the names in this book are solely from Sanskrit texts and their meanings are also in accordance with Sanskrit grammar, I give examples from texts of other languages wherever appropriate. Apart from the Upanishad-s and the Purana-s, whose treatment of OM is the focus of many books, this book also draws from Sanskrit commentaries as well as Yoga and Tantra works which have explained OM and its names in many unique ways.

This book has 109 sections, each section presents one or more specific meanings for a single name or multiple related names of OM. Apart from the meanings, each of the 109 sections offers a short explanation, a list of corresponding traditions, and translations of relevant quotations from Sanskrit texts. Most sections also provide the etymology of the name(s) explained in the section. A *mala* used for chanting a mantra typically has 109 beads, of which 108 beads are used for chanting and the head bead (*sumeru*) is used to keep track of rounds of chanting. After every complete round of chanting, the direction of moving the beads is reversed. One round of chanting covers 108 beads, beginning with the bead on one side of the *sumeru* and ending with the bead on the other side of the *sumeru*. The first 108 sections in this book are like the 108 chanting beads of a *mala*, and the last section is like the *sumeru* bead. As OM is essentially a Sanskrit word, best illuminated by Sanskrit grammar, this last section aptly explains nineteen meanings of the word OM as per the Sanskrit grammar tradition.

This book has many translations and explanations of Sanskrit words, phrases, sentences, and verses. I am a Vaishnava initiated in the tradition of Ramananda and have an unshakeable belief in the *Vishishtadvaita* philosophy. For me, as for millions of Ramanandi-s, Rama alone is the Supreme Brahman. Therefore, I have adhered to dualistic Vaishnava interpretations in my translations and explanations wherever there is a difference of opinion among interpreters. Most of the translations I offer are not literal (*shabda-anuvada*) but present the essence of the original text (*bhava-anuvada*). For additional clarity, I supply ellipsis wherever needed and also abridge the translations.

I hope the readers of this book will benefit from it. I have tried my best to keep the draft free from errors, but some errors may have still escaped the multiple rounds of proofreading. I request readers who come across any error in this edition to bring it to my notice or the publisher's notice so that it can be corrected in the next edition. For this, the reader may contact me on Twitter (`@MisraNityanand`) or write to the publisher.

Just like the meanings of OM are infinite, the list of those who have contributed to this book is endless. I cannot thank every one of them, but can only mention the most prominent ones. My Gurudeva, Jagadguru Ramanandacharya Swami Ramabhadracharya, comes first to my mind. The astounding beginning of his Sanskrit commentary on the *Isha Upanishad* is the inspiration behind this book. OM and my *ishta* Rama are the next to be mentioned, they are one and the same (pp. 38, 40, 42) and it is their grace which enabled me to complete this book in what has been the most challenging phase of my personal life. It is said that the child is the father of the man. I have experienced this firsthand, thanks to my father, who has taught me so many things in the past, and to my children Nilayaa and Niramay, who teach me something new every day. Another source of learning something new every day is the *Bharatiya-vidvat-parishat* mailing list, members of which have helped me on countless occasions while writing this book. I have relied on the works of many great commentators of the past and the present for my understanding of Sanskrit texts, I bow my head to all of them in reverence. The ever-helpful and resourceful Ami Ganatra has proofread the draft of this edition and offered many valuable comments, for which I cannot thank her enough. Another round of proofreading has been done by Arun Ayyar, whose dedication towards Krishna Yajur Veda chanting is an inspiration for everybody. Heartfelt gratitude goes to my friend Maulik Mavani who has contributed a sketch to this book. Pranav Niranjani and Sudhir Kuduchkar of Three Dot Designs have ably designed the book cover, I am heavily indebted to them. Thanks also also due to Praveen Tiwari and the Bloomsbury team for publishing the book.

My mother is motherhood personified. To her, this book is dedicated.

Nityananda Misra

Mumbai, December 2017

The OM Mala

(1)

om, tridaivat [y] a

(*ओम्, त्रिदैवत/त्रिदैवत्य* = *om, tridaivat[y]a*)

MEANING

" [having] three gods—Brahma, Vishnu, and Shiva. "

EXPLANATION

This is probably the most popular meaning of OM. The single syllable OM is composed of three sounds—*a* (as in ***a**lone*), *u* (as in *f**u**ll*), and *m* (as in ***m**ind*). As per Sanskrit *sandhi* rules, when the sounds *a* and *u* come together, the resulting sound is *o* (as in the German word ***O**ber*). Thus, *a* + *u* + *m* results in OM.

The three component sounds of OM represent Vishnu, Shiva, and Brahma, respectively. In addition to the *Yogi Yajnavalkya Smriti* and Purana-s which offer this explanation, the meanings of the three component sounds are also attested in secular sources like lexicons. As per the *Ekakshara Kosha*, the word *a* means Vishnu and the word *u* means Shiva. The lexicon gives three meanings of the word *ma* (Shiva, the moon, and Brahma) from which Brahma is taken as the meaning of the sound *m* in OM.

As per Smriti and Tantra texts, OM is also known as *tri-daivata* and *tri-daivatya.* The words *daivata* and *daivatya* are derived from the root √*div*, which is also the root of the word *deva* ("god"). The Sanskrit word *deva* is believed to be cognate with the Greek word *theos* and Latin word *deus,* with which the English word *divine* is related. Although the root √*div* has ten meanings in Sanskrit, in this context it means "to shine". Therefore, the names *tri-daivata* and *tri-daivatya* mean "having three shining gods (Brahma, Vishnu, and Shiva)".

As Brahma (the creator), Vishnu (the preserver), and Shiva (the destroyer) represent three aspects of the same Supreme Brahman in Hinduism, the purport is that OM is the Supreme Brahman. This will appear as a consistent theme across many meanings presented in this book.

TRADITION

Smriti, Purana, Tantra, commentaries.

ETYMOLOGY

a + u + m → om; tri + daivata → tridaivata;
tri + daivatya → tridaivatya.

a ▸ Vishnu; ***u*** ▸ Shiva; ***m*** ▸ Brahma. ***tri*** ▸ three; ***daivata*** ▸ deity. ***daivatya*** ▸ deity.

QUOTES

"OM is known as *tridaivata*. OM is also called *tridaivatya*; as it is Brahma, Vishnu, and Shiva."

—*Yogi Yajnavalkya Smriti*

"The sound *a* is said to be Vishnu, the sound *u* to be Shiva, and the sound *m* denotes Brahma. All three are meant by OM."

—Purana-s

"OM is Vishnu, Brahma, and Shiva."

—*Markandeya Purana*

"There is a threefold form in the sound OM; 'threefold' means consisting of Brahma, Vishnu, and Shiva."

—*Linga Purana*, its commentary

"The sound OM is called *tridaivata*."

—*Bija Varna Abhidhana*

(2)
om, udgitha, tryavasthana
(ओम्, उद्गीथ, त्र्यवस्थान = *om, udgītha, tryavasthāna*)

MEANING

"the three *loka*-s (realms)."

EXPLANATION

The word *loka*, literally "that which is seen or known", comes from the root √*lok* which means "to see". The Veda-s mention the three *loka*-s as *prithvi* (earth), *antariksha* (atmosphere), and *dyauh* (heaven). Elsewhere, the three *loka*-s are listed as *svarga* (heaven), *prithvi* (earth), and *patala* (the netherworld). Although sometimes seven and even fourteen *loka*-s are mentioned, the expression "three *loka*-s" is frequently used to mean the whole universe or creation. The three realms are also known as *triloki* in Hindu cosmology.

Earth, atmosphere, and heaven are also known respectively as *bhur*, *bhuvah*, and *svah*—the three *maha-vyahriti*-s (great mystical words) recited as part of the popular *Gayatri Mantra*. A common misconception is that the three *maha-vyahriti*-s are "added" to the Vedic mantra. The complete *Gayatri Mantra* with the *maha-vyahriti*-s is present in the thirty-sixth chapter of the Shukla Yajur Veda. The same chapter has the *Shanti Mantra* (shortened as *OM shantih shantih shantih*) which starts with the other three names—*dyauh*, *antariksha*, and *prithivi*.

As per numerous Hindu scriptures, the word OM means the three *loka*-s. Specifically, *a* means the earth, *u* the atmosphere, and *m* heaven. One of the most popular names of OM in the Upanishad-s is *udgitha*. Its three parts—*ut*, *gi*, and *tha*—

are equated with the heaven, the atmosphere, and the earth respectively in the *Chandogya Upanishad*. OM is believed to pervade the three worlds, which arose from OM as per the *Gopatha Brahmana* of the *Atharva Veda* (p. 16). This notion of OM pervading the universe is reflected in several names like *akshara* (p. 84), *hamsa* (p. 124), *sarvavyapi* (p. 156), *vishnu* (p. 206), and *vishva* (p. 208). As OM resides in all the three realms, it is also called *tryavasthana*, meaning "having three dwellings".

TRADITION

Upanishad, Smriti, Purana.

ETYMOLOGY

a + u + m → om; ut + gī + tha → udgītha;
tri + avasthāna → tryavasthāna.

a ▸ earth; ***u*** ▸ atmosphere; ***m*** ▸ heaven. ***ut*** ▸ heaven; ***gī*** ▸ atmosphere; ***tha*** ▸ earth. ***tri*** ▸ three; ***avasthāna*** ▸ dwelling.

QUOTES

"In *udgitha*, the heaven alone is *ut*, the atmosphere is *gi*, and the earth is *tha*."

—*Chandogya Upanishad*

"OM is called *tryavasthana*; as it is the earth (*bhuh*), the atmosphere (*bhuvah*), and the heaven (*svah*)."

—*Yogi Yajnavalkya Smriti*

"The sound *a* is the earth, the sound *u* is said to be the atmosphere, and the consonant *m* is proclaimed to be heaven."

—Purana-s

"OM—this means the three realms."

—Purana-s

(3)

om, tridhama, trimukha

(ओम्, त्रिधाम, त्रिमुख = *om, tridhāma, trimukha*)

MEANING

"**1** the three *agni*-s (sacred fires)

2 the father, the mother, and the guru."

EXPLANATION

Fire has held an important place in Hinduism since time immemorial. The Rig Veda starts with a prayer to Agni, the fire god. Hindus who practise *agnihotra* use three fires. The *garhapatya* ("with the householder") fire is always kept burning, the *dakshina* ("southern") fire is used to make offerings to ancestors, and the *ahavaniya* ("invoked") fire is used to perform *yajna*-s. In the *Prashna Upanishad*, these fires are identified with the vital forces of *apana*, *vyana*, and *prana* in the human body.

As per several Hindu scriptures, OM means the three fires. This is why OM is also called *tridhama* and *trimukha*. The word *dhama* ("bearer" or "holder") in this context means the site for fire. As the fires burn at three different sites (*dhama*-s), OM is called *tridhama*. As the fires are believed to eat the oblations (*havya-bhuj*), OM is called *trimukha* ("having three mouths").

The three fires are compared to the earth, the atmosphere, and the heaven in the *Maitri Upanishad*. Just as the three *loka*-s represent the entire universe, the three fires represent the fire element or the deity Agni. Agni is considered a purifier in the Veda-s and Purana-s; he is called *pavaka* ("the purifier") in many hymns of the Rig Veda. The implication is that like Agni, OM is the purifier—as evidenced by the name *sarvapavana* (p. 152).

As the source of heat and light, Agni symbolizes knowledge. In the *Gita*, Krishna says that the fire of knowledge (*jnanagni*) burns to ashes all the *karma*-s. The *Agni Purana* is an unparalleled encyclopaedia containing knowledge of many diverse fields. Like Agni, OM is also considered to be omniscient, an idea reflected in the names *sarvavid* and *sarvajna* (p. 154).

The *Manu Smriti* says that the father, the mother, and the guru are the three fires. With this, a deeper meaning of OM is the highly revered triad of the father, the mother, and the guru. The *Taittiriya Upanishad* teaches that these three are to be treated like gods in the same passage which has the popular teaching *atithi-devo bhava* ("be one who treats the guest as a god").

TRADITION

Upanishad, Smriti, Purana.

ETYMOLOGY

a + u + m → om; tri + dhāma/mukha → tridhāma/trimukha.
a, u, m ▸ the three fires. ***tri*** ▸ three; ***dhāma*** ▸ site [of fire], place, abode. ***mukha*** ▸ mouth.

QUOTES

"The sound *a* is the householder's fire, the sound *u* is the southern fire, and the sound *m* is the consecrated fire."

—*Atharva Shikha Upanishad*

"OM is called *tridhama*—the three fires ... It is known as *trimukha*—the three fires."

—*Yogi Yajnavalkya Smriti*

"OM—this means the three fires."

—Purana-s

(4)

om, udgitha, tribrahma

(ओम्, उद्गीथ, त्रिब्रह्म = *om, udgītha, tribrahma*)

MEANING

"**1** the three Veda-s **2** the three penances."

EXPLANATION

While the number of Veda-s is four, many scriptures like some Upanishad-s and the *Ramayana* mention only three—Rig Veda, Yajur Veda, and Sama Veda. The *Garuda Purana* explains that originally there was only one Veda which Vyasa divided into four. The traditional narrative is that the original single Veda consisted mostly of three kinds of verses (*rik*, *yajush*, and *sama*), and hence it was referred to as the threefold Veda. As per some texts, the fourth Atharva Veda is believed to be concealed in the three Veda-s when only three are referred to.

Many Hindu scriptures say that OM stands for the three Veda-s. As per a commentary on the *Manu Smriti*, the sound *a* corresponds to the Rig Veda, *u* to the Yajur Veda, and *m* to the Sama Veda. *Udgitha*, a name of OM, is also explained as the three Veda-s in the *Chandogya Upanishad*, with the order reversed.

The Sanskrit word *brahma* has many meanings including Veda-s, essence, penance, and the Supreme Brahman in the neuter gender; and the creator Brahma and Brahmin in the masculine gender. One of the names of OM is *tribrahma* ("triad of Veda-s"), where *brahma* means Veda.

As the word *brahma* also means penance, the name *tribrahma* can be interpreted as the three kinds of penances described in the 17th chapter of the *Gita*. Of these, the pure penance involves austerities without any desire or motive. The passionate penance is performed without sincerity for a mundane objective like fame or honour. The ignorant penance is the mortification of the body done out of attachment or to harm others. These penances correspond to the three qualities—*sattva*, *rajas*, and *tamas*—represented by OM (p. 22). Or, OM represents the threefold pure penance—that of the body, speech, and the mind.

TRADITION

Upanishad, Smriti, Purana.

ETYMOLOGY

a + u + m → om; ut + gī + tha → udgītha;
tri + brahma → tribrahma.

a ▸ Rig Veda; ***u*** ▸ Yajur Veda; ***m*** ▸ Sama Veda. ***ut*** ▸ Sama Veda; ***gī*** ▸ Yajur Veda; ***tha*** ▸ Rig Veda. ***tri*** ▸ three; ***brahma*** ▸ Veda.

QUOTES

"In *udgitha*, the Sama Veda alone is *ut*, the Yajur Veda is *gi*, and the Rig Veda is *tha*."

—*Chandogya Upanishad*

"OM is *rik*, *yajush*, and *sama*, hence called *tribrahma*."

—*Yogi Yajnavalkya Smriti*

"The Lord milked *a*, *u*, and *m* from the three Veda-s; *a* from the Rig Veda, *u* from the Yajur Veda, *m* from the Sama Veda."

—*Manu Smriti*, its commentary

"OM—this means the three Veda-s."

"*Pranava* (OM) is said to consist of the three Veda-s."

"OM is the Rig Veda, the Yajur Veda, and the Sama Veda."

—Purana-s

(5)
om
(ओम् = *om*)

MEANING

" the three strides of Vishnu."

EXPLANATION

As per the *Linga Purana* and the *Vayu Purana*, the three sounds in OM represent the three strides of Vishnu. The three strides are associated with Vishnu's Vamana incarnation. The Sanskrit word *vishnu*, which comes from the root √*vish* ("to pervade") and literally means "he who pervades", also refers to this incarnation in which Vishnu measured the universe as Vamana. The Vamana incarnation is alluded to in the *samhita*-s (mantra portions) of the Rig Veda and the Krishna Yajur Veda and is narrated in the eighth canto of the *Bhagavata Purana*. A summary follows below.

When the *asura* king Bali conquered *svarga*, Aditi (the mother of the gods) propitiated Vishnu for help. Vishnu then manifested himself as Vamana, the dwarf. Vamana went to Bali's *ashvamedha yajna* and asked him for land (space) measured by three steps. Bali agreed to this request, but his guru Shukra warned him and ordered him to go back on his word. Bali decided not to renege on his word, which infuriated Shukra. Shukra left, cursing Bali that he will lose everything. When Bali asked Vamana to take three steps, Vamana assumed a cosmic form. He measured the earth with his first step and the *svarga* with the second. As there was no space left for the third step, Bali offered his head instead. Vamana placed his foot on Bali's head, blessing him and sending him to the netherworld.

This account of Vamana and Bali (Mahabali) is unfairly portrayed by some modern-day writers as the struggle between two races. Far from being seen as an antagonist or evil, Bali is seen in a positive light in Hinduism. In fact, he is hailed as the perfect example of *atma-nivedana* (self-surrender) type of *bhakti* in Vaishnava texts. In the *Vinay-patrika*, Tulsidas praises Bali along with other exalted Vaishnava-s like Prahlada, Vibhishana, Bharata, and the *gopi*-s (cow-herdesses) of Braja.

One of the words for "a step" in Sanskrit is *krama*. As the *krama*-s of Vishnu in Vamana form are massive, he is also called *urukrama* ("one with large steps") in Vedic and Puranic texts. Hindus believe that the three steps of Vishnu (*Vishnu-krama*-s) perform the function of protection just like Vishnu does. The *Atharva Veda* has eleven verses for protection from the enemy in which the presiding deity (*devata*) is *Vishnu-krama*.

TRADITION

Purana.

ETYMOLOGY

a + u + m → om.

a, u, m ▸ three strides of Vishnu.

QUOTES

"OM—this means the three strides of Vishnu."

—Purana-s

(6)
om
(ओम् = *om*)

MEANING

"Balarama, Pradyumna, Aniruddha, and Krishna."

EXPLANATION

In Vaishnavism, the quartet of Balarama (Krishna's elder brother), Pradyumna (Krishna's son), Aniruddha (Pradyumna's son), and Krishna is commonly known as *chaturvyuha* ("quartet of manifestations"). Although the popular meaning of *vyuha* is "a military array", as in the *chakravyuha* in which Abhimanyu was killed by the Kaurava-s, the word means "manifestation" in this context. The *chaturvyuha* concept is found in Vaishnava *Agama*-s and Purana-s, and also in the *Mahabharata*, where one of the names of Vishnu in the *Vishnu Sahasranama* is *chaturvyuha* ("one who has four manifestations").

This meaning of OM as the *chaturvyuha* comes from the *Gopala Tapini Upanishad*, which is popular in the Gaudiya Vaishnava tradition of Chaitanya Mahaprabhu. The Upanishad identifies the sounds *a*, *u*, and *m* in OM with the manifestations Balarama, Pradyumna, and Aniruddha—they represent a being in the awakened state, the state of dream, and the state of deep sleep respectively. Krishna is identified with the *ardhamatra* (half mora), the fourth state (*turiya*) beyond these three.

The *ardhamatra* is the fourth component of OM, beyond the three sounds. As per the *Durga Saptashati*, it is not to be pronounced. It is, however, represented as a crescent in the iconography of OM and is variously interpreted and explained.

Commentaries on the *Gopala Tapini Upanishad* explain that the half mora represents OM in its entirety. The purport is that along with the *chaturvyuha*, OM is to be also understood as Krishna himself, the supreme divinity in the Gaudiya Vaishnava tradition.

TRADITION

Upanishad, Vaishnavism.

ETYMOLOGY

a + u + m + half mora → oṁ

a ▸ Balarama; ***u*** ▸ Pradyumna (Krishna's son); ***m*** ▸ Aniruddha (Pradyumna's son); ***half mora*** ▸ Krishna.

QUOTES

"Balarama, the son of Rohini, is born from the sound *a* [and identified with *vishva*—a being in the awakened state]. Pradyumna is born from the sound *u* and is identified with *taijasa*—a being in the state of dream. Aniruddha is born from the sound *m* and is identified with *prajna*—a being in deep sleep. The *ardhamatra* (half mora) is Krishna, on whom the universe rests."

—*Gopala Tapini Upanishad*, its commentary

(7)
om
(ओम् = *om*)

MEANING

“Vishnu, Lakshmi, and the twenty-fifth (conscious being).”

EXPLANATION

This meaning of OM, from the *Padma Purana*, combines elements from *Sankhya* and *Vaishnava* philosophies. *Sankhya* is one of the six major schools of Hindu philosophy and is closely associated with the *Yoga* school. *Sankhya* recognizes twenty-five entities (*tattva*-s). Five gross elements, five subtle elements, five organs of perception, five organs of action, mind, ego, and intellect form the set of twenty-three manifest entities. The twenty-fourth entity is the unmanifest *prakriti* (nature) and the twenty-fifth is the *Purusha*, the conscious being. This *Purusha* is what is meant by “twenty-fifth” in the *Padma Purana* explanation.

In this interpretation of OM, the sound *a* is identified with Vishnu, the sound *u* with Shri or Lakshmi (the divine consort of Vishnu), and the sound *m* with the conscious being who is a servant of both Lakshmi and Vishnu. This representation of the living being as a devotee of Lakshmi and Vishnu is echoed in the philosophy of Ramanuja’s *Shrivaishnava* tradition which recognizes Lakshmi and Vishnu as the supreme divinities and emphasizes on *sharanagati*, or seeking the protection of God. *Shrivaishnava*-s see Mahavishnu, endowed with all auspicious qualities (hence *saguna*) and devoid of all inauspicious or defiling qualities (hence *nirguna*), as the Supreme Brahman.

The *Brahmanda Purana* describes *sharanagati* as sixfold, consisting of the following—

(1) a resolve (*sankalpa*) of being agreeable to God,

(2) abandonment (*varjana*) of all that is disagreeable to God,

(3) a strong belief (*vishvasa*) that God will protect,

(4) acceptance (*varana*) of God as one's only saviour,

(5) humility (*karpanya*), and

(6) self-surrender (*atma-nikshepa*).

These components are also listed in Vaishnava *Agama*-s with minor variations. They are especially emphasized in the *Shrivaishnava* tradition of Ramanuja and the *Shri* tradition of Ramananda.

This meaning of OM appeals to Vaishnava-s disposed towards the path of devotion. Just like the philosophy of the *Gita* is useful for followers of three paths—those of action (*karma*), devotion (*bhakti*), and knowledge (*jnana*)—the various interpretations of OM across Hindu scriptures are useful for the followers of the many paths in Hinduism like Shaivism, Vaishnavism, Shaktism, Yoga, etc. As it is revered even in Buddhism, Jainism, and Sikhism, OM is the unifier of all major Indic religions.

ETYMOLOGY

a + u + m → om.

a ▸ Vishnu; ***u*** ▸ Lakshmi; ***m*** ▸ conscious being.

QUOTES

"The sound *a* denotes Vishnu. The sound *u* denotes Lakshmi. The sound *m* is said to be their servant, the twenty-fifth."

—*Padma Purana*

(8)

om

(ओम् = *om*)

MEANING

"the beginning."

EXPLANATION

As per the medieval Sanskrit lexicons *Vishva Kosha* and *Medini Kosha*, the word OM is used in the sense of beginning. This meaning of OM is rooted in Vedic and Puranic accounts. As per the *Gopatha Brahmana*, Brahma first perceived OM and then created everything—*loka*-s, deities, Veda-s, elements, directions, seasons, words, life, and senses—from the components of this sound. The *Narada Purana* states that OM and *atha* were the first words to emerge from Brahma's throat.

The meaning is reflected in several Indian religious, spiritual, and righteous practices. OM is used to start the recitation of a Vedic verse. When used thus, OM is lengthened to three morae instead of the usual two. The first verse of the Rig Veda starts with *agnimide purohitam* ("I praise Agni the priest") which is recited as *OM agnimide purohitam.* Outside the Veda-s too, OM is recited at the beginning of sacred speech. OM occurs at the beginning of many mantra-s like *om namah shivaya* and *om namo bhagavate vasudevaya* in Hinduism, the *Namokar Mantra* (*om namo arihantanam ...*) in Jainism, and the *om mani padme hum* mantra in Tibetan Buddhism. Even the Guru Granth Sahib, the Sikh scripture, starts with *Ik Onkar* where *Onkar* (p. 56) is the equivalent of OM. As per the *Gita*, noble acts like *yajna*, charity, and penance start only after the recitation of OM.

In popular culture too, OM indicates the beginning, usually of something noble or auspicious. It is used as a simile for the first king Manu by Kalidasa in the *Raghuvamsha*. In the play *Mahavira-charita*, Bhavabhuti uses OM as a metaphor to convey that the slaying of Tataka is the beginning of the demons' annihilation.

TRADITION

Smriti, *Gita*, grammar, *Kavya*, *Nataka*, dictionaries.

QUOTES

"OM is used in the sense of beginning."

—*Kosha*-s

"If not started with OM, Vedic learning trickles away. If not ended with OM, it is destroyed."

—*Manu Smriti*

"Therefore, for the students of Veda-s, enjoined actions—*yajna*, charity, and penance—commence only after reciting OM."

—*Gita*

"At the beginning of a Vedic verse, OM is lengthened."

—*Ashtadhyayi*

"You are the source of the Veda-s which begin with OM."

—The gods to Brahma, *Kumarasambhava*

"Manu was the first among kings, just as OM [is the first word] of the Veda-s."

—*Raghuvamsha*

"Vishvamitra [to himself]: 'This is verily the OM (beginning) of the Vedic study which is the annihilation of all demons.'"

—*Mahaviracharita*

(9)

om

(ओम् = *om*)

MEANING

" an expression of agreement. "

EXPLANATION

OM is an expression of agreement in response to a request or a command. It is the Sanskrit equivalent of "so be it" or "as you wish". Attested in the Upanishad-s and lexicons, this is one of the oldest meanings associated with OM. The word OM occurs thrice in the *samhita* of Shukla Yajur Veda's *Vajasaneyi Madhyandina* recension. It is first seen in the second chapter, where it is used in the sense of agreement as per traditional commentaries. In the other two cases, it denotes the Supreme Brahman.

Examples of OM in the affirmative sense are also found in Purana-s and poetic literature. The *Bhagavata Purana* narrates that when Indra saw Nara and Narayana performing penance in Badarikashrama (Badrinath), he sent Kama—the god of love—along with the *apsara*-s (celestial dancers) to entice them. Instead of being enticed by them, Narayana used his Yogic prowess to create many women who were as beautiful as Lakshmi. He then ordered Kama and his assistants to choose any one for *svarga*. They said 'OM,' chose Urvashi, and went back to Indra. Another famous use of OM in the affirmative sense also involves Indra. At the beginning of Magha's epic poem *Shishupala-vadha*, Narada carries Indra's message to Krishna, requesting him to curb the menace of Shishupala. After listening to the plea, Krishna agrees by simply saying 'OM'.

The affirmative sense of OM contrasts with the negative sense of the word *na* ("no"). The *Aitareya Aranyaka* compares OM ("yes") to truth and *na* ("no") to falsehood, and offers some worldly advice in the context of charity as follows. One who says OM and donates, gets fame and renown. One who says *na* and does not, perishes. If one donates everything, they will not have enough left for their own needs. If one donates nothing at all, the resulting infamy will harm them. Therefore, one should donate at times, and not do so at other times. Acting thus, one strikes a balance between the two and prospers.

This teaching of the *Aitareya Aranyaka* is echoed by the famous Sanskrit maxim *ati sarvatra varjayet*, which translates as "one should avoid extremes everywhere".

TRADITION

Upanishad, Purana, commentaries, *Kavya*, dictionaries.

QUOTES

"OM—this is compliance, indeed."

—*Taittiriya Upanishad*

"Saying 'OM' ('As you wish'), the servants of the deities accepted Narayana's command."

—*Bhagavata Purana*

"OM has the meaning of agreement."

—Commentaries on Shukla Yajur Veda

"Then, after listening to Narada's request, Krishna said, 'OM' ('So be it')."

—*Shishupala-vadha*

"OM is used in the sense of agreement."

—*Medini Kosha*

(10)

om

(ओम् = *om*)

MEANING

"an expression to grant permission."

EXPLANATION

When somebody asks for a permission for something, the reply OM is the Sanskrit equivalent of "Yes, you may." Attested in Upanishad-s and Sanskrit dictionaries, this meaning of OM is notably seen in the context of Vedic learning and *yajna*-s.

Various recensions of Veda-s are called *shakha*-s ("branches"). *Pratishakhya*-s ("born in every *shakha*") are texts containing phonetic rules and recitation practices of specific *shakha*-s. According to the Rig Veda's *Pratishakhya*, a student requests the guru's permission to ask a doubt by saying '*bhoh*' and the guru grants the permission by saying '*OM bhoh*' in response.

As per the *Taittiriya Upanishad*, the permission to offer oblation in a *yajna* is also given by saying OM.

Two words are commonly used in Sanskrit for permission—*anumati* and *anujna*. OM means *anujna*, which has connotations of moral instruction and spiritual learning that *anumati* does not have. In the *Brahma Sutra*, the fountainhead of Vedanta philosophy, *anujna* refers to actions which are prescribed by the scriptures. The cognate word *anujnata* is used in the *Mahabharata*, in the dialogue between Yajnavalkya and Janaka, to refer to the knowledge imparted by Yajnavalkya. In Tantric Buddhism, *anujna* is the permission given by a guru to invoke a deity and also the name of a ceremony authorizing certain spiritual practices like the use of a mantra. As *anujna,* the permission meant by OM is no ordinary permission. It connotes an instruction in morality, knowledge, or a spiritual practice by the scriptures or a guru.

TRADITION

Vedic phonetics, Upanishad, dictionaries.

QUOTES

"For an explanation, the request should be made as '*bhoh*'. In the explanation, the permission should be given as '*OM bhoh*'."

—Rigveda Pratishakhya

"Saying 'OM', one permits the act of offering to the fire."

—Taittiriya Upanishad

"Verily, OM is the syllable for granting permission, for whenever one permits anything, they say 'OM'—just this much."

—Chandogya Upanishad

"OM means permission."

—Vishva Kosha

"OM means permission—'May I offer the oblation in the fire?' 'OM, please do so.'"

—Avyaya Kosha

(11)
om, triguna
(ओम्, त्रिगुण = *om, triguṇa*)

MEANING

"[having] three qualities (*guna*-s)."

EXPLANATION

Indian philosophy recognizes three fundamental qualities called *guna*-s—*sattva* (quality of purity), *rajas* (quality of passion), and *tamas* (quality of ignorance). According to the *Yogi Yajnavalkya Smriti* and Purana-s, OM means this triad with *a* denoting *sattva*, *u* denoting *rajas*, and *m* denoting *tamas*. The *Gita* describes the three kinds of faith, worship, diet, *yajna*-s, penance, charity, renunciation, knowledge, actions, doers, intellect, resolve, and delight corresponding to the three *guna*-s. Krishna says that the three *guna*-s influence everybody, and any one *guna* dominates the other two. The essence is that at a time, one of the three *guna*-s prevails over the other two.

The three qualities are often misunderstood as good, neutral, and bad. In the *Gita*, Krishna explains that they are all deluding and binding—*sattva* binds an individual to happiness, *rajas* to action, and *tamas* to negligence. As a matter of fact, the word *guna*, from the root √*gun* ("to invite"), also means "a rope". Krishna says that one who rises above these *guna*-s becomes free of birth and death to achieve *amrita* or bliss. While the three components of OM represent the three qualities, OM itself is *gunatita*, the supreme bliss beyond the three *guna*-s. This is why OM is called *rasa* ("nectar") and described as "the essence of all essences" (p. 148) in the *Chandogya Upanishad*.

A closely related concept is the metaphoric definition of *yuga*-s. The *Bhagavata Purana* says that the different *yuga*-s (ages) exist in all beings as the influences of the *guna*-s change. *Satya Yuga* exists when the mind, intellect, and senses are dominated by *sattva*. *Treta Yuga* exists when *rajas* dominates, *Dvapara Yuga* exists when both *rajas* and *tamas* dominate, and *Kali Yuga* exists when *tamas* dominates. The Purana-s add that the greatness of Vishnu prevails in the times of *sattva*, that of Brahma in the times of *rajas*, and that of Shiva in the times of *tamas*. As OM is beyond the three qualities, its greatness prevails in all times. In other words, OM is the mantra for all situations and all times, irrespective of which *guna* dominates the individual.

The followers of Kapila's school consider OM to be *triguna* as it represents *vyanjana* (the manifest), *nirguna* (the unmanifest), and *sarva* (the whole including the two).

TRADITION

Smriti, Purana.

ETYMOLOGY

a + u + m → om; tri + guṇa → triguṇa.

a ▸ *sattva* (purity); ***u*** ▸ *rajas* (passion); ***m*** ▸ *tamas* (ignorance).
tri ▸ three; ***guṇa*** ▸ quality.

QUOTES

"OM is known as *triguna* since [its three sounds are] *sattva*, *rajas*, and *tamas*."

—*Yogi Yajnavalkya Smriti*

"*A*, *u*, and *m*—these are the three sounds. These are the three *matra*-s (morae), comprising *sattva*, *rajas*, and *tamas*."

—*Purana-s*

(12)
om
(ओम् = *om*)

MEANING

"the ending."

EXPLANATION

In addition to "the beginning" (p. 16), the word OM also means "the ending", a meaning attested in medieval and modern Sanskrit lexicons. It is believed that everything arises from OM and merges into OM. It is for this reason that OM is also called *pralaya* (p. 144), meaning "dissolution".

This meaning of OM is reflected in several Hindu scriptures, mantra-s, and religious and cultural practices. The *samhita* of the Shukla Yajur Veda ends with the proclamation that OM is the Supreme Brahman, like the endless sky. This is understood in Sanskrit commentaries as a recommendation for meditating on the sky-pervading Brahman by chanting OM. In the *Vyasa Gita*, a dialogue between Vyasa and other sages in the *Kurma Purana*, Vyasa says that OM should be properly recited at the end of the study of Veda-s. The *Manu Smriti* says that if the study of Veda is done without reciting OM at the end, the learning is destroyed. When Vedic mantra-s are used in a *yajna*, their last syllable is replaced by OM, which is lengthened and pronounced with a high pitch. For example, the Rig Veda mantra

"*agnih ... apam retamsi jinvati,*"

which means "Agni ... gratifies the creatures in the waters", is recited in a *yajna* as

"*agnih ... apam retamsi jinvatOM,*"

with the last syllable being substituted by OM. OM also occurs at the end of some mantra-s, for example a mantra used in *sandhya* worship ends with *bhur-bhuvah-svah om*, in contrast with the *Gayatri Mantra* which starts with *om bhur-bhuvah-svah*.

In modern popular culture too, OM is used at the end of several practices. Many prayer sessions end with *OM shantih shantih shantih*, a shortened form of the *Shanti Mantra*. OM is used to end meditation sessions in some contemporary techniques. Yoga classes usually end with the *shavasana* pose (the corpse posture), and OM is often chanted after this to end the class.

TRADITION

Smriti, Purana, grammar, dictionaries.

QUOTES

"If not started with OM, Vedic learning trickles away. If not ended with OM, it is destroyed."

—*Manu Smriti*

"Moreover, a twice-born Brahmin should duly recite OM at the end [of Vedic study]."

—*Kurma Purana*

"While performing a *yajna*, the last vowel and that which follows in the last word of a hymn is replaced by *pranava* (OM)."

—*Ashtadhyayi*

"OM means ending—[as in the mantra] '... *brahma bhur-bhuvah-s[u]varom*'."

—*Nipata Avyaya Upasarga Vritti, Avyaya Kosha*

(13)

om

(ओम् = *om*)

MEANING

"silence."

EXPLANATION

Medieval and modern Sanskrit lexicons list "silence" as another meaning of OM. Some traditional Vedic scholars of today believe that this meaning originates in the practice of silently reciting Vedic verses addressed to Prajapati. Such verses are recited only in the mind, and so is OM which is used to start and end them. When recited this way, OM is referred to as *kadvad om*, where *kadvad* (*kadvat*) refers to a verse containing the word *ka*, which means Prajapati.

How is it that the same OM which is called *svara* ("sound", p. 88) and *shabda* ("word", p. 162) also means silence? The answer is that in Hinduism, the Supreme Brahman is conceived as both *saguna* (with qualities) and *nirguna* (without qualities). As OM is equated with the Supreme Brahman, it is natural for it to have names and meanings which correspond to both *saguna* and *nirguna* aspects. The names like *shabda* and *svara* correspond to the *saguna* OM which is pronounced, while the meaning "silence" corresponds to the *nirguna* OM which is silent. Indeed, the *Shiva Purana* talks of a longer subtle OM which is not recited but is present only in the hearts of yogi-s.

As per multiple Purana-s, there are three kinds of *japa*-s or chanting—*vachika japa* or chanting with an audible voice, *upamshu japa* or chanting with a whispering voice, and *manasa japa* or chanting in the mind alone. The *Shiva Purana* says that OM is to be chanted mentally in the state of *samadhi* (deep concentration), while it can be chanted in a whispering voice at all times. When OM is recited as part of a Vedic mantra or chanted in a whispering voice, it is the *saguna* sound. When the same OM is chanted in the mind, it is the *nirguna* silence.

In the *Gita*, Arjuna asks who among the worshippers of the manifest *saguna* Krishna and the unmanifest *nirguna* Brahman are the highest yogi-s? Krishna answers that the *saguna* worshippers are the highest yogi-s for him and even though the *nirguna* worshippers also reach him, they experience greater pain. Tulsidas says in the *Ramcharitmanas* that the manifest *saguna* Rama and the unmanifest *nirguna* Brahman are the same, just like hailstone and water. The same can be understood about OM. The vocalized OM that is recited or whispered and the silent OM that is meditated upon are one and the same and they lead the spiritual aspirant to the same state, but the worship of the silent OM by the *manasa japa* is more difficult.

TRADITION

Dictionaries.

QUOTES

"OM means silence."

—*Nipata Avyaya Upasarga Vritti*

"OM means silence—'perform the *kadvad om*'."

—*Avyaya Kosha*

(14)

om, trimatra

(ओम्, त्रिमात्र = *om, trimātra*)

MEANING

"having three morae (instants)."

EXPLANATION

OM is called *trimatra* ("having three *matra*-s") in *Shiksha* works (texts on Vedic phonetics) and Purana-s. *Matra,* the Sanskrit equivalent of mora, is a phonological unit of time. As per a popular definition, one *matra* is the time taken to rub the left hand around the left knee. A short vowel has one *matra* and a long vowel has two. OM has three *matra*-s when recited at the start of a Vedic verse (p. 16). This is why it is called *trimatra* and is written as O3M (ओ३म्) in some traditions.

As per the Purana-s, the first *matra* of OM is called *vidyuti* ("radiant"); the second is called *tamasi* ("dark"); and the third—which is said to permeate the imperishable Brahman—is called *nirguni* ("without qualities") or *gandhari,* as it is born from the *gandhara* note (the third note in Indian classical octave).

What if an aspirant or yoga practitioner does not know that OM has three *matra*-s, and chants or meditates on OM for a time shorter than three morae? As per the *Prashna Upanishad,* there is no harm even then. The Upanishad says that those who meditate on OM for one *matra* are enlightened and return to the earth as great humans endowed with virtues. Those who meditate on OM for two *matra*-s experience great powers in lunar worlds and return to the earth. Those who meditate on OM for three *matra*-s are freed of sins and perceive the Supreme Brahman. The

Upanishad adds that individually, the three *matra*-s of OM are endowed with mortality, but when combined together, they lead to a state in which the enlightened being does not fear anything. The purport is that the three *matra*-s of OM are individually mortal but together they bestow immortality.

In Smriti-s, the three *matra*-s of OM are said to be *vyakta* (the manifest world), *avyakta* (the unmanifest nature), and *sukshma* (the being)—categories of entities in *Sankhya* philosophy. They are also identified with *adhibhuta* (the perishable material world), *adhideva* (the divine world), and *adhyatma* (the Self)—concepts explained in the eighth chapter of the *Gita*. Finally, the *Mandukya Upanishad* identifies the *matra*-s of OM with the sounds *a*, *u*, and *m*; and says that the fourth *matra* is the whole OM itself, which is *amatra* (without any measure).

TRADITION

Vedic phonetics, Upanishad, Purana.

ETYMOLOGY

tri + mātra → trimātra.

tri ▸ three; ***mātrā*** ▸ mora.

QUOTES

"OM is *trimatra*."

—*Rigveda Pratishakhya*, its commentary

"OM is known as *trimatra*, and the consonant here is Shiva."

—*Linga Purana*

"The sound *a* is said to be combined with the sound *u* (resulting in *o*); and with the sound *m*, OM is called *trimatra*."

—*Linga Purana*

(15)
om
(ओम् = *om*)

MEANING

"**1** the pervader **2** the attainer **3** the means of attaining."

EXPLANATION

The *Gopatha Brahmana* of the *Atharva Veda* has an in-depth discussion on the nature of the word OM in which thirty-six questions about OM are asked. The first of these questions is—"We ask regarding OM, what is the root?" The question is important as the ancient followers of *Nirukta* (Vedic etymology) and *Vyakarana* (grammar) believed that all words are derived from roots or verbs. Some grammarians of yore disagreed, but still most etymologies in Sanskrit literature trace words to roots.

The text then gives the answer as—"√*ap* is the root; some say it is √*av*. Similarity of meaning is closer than similarity of form. Therefore, the sound OM comes from the root √*ap*. The meaning is that which pervades (or obtains) everything." The root √*ap* has two primary meanings—"to pervade" and "to attain". The other root mentioned (√*av*) has as many as nineteen different meanings—the highest in Sanskrit (see *om*, p. 210).

As the pervader, OM is believed to transcend all boundaries of space, time, and matter. This is evidenced in the names *ananta* (p. 100), *sarvavyapi* (p. 156), and *traikalya* (p. 172). A popular verse in praise of the guru refers to this all-pervading nature as *vyaptam yena characharam tatpadam* ("that word which pervades the animate and inanimate world"). As *pada* means both "an entity" and "a word", the reference is to both Brahman and OM.

As the root √*ap* means "to attain" or "to obtain", OM also means the attainer, or the means of attaining. Describing the Supreme Brahman, the *Katha* and *Mundaka* Upanishad-s say that it is not attained by teaching, intellect, or learning; rather it is attained by those who it itself chooses. The same can be understood for OM, as it is the name of the Supreme Brahman (see *om*, p. 36). Whoever OM attains, attains OM. This is how OM is to be understood as the attainer.

OM can also be explained as the means of attaining. OM is described as the means of attaining Brahman in the *Taittiriya Upanishad* as "The eloquent (learned) Brahmin chants OM and says, 'May I attain Brahman;' and indeed obtains Brahman." One of the names of OM is *tara*, which similarly means the "the means of liberation" (see p. 170).

TRADITION

Veda, commentaries.

ETYMOLOGY

√āp + ḍom → om.

√*āp* ▸ **1** to pervade **2** to obtain; ***ḍom*** ▸ an assumed *uṇādi* suffix indicating the performer or means of an action.

QUOTES

"What is the root of OM? The root is √*ap*. ... Therefore OM is derived from √*ap*. The meaning is it pervades everything."

—*Gopatha Brahmana*

"OM is derived from the root √*ap* or the root √*av*."

—Commentary on Shukla Yajur Veda

(16)

om

(ओम् = *om*)

MEANING

"an expression for removal or warding off."

EXPLANATION

As per the *Medini Kosha,* the word OM is used in the sense of *apakriti* ("removal, separation")—to be understood as the removal of evil or sins (*papa*). Vedic texts mention that the chanting of OM drives away evil. As per the *Aitareya Brahmana,* the reciter of the Yajur Veda wards off evil accrued to the host with the divine word OM and the mundane word *tatha.* The *Jaiminiya Brahmana* says that when specific mantra-s of the Sama Veda are recited with OM, which is truth, all evil is destroyed.

Apakriti also refers to the removal of sorrow (*duhkha*) and debts (*rina*-s). The Rig Veda uses the word in the context of sorrow as "O Aditya-s, you know how to remove sorrows." The *Manu Smriti,* the *Ramayana,* and the Purana-s speak of *apakriti* (removal or repayment) of the debts to gods, guru, and ancestors.

This meaning has parallels in the names *Hari* and *Hara* of Vishnu and Shiva respectively. Both mean "one who removes", and the removal is understood to be that of evil or sins.

TRADITION

Dictionaries.

QUOTES

"OM is used in the sense of removal."

—*Medini Kosha*

(17)
om
(ओम् = *om*)

MEANING

"an expression uttered on an auspicious occasion."

EXPLANATION

The *Medini Kosha* adds that OM is used in the sense of auspiciousness. OM does not mean auspiciousness, rather it is uttered on auspicious occasions and is believed to bestow auspiciousness on the speaker and the listener. The *Narada Purana* states that OM and *atha* were the first words uttered by Brahma, and therefore both are auspicious. This is why OM and *atha* are used when beginning something. Many philosophical texts like the *Yoga Sutra* begin with *atha* while the *Chandogya* and *Mandukya* Upanishad-s begin with OM. Panini's grammar begins with *atha* while the *Mugdhabodha* grammar begins with OM as *om namah shivaya*—which is explained in Durgadasa's commentary as "Salutations to OM, for auspiciousness" in addition to the popular meaning "OM, salutations to Shiva."

TRADITION

Purana, dictionaries.

QUOTES

"OM and the word *atha*—these two came out first, piercing the throat of Brahma. Therefore, both are auspicious."

—*Narada Purana*

"OM is used in the sense of auspiciousness."

—*Medini Kosha*

(18)

om, omkara

(ओम्, ओंकार = *om, oṃkāra*)

MEANING

“ the uplifter, that which raises [something] upwards. ”

EXPLANATION

Smriti and Purana works as well as Upanishad-s state that OM or *omkara* is called so because it is the uplifter which raises the vital forces (*prana*-s), the body, or the devotee (*bhakta*). This idea of raising occurs notably in the *Chandogya Upanishad*, which describes how an atman leaves the body at the time of death thus: “And then, when this atman departs from this body, it goes up by these very rays; or it goes up chanting OM.” The purport is that the enlightened atman departs the body through the *brahma randhra* (aperture in the head), meditating on OM.

Two Upanishad-s of the Atharva Veda say that *omkara* is called so due to *urdhvam* (“upwards”) and *utkrama* (“taking, leading”). In sacred and grammatical texts, such definitions or explanations of a word without any clear derivation are called *nipatana*-s. The Upanishad-s state that OM uplifts the vital forces (*prana*-s). The *Dipika* commentary explains that OM takes the *prana*-s with the mind and the [digestive] fires to the head via the central *sushumna* channel (*nadi*), piercing the six *chakra*-s.

Similar explanations for the names OM and *omkara* are found in Smriti and Purana texts. The *Yogi Yajnavalkya Smriti* says that OM is called so because it raises (*unnamayati*) the whole body. Here “raises” is to be understood in the sense of “making upright” or “rejuvenating”. Accordingly, the import is that the chanting of OM is instrumental in perfecting the straight-back or upright Yoga poses for meditation. The *Skanda Purana* mentions that OM is called so as it raises (*unnayate*) the devotee who chants it. As per the *Linga Purana*, that alone which raises upwards is *omkara*. The *Shiva Toshini* commentary on the Purana explains this as follows—when OM is uttered, it raises the entire [subtle] body upwards.

TRADITION

Upanishad, Yoga, Smriti, Purana.

ETYMOLOGY

From **ūrdhva + utkrāma, ut + √nī**, or **ut + √nam + ṇic.** ***ūrdhva*** ▸ upwards; ***utkrāma*** ▸ leading, taking. ***ut* + √*nī*** ▸ to raise, to lift up. ***ut* + √*nam*** ▸ to rise, to ascend; ***ṇic*** ▸ suffix in the causative sense.

QUOTES

"As merely on being pronounced, it makes the vital forces (*prana*-s) move upwards, it is called *omkara*."

—Upanishad-s

"When pronounced, it raises (uprights) the body all over—from the toe to the head. Hence it is called *omkara*."

—*Yogi Yajnavalkya Smriti*

"Since it raises the devotee (chanting it), it is called OM."

—*Skanda Purana*

"That alone which raises upwards is proclaimed as *omkara*."

—*Linga Purana*

(19)

om, pranava

(ओम्, प्रणव = *om, praṇava*)

MEANING

"the Supreme God, or the Supreme Brahman."

EXPLANATION

OM is equated with the Supreme Brahman by several Hindu scriptures starting from the Vedic texts to Purana-s and the *Yoga Sutra*. The Shukla Yajur Veda's *Madhyandina Samhita* ends by saying that OM is Brahman. Commentaries explain that OM is the name (*nama*) or symbol (*pratima*) of Brahman. The *Gopatha Brahmana*, the *Taittiriya Aranyaka*, and multiple Upanishad-s reiterate that OM is Brahman. The *Narada Purana* explains that *pranava* (OM) is the *vachaka* (indicator) and Brahman is the *vachya* (indicated).

In the *Yoga Sutra*, Patanjali says that *pranava* is the indicator of *Ishvara*. As per Patanjali, *Ishvara* is a specific *Purusha* free from afflictions, actions, fruits of actions, and impressions; in whom is the unsurpassed seed of omniscience; who is the guru of the earliest ones; and who is not limited by time. Patanjali then mentions chanting of OM and meditation on *Ishvara*. Vyasa's commentary explains that the Supreme Brahman is revealed by the combination of chanting of OM and meditation on *Ishvara*.

The *Vaijayanti Kosha* begins with a beautiful verse which says, "Salutations to the guru of the earliest guru-s who is called Brahman, who is the entity meant by the word OM, and who is the *vachya shakti* and the *vachaka shakti*." The reference is to the two powers in a mantra—the divinity which the mantra invokes is the *vachya shakti* and the mantra itself is the *vachaka shakti*. The *Vaijayanti Kosha* verse implies that for the mantra OM, both the *vachya shakti* and the *vachaka shakti* are the same, i.e. there is no difference between Brahman and OM even though the latter is the indicator and the former is the indicated.

TRADITION

Veda, Upanishad, Purana, Yoga, dictionaries.

QUOTES

"OM is the Supreme Brahman, [like] the [endless] sky."

—Shukla Yajur Veda

"OM is the name or image (symbol) of Brahman."

—Commentary on Shukla Yajur Veda

"Verily, *pranava* (OM) is the Supreme Brahman."

—*Gopatha Brahmana*

"OM—this is the Supreme Brahman."

—*Taittiriya Aranyaka, Taittiriya Upanishad*

"O Satyakama! Certainly, that which is OM is the qualified Brahman and also the unqualified Brahman."

—*Prashna Upanishad*

"The indicated is the Supreme Brahman and the indicator is known to be *pranava* (OM)."

—*Narada Purana*

"His indicator (name) is *pranava* (OM). The Supreme God is indicated (meant) by *pranava* (OM)."

—*Yoga Sutra*, its commentary

(20)

om

(ओम् = *om*)

MEANING

"Rama."

EXPLANATION

In the *Valmiki Ramayana*, Brahma describes Rama as *omkara*. In the *Adhyatma Ramayana*, Ahalya says the same while praising Rama after her salvation. OM is often equated with Rama in the Rama-centric Vaishnava sects like the *Ramananda Sampradaya*. One of the most valued Upanishad-s of the Ramanandi-s is the *Rama Tapini Upanishad* in which Rama is extolled as *omkara* (OM), the seed of the Veda-s. Another important work is the *Rama Stavaraja Stotra*, in which one of the names of Rama is *pranava* (OM). In the *Vaishnava Matabja Bhaskara* of Ramananda, the seed-sound of Rama is called *pranavi* ("having OM in it").

OM is called *tara* (p. 170) and also *taraka* (in *Tarasara Upanishad*), both words mean "the saviour". Similarly, the *Rama Tapini Upanishad* says that the six-syllabled mantra of Rama is *taraka*. The Upanishad further says that the mantra of Rama is same as OM with its six syllables being the *a, u, m,* half mora, *bindu,* and *nada* of OM. The *Harita Smriti* says that the mantra *shriramaya namah*, meaning "Salutations to Rama who is with Shri (Sita)", is called *taraka brahma*. As per the Smriti, Shiva gives this mantra to all those who die in Varanasi. In the *Rama Stavaraja Stotra*, Vyasa tells Yudhishthira that the mantra *shrirama*, which means "O auspicious Rama" or "O Rama with Shri (Sita)", is supreme and is called *taraka* and *brahma*.

Elsewhere, the name Rama itself is equated with OM. In the *Maha Ramayana*, Shiva tells Parvati that the word OM is another form of the word *rama* (राम). This is explained as follows. The word *rama* is split into its components as *r* + *a* + *m* + *a*. The last *a* is elided (*varna-lopa*), and the first two undergo an exchange of letters (*varna-viparyaya*) to result in *a* + *r* + *m*. The *r* then changes to *u* (*varna-vikriti*), giving *a* + *u* + *m* which becomes OM. These operations of elision, exchange, and transformation can be explained by the Paninian rule which covers *prishodaradi* words. Incidentally, the word *rama* has three morae and hence is also *trimatra* (p. 28) like OM.

In the *Ramcharitmanas*, Tulsidas says that the name of Rama comprises Brahma, Vishnu, and Shiva. OM is similarly considered as standing for this trinity (p. 2). Tulsidas further says that Rama's name is like *veda-prana*—the life (*prana*) of the Veda-s. Commentaries on the work interpret *veda-prana* as OM. OM is similarly considered to be the source or the Self of the Veda-s, as it is called *vedabija* (p. 110) and *vedatma* (p. 202).

TRADITION

Upanishad, *Ramayana*, Vaishnavism.

QUOTES

"Salutations to Rama who is OM, the seed of the Veda-s. Salutations! Salutations!!"

—*Ramapurva Tapini Upanishad*

"Brahma said, 'O Rama! You [alone] are the sound OM'."

—*Valmiki Ramayana*

"Ahalya said, 'O Rama! You are expressed by the sound OM'."

—*Adhyatma Ramayana*

(21)

om

(ओम् = *om*)

MEANING

"Lakshmana, Shatrughna, Bharata, and Rama."

EXPLANATION

This interpretation of OM is given by the *Rama Tapini Upanishad.* The four Raghu princes are said to be the four parts of OM—*a, u, m,* and the *ardha-matra* (half mora), and correspond to the four *vibhu*-s (masters) of the four states of consciousness. Lakshmana is the sound *a* and *vishva,* the Self in the awakened state; Shatrughna is the sound *u* and *taijasa,* the Self in the dreaming state; Bharata corresponds to *m* and *prajna,* the Self in the state of deep sleep; and Rama is the half mora and Brahman, who the Self realizes in the fourth state. This identification of the components of OM with *vishva* (*vaishvanara*), *taijasa, prajna,* and Brahman is the same as that in the *Mandukya Upanishad* (see *triprajna,* p. 180). The *Rama Tapini Upanishad* further identifies the four with the Raghu princes, just like the *Gopala Tapini Upanishad* identifies them with the *chaturvyuha* (p. 12).

In the *Ramcharitmanas,* Tulsidas presents a metaphor based on this interpretation of OM while describing the wedding of the four Raghu princes with the four princesses of Mithila. Tulsidas says, "The beautiful princesses appear effulgent in the same pavilion with their handsome grooms, as if the four states (*avastha*-s) are resplendent with their *vibhu*-s in the heart of the living being." This is explained in commentaries as follows: Urmila is the awakened state (*jagrat*) and her lord is Lakshmana who is *vishva,* Shrutikirti is the state of dream (*svapna*) and her lord is Shatrughna who is *taijasa,* Mandavi is the state of deep sleep (*sushupti*) and her lord is Bharata who is *prajna,* and finally Sita is the fourth state (*turiya*) and her lord is Rama who is the Supreme Brahman.

Elsewhere in the *Ramcharitmanas,* after naming the Raghu princes, the sage Vasishtha tells Dasharatha, "O king, your four sons are the essence (*tattva*) of the Veda-s." The word *veda-tattva* is interpreted in commentaries as OM, as it is the essence of the Veda-s. This interpretation is also rooted in the description of OM found in the *Rama Tapini Upanishad.*

TRADITION

Upanishad, Vaishnavism.

ETYMOLOGY

a + u + m + half mora → om.

a ▸ Lakshmana; ***u*** ▸ Shatrughna; ***m*** ▸ Bharata; ***half mora*** ▸ Rama.

QUOTES

"Lakshmana, indicated by (arisen from) the sound *a,* is *vishva*—a being in the awakened state. Shatrughna, indicated by the sound *u,* is identified with *taijasa*—a being in the state of dream. Bharata, indicated by the sound *m,* is identified with *prajna*—a being in deep sleep. Rama, identified with the half mora, is the Supreme Brahman who has the form of bliss alone."

—*Ramottara Tapini Upanishad*

(22)

om

(ओम् = *om*)

MEANING

"Brahma (Jambavan), Vishnu (Sugriva), Shiva (Hanuman), Shatrughna, Bharata, Lakshmana, Sita, and Rama."

EXPLANATION

This explanation of OM is found in the *Tarasara Upanishad.* The name of the Upanishad, *Tarasara,* means the essence (*sara*) of OM (*tara,* p. 170). The explanation breaks down OM into eight parts and equates them with octet of Rama's court.

The first three parts of OM are the letters *a, u,* and *m* as usual. Here *a* is said to be the source of Brahma who is equated with Jambavan. Jambavan is born from Brahma as per the *Ramayana.* Vishnu, equated with Sugriva, is said to arise from *u* which is the first letter of Upendra, one of the names of Vishnu. Vishnu is often identified with Surya—both are called Aditya and Hari. As per the *Ramayana,* Sugriva is born from Surya and is the leader of the *vanara*-s, also called *hari* in Sanskrit. The letter *m* is said to be the origin of Shiva, who is equated with Hanuman. Shiva is identified with Hanuman in several Hindu scriptures.

The next three components of OM are the *bindu* (nasal sound), *nada* (resonance), and *kala* (simply understood as morae). These three are equated with Shatrughna, Bharata, and Lakshmana respectively by the Upanishad. Lakshmana is also described as the earth-bearer, i.e. the Shesha serpent.

The seventh component of OM is the *kalatita* ("beyond the *kala*-s") Sita, described as the Supreme Goddess (*bhagavati*) herself. In the Ramanandi sect, Sita is considered the first guru and the power (*shakti*) of Rama. In the *Adhyatma Ramayana*, Sita tells Hanuman that she is the original *prakriti* responsible for the creation, protection, and dissolution of the world.

Finally, the Upanishad says that the eighth component of OM is even beyond Sita. This is Rama, the Supreme Brahman.

TRADITION

Upanishad, Vaishnavism.

ETYMOLOGY

a + u + m + bindu + nāda + kalā + kalātītā + para → om.

a ▸ Brahma/Jambavan; ***u*** ▸ Vishnu/Sugriva; ***m*** ▸ Shiva/ Hanuman; ***bindu*** ▸ Shatrughna; ***nāda*** ▸ Bharata; ***kalā*** ▸ Lakshmana; ***kalātītā*** ▸ Sita; ***para*** ▸ Rama.

QUOTES

"Brahma, who arose from the sound *a*, is known as Jambavan. Vishnu, who arose from the sound *u*, is the leader of the *vanara*-s (i.e. Sugriva). And Shiva, who arose from the sound *m*, is declared to be Hanuman. The *bindu*, also called *Ishvara*, is the sovereign Shatrughna himself. The *nada*, also called *Shankha*, is to be known as the immensely powerful Bharata. From the *kala* comes Lakshmana, who is *Purusha* himself and the bearer of the earth (the Shesha serpent). Beyond the *kala* is the Supreme Goddess herself, who is called Sita. And beyond her is the Supreme Brahman and the most eminent *Purusha*—the auspicious Rama."

—*Tarasara Upanishad*

(23)

om, pranava

(ओम्, प्रणव = *om, praṇava*)

MEANING

"Devi (Shakti)."

EXPLANATION

In Shaktism, one of the five major Hindu *sampradaya*-s (sects), the goddess Devi or Shakti is the supreme divinity. The *Devi Bhagavata* is one of the major texts in Shakti-centric traditions. The Purana repeatedly identifies Devi with OM. In the first canto, Devi is described by the Veda-s as the half mora of *udgitha* (OM). This is similar to the half mora, which is said to represent OM in its entirety, being identified with Krishna (p. 12) and Rama (p. 38) in the Upanishad-s.

In the seventh canto of the Purana, the gods praise Devi and say that she is the meaning of *pranava*. Applying the principle of non-difference between *vachya* and *vachaka* referred to in the *Shiva Purana* (p. 73), this can be understood as OM and Devi being the same. Further in the same canto, the gods say that Devi is *hrim* as well as OM. *Hrim* is a seed sound (*bija*) used in many Shakti-centric mantra-s. In Shaktism, *hrim* is sometimes referred to as the *shakta pranava* ("the OM of Shaktism"). The verse identifies Devi with both *hrim*, the *shakta pranava*, and OM, the universal *pranava*. Still further in the same canto, the gods praise Devi as *pranavatmika* ("she whose true nature is OM)."

Another major text in Shaktism is the *Devi Mahatmya* (also known as *Durga Saptashati*), which is a part of the *Markandeya Purana*. In the fourth chapter of the *Devi Mahatmya*, Indra and the gods extol Devi as *shabdatmika* ("she who is *shabda* itself"). *Shabda* here refers to OM; the word *shabda* is one of the names of OM (p. 162). Four major commentaries interpret the word *shabdatmika* in the verse as either *Shabda Brahman* or *Nada Brahman*, which are both identified with OM (pp. 164, 189). In the same verse, Devi is described as the resting place of the three Veda-s. OM is similarly seen as *tribrahma* (p. 8), the abode of the three Veda-s.

TRADITION

Purana, Shaktism.

QUOTES

"We revere the goddess of the universe (Devi) who really is the meaning of OM."

—*Devi Bhagavata*

"Salutations to her whose form is OM and the sound *hrim*."

—*Devi Bhagavata*

"Salutations to you, whose nature is OM."

—*Devi Bhagavata*

"O Devi! You have the form of the word (OM). You are the abode of the extremely pure verses of the Rig Veda and the Yajur Veda. You are the abode of the verses of the Sama Veda, the recitation of whose words is made mellifluous by *udgitha*. You are the triad [of gods]. You are *bhagavati* (abounding in the six riches). You are the *varta* (farming, enterprise, and animal husbandry) for the life of the living beings. You are the destroyer of the greatest misfortunes for all the realms."

—Gods to Devi, *Durga Saptashati*

(24)
om
(ओम् = *om*)

MEANING

"*pranayama*—inhalation, holding the breath, and exhalation."

EXPLANATION

Pranayama ("regulation of breath") is one of the eight limbs of Patanjali's *Ashtanga Yoga.* In the *Yoga Sutra*, Patanjali defines *pranayama* as the control of inhalation and exhalation done after the accomplishment of an *asana* (a steady and easy pose). In two verses that are common to the *Jabala Darshana Upanishad*, the *Devi Bhagavata*, and the *Yoga Yajnavalkya*, *pranayama* is said to be OM as it is full of OM. The purport is that *pranayama* is performed along with the chanting of OM.

The texts associate the three sounds of OM with the three stages of *pranayama*, described as follows by the Upanishad and the *Yoga Yajnavalkya.* In the first stage called *puraka*, air is to be inhaled slowly using the *ida nadi* (left nostril) while meditating on the sound *a* for sixteen *matra*-s (morae). In the second stage called *kumbhaka*, air is to be held inside for sixty-four *matra*-s while meditating on the sound *u*. In the third stage called *rechaka*, air is to be exhaled using the *pingala nadi* (right nostril) while meditating on the sound *m* for thirty-two *matra*-s. The three stages are to be then repeated but with opposite nostrils, i.e. with inhalation using the right nostril and exhalation using the left nostril. This cycle is to be continued all over again, starting with the left nostril. The Upanishad declares that six months of daily practice of this *pranayama* makes one an aspirant, and one year of practice leads to the knowledge of Brahman. Nilakantha's commentary on the *Devi Bhagavata* states differently that *puraka* should last thirty-two *matra*-s and *rechaka* sixteen *matra*-s.

The description of the *sagarbha pranayama* in the *Gheranda Samhita,* one of the principal hatha yoga texts, further connects *pranayama* with OM. In this *pranayama,* the practitioner inhales repeating *a* for sixteen *matra*-s and contemplating on Brahma, whose quality is *rajas* and complexion is red. The breath is then held while repeating *u* for sixty-four *matra*-s and contemplating on Vishnu, whose quality is *sattva* and complexion is dark blue. This is followed by exhalation while repeating *m* for thirty-two *matra*-s and meditating on Shiva, whose quality is *tamas* and complexion is white. As here, OM is associated with the three gods (p. 2) and the three *guna*-s (p. 22) elsewhere too.

TRADITION

Upanishad, Purana, Yoga.

ETYMOLOGY

a + u + m → om.

a ▸ inhalation (*pūraka*); ***u*** ▸ holding the breath (*kumbhaka*); ***m*** ▸ exhalation (*recaka*).

QUOTES

"*Pranayama* is said to be achieved by *rechaka* (exhalation), *puraka* (inhalation), and *kumbhaka* (holding breath). *Rechaka, puraka,* and *kumbhaka* are said to be the same as the three syllables [of OM]. Brahman alone is proclaimed to be *pranava* (OM), and *pranayama* is full of OM."

—*Jabala Darshana Upanishad, Devi Bhagavata, Yoga Yajnavalkya*

(25)

om

(ओम् = *om*)

MEANING

"Brahma (the four-headed creator)."

EXPLANATION

Though a part of the Hindu *trimurti* (trinity of gods), Brahma is hardly worshipped in Hinduism. Very few temples of Brahma exist in places like Pushkar (Rajasthan), Khedbrahma (Gujarat), Dudhai (Uttar Pradesh), and Kodakkal (Kerala). There are no notable Hindu denominations dedicated to Brahma, and even the *Brahma Sampradaya* which carries his name is a Vaishnava lineage. However, there are several instances in the Purana-s and epics where he is identified with OM or the Supreme Brahman.

In the *Matsya Purana*, when the deities are defeated by the demon Tarakasura, they go to Brahma for help. Propitiating him, the deities say, "You are the sound OM. You, the Supreme Brahman, are born first for the creation of this universe with infinite diversity. After the creation, you are the embodiment of *sattva* (Vishnu), and you are also Rudra desirous of destroying. Salutations to you." Here, the four-headed Brahma is identified with OM, the three *guna*-s, and the three actions—the creation, the preservation, and the destruction of the universe. The deities add that it is Brahma who the Veda-s and yogi-s praise.

In the *Garuda Purana*, the mantra *om hrim hrim* is listed in a collection of secret mantra-s taught by Shiva himself. Here, it is said that OM represents Brahma as its seed, the first *hrim* represents Vishnu, and the second *hrim* represents Shiva. A name of OM is *brahmabija* (p. 110), which can mean the seed of the Veda-s, the seed of Brahman, or the seed of Brahma—all three are meant with *brahma* at the beginning of the compound.

Perhaps the most beautiful prayer to Brahma in Sanskrit literature is the twelve-verse *stuti* by the gods in the second canto of Kalidasa's epic *Kumarasambhava.* Like in the *Matsya Purana*, here too the deities are tormented by Tarakasura. The gods say, "Salutations to you! Before creation, you are one. Afterwards, for the division of the three *guna*-s, you assume multiplicity as the *trimurti.*" This description of Brahma is similar to OM being described as having three *guna*-s (p. 22) and representing the *trimurti* of Brahma, Vishnu, and Shiva (p. 2). The deities further praise Brahma by saying, "Expressing your greatness through three states, you alone become the cause of destruction, preservation, and creation." Associating Brahma with OM, they say, "You are the source of the sacred words (Veda-s) which begin with OM, which are recited with three accents, which propound *yajna*, and which result in obtaining *svarga.*" Explaining the *om hrim hrim* mantra, the *Garuda Purana* states that OM is the seed of Brahma whereas here, Brahma is said to be the cause of OM.

TRADITION

Purana, *Kavya.*

QUOTES

"You (Brahma) are the sound OM."

—*Matsya Purana*

"The sound OM is the seed mantra of Brahma."

—*Garuda Purana*

(26)

om, panchakshara

(ओम्, पञ्चाक्षर = *om, pañcākṣara*)

MEANING

"having five imperishable parts."

EXPLANATION

In the *Ganesha Sahasranama* of the *Ganesha Purana*, one of the names of Ganesha is *panchaksharatma*. Traditionally, this name is understood as "one whose form is OM" with the word *panchakshara* ("having five imperishables") meaning OM and the word *atma* interpreted as body or form. The word *atma* (*atman*), usually used for the Self, also means the body in Sanskrit.

The five imperishable parts of OM are the three sounds (*a*, *u*, and *m*), *bindu* (nasal element), and *nada* (resonance). These parts are associated with Shiva's five heads in the *Shiva Purana*. Shiva tells Brahma and Vishnu that *a* arose first from his northern face, followed by *u* from his western face, *m* from his southern face, *bindu* from his eastern face, and *nada* from his middle face. Shiva says that the five parts then combined into one to result in the monosyllable OM.

The mantra *namah shivaya* is also called *panchakshara*, as it has five syllables. The *Shiva Purana* states that this *panchakshara* mantra was born from OM, with the five syllables *na*, *mah*, *shi*, *va*, and *ya* coming from *a*, *u*, *m*, *bindu*, and *nada* respectively. This is another reason why OM is *panchakshara*, which can be interpreted as "having the five-syllabled mantra".

Also associated with the five parts of OM mentioned above are the five cosmic actions. These are described by Shiva in the

Shiva Purana just before he describes the origin of the five parts of OM. The five actions (see also p. 52) are *srishti* (creation), *stithi* (preservation or maintenance), *samhara* (annihilation), *tirobhava* (disappearance), and *anugraha* (liberation or blessing). Shiva further connects these activities with the five elements—everything is created by earth, sustained by water, destroyed by fire, taken away by the wind, and blessed by the ether. Shiva says that his five faces, which correspond to the five parts of OM, carry out these five actions.

In the same chapter, the *Shiva Purana* mentions five deities instead of the usual trinity (see *om*, p. 2). Shiva says that creation is performed by Brahma, preservation by Vishnu, annihilation by Rudra, disappearance by Mahesha, and blessing by Shiva himself. These five deities correspond to the five parts of OM.

TRADITION

Purana, commentaries.

ETYMOLOGY

pañca + akṣara → pañcākṣara.

pañca ▸ five; ***akṣara*** ▸ imperishable [part].

QUOTES

"Ganesha has the form of *panchakshara*. The five *akshara*-s of OM—the sound *a*, the sound *u*, the sound *m*, *bindu*, and *nada*—are the form of Ganesha."

—*Ganesha Sahasranama*, its commentary

"There are five components of OM—the sound *a*, the sound *u*, the sound *m*, *bindu*, and *nada*."

—*Bhagavata Purana* commentary

(27)
om
(ओम् = *om*)

MEANING

"Brahma, Vishnu, Hara, Maheshvara, Sadashiva, and supreme Shiva."

EXPLANATION

The *Kailasa Samhita* in the *Shiva Purana* offers another fivefold interpretation of OM where the components *a*, *u*, *m*, *bindu*, and *nada* are said to be Brahma, Vishnu, Rudra, Maheshvara, and Sadashiva respectively. The five deities are associated with the five cosmic activities called *panchakritya*-s in the *Shaiva Siddhanta* tradition of Tamil Nadu. The five activities are *srishthi* (creation), *palana* (sustenance), *samhara* (destruction), *tirobhava* (concealment), and *anugraha* (grace). The first three constitute the cosmic cycle in several Indian philosophies. *Tirobhava* is the concealment of the nature of the atman, the world, and Shiva. *Anugraha* is the grace of Shiva which grants knowledge and liberation to the atman. As per the Tamil work *Tirumantiram*, the five activities are represented by the dance of Nataraja, a form of Shiva immortalized in art by the Chola dynasty sculptures. This is illustrated on the facing page.

The five cosmic activities of Shiva are recognized in Kashmir Shaivism also, where works like *Svacchanda Tantra* formally define the activities. The first verse of *Pratyabhijna Hridaya* describes Shiva as one who is constantly engaged in the five activities. As per the *Lakshmi Tantra*, the five activities are the functions of Shri, the independent power of Narayana.

TRADITION

Purana, *Shaiva Siddhanta*, Kashmir Shaivism, Dramatics.

ETYMOLOGY

a + u + m + bindu + nāda → om.

a ▸ Brahma; ***u*** ▸ Vishnu; ***m*** ▸ Rudra; ***bindu*** ▸ Maheshvara; ***nāda*** ▸ Sadashiva.

QUOTES

"The sound *a* is the creator Brahma, *u* is the protector Vishnu, and *m* is the destroyer Hara (Rudra). The *bindu* is the deity Maheshvara, proclaimed to be concealment. The *nada* is said to be Sadashiva, bestowing grace on everybody. After meditating above the *nada*, the most supreme Shiva [is seen]."

—*Shiva Purana*

(28)
om
(ओम् = *om*)

MEANING

"**1** the pervader and the first, the superior and the equanimous, and the establishment and the dissolution
2 all-pervading, the most superior, and all-powerful
3 the Supreme Brahman as Narasimha."

EXPLANATION

The *Mandukya Upanishad* gives an esoteric meaning of OM by tracing its components to various concepts. It says that the sound *a* comes from *apti* (obtaining) or *adimat* (being first), *u* comes from *utkarsha* (superiority) or *ubhaya* (being both), and *m* comes from *miti* (establishment) or *apiti* (dissolution). Putting them together, OM means that which is all-pervading, first, superior, equanimous, establishment, and dissolution. The Upanishad states that one who knows this about the components of OM obtains all desires and becomes foremost, exalts his tradition of knowledge and stays equanimous in both worlds, and establishes everything and becomes the [place of] dissolution also.

A similar explanation of the three components of OM is found in the *Nrisimha Uttara Tapini Upanishad*, which establishes Narasimha as the Supreme Brahman. As per this Upanishad, the sound *a* comes from *aptatama* (the most pervading), *u* comes from *utkrishtatama* (the most superior), and *m* comes from *mahavibhuti* (having great power). In the eighth canto of the *Bhagavata Purana*, the word *mahavibhuti* is used as part of the refrain in twelve consecutive verses of Brahma's prayer to Vishnu.

Combining the Upanishad explanations together, OM means that which is omnipresent, the most superior, and omnipotent.

The Upanishad equates all the three component sounds of OM with Narasimha, who is described as Brahman, the Supreme atman. This implies a three-way identity: OM is the same as Narasimha who is Brahman. This understanding is in accordance with the philosophy of the *Narasimha Sampradaya* (a tradition with very few followers today) which identifies Narasimha as the Supreme Brahman.

TRADITION

Upanishad, Vaishnavism.

ETYMOLOGY

a + u + m → om.

a ▸ (see below); ***u*** ▸ (see below); ***m*** ▸ (see below).

QUOTES

"The first mora is *a* which means obtaining or being first ... the second mora is *u* which means exaltation or being both ... the third mora is *m* which means establishment or dissolution."

—*Mandukya Upanishad*

"The sound *a* means the most pervading, ... the sound *u* means the most exalted ... the sound *m* means all-powerful."

—*Nrisimha Uttara Tapini Upanishad*

"The sound *a* means Narasimha, the Supreme atman Brahman ... the sound *u* means Narasimha, the Supreme atman Brahman ... the sound *m* means Narasimha, the Supreme atman Brahman."

—*Nrisimha Uttara Tapini Upanishad*

(29)
omkara/onkara
(ओंकार/ओङ्कार = oṃkāra/oṅkāra)

MEANING

"the exclamation or the sound OM."

EXPLANATION

As per the *Pratishakhya*-s of Shukla and Krishna Yajur Veda, the suffix *kara* indicates a sound of speech and the name of any sound is the sound followed by the suffix *kara*. In the grammar tradition, a *varttika* (auxiliary rule) by Katyayana says that the *kara* suffix is used in the sense of imitation of a sound. Thus, *a-kara*, *u-kara*, and *ma-kara* are the names of the sounds *a*, *u*, and *m* respectively. This is why the five elements used in Tantric practice (*madya*, *mamsa*, *matsya*, *mudra*, and *maithuna*) are referred to as *pancha-makara*-s ("the five Ms"), and the five signs of a Sikh in Sikhism (*kesh*, *kangha*, *kirpan*, *kara*, and *kachera*) are called *panch kakar*-s ("the five Ks").

Kaiyata's commentary on the *Mahabhashya* says that the suffix *kara* is also seen after words in some cases. This explains words like *humkara* ("grunting sound") and *chitkara* ("shouting sound"), and similarly *omkara*. The word *omkara* literally means "the sound OM". As it means a sound, the name *omkara* refers to the *saguna* aspect of OM, the *svara* (p. 88) or the *shabda* (p. 162). In contrast, names like *niranjana* (p. 134) refer to the *nirguna* aspect of OM. The existence of these two kinds of names imply that OM is seen as both *saguna* and *nirguna* in Hindu traditions.

Along with *pranava*, *omkara* is one of the most popular names of OM. It is mentioned and equated with *pranava* in Smriti and

Purana texts, and also in the famous dictionary *Amara Kosha.* It is noteworthy that both names have three syllables each (*om-ka-ra* and *pra-na-va*) and can be called *tryakshara* (p. 192).

Both *omkara* (ओंकार) and *onkara* (ओङ्कार) are valid spellings which represent two different pronunciations of the same name. The former pronunciation is due to the letter *m* changing to the *anusvara* (nasal vowel modifier) in accordance with a mandatory rule of Sanskrit grammar. The *anusvara* optionally changes to a homoorganic nasal consonant when followed by a plosive. This gives rise to the latter alternative pronunciation. The *onkara* spelling and pronunciation are also seen in Sikhism, where the spelling *Ik Onkar* is more common than *Ik Omkar.*

TRADITION

Smriti, Purana, grammar, dictionaries.

ETYMOLOGY

om + kāra → oṃkāra/oṅkāra.

om ▸ OM; ***kāra*** ▸ suffix to denote a sound or a word.

QUOTES

"*Omkara* is *Pranava.*"

—*Yogi Yajnavalkya Smriti*

"That sound *omkara* alone is *pranava* in this world."

—*Linga Purana*

"Suffix *kara* occurs after sounds, e.g. *akara.* At some places, it occurs after a group of sounds (a word) too."

—Grammar commentaries

"*Omkara* and *pranava* are synonymous."

—*Amara Kosha*

(30)

pranava

(प्रणव = *praṇava*)

MEANING

"**1** eminently praised **2** the means of praise or worship."

EXPLANATION

Pranava is one of the most popular and the most ancient names of OM. Attested in popular dictionaries, the name is first used in the Shukla Yajur Veda, which ends with the proclamation that OM is Brahman (p. 36). It is used five times in the *Chandogya Upanishad* which starts with OM. The name is used frequently in both sacred texts (Upanishad-s, Purana-s, Smriti-s, etc.) and secular texts (Panini's grammar, poems, plays, dictionaries, etc.).

The word *pranava* is derived from *pra* + √*nu*, where the root √*nu* means "to praise" or "to worship" and the prefix *pra* has the sense of "especially" or "eminently". Accordingly, *pranava* means that which is eminently praised. The *Chandogya Upanishad* states that one who eminently praises OM enters (takes refuge in) it and becomes fearless and immortal. The verb used here for eminent praise is *pranauti*, which is also from *pra* + √*nu*. OM is *pranava* as it is praised generously by the Upanishad-s, the Smriti-s, the *Gita*, and the Purana-s.

With the same etymology, another meaning of *pranava* is "the means of praising or worshipping". Not only is OM praised, it is also used in mantra-s as a means (*sadhana*) for praising Brahman or one's desired (*ishta*) deity. The *Aitareya Brahmana* uses the verb *pranauti* four times, thrice in the context of pronouncing OM with mantra-s used for praising deities. When OM is chanted independently, it is a means to praise Brahman. When it is used as a part of a mantra, it is a means to propitiate or worship a specific deity like Shiva, Vishnu, Ganesha, Rama, Durga, etc.

The use of OM for worshipping Shiva has been specially noted. The *Linga Purana* states that Shiva is to be worshipped on top of the *linga* using *pranava* alone. In the *Shiva Gita* of the *Padma Purana*, Shiva says, "There does not exist a greater devotee of mine than one who eminently worships me with *pranava* after putting on ash (*bhasma*)." Shiva further says, "One who regularly worships me with OM—along with offering sacred grass, *bilva* leaves, or mountain flowers—is dear to me."

TRADITION

Purana, dictionaries, commentaries.

ETYMOLOGY

pra + √nu + ap → praṇava.

pra* + √*nu ▸ to praise eminently, to worship; ***ap*** ▸ suffix indicating object or means of an action.

QUOTES

"It is known as *pranava*, as it is eminently praised much more than everything else by all those desirous of supreme liberation."

—*Skanda Purana*

"*Omkara* and *pranava* are synonymous. *Pranava* is that which is eminently praised."

—*Amara Kosha*, its commentaries

"*Pranava* is that with which Brahman or one's *ishta* deity is eminently praised or worshipped."

—*Shabdakalpadruma Kosha*

(31)

pranava

(प्रणव = *praṇava*)

MEANING

“1 the guide, that which leads forward
2 the initiator, that which inspires
3 the lover, that which loves.”

EXPLANATION

The *Skanda Purana* derives *pranava* from the root *pra* + √*ni*, among whose many meanings the primary one is “to lead”, or “to take”. The Purana says that *pranava* is called so because it leads those who serve it to the supreme state (*moksha*). The word *neta* (“leader”), used in two names in the *Vishnu Sahasranama*, also derives from the root √*ni*. The name *yogavidam neta* of Vishnu is explained by a commentary as “he who leads devotees to *moksha*”, similar to the *Skanda Purana* explanation above.

The derivation of *pranava* from *pra* + √*ni* is alluded to in the *Maitri Upanishad*, which describes OM as the *praneta* (“initiator”) named *pranava*. Ramatirtha’s commentary confirms this by stating that OM is called *pranava* for the very reason that it is *praneta*, or the initiator of all actions. While the same derivation is implied here as suggested by the *Skanda Purana*, the sense of *pra* + √*ni* in this derivation is “to inspire”. The same sense of the root is used to explain the word *prana* in the *Aitareya Brahmana*. Just before describing how Prajapati obtained OM, the text states that the rising sun inspires (*pranayati*) all beings to move, hence it is called *prana*. Incidentally, OM is identified with both *prana* (*pranava*, p. 66) and the sun (*aditya*, p. 94).

The word *praneta,* which means "eminent leader" in addition to "initiator", is used in many Vedic hymns to describe the deity of the hymn. It is found in the *samhita*-s of the Rig Veda, the Yajur Veda, and the Atharva Veda. In the Rig Veda, Indra is called *praneta* four times, Agni and Marut-s twice each, and Varuna and Bhaga once each. The riches of Indra are called *praneta* in the Rig Veda as they delight; and Prajapati is also called *praneta* in the *Taittiriya Brahmana.*

The root *pra* + √*ni* also means "to love": the Sanskrit word *pranaya* ("love") is derived from *pra* + √*ni.* Thus, *pranava* also means that which loves. OM loves everybody, for it is called *narayana* which means the refuge of entire humanity (p. 132).

TRADITION

Upanishad, Purana.

ETYMOLOGY

From **pra + √nī.**

pra + √***nī*** ▸ **1** to guide, to lead **2** to inspire **3** to love.

QUOTES

"'To the *praneta* named *pranava*' means that it (OM) is the initiator of all actions—for this reason alone it is named *pranava.*"

—Commentary on *Maitri Upanishad*

"As it leads its worshipper to the supreme state, hence [it is called] *pranava.*"

—*Skanda Purana*

(32)
pranava
(प्रणव = *praṇava*)

MEANING

"the boat or ship to cross the worldly ocean."

EXPLANATION

The *Shiva Purana* splits *pranava* into *pra* and *nava* and explains that the former stands for *prakriti* (cause of the material world), while the latter means a ship or a boat. The meaning of *pranava*, then, is the vessel to cross the ocean of the world. OM is also called *tara* (p. 170) where the sense of crossing of the material ocean is expressed. In addition, the second sound of OM is called *karna* (p. 192), which means an oar used to steer a boat.

The words *nau* and *nava* in Sanskrit refer to a ship or a boat. The cognate words in Greek and Latin are *naus* and *navis* respectively, from where several English words—*naval, navy, navigate,* and *nautical*—are derived directly or indirectly.

TRADITION

Purana.

ETYMOLOGY

pra + nava → praṇava.

pra ▸ (*prakṛti*) ocean of the world; ***nava*** ▸ boat (variant of *nāva*).

QUOTES

"The wise certainly know *pranava* as the *nava,* another [word for] boat, for *pra,* the ocean of world arising from *prakriti.*"

—*Shiva Purana*

(33)

pranava

(प्रणव = *praṇava*)

MEANING

"'there is no material world or illusion for you.'"

EXPLANATION

In another meaning, the sage Suta tells other sages in the *Shiva Purana* that *pranavah* (*pranava*) has three parts—*pra* stands for *prapancha* which means material world or *maya* (illusion), *na* means "no", and *vah* means "of you all". *Pranavah* is the proclamation that there is no *prapancha* for you. The essence is that OM is the redeemer from materialism and *maya.*

The interpretation of *pra* as *prakriti* or *prapancha* follows a Sanskrit maxim (*nyaya*) which says that when a part of a name is mentioned, the whole name is to be understood. Applying this maxim, Sanskrit commentaries sometimes give esoteric meanings of words.

TRADITION

Purana.

ETYMOLOGY

pra + na + vaḥ → praṇavaḥ.

pra ▸ (*prapañca*) **1** material world **2** illusion, *maya*; ***na*** ▸ no; ***vaḥ*** ▸ your (plural).

QUOTES

"They (the wise) know *pranava* as there is no (*na*) material world (*prapancha*) for you (*vah*)."

—*Shiva Purana*

(34)

pranava

(प्रणव = *praṇava*)

MEANING

" that which completely leads you [to liberation]. "

EXPLANATION

In this meaning from the *Shiva Purana*, the sage Suta splits the inflected form *pranavah* into *prana*, which is said to come from the root *pra* + √*ni*, and *vah* which means "you all". Suta tells other sages that OM is called *pranava* as "it completely leads you all to *moksha*."

The difference between this meaning and *pranava* as explained earlier from *pra* + √*ni* (p. 60) is that here the object is explicitly specified as "you all", emphasizing the universal nature of OM as a means of liberation.

TRADITION

Purana.

ETYMOLOGY

pra + na + vaḥ → praṇavaḥ.

pra ▸ completely; ***na*** ▸ (from √*nī* + *ḍa*) one who leads; ***vaḥ*** ▸ you all.

QUOTES

"As it completely (*pra*) leads (*na*) you all (*vah*) to liberation (*moksha*), the wise know it to be *pranava*."

—*Shiva Purana*

(35)
pranava
(प्रणव = *praṇava*)

MEANING

“**1** eminent bestower of new knowledge **2** always new.”

EXPLANATION

The *Shiva Purana* explains *pranava* alternatively as *pra* + *nava* (“new”). *Nava* is cognate with Greek *neos* (used in words like *neo-classical*) and English *new*. The Purana says that *nava* refers to the divine knowledge, which is ever new, and that which specially (*pra*) endows the noble with this knowledge is *pranava*.

A commentary on the *Vishnu Sahasranama* explains *pranava* as always new. This applies to OM also; OM is always new as it is endless (*ananta*, p. 100) and unchanging (*avyaya*, p. 102).

TRADITION

Purana, commentaries.

ETYMOLOGY

pra + nava → praṇava.

pra ▸ eminently; ***nava*** ▸ new.

QUOTES

“The divine knowledge is ever new. The wise know *pranava* as that which eminently (*pra*) makes the noble [endowed with] *nava*, the ever new divine knowledge which is pure by nature.”

—*Shiva Purana*

“Ever new, hence *pranava*.”

—Commentary on *Vishnu Sahasranama*

(36)

pranava

(प्रणव = *praṇava*)

MEANING

"*prana* (vitality, or the vital force)."

EXPLANATION

Smriti and Purana texts associate the word *pranava* with *prana*, identifying OM as the giver of *prana* or as *prana* itself. The *Talavakara Aranyaka* also compares OM with *prana*.

OM is described as the giver of *prana* (life) to the Veda-s, deities, body, speech, and mind. OM gives life to the Veda-s as Vedic mantra-s are chanted with OM, whose recitation is believed to preserve Vedic learning (p. 17). OM is the giver of life for the deities as per the *Chandogya Upanishad* which states that the deities entered OM to achieve immortality when they were seen by Death (p. 129). In Upanishad, Purana, and Yoga texts, OM is identified with the process of breathing (see p. 46), which gives life to the mortal body. As the ultimate essence of speech (p. 148), OM gives life to speech. Finally, as OM is identified with the Supreme Brahman, it is believed to give life to the mind, for the *Kena Upanishad* says, "Know that to be Brahman which is not thought of by the mind, but due to which the mind thinks."

The Shiva Purana defines *pranava* as the *prana* of all beings, where *prana* stands for both life and the fivefold vital force. The five types of vital forces are *prana* (ingestive force in the heart), *apana* (excretory force in the intestines), *samana* (digestive force in the centre), *udana* (vocal force in the throat), and *vyana* (nictitative and similar forces in the body).

OM is identified with Vishnu (p. 206), who is called *prana* and *pranada* ("the giver of *prana*") in the *Vishnu Sahasranama.* OM is identified with Agni (p. 6), who is called *pranada* in the Yajur Veda. OM is also identified with the Supreme Brahman (p. 36), and the *Brahma Sutra* says that *prana* means Brahman in the Veda-s. As per the *Chandogya Upanishad,* all beings dissolve into *prana* and originate from *prana*; OM is seen similarly (p. 144).

As OM is said to be both *prana* and the bestower of *prana*, it can be understood as *prana* of even *prana*. Vedic texts describe Brahman, whose name is OM, as *pranasya pranah,* meaning "*prana* of even *prana*".

TRADITION

Veda, Smriti, Purana.

ETYMOLOGY

prāṇa → praṇava.

prāṇa ▸ vital force.

QUOTES

"That which is OM is the fire, speech is the earth. OM is the wind, speech is the atmosphere. OM is the sun, speech is the sky. OM is the vital force, speech is speech itself."

—*Talavakara Aranyaka*

"The three-syllabled OM is called *pranava* since it gives *prana* (life) to the four Veda-s, deities, body, speech, and mind."

—*Yogi Yajnavalkya Smriti*

"As this *pranava* is surely the *prana* (life or vital force) of all beings from Brahma to the unmoving, hence it is called *pranava.*"

—*Shiva Purana*

(37)

pranava

(प्रणव = *praṇava*)

MEANING

"that which makes one bow down."

EXPLANATION

Two Upanishad-s of the Atharva Veda derive *pranava* from the root *pra* + √*nam.* The root √*nam* means to "to bow down". The words *namas* (नमस्, "act of bowing down") and *pranama* (प्रणाम, "salutation") come from this root. The greeting *namaste* ("salutation to you") derives from *namas.* The word *namas* can change to *namo* or *namah* as per rules of *sandhi.* It occurs five times in the refrain *namastasyai namastasyai namastasyai namo namah* ("salutation to her, salutation to her, salutation to her, salutation, salutation") from the *Durga Saptashati. Namas* is a part of many mantra-s like *om namah shivaya* and *om namo bhagavate vasudevaya.* Its Prakrit form *namo* (णमो) occurs five times in the *Namokar Mantra* recited to pay obeisance to the five *parameshthi*-s (supreme ones) in Jainism. Interestingly, the Jain tradition derives OM from the initial sounds of the *parameshthi-s*—***a**rihanta*-s (conquerors of inner enemies), ***a**sarira*-s (the liberated *siddha*-s), ***a**yariya*-s (spiritual teachers), ***u**vajjhaya*-s (preceptors), and ***m**uni*-s (sadhus). The sounds combine as per rules of *sandhi* to give *a+a+a+u+m* = OM.

The two Upanishad-s state that OM is called *pranava* since it makes Brahmins bow down to the Supreme Brahman and makes all beings bow down [to Brahman, the *ishta*, guru, etc.]. Indeed, as the beginning of many important mantra-s containing *namas,*

OM is what initiates or inspires aspirants to bow down to the object of worship or meditation.

The *Satya Bhashya* on the *Vishnu Sahasranama* explains the name *pranava* as *pranamayati iti* ("that which causes somebody to bow down"), adding that an alternate reading is *pranama* (प्रणम). Grammatically, *pranama* is the word derived from *pra* + √*nam*. The Upanishad-s and commentaries do not say how it becomes *pranava*, but a *prishodaradi* derivation can be assumed to account for *m* changing to *v*.

TRADITION

Upanishad, commentaries.

ETYMOLOGY

pra + √nam + ṇic + ac → praṇava.

pra + √***nam*** ▸ to bow down to, to pay obeisance to; ***ṇic*** ▸ suffix to denote causative sense; ***ac*** ▸ suffix to denote the doer.

QUOTES

"Then, why is it called *pranava*? Since on merely being pronounced it makes the Brahmins specially bow to the Supreme Brahman which is the *rasa* having the Rig Veda, the Yajur Veda, the Sama Veda, and the Atharva Veda as its limbs—hence it is called *pranava*."

—*Atharva Shira Upanishad*

"Certainly, OM makes all the beings especially bow down. It is therefore called *pranava*."

—*Atharva Shikha Upanishad*

"*Pranava* is that which makes one bow down."

—Commentary on *Vishnu Sahasranama*

(38)

pranava

(प्रणव = praṇava)

MEANING

"1 protector of life, vital forces, and living beings 2 that which loves living beings 3 pervader of vital forces and living beings 4 that which causes living beings to grow."

EXPLANATION

The *Linga Purana* explains the word *pranava* as *prana* (प्राण) + *avati*. Of the many meanings of *prana*, three—life, the five vital forces, and living beings—are applicable here. The verb *avati* is from the root √*av*, which has nineteen meanings (p. 210). Four meanings—to protect, to love, to enter or pervade, and to cause to grow—apply here. The Purana does not say how the first vowel in *prana* (प्राण) becomes short in *pranava* (प्रणव); it is to be understood that the irregular word is of the *prishodaradi* type. Similarly, *prana* + *ava* should result in the form *pranava* (प्रणाव) with a long middle vowel as per *sandhi* rules, but the exception here is like in the case of *shakandhvadi* words.

In *shakandhvadi* words like *manisha* ("intellect"), from *manas* ("mind") + *isha* ("movement"), the last vowel and any following consonants in the first word are effectively deleted in *sandhi*. Thus, in *manas* + *isha*, the ending *as* of *manas* is deleted to give *man* + *isha* = *manisha*. Similarly, *prana* + *ava* here results in *pran* + *ava* = *pranava* with all short vowels. Another example is *patat* ("falling") + *anjali* ("cupped hands") = *patanjali*.

Due to the multiple meanings of the both parts *prana* and *ava*, many meanings of *pranava* (OM) are implied by the *Linga*

Purana explanation. That which protects life, vital forces, and living beings is *pranava*. As the breath (p. 66), OM protects and sustains life and the vital forces. As the protector from death (p. 129), OM protects living beings.

That which loves all living beings is *pranava*. OM is described as the refuge of all humans and all living beings (p. 132): it accepts every living being as its own.

That which pervades vital forces or living beings is *pranava*. OM pervades *prana*; it is the *prana* of even the fivefold *prana* (p. 67). OM pervades yogi-s; the *Shiva Purana* states that the subtle OM is located in their hearts. OM pervades living beings too; Krishna says in the *Gita* that *ishvara*, whose name is *pranava* (p. 36), resides in the hearts of all living beings.

Finally, that which causes living beings to grow is *pranava*. Purana-s say that OM is called *brahma* because of growth or expansion (p. 108). The *Linga Purana* adds that Brahman is called so because it nourishes living beings and makes them grow.

TRADITION

Purana.

ETYMOLOGY

√av + ac → ava; prāṇa + ava → praṇava.

√av ▸ **1** to protect **2** to love **3** to enter, to pervade **4** to grow; ***ac*** ▸ suffix to denote performer of an action; ***prāṇa*** ▸ **1** life **2** one of the five vital forces **3** a living being.

QUOTES

"It protects/loves/pervades/grows life/vital forces/living beings, therefore it is known as *pranava*."

—*Linga Purana*

(39)

pranava, omkara

(प्रणव, ओंकार = *praṇava, oṃkāra*)

MEANING

"Shiva."

EXPLANATION

In the many schools of Shaivism, one of the largest Hindu denominations, Shiva is the Supreme Brahman—seen as both *sakara* (with form) and *nirakara* (without [anthropomorphic] form, as *linga*). It is not surprising then that OM is identified with Shiva in several Purana-s. Just like the *Yoga Sutra* says that *pranava* is the name of Brahman and its repetition is the contemplation of Brahman (p. 36), the *Linga Purana* says that *pranava* is the foremost name of Shiva and its repetition leads to the contemplation of Shiva. The Purana also describes Shiva as the *jagadguru* (universal preceptor) named *omkara*.

In the *Matsya Purana*, all the three sounds of OM are indirectly identified with Shiva. While praising Shiva in a *stotra*, Shukra says Shiva alone is the three Veda-s in *pranava*. The three Veda-s correspond to the sounds *a*, *u*, and *m* in OM (p. 8). This identification is made explicit in the *Skanda Purana*, where Brahma praises Shiva by saying that he alone is the sounds *a*, *u*, and *m* of OM. In the *Shiva Purana*, Shiva himself tells Parvati that there is no difference between *pranava* and Shiva.

In the Kaula work *Karpuradi Stotra*, attributed to Mahakala, goddess Kali is described as *tryakshare'ti*. A commentary parses this as *ati-tryakshare* and explains it as "she who has surpassed even the *tryakshara* (Shiva)". As *tryakshara* is also a name of OM

(p. 192), the commentary identifies OM with Shiva.

Omkareshvara in Madhya Pradesh is one of the twelve *jyotirlinga*-s (effulgent emblems) of Shiva. Although the word *omkareshvara* is commonly understood as the "lord of OM", it can also be interpreted as "he whose lord is OM" and "he who is the lord and OM [both]".

TRADITION

Purana, Shaivism.

QUOTES

"*Pranava* is the indicator of the Supreme Self [known as] Shiva. *Pranava* is superior to even the words Shiva and Rudra. The contemplation of Shiva, which is indicated by *pranava*, is also [achieved] by chanting it."

—*Linga Purana*

"Above the *nada* (sound), one should meditate on Shiva, who is known as *omkara* and who is the preceptor of the whole world."

—*Linga Purana*

"To Shiva, who is the Rig Veda, the Yajur Veda, and the Sama Veda in *Pranava* (OM)."

—*Matsya Purana*

"Sadashiva! Salutations to you. Your form (sign) is OM. You are the sound *a*, you are the sound *u*, and you are the sound *m*."

—*Skanda Purana*

"Shiva said, 'I, the omnipresent Shiva, am established in the *ekakshara* OM. Shiva is *pranava* and *pranava* is Shiva, since there is no difference at all between that which is expressed (*vachya*) and that which expresses it (*vachaka*).'"

—*Shiva Purana*

(40)

udgitha, trimatra

(उद्गीथ, त्रिमात्र = *udgītha, trimātra*)

MEANING

"the sun, the air, and the fire."

EXPLANATION

One of the famous names of OM is *udgitha*. The *Chandogya Upanishad* splits the name into three parts—*ut*, *gi*, and *tha*—and explains them as the sun (Surya), the air (Vayu), and the fire (Agni) respectively. Commentaries explain this as follows—*ut* refers to ***utthana*** or the sun's act of rising, *gi* refers to ***girana*** or the air's act of swallowing fire or fragrance, and *tha* refers to ***sthana*** or the fire's property of being the site for the sacred *yajna*. OM refers to the three gods together.

The triad of Surya, Vayu, and Agni has a unique place in Vedic Hinduism. A verse in the Rig Veda is a prayer to this triad—"May Surya protect us from heavenly beings, Vayu from atmospheric troubles, and Agni from enemies on earth." The *Nirukta* tradition believes that there are only three deities—Agni on earth, Vayu (or Indra) in atmosphere, and Surya in the heavens. In the same context, Yaska says in the *Nirukta* that only the one Supreme God is worshipped in many ways, and the other deities (Agni, Vayu, Surya, etc.) are like the limbs of the one God. Indeed, in a hymn addressed to Vishvedeva-s ("all gods") in the Rig Veda, a verse states that the wise call the same entity variously (*ekam sad vipra bahudha vadanti*)—Aditya (Surya) is called Indra, Mitra, Varuna, Agni, Garuda, Yama, or Matarishva (Vayu). The verse explains not only the underlying unity of many gods in Hinduism (they are all aspects of one God), but also the concept of *ishta-devata* or desired deity. Just like all gods are seen as Surya here, all deities in Hinduism are considered manifestations of the *ishta-devata*—be it Surya, Agni, or Vayu; or Ganesha, Vishnu, Shiva, Devi, Rama, or Krishna.

The *Jaiminiya Aranyaka* presents Surya, Vayu, and Agni as the essences of the three *loka*-s and compares each to OM, the essence of speech. The triad is called the luminous form of OM in the *Maitri Upanishad* (p. 176).

The *Yogi Yajnavalkya Smriti* says that one of OM's names is *trimatra* (p. 28)—the fire, the air, and the sun. The word *matra* here means constituents or retinue (royal attendants). The essence is that the three gods considered supreme in the *Nirukta* tradition are the three constituents or three attendants of OM.

TRADITION

Upanishad, Smriti.

ETYMOLOGY

ut + gī + tha → udgītha; tri + mātrā → trimātra.

ut ▸ sun; ***gī*** ▸ air; ***tha*** ▸ fire. ***tri*** ▸ three; ***mātrā*** ▸ **1** constituent, part **2** attendants, retinue, insignia.

QUOTES

"The sun alone is *ut*, the air is *gi*, and the fire is *tha*. ... That *udgitha* (OM) is the fire, the air, and the sun."

—*Chandogya Upanishad*

"OM is called *trimatra* due to the fire, the air, and the sun."

—*Yogi Yajnavalkya Smriti*

(41)
udgitha
(उद्गीथ = *udgītha*)

MEANING

"vital force (*prana*) and speech."

EXPLANATION

The word *udgitha* is explained as the pair of vital force and speech in the *Brihad Aranyaka Upanishad*. The context is an allegorical account as follows (the same account occurs in the *Chandogya Upanishad* with some differences).

The gods and demons, sons of Prajapati, were engaged in a battle for the three worlds. The heavily outnumbered gods asked the presiding deities of the senses to chant the *udgitha* (OM) for their victory. One after the other, the deities of speech, smell, vision, hearing, and mind chanted the *udgitha*. All five of them dedicated the fruit of chanting to the gods but kept the merit for themselves. Coming to know of their chanting, the demons struck them down with evil. This is why the senses of speech, smell, vision, hearing, and mind are associated with both good and evil actions. The gods then asked the vital force (*prana*) to chant the *udgitha*. The *prana* did not keep the merit for itself. When the demons tried to strike the *prana* with evil, they were themselves destroyed and scattered. The *prana* then freed the other five deities from evil, transforming them into Agni (fire), Vayu (wind), Surya (sun), the directions, and Chandra (moon). Following this, the *prana* chanted to obtain food for eating, and nourished the five deities also with it. The *prana* then came to be known as the essence of all limbs of the body.

The Upanishad states that they who know this are the nourishers of their dependents, and their rivals are powerless. The purport is that just as the *prana*, which chanted the *udgitha* without partaking of the merit, was not harmed and became the nourisher of others, a person with selfless benevolence is not harmed and becomes the nourisher of others.

The Upanishad then says that this *prana* and speech are together known as *udgitha*, with *ut* meaning the *prana* (vital force) and *githa* meaning speech. In the account, the *prana* and its chanting (the speech) protected the gods from the demons and made them prevail. *Udgitha* or OM is also described as that which protects—the *Kurma Purana* says that OM is called so because of its function of protection (see *om*, p. 210).

TRADITION

Upanishad.

ETYMOLOGY

ut + gītha → udgītha.

ut ▸ vital force; ***gītha*** ▸ speech.

QUOTES

"The vital force (*prana*) alone is *ut*, [since] by the vital force all this is upheld (***uttabdha***). Speech alone is *githa* [since the sacred speech is sung]. That which is *ut* and *githa* is *udgitha*."

—*Brihad Aranyaka Upanishad*

(42)
udgitha
(उद्गीथ = *udgītha*)

MEANING

" vital force (*prana*), speech, and food."

EXPLANATION

This meaning comes from the *Chandogya Upanishad*, which begins with the word OM. The Upanishad says in the beginning that one should worship the imperishable syllable OM, which is *udgitha*. Later, the Upanishad says that the individual syllables of the word *udgitha*—*ut*, *gi*, and *tha*—should also be worshipped and then gives their meanings. As per Sanskrit *sandhi* rules, when the sound *g* follows the sound *t*, the latter changes to the sound *d*. For example, *sat* ("true, good") and *guru* ("spiritual teacher") combine to result in the word *sadguru* ("the genuine teacher"). Similarly, *ut* becomes *ud* when it is followed by *gi*.

The first syllable *ut* is explained by the Upanishad as vital force or breath, since one rises by the means of breath. The prefix *ut* means upwards, as in *uttishthati* ("gets up"). The purport is that as long as one possesses the vital force and breathes, they are able to rise from sleep and stand up. Metaphorically, rising from sleep is the first step towards obtaining a goal. A popular verse of *Katha Upanishad*, as translated by Swami Vivekananda, says "Arise, awake, and stop not till the goal is reached."

The second syllable *gi* is explained by the Upanishad as speech. This is derived from the root √*gri* ("to speak"). A cognate word for speech is *gir*, which is why Sarasvati is called *girdevi* ("goddess of speech").

The third syllable *tha* is explained by the Upanishad as food. This is derived from the root √*stha* ("to rest"). Food is called *tha* because all life rests on (depends on) food.

Taken together, the word *udgitha* stands for the triad of vital force, speech, and food. The meaning is an extension of the "vital force and speech" meaning presented in the *Brihad Aranyaka Upanishad* passage on vital force (p. 76), where the vital force protects the gods using speech and nourishes the deities using food. Similarly, OM is seen as both the protector (see OM, on p. 210) and the nourisher (see *gunajivaka*, p. 122).

Paul Deussen, who translated sixty Upanishad-s into German, remarks in this context that the interpretation of *udgitha* as the vital force, speech, and food corresponds to the three main activities of humans—breathing, speaking, and eating.

TRADITION

Upanishad.

ETYMOLOGY

ut + gī + tha → udgītha.

ut ▸ vital force; ***gī*** ▸ speech; ***tha*** ▸ food.

QUOTES

"The vital force (*prana*) alone is *ut*, for one rises (*uttishthati*) by means of the vital force. Speech is *gi*, for speeches are called *girah*. Food is *tha*, for it is in food that all this (living world) is subsisting (*sthita*)."

—*Chandogya Upanishad*

(43)
udgitha
(उद्गीथ = udgītha)

MEANING

"that which is sung aloud."

EXPLANATION

In the Sama Veda, each verse (*saman*) in a *stotra* has five parts of which the third is called *udgitha*. The chanting of *udgitha* begins with OM. Sama Veda's *Chandogya Upanishad*, which mentions *udgitha* more than 60 times, says that this is why the word *udgitha* denotes OM.

Grammatically, the word *udgitha* is derived from the root √*gai* ("to sing"). The words *gana* and *gita*, both meaning "a song", are from the same root √*gai*. The prefix *ut*, which changes to *ud* (p. 78), in *udgitha* means "high" or "aloud". Thus, *udgitha* literally means "that which is sung aloud". In the *Shvetashvatara Upanishad*, Brahman is described as *udgita* (उद्गीत), which has the same meaning as *udgitha* (उद्गीथ). A cognate word is *udgata* (उद्गाता) which means a singer of the Sama Veda. In the *Gita*, Krishna says that among the Veda-s, he is the Sama Veda. The *Chandogya Upanishad* proclaims *udgitha* to be the essence (*rasa*) of Sama Veda. OM is thus the essence of the foremost Veda—it is described in the Upanishad as the essence of all essences (p. 148). In the *Durga Saptashati*, Indra and the gods praise Shakti as the resting place of the Veda-s, the recitation of whose words is made mellifluous by *udgitha* (p. 45).

While the name *udgitha* is rarely mentioned in the Purana-s and *Itihasa*-s, there is description of OM being sung or chanted aloud at several places. In the *Mahabharata*, Bhishma narrates Vishnu's display of his universal form to Narada. Narada sees Vishnu, who has hundreds of heads, "singing aloud" OM with one of his mouths. The *Kurma Purana* similarly has a description of Shiva's cosmic form, akin to thousands of suns, in which he is described as "singing aloud" *pranava* (OM).

In addition to being the name of the central part of a Sama Vedic *stotra* and the sound OM, *udgitha* also refers to the act of singing. In this context, *udgitha* refers to the singing of the Sama Veda in general and its second chapter in particular.

TRADITION

Upanishad, Smriti, Purana, *Mahabharata*.

ETYMOLOGY

ut + √gai + thak → udgītha.

ut* + √*gai ▸ to sing or chant aloud; ***thak*** ▸ suffix indicating object of the action.

QUOTES

"Then, verily, what is *udgitha* is *pranava* (OM). What is *pranava* (OM) is *udgitha*."

—*Chandogya Upanishad*

"OM is known as *udgitha*."

—*Yogi Yajnavalkya Smriti*

"Vishnu was singing aloud OM with [one] mouth."

—Bhishma's description, *Mahabharata*

"Shiva was singing aloud the great OM with his mouth."

—*Kurma Purana*

(44)

udgitha, suryantargata

(उद्गीथ, सूर्यान्तर्गत = *udgītha, sūryāntargata*)

MEANING

" the golden being in the interior of the sun. "

EXPLANATION

The *Yogi Yajnavalkya Smriti* mentions *suryantargata* ("existing inside the sun") as one of the names of OM. An explanation which alludes to this name is offered by the *Chandogya Upanishad* for the name *udgitha* of OM. While describing the godly (*adhidaivata*) aspect of meditating on OM, the Upanishad mentions a golden *Purusha* (being) who is seen within the sun. This *Purusha* has a golden beard and golden hair, and is golden all over—down to the tips of his nails. The eyes of this *Purusha* are described as resembling blooming lotuses. The Upanishad says that the *Purusha* is called *Ut* as he has "risen above" (*udita* = *ut*, "above", + *ita*, "gone") all evil, and one who knows this also rises above all sins. The Upanishad adds that the Rig Veda and the Sama Veda are the singers (*githa*-s) of this *Ut*, and so he is also called *Udgitha*. For the same reason, one who sings of *Ut* is called *udgata* (a singer of the Sama Veda). This *Ut* is said to be the ruler of the worlds beyond the solar orb and the ruler of the gods' desires.

The *Purusha* inside the sun is also mentioned in the *Isha Upanishad*, where the aspirant beseeches Surya, the sun-god, to gather his radiance and allow them to see his most auspicious form. The aspirant then says, "That *Purusha* [inside the sun]—that I am." This implies that the living being (*jivatma*) is similar to the Brahman as the former is a part (*amsha*) of the latter.

In the *Rama Stavaraja Stotra,* Rama is called *aditya-mandala-gata* ("situated in the orb of the sun"). In the same hymn, Rama is identified with OM as he is called *pranava* (p. 38). In the *Valmiki Ramayana,* Sumitra describes Rama as "the sun of even the sun", alluding to Rama's identification with the Upanishad-s' golden *Purusha* inside the sun.

In his commentary on the *Isha Upanishad,* Raghavendra Swami interprets the appellation *surya* of the sun as *suryantargata,* the supreme divinity inside the sun.

TRADITION

Upanishad, Smriti.

ETYMOLOGY

ut + gītha → udgītha;

sūrya + antargata → sūryāntargata.

ut ▸ the golden being inside the sun; ***gītha*** ▸ singer; ***sūrya*** ▸ the sun; ***antargata*** ▸ existing inside (literally, "gone inside").

QUOTES

"Now, this golden being seen in the interior of the sun, ... its name is *Ut* ... the Rig Veda and the Sama Veda are its singers (*githa-s*), hence it is known as *udgitha.*"

—*Chandogya Upanishad*

"OM is known by synonyms like *suryantargata.*"

—*Yogi Yajnavalkya Smriti*

(45)
akshara
(अक्षर = *akṣara*)

MEANING

" 1 indestructible **2** imperishable, undying **3** liberation **4** syllable **5** letter **6** atman **7** Shiva **8** Vishnu **9** Brahman."

EXPLANATION

OM is called *akshara* in the *Chandogya Upanishad* and the *Gita*. The word *akshara* is the opposite of *kshara*, which comes from the root √*kshi* ("to destroy") or √*kshar* ("to melt, to perish"). Therefore, as the *Nirukta* and the *Mahabhashya* explain, the literal meaning of *akshara* is that which cannot be destroyed (by others) or that which does not perish or die (on its own). As OM is said to be eternal (see *dhruva*, p. 112), it is both indestructible and imperishable. Hence, it is called *akshara*.

There are many other meanings of the word *akshara* related to OM. The *Amara Kosha* says that *akshara* also means liberation (*moksha*). The name *tara* of OM also means liberation (p. 170).

A syllable, i.e. a segment of speech with only one vowel sound, is also called *akshara* in Sanskrit. This is why *na-mah shi-va-ya* is called the *panchakshara mantra*, as it has five (*pancha*) syllables. OM consists of only one vowel sound, hence it is an *akshara*. As it is considered the supreme syllable, it is called the principal syllable (*ekam aksharam*) in the *Gita* (p. 120).

Akshara also means a letter or symbol of an alphabet or script. The word OM is often written as ओम् where it has two letters (a vowel and a consonant). However, it is also written as ॐ. As it is a special letter or symbol in its own, OM is called *akshara*.

In chapter 15 of the *Gita*, Krishna uses the word *kshara* for the body and *akshara* for the atman. The names *narayana* (p. 132) and *vibhu* (p. 204) also associate OM with the atman.

In the *Shabda Ratnavali* dictionary, Shiva and Vishnu are listed among the meanings of the word *akshara*. OM is identified with both—see *omkara* (p. 56) and *dhruvakshara* (p. 112).

Finally, the word *akshara* means the Supreme Brahman. It is used in this sense in the Rig Veda and the Upanishad-s. OM is also identified with the Supreme Brahman (p. 36).

TRADITION

Upanishad, *Gita*, grammar, dictionaries.

ETYMOLOGY

a + kṣara → akṣara.

a ▸ (from *na*) not; ***kṣara*** ▸ that which is destroyed or perishes.

QUOTES

"One should worship OM, [known as] *akshara* and *udgitha*."

—*Chandogya Upanishad*

"Of all speech, I am OM—the chief *akshara*."

—*Gita*

"Know *akshara* to be that which is not *kshara*. That which is not destroyed, or does not perish, is *akshara*."

—*Mahabhashya*

"The word *akshara* means OM."

—*Anekartha Kosha*

(46)
akshara
(अक्षर = *akṣara*)

MEANING

"**1** the pervader **2** the devourer **3** water."

EXPLANATION

Apart from taking it as the opposite of *kshara,* the word *akshara* can be derived directly from the root √*ash* and the suffix *sara* following the *Unadi Sutra*-s and rules of Paninian grammar.

The root √*ash* means "to pervade" and so the word *akshara* means the pervader. In the context of OM, this can be understood as the pervader of the universe (see *om,* p. 30). Or, as the *Vachaspatya* dictionary explains, OM is called *akshara* as it pervades the Veda-s—all mantra-s of Veda-s begin with OM. OM is also described as pervading all speech in the *Chandogya Upanishad* (see p. 169)—this is another interpretation.

There is another root √*ash,* which means "to eat" or "to devour". While its conjugations are different, *akshara* is derived in exactly the same manner from this root also. Accordingly, the word *akshara* means that which devours. In the context of OM, this can be explained in several ways. OM is believed to be the beginning and end of everything, which is the reason it is also called *pralaya* (p. 144). As everything dissolves in OM, it is seen as the devourer (destroyer) of the universe.

Or, OM can be understood as Kala, which is beyond the past, present, and future (see *traikalya,* p. 172). In chapter 10 of the *Gita,* Krishna compares himself with OM. In the next chapter (verse 11.32), he says that he is the mighty Kala who destroys the worlds and who is engaged in destroying people in the battlefield. This is the line that J. Robert Oppenheimer said he remembered at the time of the first nuclear explosion carried out on July 16, 1945. Oppenheimer quoted the translation "Now, I am become Death, the destroyer of worlds." Arjuna vividly describes the devouring form of Krishna as "O Vishnu! With your flaming mouths, you are devouring the worlds from all sides and licking them again and again. Filling the whole universe with brilliance, your intense rays are fiercely burning it."

In the Rig Veda, the word *akshara* is used for water, as it pervades (i.e., obtains) one place from another. OM is also called *rasa* (p. 148), one of whose meanings is water. OM is equated with *Apas*, the deities of water, in a *sandhya* mantra (*ibid*).

TRADITION

Grammar, commentaries, dictionaries.

ETYMOLOGY

√aś + saran → akṣara.

√aś ▸ **1** to pervade **2** to eat, to devour; ***saran*** ▸ suffix indicating performer of the action.

QUOTES

"Or, *akshara* results from the root *ash* followed by the suffix *saran*. That which pervades is called *akshara*."

—*Mahabhashya*

"That which pervades or devours is *akshara*."

—Commentary on *Vishnu Sahasranama*

"The word *akshara* means OM."

—*Anekartha Kosha*

(47)
svara
(स्वर = *svara*)

MEANING

"1 the sound **2** the vowel

3 one of the seven musical notes."

EXPLANATION

In the Upanishad-s, OM is referred to as *svara*, which comes from the root √*svri* ("to make a sound"). *Svara* refers to any sound in general; even the air breathed through the nose is called *svara* as it makes a low sound. OM in particular is called *svara* as it is seen as the most distinguished sound (p. 146). The *Mahanarayana Upanishad* refers to OM as the *svara* recited at the beginning of Veda-s. For this reason, OM is also called *vedadi* (p. 198). The *Chandogya Upanishad* refers to OM as *svara* several times. The Upanishad gives the reason as follows—"When one learns the Rig Veda, one makes the sound (*svarati*) OM with reverence; and similarly, for the Sama Veda and the Yajur Veda."

The word *svara* also refers to a vowel, in contrast with *vyanjana* which means a consonant. The *Shiva Tattva Rahasya*, a commentary on the 108 names of Shiva in the fifth *samhita* of the *Skanda Purana*, states that OM is designated as a vowel because it is mostly a vowel—the vowel part of OM (*o*) has two *matra*-s while its consonant part (*m*) has only half a *matra*.

The seven notes of Indian music are also called *svara*-s. These are named in the *Amara Kosha* as *shadja*, *rishabha*, *gandhara*, *madhyama*, *panchama*, *dhaivata*, and *nishada*. These seven notes are said to be the natural notes of the peacock, the cows, the goat and sheep, the heron, the cuckoo, the horse, and the elephant respectively. In the *Bhagavata Purana*, Narada's lute is said to be adorned with *Svara Brahman*. As per commentaries, this implies that the seven notes themselves are Brahman, or OM. It is noteworthy that the *Chandogya Upanishad*, which refers to OM as *svara*, represents the tradition of music as it is an Upanishad of the Sama Veda, from which Indian classical music originates. The word *chandogya* itself means "belonging to the singers of *chandas*", where *chandas* refers to the verses of the Sama Veda.

TRADITION

Upanishad, commentaries.

ETYMOLOGY

√svṛ + ac/gha → svara.

√svṛ ▸ to make a sound; ***ac*** ▸ suffix to denote performer of an action; ***gha*** ▸ suffix to denote means of an action

QUOTES

"The *svara* (OM) which is uttered at the beginning of the Veda-s and firmly established in *Vedanta* philosophy ...."

—*Mahanarayana Upanishad*

"As one sees fish in water, Death saw the deities there in the Rig Veda, the Yajur Veda, and the Sama Veda. Knowing this, they arose from the Rig Veda, the Yajur Veda, and the Sama Veda and entered *svara* (OM) itself."

—*Chandogya Upanishad*

"*Svara* means a vowel, and here that is *pranava* (OM), for a general term can refer to the specific."

—*Shiva Tattva Rahasya*

(48)
svara
(स्वर = *svara*)

MEANING

"1 self-resplendent, that which shines by itself
2 that which makes others take delight in itself
3 that which takes delight in one's own
4 that which gives itself."

EXPLANATION

The name *svara* of OM has been derived as a compound in several ways. In the *Mahabhashya* and the *Sangita Sudhakara* (a commentary on the *Sangita Ratnakara*), *svara* is explained as "self-resplendent", derived from *sva* ("own") and √*raj* ("to shine"). While the contexts in the works are vowel in grammar and Shiva in music respectively, the explanation applies to OM also as it is uncreated (p. 96) and resplendent (p. 194).

While explaining the word *svara* used for OM in the *Chandogya Upanishad*, Swami Ramabhadracharya's *Raghavakripa* commentary derives *svara* in three additional ways—

(1) OM is *svara* since it is the Supreme Brahman which causes aspirants to take delight in itself. This derivation uses the root √*ram* ("to delight"), from which comes the name Rama which is explained as "one who causes [devotees] to delight". OM is identified with both Rama and bliss in Upanishad-s (p. 41).

(2) OM is *svara* as it takes delight in its own, i.e. the Veda-s. This derivation uses the meaning "one's own" of *sva*. The Veda-s are considered to be the body or essence of OM (p. 202), so they are its own and OM relishes in their sacred speech.

(3) OM is *svara* as it is the Supreme Brahman which gives itself. This explanation derives the word from √*ra* ("to give") and alludes to the *Mundaka Upanishad* assertion which says that the Supreme Brahman is attained by only those whom it chooses itself (p. 31).

TRADITION

Grammar, music, Upanishad commentaries.

ETYMOLOGY

sva + √rāj + ḍa → svara; sva + √ram + ṇic + ḍa → svara; sva + √ram + ḍa → svara; or **sva + √rā + ḍa → svara.**

sva ▸ **1** self **2** one's own; ***√rāj*** ▸ to shine, to be resplendent; ***ḍa*** ▸ suffix to denote performer of an action. ***√ram*** ▸ to play, to delight; ***ṇic*** ▸ suffix in causative sense. ***√rā*** ▸ to give, to bestow.

QUOTES

"The deities entered *svara* (OM) itself."

—*Chandogya Upanishad*

"*Svara*-s are those that shine by themselves."

—*Mahabhashya*

""That which shines by itself," since it delights independently of anything else. The etymology of the word *svara* is also being said by this [phrase]."

—Commentary on *Sangita Ratnakara*

"*Svara*, which is radiant by itself. Or, *svara* is that which makes [aspirants] take delight in itself, i.e. the supreme lord. Or, *svara* is that which takes delight in its own, i.e. the Veda-s. Or, *svara* is that which gives itself, i.e. the Supreme Brahman."

—Commentary on *Chandogya Upanishad*

(49)

adibija

(आदिबीज = *ādibīja*)

MEANING

"**1** the first seed **2** the first seed sound **3** the original cause **4** the ultimate cause, the cause of all causes."

EXPLANATION

In Tantra traditions, a name of OM is *adibija* ("the initial seed"). The *Gopatha Brahmana* narrates how Prajapati created everything in the universe from the components of OM (see *om*, p. 16). Therefore, OM is considered the first seed of creation.

The word *bija* also refers to seed sounds used in mantra-s. A *bija* (seed sound) is a mystic syllable chanted as part of a mantra or by itself. For example, in the Upanishadic six-syllabled mantra *ram ramaya namah*, the syllable *ram* is the seed sound which represents fire. The seed sound for many mantra-s since time immemorial, OM is *adibija*—the first and foremost seed sound.

The word *bija* also means a cause. OM is the original cause of the universe—everything is believed to arise from it (see *pralaya*, p. 144). In the *Gita*, Krishna says that he is the source of the twofold *prakriti* (material nature and life from which all beings arise), the origin of the world, and the *bija* (cause) of all beings. In the same context, Krishna identifies himself with OM. Alternatively, *adi* is *prakriti*—the cause of everything—and the controller or cause of *prakriti* itself is OM. OM has been explained as the boat to cross *prakriti* (see *pranava*, p. 62).

In addition, the word *adi* also means a cause. With both *adi* and *bija* meaning cause, we get another meaning of the word *adibija* as "the cause of all causes" or "the ultimate cause". The creator Brahma is the cause of the universe and OM is the cause of even Brahma, who is represented by the first sound of OM (see *om*, p. 2).

In the *Bhagavata Purana*, *adibija* is used twice for Vishnu, once each in prayers by Gajendra (the elephant king) and Bhumi (the earth). Vishnu is identified with OM at many places (p. 206) and there are many names common to Vishnu and OM.

The word *adibija* is famously used for OM at the beginning of the *Jnaneshvari*, a commentary in Marathi on the *Gita*. The work identifies OM with Ganesha, saying that the sound *a* is Ganesha's feet, the sound *u* is his paunch, and the sound *m* is the great *mandala* in the form of his head.

TRADITION

Tantra, commentaries.

ETYMOLOGY

ādi + bīja → ādibīja.

ādi ▸ **1** first **2** original; ***bīja*** ▸ **1** seed **2** seed sound of a mantra **3** cause.

QUOTES

"The sound OM is called *adibija*."

—*Pranatoshini*

"Where the three—*a*, *u*, and *m*—meet, there pervades *Shabda Brahman* (or Veda); I bow to that *adibija* (OM) with the grace of the auspicious guru."

—*Jnaneshvari*

(50)
aditya
(आदित्य = *āditya*)

MEANING

“1 Surya (the sun god) **2** the lord of the earth **3** the essence of speech **4** the mantra of the sacred cow.”

EXPLANATION

Vedic texts identify OM with the sun or *aditya*, another name of OM as per Smriti and Tantra texts. The *Jaiminiya Brahmana* identifies OM with the sun. The *Chandogya Upanishad* says that the sun is OM as it moves around pronouncing OM.

Literally, *aditya* means the son of Aditi, the mother of the gods. The names Diti and Aditi derive from the root √*do* which means “to cut”, “to divide”, or “to destroy”. *Diti* means the act of cutting, and *aditi* connotes the negation of *diti*. The sons of Diti are the destructive *daitya*-s, while the sons of Aditi are the constructive and immortal *aditya*-s (gods). While *aditya* refers to deities in general, the word specifically refers to Surya, the sun god. Surya has been revered in Hinduism right from the Rig Veda, which has several hymns addressed to Surya. The sun-worshipping Saura tradition, in which Surya is the Supreme Brahman, is one of the five Puranic sects (*sampradaya*-s) with the other four being Shaiva, Vaishnava, Shakta, and Ganapatya. The Saura tradition was popular during the Gupta empire and also in medieval India when the magnificent sun temples at Modhera and Konark were built. While the tradition is virtually non-existent today, Surya worship takes place in festivals like Chhath, celebrated in eastern India and Nepal.

The word *aditi* means that which cannot be cut, split, or destroyed. As per the *Nighantu Kosha*, it is used in the Veda-s for the earth (which is undivided), speech (which is imperishable), and the cow (which is not to be slaughtered). And so, the word *aditya* also means something belonging to the earth, speech, or the sacred cow—the name *aditya* in the *Vishnu Sahasranama* is explained by Adi Shankara as "the lord of the earth". As an appellation of OM, *aditya* means (1) the lord of the earth, as OM pervades it (p. 208); (2) the essence of speech, as OM is called *rasa* (p. 148) and *vedatma* (p. 202); (3) the mantra for the sacred cow, as she is called *pranavedya* ("praised by OM") in the *Gosahasranama Stotra* which gives 1,000 names of the cow.

TRADITION

Upanishad, Smriti, Tantra.

ETYMOLOGY

aditi + ṇya → āditya.

aditi ▸ **1** Aditi, the mother of the gods including Surya (the sun god) **2** the earth **3** speech **4** cow; ***ṇya*** ▸ a suffix in the sense of "offspring" or "belonging to".

QUOTES

"This syllable (OM) is that sun."

—*Jaiminiya Brahmana*

"That sun is verily *udgitha*. It is *pranava*, as it moves [in the sky] pronouncing OM. ... The sun is *udgitha* (OM)."

—*Chandogya* and *Maitri* Upanishad-s

"The sound OM is known as *aditya*."

—*Yogi Yajnavalkya Smriti, Lakshmi Tantra*

(51)
advaita
(*अद्वैत = advaita*)

MEANING

"1 without a second, undivided, the only one
2 not coming from the two *prakriti*-s."

EXPLANATION

A name of OM is *advaita* as per the Tantra work *Pranatoshini*. The word *dvaita* means that which has undergone a twofold division. *Advaita* means without any such division, i.e. "without a second" or "the one and only one" (*eka*). OM is *advaita* as it is a monosyllable (p. 120), pronounced without any division into its component sounds. Or, OM is *advaita* as it is identified with Brahman (p. 36), the one and only supreme divinity.

In the *Rama Stavaraja Stotra*, Rama is called *advaita*. The *Raghavakripa* commentary explains this as follows—*dvita* (द्वीत) refers to one who has "come from" (*ita*) "two" (*dvi*), i.e. one who is born from a mother and a father. The word *dvaita* has the same meaning as *dvita*. The opposite of *dvaita* is *advaita*, which refers to one who is born without a mother and a father, or one who has a divine birth. OM can be understood similarly by interpreting *dvi* as the two *prakriti*-s. In chapter 7 of the *Gita*, Krishna says that the eightfold material nature and spiritual nature are his two *prakriti*-s which are the source of all beings, while Krishna himself is the origin and end of the entire creation. All beings are *dvaita* as they arise from the two *prakriti*-s. The Supreme Brahman, as OM or Krishna, is *advaita* as it does not arise from these two *prakriti*-s. Rather, it is their source.

In the *Kurma Purana*, OM is described as *advaita* by Vyasa and is identified with Shiva. Vyasa describes Shiva as follows—"This deity Mahadeva is the pure and supreme Shiva. He is that *advaita* syllable (OM) and that Supreme Brahman inside the sun." Just like Shiva in this verse, OM is also identified with the Supreme Brahman (p. 36) and the *Purusha* inside the sun (*suryantargata*, p. 82).

In the *Garuda Purana*, Suta narrates to Shaunaka a beautiful hymn that was originally narrated by Brahma to Narada. The hymn is called the *Achyuta Stotra* and is devoted to Vishnu. In this hymn, Vishnu is twice described as the supreme *advaita* and the imperishable *advaita*.

TRADITION

Purana, Tantra.

ETYMOLOGY

a + dvaita → advaita.

a ▸ (*na*) not; ***dvaita*** ▸ **1** divided into two **2** arising from two.

QUOTES

"The sound OM is called *advaita*."

—*Pranatoshini*

(52)
anadi
(अनादि = *anādi*)

MEANING

"1 without a beginning **2** without an origin, uncreated **3** ungraspable, inconceivable **4** the source of *prana*.**"**

EXPLANATION

The Tantra work *Pranatoshini* says that OM is called *anadi*. The word *adi* means both "beginning" and "cause" or "origin". Therefore, *anadi* means "without a beginning in time" and also "without any origin" (i.e. unborn or uncreated).

OM is without a beginning as it is eternal (p. 112) and beyond time (p. 172). Vyasa's commentary on Patanjali's *Yoga Sutra* states that the relation of word and meaning—such as the one between OM and Brahman—is eternal, i.e. the word OM, the meaning Brahman, and their relation are all eternal.

OM is described as unborn (*aja*) in the *Atharva Shira Upanishad* (p. 118), hence it is *anadi*—without a cause or origin.

The word *adi*, from *a* + √*da* ("to receive" or "to grasp"), literally means that which is grasped. That which cannot be grasped or understood is *anadi*, as the *Satya Bhashya* explains while commenting on the name *anadi* in the *Vishnu Sahasranama*. This interpretation applies to OM also. The *Mandukya Upanishad* describes the Supreme Brahman, identified with OM, as *agrahya* ("ungraspable") and *achintya* ("inconceivable").

The word *anadi* can also be split as *ana* + *adi*. In the *Chandogya Upanishad*, the word *ana* is used to refer to the vital force (*prana*). It comes from √*an* ("to breathe"), the root for the names of all five vital forces (*prana*, *apana*, *samana*, *udana*, and *vyana*). With *ana* as *prana* and *adi* as source, *anadi* means the source of *prana*, as OM is described in several texts. The *Yogi Yajnavalkya Smriti* states that OM gives *prana* to Veda-s, deities, body, speech and mind (p. 67). The *Atharva Shikha Upanishad* describes that OM releases the *prana*-s during creation (p. 118), having united with them during dissolution.

In the *Gita*, Krishna says that Brahman (*paramatman*) is imperishable (*avyaya*) as it is beginningless (*anadi*) and without qualities (*nirguna*). This can be interpreted as a description of OM, which is equated with the Supreme Brahman (p. 36); is called *parama* (p. 138); and has the names *avyaya* (p. 102), *anadi*, and *nirguna* (p. 23).

In the *Mahabharata*, Bhishma tells Yudhishthira that *vak* (Vedic speech) is *anadi-nidhana*—without beginning or end. As OM is the essence of *vak* (p. 148), it is also without beginning or end. *Anadi-nidhana* is the first word of the *Vakyapadiya* which begins with the description of the *Shabda Brahman* (see p. 162).

TRADITION

Tantra.

ETYMOLOGY

an + ādi → anādi;

ana + ādi → anādi.

an ▸ (*na*) not; ***ādi*** ▸ 1 beginning 2 cause, origin. ***ana*** ▸ vital force, *prana*.

QUOTES

"The sound OM is called *anadi*."

—*Pranatoshini*

(53)
ananta
(अनन्त = *ananta*)

MEANING

"**1** infinite, endless **2** Vishnu **3** Shesha **4** Balarama **5** the sky."

EXPLANATION

Ananta is a name of OM as per Upanishad and Smriti texts. The word comes from *na* ("not") + *anta* ("end"). When compounded, *na* changes to *an* before vowel sounds as per rules of Sanskrit grammar. This is similar to the Greek prefix *an*- from which comes the English prefix *a*- in words like *amoral.* A few English words like *anarchy* have the full prefix *an*-. The English word *end* is believed to be related to the Sanskrit *anta.*

The word *ananta* primarily means "without an end" or "infinite". It occurs many times in Vedic texts. Upanishad and Smriti texts say that OM is called *ananta* because it is experienced to be without any end by sages, deities, and humans.

OM is identified with Vishnu (p. 206), who is called *ananta* twice in the *Vishnu Sahasranama.* Four more names of Vishnu in the hymn begin with *ananta—anantajit* ("conqueror of infinite worlds"), *anantatman* ("the infinite Self"), *anantarupa* ("having infinite forms"), and *anantashri* ("having infinite powers").

Ananta is also a name of Shesha, the lord of the serpents, as per the *Amara Kosha.* In the *Vishnu Purana,* sage Parashara tells Maitreya that even the gods cannot describe or fully know the prowess, power, nature, and form of Shesha who is called *ananta* since none of the *gandharva*-s, *apsara*-s, *siddha*-s, *kinnara*-s, *naga*-s, and *charana*-s can perceive the extent of his virtues.

Krishna's elder brother Balarama is also called Ananta, as he is an incarnation of Shesha as per the *Mahabharata* and the *Bhagavata Purana*. Balarama has been worshipped independently in several parts of India. The *Arthashastra* of Chanakya mentions the worshippers of Sankarshana (Balarama) and Bhasa's play *Svapna-vasavadatta* begins with a prayer to Balarama.

As per the *Amara Kosha*, *ananta* also means the sky. The *Madhyandina Samhita* of the Shukla Yajur Veda compares OM, the Supreme Brahman, with the endless sky (p. 36). The sky is also called *akasha* in Sanskrit and the *Brahma Sutra* uses the word *akasha* for the Supreme Brahman, whose name is OM.

TRADITION

Upanishad, Smriti.

ETYMOLOGY

an + anta → ananta.

an ▸ (from *na*) not (here meaning without); ***anta*** ▸ end.

QUOTES

"As OM leads to the place where there is no end and as its end is not obtained by anybody among sages, deities, and humans—it is proclaimed as *ananta*."

—*Yogi Yajnavalkya Smriti*

"Then, why is it (OM) called *ananta*? Because on merely being pronounced, its endlessness is experienced horizontally, upwards, and downwards—hence it is called *ananta*."

—*Atharva Shira Upanishad*

(54)
avyaya
(*अव्यय = avyaya*)

MEANING

“1 indeclinable, having no inflection
2 imperishable, undecaying 3 inexhaustible.”

EXPLANATION

Sanskrit is a highly inflected language where most nouns, pronouns, and adjectives have different forms according to the gender, case, and number. For example, the noun *mitra* denotes the sun (*mitrah* or मित्रः) in the masculine gender, Lakshmana's mother Sumitra (*mitra* or मित्रा) in the feminine, and a friend (*mitram* or मित्रम्) in the neuter. In all the three genders, the word is inflected differently depending on the case (nominative, accusative, instrumental, dative, ablative, genitive, locative, or vocative) and the number (singular, dual, or plural). Words which are not inflected and stay the same in all genders, cases, and numbers are called *avyaya*-s (indeclinables) in grammar.

One of OM's names is *avyaya* as per the *Gopatha Brahmana* and the Tantra work *Bija Varna Abhidhana.* The Brahmana gives the reason as OM being the same in all genders, all cases, and all numbers. This is the reason why the opening line *om namah shivaya* of the *Mugdhabodha* grammar is explained by Durgadasa as both “OM, salutations to Shiva” and “Salutations to OM, for auspiciousness”. The word OM is taken to be in the nominative and dative cases in the two interpretations. Though Sanskrit has many indeclinables, OM is the most eminent and the only one to be specifically named *avyaya.*

Another meaning of *avyaya* is "imperishable". OM is called *avyaya* as it is believed to never decay or get destroyed. Names like *akshara* (p. 84), *anadi* (p. 98), *ananta* (p. 100), *dhruva* (p. 112), and *pralaya* (p. 144) also express this idea.

As *vyaya* also means an expense or spending, *avyaya* means that which cannot be spent, i.e. inexhaustible. OM is considered the bestower of knowledge that is ever new (p. 65), and thus symbolizes the supreme knowledge. In addition, OM is called *sarvavid*, one of whose meanings is "complete knowledge" (p. 154). Knowledge is considered an inexhaustible wealth in Indian tradition. A saying (*subhashita*) in Sanskrit goes "the wealth of knowledge always increases on being spent."

Avyaya is a name of Vishnu in the *Vishnu Sahasranama*, where he is also called *avyaya nidhi* ("the inexhaustible treasure") and *avyaya bija* ("the undecaying seed").

TRADITION

Veda, Tantra, grammar.

ETYMOLOGY

a + vyaya → avyaya.

a ▸ (from *na*) not; ***vyaya*** ▸ **1** change **2** decay **3** expenditure.

QUOTES

"The word OM is true to its name, it never changes. That which is same in all three genders and all cases and numbers and which never changes in anything is called *avyaya*."

—Gopatha Brahmana

"The sound OM is called *avyaya*."

—Bija Varna Abhidhana

(55)
bhavanashana
(भवनाशन = *bhavanāśana*)

MEANING

"**1** destroyer of worldly existence
2 devourer of worldly existence."

EXPLANATION

This is one of the names of OM mentioned in the Tantric work *Pranatoshini.* The name is a compound of two words—*bhava* and *nashana.* The first word *bhava* is from the root √*bhu* ("to exist"), which is the first among the nearly 2,000 roots in the *Dhatupatha.* The second word *nashana* is a causative form derived from the root √*nash* ("to disappear" or "to perish"). The words *nashta* (नष्ट, "destroyed") and *nashvara* (नश्वर, "perishable") come from the same root. The compound *bhava-nashana* therefore means the destroyer (*nashana*) of worldly existence (*bhava*). OM is the destroyer of worldly existence as it is the means of liberation (p. 170) and it takes across the ocean of mortality (p. 62).

Alternatively, the compound *bhavanashana* can be split as *bhavana* + *ashana.* When parsed this way, the word means the devourer of worldly existence. While *bhavana* is from the same root as *bhava* and has the same meaning ("worldly existence") in this context, the word *ashana* is from the root √*ash* ("to eat"). This root was mentioned along with the root √*ash* ("to pervade") in the derivation of the word *akshara* (p. 86), also a name of OM. The word *ashana* means food as well as the act of eating. Its opposite is *anashana* (fasting), from which comes the Hindi word *anshan* used in phrases like *amaran anshan* (fast-unto-death). With this, *bhavanashana* as an exocentric compound literally means "that due to which there is devouring of wordly existence" (*bhavanasya ashanam yena*) or "that whose food is worldly existence" (*bhavanam ashanam yasya*). The implied meaning is "the devourer of worldly existence".

Bhavanashana occurs as one of the names of Vishnu in the *Vishnu Sahasranama* of the *Garuda Purana.* Shiva is also described as *bhavanashana* in the *Linga Purana.* The feminine form of the word is *bhavanashini,* which is one of Lalita's names in the *Lalita Sahasranama* and a name of the Sarayu River in the Purana-s.

TRADITION

Tantra.

ETYMOLOGY

bhava + nāśana → bhavanāśana;
or bhavana + aśana → bhavanāśana.

bhava ▸ world, mortal existence; ***nāśana*** ▸ destroyer. ***bhavana*** ▸ birth, mortal existence; ***aśana*** ▸ **1** the act of eating **2** food.

QUOTES

"The sound OM is called *bhavanashana.*"

—*Pranatoshini*

(56)

bindushakti

(**बिन्दुशक्ति** = ***binduśakti***)

MEANING

"1 power as an infinitesimally small point or dot **2** that whose power lies in the *bindu* **3** Apas (the waters) **4** the power in the centre of the eyebrows."

EXPLANATION

Bindu in Tantric cosmology refers to the infinitesimal point, full of power, from which the universe manifests, as described in the *Prapancha Sara Tantra*. *Bindu* is described variously in different Tantra works. In general, *bindu* means "a small drop". The word also occurs in the Atharva Veda where it refers to the sun and two cosmological dots—the dot arising from Brahman and the golden dot arising from the ocean.

OM is known as *bindushakti* in the Tantra works *Bija Varna Abhidhana* and *Pranatoshini*. The word can be grammatically parsed and explained in multiple ways. As an appositional determinative compound, *bindushakti* means power (*shakti*) as a point (*bindu*). The *Prapancha Sara Tantra* describes that during the process of creation, *Prakriti* first appears as a dense *bindu*. When the *bindu* splits, from it emerges the unmanifest sound which is *Shabda Brahman*. *Shabda Brahman* is often identified with OM (p. 189). This *Shabda Brahman* or OM is latent in the *bindu* which is full of power.

Or, as an exocentric compound, *bindushakti* means that whose power lies in the *bindu*. OM represents the Veda-s (p. 8) which are described by the *Gopatha Brahmana* as consisting of *bindu*-s of *soma* (nectar), which has the power of granting immortality. Therefore, OM as the Veda-s is *bindushakti*, for its power lies in the *bindu*-s of *soma* contained in the Veda-s.

As a dependent determinative compound in the genitive case, *bindushakti* means the power of *bindu*-s. As per the *Amara Kosha*, *bindu* means a drop of water. The power of *bindu*-s, then, is Apas, the deities associated with waters. OM is identified with Apas in a popular *sandhya* mantra (p. 148) and is also called *akshara* (p. 84), one of whose meanings in Vedic texts is water.

Finally, as a dependent determinative compound in the locative case, *bindushakti* can be interpreted as the power in the *bindu*. As per the *Medini Kosha*, one of the meanings of *bindu* is the region between the eyebrows. OM is described as the aura or light which shines between the two eyebrows in the *Yogi Yajnavalkya Smriti* and the *Gheranda Samhita* (p. 194). In addition, OM is called *vibhu* (p. 204) which means all-powerful. Therefore, OM is the power located between the eyebrows.

TRADITION

Tantra.

ETYMOLOGY

bindu + śakti → binduśakti.

bindu ▸ **1** dot, drop, or point **2** drop of water **3** centre of the eyebrows; ***śakti*** ▸ power, energy.

QUOTES

"The sound OM is called *bindushakti*."

—Tantra works

(57)

brahma, parabrahma

(ब्रह्म, परब्रह्म = *brahma, parabrahma*)

MEANING

"**1** that which [is supreme and] grows or expands

2 that which [is supreme and] makes others grow or expand

3 the [supreme] Brahman

4 the [supreme] abode of growing virtues."

EXPLANATION

Among the names of OM, the *Atharva Shira Upanishad* lists *param brahma*, which when compounded becomes *parabrahma*. The Upanishad says that OM is *para* ("supreme") because it is *para*, *apara*, and *parayana*—the *Dipika* commentary explains these as *saguna*, *nirguna*, and the supreme refuge, respectively. The Upanishad adds that OM is *brahma* as it is expanded and also expands others using its expanse. This draws on the meaning "to grow" of the root √*brimh*, from which *brahman* is derived with the suffix *man*. The word *brahma* (ब्रह्म) is the nominative singular form of the base word *brahman* (ब्रह्मन्) in the neuter gender. As OM is both *param* and *brahma*, it is called *param brahma*. The *Yogi Yajnavalkya Smriti* explains the name differently by saying that OM is the mouth of the Veda-s (also called *brahma*), the *Shabda Brahman*, and it leads to the Supreme Brahman.

In the *Pratishakhya* of the Rig Veda, OM is referred to as *brahma*. The *Brahmanda Purana* and the *Vishnu Purana* state that OM is called *brahma* because of its greatness or expansiveness (*brihat-tva*) and its quality of expanding (*brimhana-tva*). Both *brihat* and *brimhana* derive from the same root √*brimh*.

The suffix in *brahma* can also be interpreting in the sense of location. Accordingly, *brahma* is explained as "that where virtues grow" in some Vaishnava texts. OM is also the abode of growing virtues; one of its names is *gunajivaka* (p. 122). This interpretation stresses the *saguna* aspect of Brahman and OM.

TRADITION

Upanishad, Vedic phonetics, Smriti, Purana.

ETYMOLOGY

√bṛṃh + manin → brahman,
or √bṛṃh + ṇic + manin → brahman;
para + brahman → parabrahman.

√bṛṃh ▸ to grow or expand; ***manin*** ▸ suffix to denote performer or location of an action. ***ṇic*** ▸ causative suffix. ***para*** ▸ supreme.

QUOTES

"Then, why is it (OM) called *param brahma*? As it is *saguna, nirguna,* and the supreme refuge and it is expansive and expands [others] by means of its expanse, it is called *param brahma.*"

—*Atharva Shira Upanishad*

"This *brahma* (OM), greatest of all, is the eternal door to *svarga* for the student and the instructor."

—*Rigveda Pratishakhya*

"It is explained as the mouth of all speech and the threefold Veda-s and the omnipresent *Shabda Brahman.* It leads to the Supreme Brahman—hence it is known as *param brahma.*"

—*Yogi Yajnavalkya Smriti*

"OM is called *brahma* because of growth or expansion."

—Purana-s

(58)
brahmabija, vedabija
(ब्रह्मबीज, वेदबीज = *brahmabīja, vedabīja*)

MEANING

" the seed (source) of the Veda-s. "

EXPLANATION

OM is called *brahmabija* in the *Bhagavata Purana* and Tantra works, and similarly *vedabija* in some Purana-s. As per the *Amara Kosha, brahma* also means Veda-s. This is why a student of Veda-s is called a *brahmachari.* As OM is the source of the three Veda-s (p. 8), it is called *brahmabija* and *vedabija.*

TRADITION

Purana, Tantra.

ETYMOLOGY

brahma + bīja → brahmabīja; veda + bīja → vedabīja.

brahma ▸ the Veda-s; ***bīja*** ▸ seed, source. ***veda*** ▸ the Veda-s.

QUOTES

"Conquering (regulating) the breath, one should conquer their mind without forgetting the *brahmabija* (OM)."

—*Bhagavata Purana*

"The sound OM is called *brahmabija.*"

—*Bija Varna Abhidhana*

"I worship her whose true form is *vedabija* (OM), and who is the mother of the Veda-s."

—*Devi Bhagavata*

(59)

brahmakshara

(ब्रह्माक्षर = *brahmākṣara*)

MEANING

"**1** the syllable of Brahman
2 the syllable explaining Brahman."

EXPLANATION

The *Trikanda-shesha* dictionary says the word *brahmakshara* means OM. A commentary explains that OM is the "syllable of Brahman", i.e. *Shabda Brahman* or Brahman as a syllable (p. 189). The *Bhagavata Purana* uses the word *brahmakshara* twice for OM. Commentaries explain it as the syllable which explains Brahman (*brahma-pratipadaka*) or the syllable whose subject is Brahman (*brahma-pratipadya*).

TRADITION

Purana, dictionaries, commentaries.

ETYMOLOGY

brahma + akṣara → brahmākṣara.

brahma ▸ Brahman; ***akṣara*** ▸ syllable, sound.

QUOTES

"One should repeat in the mind the pure and supreme *brahmakshara* (OM) which is composed of three sounds."

—*Bhagavata Purana*

"[The word] *brahmakshara* means *omkara*. *Brahmakshara*—the sound of Brahman."

—*Trikanda-shesha* dictionary, its commentary

(60)

dhruva, dhruvakshara

(ध्रुव, ध्रुवाक्षर = *dhruva, dhruvākṣara*)

MEANING

"**1** Vishnu **2** the eternal [syllable or imperishable] **3** that [syllable] which approaches spiritual aspirants."

EXPLANATION

The Tantra work *Bija Varna Abhidhana* lists *dhruva* as a name of OM. This name is also alluded to in the *Mahabharata* where Vishnu is called *dhruvakshara*, which Nilakantha's commentary explains as he who is the same as the *pranava* syllable (OM). The *Vishnu Smriti* also addresses Vishnu as *dhruvakshara*. In these examples, *dhruvakshara* refers to Vishnu who is identified with OM (also see p. 206). In the *Vishnu Sahasranama*, two of Vishnu's names are *sthavira dhruva* and *dhruva*.

The word *dhruva* comes from the root √*dhru* which surprisingly means either "to go" (*gati*) or "to be fixed" (*sthairya*), depending on the context. In case of the word *dhruva*, the sense of the root is to be fixed or firm. The *Vachaspatya* dictionary lists twenty-five meanings of *dhruva* including stable, certain, eternal, sky, Vishnu, Shiva, and the banyan tree. The astronomical work *Surya Siddhanta* refers to the North Star and the South Star, which appear as fixed, as two *dhruva* stars.

When used for OM, *dhruva* means "eternal" or "timeless". This is because OM is understood to be without a beginning (*anadi*, p. 98) or an end (*ananta*, p. 100), and traverses time (*traikalya*, p. 172). As OM is a syllable (*akshara*) that is eternal, it is called *dhruvakshara*, which means means "the eternal syllable".

Or, taking the word *akshara* to mean imperishable, *dhruvakshara* means "eternally imperishable". This meaning is also reflected in the explanation of *tryakshara*, a name of OM and Shiva, as "imperishable in three times—past, present, and future" (p. 192).

In his commentary on the *Vishnu Sahasranama*, Baladeva Vidyabhushana takes the "to go" sense of √*dhru* and explains *dhruva* as he who approaches or follows the solitary or single-minded devotees (*bhakta*-s). OM is similarly explained as that which goes or approaches as both √*ap* (p. 30) and √*av* (p. 210), roots from which it is derived, have this sense.

TRADITION

Mahabharata, Tantra, commentaries.

ETYMOLOGY

√dhru + ac → dhruva; dhruva + akṣara → dhruvākṣara.

√dhru ▸ **1** to go **2** to be fixed or stable; ***ac*** ▸ suffix to denote performer of an action. ***dhruva*** ▸ **1** fixed, eternal; **2** that which goes or approaches ***akshara*** ▸ syllable.

QUOTES

"... Vishnu, who has been called the eternal syllable (OM)."

—*Mahabharata*

"*Dhruvakshara* means he who in reality is the syllable called *pranava* (OM)."

—Commentary on *Mahabharata*

"The sound OM is called *dhruva*."

—*Bija Varna Abhidhana*

"He who follows single-minded devotees is *dhruva*."

—Commentary on *Vishnu Sahasranama*

(61)
divya
(दिव्य = *divya*)

MEANING

"1 heavenly, celestial 2 supernatural, divine 3 beautiful, charming."

EXPLANATION

Another name of OM as per the *Yogi Yajnavalkya Smriti* is *divya*. *Divya* has a great many meanings in Sanskrit—as many as 29 are listed in the *Vachaspatya* dictionary. The word *divya* and also *deva*, the word for deity, derive from the root √*div* which has ten meanings—the second highest among all roots in the *Dhatupatha*. *Divya* is one of the most frequently used words in Hindu scriptures—it occurs hundreds of times in Vedic texts, 16 times in the *Gita*, more than 200 times in the *Ramayana*, and more than 1,000 times in the *Mahabharata*.

The primary meaning of *diyva* is that which is born in, found in, or belongs to *dyaus* (the heaven or the skies). For example, the heavenly pleasures are called *divya* in the *Gita*. OM is called *divya* as it pervades all the three *loka*-s including heaven. Heaven in this context can also refer to *Goloka*, *Saketa*, or *Vaikuntha*—the supreme abodes of Krishna, Rama, and Vishnu respectively. OM is identified with all three deities (pp. 12, 38, and 206). In the *Gita*, the adjective *divya* is used thrice to describe the supreme being or Krishna.

The word *divya* also means divine, supernatural, or beyond worldly limits. The supernatural vision that was given to Sanjaya by Veda Vyasa is referred to as *divya chakshu* (divine eye) or *divya drishti* (divine vision). In the eleventh chapter of the *Gita*, Krishna gives the same *divya chakshu* to Arjuna when revealing his universal form (also called *divya rupa*) which is seen by both Arjuna and Sanjaya. Krishna uses the word *divya* in the *Gita* several times—to describe his birth, actions, powers, and forms. Coming back to OM, it is called *divya* as it is said to represent the divine supernatural state which is beyond the worldly states of waking, dreaming, and deep sleep (p. 180). As the *bija* or seed, it is OM which makes a *mantra* divine or supernatural—a reason why it is also known as *divyamantra* (p. 116).

Another prominent meaning of *divya* is beautiful or charming. OM is seen as a riveting syllable or mantra that charms the minds of yogi-s—this is why they always meditate on OM with the *bindu*, as a popular verse says. The *Linga Purana* describes the eight-syllabled mantra *om namo narayanaya* as *parama-shobhana* ("supremely beautiful"). The mantra is supremely beautiful as it contains the supremely beautiful (or *divya*) syllable OM.

TRADITION

Smriti.

ETYMOLOGY

div + yat → divya.

div ▸ **1** heaven **2** sky; ***yat*** ▸ suffix having the sense of "born in", "found in", "originating from", "belonging to", etc.

QUOTES

"OM is known as *divya*."

—*Yogi Yajnavalkya Smriti*

(62)
divyamantra
(दिव्यमन्त्र = *divyamantra*)

MEANING

"**1** the divine mantra **2** that which makes a mantra divine **3** that which makes the Vedic *samhita*-s divine."

EXPLANATION

OM is called *divya-mantra* in the *Amrita Nada Upanishad* and the *Garuda Purana*. There are many meanings of both *divya* (p. 114), also a name of OM, and *mantra*, which comes from √*mantr* ("to speak secretly"). A mystic formula is called a *mantra* as it is given secretly and chanted in isolation. A consultation by a king's minister (*mantri*) is called a *mantra* since it is often passed on secretly. The *samhita* portion of the four Veda-s is also called *mantra*, and so is Vishnu in the *Vishnu Sahasranama*. Of the many meanings of *divyamantra*, three are explained here.

As an appositional determinative (*karmadharaya*) compound, *divyamantra* means "divine mantra"—the mantra OM is believed to be divine as it is the name of the Supreme Brahman (p. 36).

As an exocentric (*bahuvrihi*) compound, *divyamantra* means "that due to which a mantra is divine". OM is a part of many powerful mantra-s like *om namah shivaya* and *om namo narayanaya* which are made divine by the seed OM. In the *Linga Purana*, Dhruva asks Vishvamitra how to attain a place above all. Vishvamitra instructs Dhruva to chant *om namo'stu vasudevaya*, saying that it is a "*divya* mantra [as it is] endowed with OM".

Finally, interpreting *mantra* as Vedic *samhita*-s, *divyamantra* can be understood as "that which makes the *samhita*-s divine".

OM is used at the beginning and end when reciting verses from Vedic *samhita*-s. It is considered the essence (p. 202) and origin of the Veda-s (p. 198). Or, the *samhita*-s are made divine by OM because they mention OM as the name of Brahman (p. 36).

The word *divyamantra* is used in the Kolagallu inscription (c. 967 CE) in Bellary, Karnataka. The inscription describes the installation of a statue of Karttikeya and states that a Brahmin named Gadadhara consecrated it with the *divyamantra*, which possibly refers to OM. The inscription is important as it records the migration of Gadadhara from a village in north Bengal to Bellary, nearly 2,000 km away.

TRADITION

Upanishad, Purana, inscriptions.

ETYMOLOGY

divya + mantra → divyamantra.

divya ▸ celestial, heavenly, divine; ***mantra*** ▸ mantra.

QUOTES

"By [chanting] the *divyamantra* (OM) repeatedly, one should remove one's impurities."

—*Amrita Nada Upanishad*

"Therefore, even one who is omniscient should narrate the *Bhagavata Purana* daily after chanting the *divyamantra* (OM)."

—*Garuda Purana*

"For the purpose of achieving a place in *svarga*, this [statue] was consecrated with the *divyamantra* (OM) by Gadadhara, native of Tada village and illuminator the Varendri region."

—Kolagallu inscription

(63)
eka
(एक = *eka*)

MEANING

" **1** the one **2** chief, principal **3** the best **4** the only one. "

EXPLANATION

The word *eka* comes from the root √*i* ("to go"). Narayana's commentary on the *Unadi Sutra* explains that *eka* is that which goes to or pervades all numbers. The purport is that all natural numbers are divisible by *eka*, or the number one. The word *eka* has many other meanings; some of them are discussed in Patanjali's *Mahabhashya* on Panini's *Ashtadhyayi*.

The *Atharva Shira Upanishad* says that OM is called *eka* because it is the one unborn which unites with *prana*-s and releases them. The *Dipika* commentary explains that *prana*-s here stands for Veda-s or speech. The Upanishad then cites a mantra from the *Paippalada Samhita* of the Atharva Veda which goes thus—"Some take recourse to a means; some in the south, the west, the north, and the east take recourse to another means; all of them come together here and concurrently that one existent entity moves among all beings." The purport is that OM is that one eternal entity which lives among all beings.

In addition, the word *eka* also means chief or principal. OM is *eka* as it is the principal mantra—the *Yogi Yajnavalkya Smriti* says that it is the leader (*nayaka*) among all mantra-s. It is also the principal syllable, the principal sound, and the principal word as indicated by its names *akshara* (p. 84), *svara* (p. 88), and *shabda* (p. 162).

The word *eka* also means "the best". Another name of OM is *parama* (p. 138), one of whose meanings is also "the best".

Finally, *eka* also means *kevala*, or "the only one". From *kevala* comes the word *kaivalya* for liberation. Literally, *kaivalya* means the state of being alone, i.e. without any bondage. OM is *eka* as it is the only Supreme Brahman (p. 36). The word *eka* occurs in this sense in the Rig Veda in a hymn dedicated to Vishvakarma. The verse goes thus—"He has eyes, mouths, arms, and feet on all sides; he produces heaven and earth, inspiring them with his arms and feet; he is the *eka* (only) deity."

The *Vishnu Sahasranama* lists the name *ekatma* ("the chief atman") as well as *eka* ("the one") for Vishnu.

TRADITION

Upanishad.

ETYMOLOGY

√i + kan → eka.

√*i* ▸ to go; ***kan*** ▸ suffix indicating performer of an action.

QUOTES

"Then, why is it called *eka*? As it dissolves all *prana*-s, and though unborn becomes one with them by dissolution and releases them [during creation], hence it is called *eka*."

—*Atharva Shira Upanishad*

(64)

ekakshara

(एकाक्षर = *ekākṣara*)

MEANING

"1 the monosyllable **2** the principle syllable **3** the best syllable **4** the only imperishable."

EXPLANATION

This popular name of OM occurs in Smriti-s, Purana-s, the *Mahabharata*, the *Gita*, and even secular texts like the *Chanakya Niti*. The previous section presented four meanings of *eka* as per the *Amara Kosha* and the *Medini Kosha*. Accordingly, four meanings of *ekakshara* are given here.

Ekakshara means a monosyllable, or a word with just one syllable. OM has only one syllable, hence it is called *ekakshara*. OM is also called *tryakshara* (p. 192) and *panchakshara* (p. 50).

Ekakshara also means the main syllable. Across all syllables, OM is believed to be the foremost. In chapter 10 of the *Gita*, Krishna says that he is *ekam aksharam*, understood in most commentaries as OM and explained in the *Raghavakripa* commentary as the "principal syllable" OM.

As *eka* also means "the best" or "the most praiseworthy", the word *ekakshara* means "the best syllable". The syllable OM is the most praised syllable in Hindu scriptures.

Finally, *eka* also means "the only one". When considering this meaning of *eka*, the meaning "syllable" of *akshara* is to be discarded (since OM is not the only syllable) and the meaning "imperishable" of *akshara* is to be accepted. *Ekakshara* then means "the only imperishable". OM is the only imperishable—it is without beginning (*anadi*, p. 98) or end (*ananta*, p. 100) and is *pralaya* (p. 144), i.e. that in which everything dissolves.

As mentioned before, Vishnu is called *eka* and *ekatma* in the *Vishnu Sahasranama.* The Rig Veda talks about *ekam sad*, the one entity (deity) described variously (p. 74).

The Hindi/Punjabi word *ik* (इक/ਇੱਕ) derives from the Sanskrit *eka.* Therefore, the phrase *Ik Onkar* of Sikhism can be understood in several ways as "the one *Onkar*", "*Onkar*, the principal one", "*Onkar*, the most praiseworthy", and "*Onkar*, the only one".

TRADITION

Smriti, Purana, *Mahabharata, Gita, Chanakya Niti.*

ETYMOLOGY

eka + akṣara → ekākṣara.

eka ▸ **1** the number one **2** main **3** best, most eminent **4** the only one, solitary; ***akṣara*** ▸ **1** syllable **2** imperishable.

QUOTES

"*Ekakshara* is the Supreme Brahman. *Ekakshara* means OM."

—*Manu Smriti*, its commentaries

"OM—this eternal *ekakshara*—is Brahman."

—*Vishnu Purana*

"The *ekakshara* OM is Brahman."

—*Mahabharata*

"One who dies pronouncing OM—the *ekakshara* Brahman—and remembering me, achieves the supreme state."

—*Gita*

"... to the guru, who gives the *ekakshara* mantra (OM)."

—*Chanakya Niti*

(65)

gunabija, gunajivaka

(गुणबीज, गुणजीवक = guṇabīja, guṇajīvaka)

MEANING

"1 the origin and nourisher of virtues
2 the seed of the three *guna*-s
3 the origin and nourisher of living beings
4 the origin and nourisher of the universe."

EXPLANATION

These related names of OM are listed in the Tantra works *Prapancha Sara Tantra* and *Pranatoshini*. As the word *guna* has many meanings, many interpretations are possible.

One of the meanings of *guna* is "a virtue", as opposed to *dosha* which means "a vice". This sense of *guna* gives the first meaning as "origin/nourisher of virtues". OM is called *brahman*, one of whose meanings is "where virtues grow" (p. 108). In the *Vishishtadvaita* philosophy, Brahman is conceived as the abode of all auspicious qualities (virtues) and devoid of all undesirable qualities (vices).

Guna also refers to the three qualities—*sattva*, *rajas*, and *tamas*—which correspond to the three syllables of OM (p. 22). The *Nada Bindu Upanishad* describes OM as a *hamsa* (p. 124) whose feet are *rajas* and *tamas* and whose body is *sattva*.

The word *guna* also means subordinate or secondary, as opposed to *pradhana* which means primary. The living beings are *guna*-s as they are secondary to Brahman. The *Taittiriya Upanishad* says that all beings arise from Brahman and live depending on Brahman after being born. The Upanishad also identifies OM with Brahman. Therefore, OM is both *gunabija*, the origin of the living beings, and *gunajivaka*, the nourisher of the living beings.

Finally, *guna* refers to the entire universe which is made of the three *guna*-s. The universe is called *trigunatmaka* ("of the form of the three *guna*-s") in the *Bhagavata Purana*. OM is the origin of the universe as per the *Gopatha Brahmana*, which describes how Brahma created everything in the universe from the components of OM (p. 16). As vital force, food, and the sun (p. 158), OM is also the nourisher of the universe.

In the *Vishnu Sahasranama*, Vishnu is similarly called *gunabhrit*. The name means the supporter or nourisher of *guna*-s. Various commentaries interpret *guna* differently as the three qualities, virtues, living beings, or the universe.

TRADITION

Tantra.

ETYMOLOGY

guṇa + bīja → guṇabīja;
guṇa + jīvaka → guṇajīvaka.

guṇa ▸ **1** a virtue **2** one of the three *guṇa*-s **3** secondary, living beings (as opposed to the primary Brahman) **4** the universe; ***bīja*** ▸ seed, source, origin. ***jīvaka*** ▸ nourisher, life-giver.

QUOTES

"The sound OM is called *gunabija*."

—*Prapancha Sara Tantra*

"The sound OM is called *gunajivaka*."

—*Pranatoshini*

(66)

hamsa

(**हंस = *haṃsa***)

MEANING

"1 a swan 2 that which leads to the sun 3 all-pervading 4 the destroyer of sins."

EXPLANATION

The *Nada Bindu Upanishad* presents OM as a swan (*hamsa*), riding which one gets free from karma-s and all sins. The sounds *a*, *u*, and *m* are its right wing, left wing, and tail respectively; while the half mora is its head. Its feet are the qualities of passion (*rajas*) and ignorance (*tamas*), its body is the quality of purity (*sattva*), its two eyes are morality and immorality, and different parts of its body correspond to the seven *loka*-s.

Smriti and Tantra works mention that OM is called *hamsa*. The word *hamsa* comes from the root √*han* ("to go" and also "to kill or destroy"). Many meanings of *hamsa*—for example a swan, the sun, a kind of horse, a specific vital force—denote something that moves in a distinguished way. The *Yogi Yajnavalkya Smriti* states that OM is called *hamsa* as it leads to the OM of the sun.

The word *hamsa* also means Vishnu, Supreme Brahman, a type of yogi, and a specific mantra as per the *Medini Kosha*. Brahman is called *hamsa* in the *Shvetashvatara Upanishad*; the *Raghavakripa* commentary explains the reason: Brahman can go everywhere and is the destroyer of sins. Similar explanations can be used for OM—OM is called *hamsa* because it is all-pervading (see *sarvavyapi*, p. 156) and the destroyer of worldly existence (see *bhavanashana*, p. 104).

The name *hamsa* is also a metaphor for *viveka* (discernment), or separating the essential from the non-essential. The *hamsa* (swan) is believed to have an ability to separate milk from a mixture of milk and water. In similes and metaphors involving the *hamsa*, milk and water are often compared with right and wrong, virtues and vices, the transcendental and the mundane, and the good and the bad, respectively. Furthermore, *viveka* is often seen as an essential means of knowledge and liberation. OM is similarly seen as a means of liberation (p. 170). With this in mind, the name *hamsa* suggests that OM is the possessor and bestower of *viveka* which leads to *jnana* and *moksha*.

TRADITION

Upanishad, Smriti, Tantra.

ETYMOLOGY

√han + sa/ac → haṃsa.

√han ▸ **1** to go, to move; **2** to strike, to slay, to destroy; ***sa, ac*** ▸ suffixes to indicate the performer of an action.

QUOTES

"The sound *a* is the right wing, the sound *u* is the left wing, the sound *m* is its tail, and the half mora is its head."

—*Nada Bindu Upanishad*

"OM is known as *hamsa*. ... Its meditation in the heart always pierces the [subtle] body and leads one to the OM of the sun, hence it is called *hamsa*."

—*Yogi Yajnavalkya Smriti*

"OM is known as *hamsa*."

—*Lakshmi Tantra*

(67)
ishana
(ईशान = īśāna)

MEANING

“1 ruler, master **2** radiant, lustrous **3** Vishnu **4** Shiva.”

EXPLANATION

The *Atharva Shira Upanishad* says that *ishana* is a name of OM because it rules over all gods. The Upanishad quotes a verse from a hymn dedicated to Indra in the Rig Veda—“O brave Indra, you are omniscient, you are the master of this animate world, and you are the master of the inanimate. We praise you exceedingly like unmilked cows [overflowing with milk].” The word *ishana*, common in Veda-s, occurs twice in this verse.

Ishana comes from the root √*ish* which means to rule over, or to have power or sovereignty. The words *isha* and *ishvara*, which mean “master” or “lord”, come from the same root. The *ana* suffix in *ishana* has the sense of nature or habit. Literally, *ishana* means one whose nature is to rule over, i.e. a natural ruler.

As per the *Medini Kosha*, *ishana* means light or lustre in the neuter gender. The *Shabda Kalpadruma* adds that *ishana* also means “having light” (lustrous or brilliant) in all three genders. The *arsha·adi* suffix is implied in this sense. Since the *Atharva Shira Upanishad* mentions *ishana* in the masculine form as a name of OM, it means lustrous or brilliant. Some other names like *svara* (p. 90) and *vaidyuta* (p. 194) also mean the same.

Ishana is a name of Vishnu as per the *Vishnu Sahasranama*. At the start of the *Mahabharata*, the sage Ugrashravas describes Vishnu as *ishana* and also as *ekakshara*, meaning OM (p. 120).

The *Amara Kosha* lists *ishana* among the 48 names of Shiva, who is identified with OM in several scriptures (p. 72). As per the Purana-s, Ishana is one of Shiva's eight *murti*-s (forms) and is associated with the sun. In the *Durga Saptashati*, the Ishana form of Shiva is described as *dhumra-jatila* ("having smoke-coloured locks"). As per the *Brihat Jabala Upanishad*, *Ishana* is one of the five forms of Shiva which corresponds to the ether element. The fifth face of Shiva which points upwards corresponds to Ishana. The iconographic work *Rupamandana* states that this fifth face is beyond the reach of even yogi-s, and hence it is not shown while making a *mukha-linga* (a *linga* with faces).

Ishana is the name of one of the eleven Rudra-s, and this is why the word *ishana* also refers to the number eleven. The *Shvetashvatara Upanishad* uses the word *ishana* for the Supreme Brahman. The feminine form *Ishani* is a name of Durga in the Tantra tradition.

TRADITION

Upanishad.

ETYMOLOGY

√īś + cānaś → īśāna.

√īś ▸ to lord over, to have power or sovereignty; ***cānaś*** ▸ suffix indicating one's nature or habit.

QUOTES

"Then, why is it called *ishana*? Along with the ruling mother *shakti*-s, it rules over all gods. Therefore it is called *ishana*."

—*Atharva Shira Upanishad*

"... after bowing to Hari, who is *ishana* and who is OM."

—Ugrashravas to Rishi-s, *Mahabharata*

(68)

lokasara

(लोकसार = *lokasāra*)

MEANING

" **1** the essence of the universe **2** the nectar for humanity. "

EXPLANATION

The word *lokasara* is explained as OM in the commentary by Adi Shankara on the *Vishnu Sahasranama* from the *Mahabharata*. Explaining the name *lokasaranga* of Vishnu, Adi Shankara cites a verse from the *Chandogya Upanishad* to interpret *lokasara* as an appellation of OM. The cited verse and the one that follows it narrate how Prajapati (Brahma) perceived OM. Prajapati first meditated on all the *loka*-s, as a result of which he perceived the three Veda-s. Then, Prajapati meditated on the three Veda-s, as a result of which he perceived the three utterances—*bhur, bhuvah,* and *svah.* And when Prajapati meditated on these three utterances, he perceived OM. The purport of the verses is that the essence of the three realms (which comprise the entire universe) are the three Veda-s, the essence of the three Veda-s are the three utterances, and the essence of the three utterances is OM. OM is the ultimate essence (*sara*) of the universe (the *loka*-s), hence it is called *lokasara.*

Adi Shankara says that as Vishnu is to be achieved by the chanting of OM or *lokasara,* he is called *lokasaranga.* Coincidentally, *lokasaranga* is also listed as a name of Shiva in the *Shiva Sahasranama* of the *Linga Purana.*

The notion of OM being the ultimate essence is echoed in its name *rasa* ("essence", p. 148). The *Chandogya Upanishad* calls

OM the most superior essence of essences (p. 148). In the Tantra tradition, OM is called *tritattva*, meanings "the triad of essences".

The Sanskrit word *loka* also means "people" or "humanity". This sense is present in the words used for democracy in some Indian languages, e.g. *loktantra* (Hindi) and *lokshahi* (Marathi and Gujarati). The word *sara* also means "nectar" in Sanskrit. Accordingly, the word *lokasara* can be understood as "the nectar for humanity". OM is described as *amrita*, which means both "nectar" and "immortal", in the *Chandogya Upanishad*. The Upanishad says that the gods achieved immortality when they entered the sound OM, and further adds that anybody who knows OM and "enters" it (takes refuge in it) becomes free from death. This freedom from death is to be understood as *moksha*, or freedom from cycles of birth and death.

TRADITION

Commentaries.

ETYMOLOGY

loka + sāra → lokasāra.

loka ▸ **1** one of the three, seven, or fourteen realms which comprise the universe **2** mankind, humanity; ***sāra*** ▸ **1** essence, core, purport **2** nectar.

QUOTES

"Or, 'Prajapati meditated on the *loka*-s'—from this Vedic verse, *lokasara* means OM."

—Adi Shankara's commentary on *Vishnu Sahasranama*

(69)

mantradi, mantradya

(मन्त्रादि, मन्त्राद्य = *mantrādi, mantrādya*)

MEANING

"1 the beginning of mantra-s **2** the source of mantra-s **3** the first mantra **4** the foremost mantra."

EXPLANATION

These are names of OM as per three Tantra works. Bhaskara Raya's commentary on the *Lalita Sahasranama* also explains the word *mantradi* as OM, citing the *Matrika Kosha.*

The derivation of *mantra* from the root √*mantr* ("to speak secretly") has been explained already (p. 116). In the *Nirukta,* Yaska derives the word from *manana* ("deliberation"), i.e. from √*man* ("to think"). The *Rama Tapini Upanishad* derives the word from *manana* ("meditation") and *tranana* ("protection") and the *Brihat Tantra Sara* similarly derives it as ***mana**nat **tra**yate,* i.e. mantra is that which "protects on being meditated upon".

The word *adi* means "beginning", "cause", and "first". The word *adya* means "occurring at the beginning" (i.e. "first") and also "the most eminent". Accordingly, four meanings of the two names *mantradi* and *mantradya* are explained here.

Mantradi means the beginning of the mantra-s. As mentioned earlier, OM occurs at the beginning of many mantra-s like *om namah shivaya, om namo bhagavate vasudevaya,* and *om mani padme hum*; hence it is called *mantradi.* OM is also recited at the beginning of Vedic mantra-s (p. 16), therefore it is *mantradi.*

As *mantra* also refers to the *samhita* portion of the Veda-s, the word *mantradi* means the cause, source, or origin of Vedic *samhita*-s. As per the *Gopatha Brahmana*, Brahma created the Rig Veda, the Yajur Veda, and the Sama Veda from the three *matra*-s of OM (p. 28), and the Atharva Veda from the latent *v matra*. This is why OM is *mantradi*, the source of Vedic mantra-s.

Mantradi and *mantradya* also mean "the first mantra". OM is said to be the first word to come out from the throat of Brahma along with *atha* (p. 16). While both the words OM and *atha* are considered auspicious, OM is a mantra but *atha* is not. Therefore, OM is the first mantra. Alternatively, if *mantra* is understood as the *samhita* portion of the Veda-s, then *mantradi* and *mantradya* mean the first Vedic *samhita*. The *Bhagavata Purana* states that in the *Satya Yuga*, there was only one Veda which was OM (p. 201).

Finally, *mantradya* also means the foremost or the most eminent mantra. The *Yogi Yajnavalkya Smriti* mentions that OM is the leader (*nayaka*) among all mantra-s.

TRADITION

Tantra.

ETYMOLOGY

mantra + ādi → mantrādi;
mantra + ādya → mantrādya.

mantra ▸ **1** mantra-s **2** Vedic *samhita*-s; ***ādi*** ▸ **1** beginning **2** source, cause; **3** first. ***ādya*** ▸ **1** first **2** best, most eminent.

QUOTES

"The sound OM is called *mantradi*."

—*Bija Varna Abhidhana*

"The sound OM is called *mantradya*."

—*Matrika Kosha, Pranatoshini*

(70)

narayana

(नारायण = *nārāyaṇa*)

MEANING

"1 the pervader of atman-s, elements, and the world 2 the refuge of humans and atman-s 3 connected with the world."

EXPLANATION

As per Smriti and Tantra texts, *narayana* is a name of OM. Many meanings of the word *narayana* are explained in Smriti-s, Purana-s, and commentaries. The meanings presented in this section are based on a dialogue between Shiva and Parvati on the word *narayana* in the *Padma Purana.*

All the atman-s are collectively known as *nara* (नार) and they are the abode (*ayana*) of OM which resides in them. Therefore, OM is *narayana.* The elements are also called *nara* and OM, which pervades them too, is *narayana.* Finally, the entire world including both sentient and insentient entities is also called *nara.* As it is the abode of OM, OM is *narayana.* These three meanings are also indicated by the name *sarvavyapi* (p. 156). In all the three, the word *ayana* is interpreted as abode, like in the word *Ramayana* whose primary meaning is "the abode of Rama".

The word *ayana* also means refuge—as in the word *parayana* ("final refuge")—and one meaning of *nara* is humankind. OM is the refuge of the entire humankind, and so it is *narayana.* Moreover, as OM is the refuge of all atman-s, collectively called *nara*, it is named *narayana.* The last two meanings are confirmed by the *Chandogya Upanishad* account in which the gods achieve immortality when they enter OM (p. 129).

Another meaning of *ayana* is movement or motion, and that of *nara* (नार) is the world or the universe. Therefore, *narayana* also means that which moves with the world. The world is believed to be constantly moving or changing. The Sanskrit word for the world is *jagat* ("that which moves") which comes from the root √*gam* ("to go"). OM moves with the world as it is inseparable from the latter (p. 208).

Narayana is one of the most popular names of Vishnu. It is a part of the eight-syllabled mantra *om namo narayanaya.* As a name of Vishnu, *narayana* is explained by the *Manu Smriti* as follows—water is called *nara* (नार) as it is born from Nara (नर), the Supreme Brahman. Since water is the original abode of Vishnu, he is called *Narayana. Narayana* is also a name of Krishna; in the *Mahabharata*, Krishna's army which fought on the side of Duryodhana in the Kurukshetra war was called *narayani sena* ("the army of Narayana").

TRADITION

Smriti, Tantra.

ETYMOLOGY

nāra + ayana → nārāyaṇa.

nāra ▸ **1** atman-s **2** the elements **3** humankind **4** the world; ***ayana*** ▸ **1** abode, dwelling **2** refuge **3** going [with].

QUOTES

"OM is known as *narayana.*"

—*Yogi Yajnavalkya Smriti*

"The sound OM is called *narayana.*"

—*Lakshmi Tantra*

(71)
niranjana
(निरञ्जन = *nirañjana*)

MEANING

"**1** pure, spotless, unstained **2** without darkness **3** without ignorance **4** without the burden of karma."

EXPLANATION

This name of OM is attested in the *Yogi Yajnavalkya Smriti* and the *Naigama Kosha.* The word *anjana* primarily means kohl (*kajal*), a cosmetic used historically in India for eye make-up. Due to its black colour, *anjana* connotes stain, darkness, and ignorance. With the prefix *nir* denoting absence, *niranjana* means without any stain, without darkness, or without ignorance. OM is called *niranjana* as it is considered pure (*sarvapavana*, p. 152), brilliant (*divya*, p. 114), and omniscient (*sarvavid*, p. 154).

As kohl is an ointment, it also connotes karma, which sticks to an individual. The burden of karma is often called *karma lepa* ("the coating of karma"). The *Isha Upanishad* says that karma does not stick to one who performs actions while dedicating them to God and desires to live for a hundred years. Thus, *niranjana* means without the burden or coating of karma. This is how some commentaries explain *niranjana*, used for Brahman and karma-yogi, in the *Shvetashvatara* and *Mundaka* Upanishad-s. OM as the Supreme Brahman is free from all karma, just like Krishna who says in the *Gita* that karma-s do not taint him.

The name *niranjana* again stresses the *nirguna* aspect of OM, as seen in the meaning of "silence" (p. 26). The phrase *alakh niranjan* is used to describe the *nirguna* God in many medieval works and traditions. The word *alakh* derives from Sanskrit *alakshya* ("invisible"), while *niranjan* comes from Sanskrit *niranjana*, which is used in Upanishad-s, Smriti-s, Purana-s (*Niranjana* is one of the 1,000 names of Shiva listed in the *Linga Purana*), and Tantra works. The *Ramcharitmanas* of Tulsidas uses both words, independently, four times each to describe the *nirguna* aspect of God. The phrase *alakh niranjan* was popularly used in medieval India among the Nath, Yoga, Sikh, and even Sufi traditions. In the hatha yoga lineage, Niranjana is the name of one of the *siddha*-s (accomplished masters). Sadhu-s (ascetics) in the Nath and hatha yoga traditions beg for alms crying "*alakh niranjan*". Kabir refers to God as *alakh niranjan* in several compositions. Both words are used more than a hundred times (including nine times together) in the *Guru Granth Sahib*, the holy book of the Sikhs. The words are also used by Sufi poets Qutaban and Malik Muhammad Jayasi to describe God in their works *Mrigavati* and *Padmavat*.

TRADITION

Smriti, dictionaries.

ETYMOLOGY

nir + añjana → nirañjana.

nir ▸ prefix meaning without, freed of, or gone beyond; ***añjana*** ▸ night, darkness (literally, kohl or *kajal*).

QUOTES

"OM is known as *niranjana*."

—*Yogi Yajnavalkya Smriti*

"The mantra OM is called *niranjana*."

—*Naigama Kosha*

(72)

pancharashmi

(पञ्चरश्मि = *pañcaraśmi*)

MEANING

" **1** having five rays **2** having five strings or reins. "

EXPLANATION

OM is called *pancharashmi* in Tantra works. The medieval *Brihat Tantra Sara* traces the name to the work *Yaksha Damara*. The chapter on OM in the *Prapancha Sara Tantra*, ascribed to Adi Shankara, lists five states of yogi-s—waking, dreaming, deep sleep, the fourth state, and the tranquil state beyond the fourth. A commentary associates these states with the five 'rays' of OM—*bija* (origin), *bindu* (dot or nasal sound), *nada* (resonance or sound), *shakti* (power), and *laya* (rhythm) respectively.

In the Rig Veda, Soma and Pushan's chariot, said to travel everywhere, is called *pancharashmi* (having five reins). The five reins are explained as the five seasons—*vasanta* (spring), *grishma* (summer), *varsha* (monsoon), *sharad* (autumn), and *hemanta-shishira* (pre-winter and winter taken as one season). Pushan is one of the twelve Aditya-s. The *Amara Kosha* lists *pushan* ("the nourisher" or "that which grows") as one of the thirty-seven words for the sun, often identified with OM (see *aditya*, p. 94). As the five rays mentioned above belong to Pushan, he is also *pancharashmi*. Thus, OM as Pushan or the sun is *pancharashmi*, having five reins [in his chariot].

The sun is also called *pancharashmi*, since it is described as having rays of five different colours. The *Chandogya Upanishad* describes the sun as brown, white, blue, yellow, and red. The arteries emanating from the heart are described by the Upanishad as having five essences corresponding to these five colours of the sun. Elsewhere, OM is also described as residing in the heart (see *tryavasthana*, p. 188).

In the esoteric work *Tara Bhakti Rahasya Dipika*, the word *pancharashmi* is used for the five-syllabled mantra *om hrim strim hum phat.* This mantra is used to worship the Tantric goddess Tara (also called Ugra Tara).

In the Buddhist Tantric tradition, the word *pancharashmi* is explained as the five-coloured rays of the sounds *ya*, *ra*, *la*, *va*, and *ha* which represent the five elements. OM is also associated with the five elements; it is said to be their origin in the *Gopatha Brahmana* (p. 16).

TRADITION

Tantra.

ETYMOLOGY

pañca + raśmi → pañcaraśmi.

pañca ▸ five; ***raśmi*** ▸ **1** string **2** ray.

QUOTES

"The sound OM is called *pancharashmi*."

—Tantra works

(73)
parama
(परम = *parama*)

MEANING

"**1** that which measures the Supreme Brahman
2 that which expresses (as a sound) the Supreme Brahman
3 that which throws off or kills the [internal] enemies
4 best, supreme **5** principal, main **6** the first
7 the leader **8** Shiva."

EXPLANATION

As per the *Vishva Kosha*, the word *parama* means OM. It is used in this sense by Kalidasa in the epic *Kumarasambhava.* The word derives from *para* ("Brahman", and also "enemy") and one of the three roots—√*ma* (मा, "to measure", "to sound"), √*mi* (मि, "to throw"), or √*mi* (मी, "to injure, to kill"). The first three meanings given above are the corresponding literal meanings of the word *parama* that apply to OM. OM measures Brahman as it is the mantra to perceive Brahman (*tara*, p. 170). OM expresses Brahman as it is the name of Brahman (p. 36). OM throws away or annihilates the internal enemies as it nourishes virtues (p. 122) and exhausts vices (p. 166).

The word *parama* has many conventional meanings in Sanskrit, including the last five meanings listed above. All of these apply to OM. *Parama* means the best or supreme; OM is considered the supreme mantra (p. 130). *Parama* means principal or main; OM is called the principal syllable by Krishna in the *Gita* (p. 85). *Parama* means the first; OM is considered the first seed sound (p. 92) and the first Veda (p. 198). *Parama* also means the leader; OM is called *pranava* as it leads forward (p. 60) and leads one completely to liberation (p. 64). Finally, *parama* is a name of Shiva; OM is also identified with Shiva (p. 72).

The word *parama* occurs as a part of the words *paramatma* ("supreme atman") and *parameshvara* ("supreme lord"), used for the Supreme Brahman. Both words are names of Vishnu in the *Vishnu Sahasranama*. The PARAM series of supercomputers designed in India gets its name from the Sanskrit word *parama*.

TRADITION

Dictionaries, *Kavya*.

ETYMOLOGY

para + √mā + ka → parama, para + √mi + ḍa → parama,
or **para + √mī + ḍa → parama.**

para ▸ **1** Supreme Brahman **2** an enemy; ***√mā*** ▸ **1** to measure **2** to make a sound. ***√mi*** ▸ to cast off, to throw. ***√mī*** ▸ to injure, to hurt. ***ka, ḍa*** ▸ suffixes to denote performer of an action.

QUOTES

"The word *parama* is also said to mean the sound OM."

—*Vishva Kosha*

"Then, the group of sages departed after saying *parama*. After saying *parama*, i.e. after saying OM."

—Kalidasa's *Kumarasambhava*, its commentary

(74)
paramakshara
(परमाक्षर = *paramākṣara*)

MEANING

" 1 the supreme syllable

2 the supreme and imperishable [Brahman]. "

EXPLANATION

OM is called *paramakshara* in the *Brahma Upanishad* and the *Shiva Purana.* The *Taittiriya Aranyaka* alludes to this name of OM, in the uncompounded form, thus: "OM—this mantra represents the three Veda-s, this is speech, and this is the *parama akshara.*" The *Aranyaka* then quotes an esoteric mantra from the Rig Veda which goes "the gods depend and rest in the skies on the *parama akshara* of the Vedic verses." One of the meanings of this mantra by Sayana interprets *parama akshara* as the unsurpassed OM. In chapter 8 of the *Gita,* Arjuna asks Krishna the definition of Brahman, to which Krishna replies by saying that Brahman is *akshara parama.* Later, in chapter 11, when Krishna displays his universal form, Arjuna extols him by saying, "You are the *parama akshara,* worthy of knowing." In both places, *akshara parama* or *parama akshara* can be understood as OM. Thus, the name *paramakshara* is rooted in the Rig Veda and is alluded to in several Hindu scriptures.

The word *parama* has many meanings applicable to OM (p. 138). All of them can be considered, but for simplicity only one ("supreme") is taken here. As *akshara* means "a syllable", *paramakshara* means the most eminent or supreme syllable, as OM has already been explained (p. 120).

The second meaning of *akshara* considered here is "imperishable". With this, *paramakshara* means the supreme imperishable. OM is seen as both supreme, as it is omnipotent (p. 204), and imperishable, as it is without decay (p. 102).

The word *paramakshara-vigraha* ("the form of the *parama akshara*" or "one whose form or expression is *parama akshara*") is used as a name to describe several deities. It is one of the 1,000 names of Krishna in the *Krishna Sahasranama* and also one of the 1,000 names of the guru in the *Guru Sahasranama* from the astrological work *Brihad Jyotisha Arnava*. In the *Ishvara Pratyabhijna Karika*, one of the foundational texts of the *Pratyabhijna* school of Kashmir Shaivism, Shiva is described as *paramakshara-vigraha*. *Paramakshara* can be interpreted as OM in these names and descriptions.

TRADITION

Upanishad, Purana.

ETYMOLOGY

parama + akṣara → paramākṣara.

parama ▸ supreme; ***akṣara*** ▸ **1** syllable **2** imperishable.

QUOTES

"There, Brahman is resplendent in four states—as Brahma in the awakened state, as Vishnu in dream, as Shiva in deep sleep, and the fourth [state] is the *paramakshara* (OM)."

—*Brahma Upanishad*

"Then, even when the *paramakshara* OM split, Brahma and Vishnu did not understand the purpose of the division."

—*Shiva Purana*

(75)

prabhu

(प्रभु = *prabhu*)

MEANING

"**1** capable **2** master, lord **3** eternal **4** protector **5** eminent."

EXPLANATION

In the Tantra work *Pranatoshini*, one of OM's names is *prabhu*, which as per the *Yogi Yajnavalkya Smriti* is how the followers of Hiranyagarbha like to call OM. Hiranyagarbha is the first teacher of Yoga as per Bhishma's account in the *Mahabharata*.

Prabhu, from the root *pra* + √*bhu* ("to have power"), means "capable" or "powerful". As per Tantra texts, *prabhu* is one who has the power of both restraining (*nigraha*) and showering grace (*anugraha*). Restraining the evil and showering grace on the devotees are two key aspects of avatars like Krishna and Rama, who are both identified with OM (pp. 12, 38). Names of OM like *bhavanashana* (p. 104) and *sarvapavana* (p. 152) indicate its restraining and grace-showering powers.

The word *prabhu* also means a ruler or a leader. As explained under the name *ishana* (p. 126), OM is described as the ruler of all gods. The *Yogi Yajnavalkya Smriti* says that OM is the leader among all mantra-s. In the *Arthashastra*, Chanakya says that treasury (*kosha*, symbolizing riches) and sceptre (*danda*, symbolizing punishment) comprise the powers of a *prabhu* or a ruler. OM is described as the bestower of knowledge (p. 65) and the inexhaustible treasure (p. 103). OM is also called *rudra* (p. 150), the Brahman which makes the evildoers cry. This indicates its power to administer punishment.

Some other meanings of *prabhu* as per Sanskrit dictionaries are "eternal", "protector", and "eminent". OM is eternal as it is without beginning (*anadi*, p. 98) or end (*ananta*, p. 100)—this is why it is also called *dhruva* (p. 112) and *tryakshara* (p. 192). The name *pranava* of OM is explained as the protector of *prana*—life, vital forces, or living beings (p. 70). The word OM itself is derived in Paninian grammar from the root √*av*, whose first meaning is "to protect" (p. 210). Finally, OM is eminent as it is eminently praised (*pranava*, p. 58). The name *eka* (p. 118) of OM also means eminent.

The word *prabhu* occurs many times in Vedic texts, often in conjunction with the word *vibhu*, which is another name of OM (p. 204). In the fifth chapter of the *Gita*, the words *prabhu* and *vibhu* are used in successive verses. Vishnu is called *prabhu* twice in the *Vishnu Sahasranama*. *Prabhu* is also a name of Shiva in the *Shiva Sahasranama* occurring in the *Mahabharata*.

TRADITION

Smriti, Tantra.

ETYMOLOGY

pra + √bhū + ḍu → prabhu.

pra + √***bhū*** ▸ to be capable, to eminently exist; ***ḍu*** ▸ suffix to denote performer of an action.

QUOTES

"*Pranava*, the most eminent means of Yoga, is called *prabhu* by the followers of Hiranyagarbha."

—*Yogi Yajnavalkya Smriti*

"The sound OM is called *prabhu*."

—*Pranatoshini*

(76)

pralaya

(प्रलय = *pralaya*)

MEANING

"**1** that where everything dissolves or disappears
2 having a distinguished rhythm **3** musical time (*tala*)."

EXPLANATION

Pralaya is a name of OM as per the *Atharva Shikha Upanishad*. The Upanishad says that since OM dissolves all *prana*-s, it is called *pralaya*. OM, seen as the protector of the *prana*-s (see p. 70), is established here as the final destination of *prana*-s too. Vishnu is similarly called *prana-nilaya* ("abode of *prana*") and *sarvasu-nilaya* ("abode of all *prana*-s") in the *Vishnu Sahasranama*.

In the very first verse of its famous second chapter titled *omkara-nirnaya* ("Ascertainment of OM"), the *Yogi Yajnavalkya Smriti* says that the mantra-s that begin with OM grant all the four fruits (righteousness, prosperity, wishes, and liberation), since they arise from it and also dissolve in it. The Smriti uses the word *praliyante* ("they dissolve"), from the root *pra* + √*li* ("to dissolve"). Later, the Smriti lists *pralaya*, which also derives from *pra* + √*li*, as a name of OM.

As per the Apte Sanskrit-Hindi dictionary, *pralaya* means OM since everything arises from OM and dissolves in OM.

As an exocentric compound, the word *pralaya* also means that whose rhythm (*laya*) is distinguished (*pra*). Rhythm or *laya* is one of the five rays of OM (p. 136). OM is *pralaya* as its *laya* is distinguished, for it corresponds to a state even beyond the fourth as per the *Prapancha Sara Tantra* (p. 136).

As *laya* also refers to musical rhythm, *pralaya* means "that with [three] eminent rhythms", i.e. *tala*. *Tala* is the measure of time in Indian music and its three rhythms (*laya*-s) are *vilambita* (slow), *madhyama* (medium), and *druta* (fast). OM is associated with time (p. 172) and *tala* measures time in music. OM is identified as *Nada Brahman* (p. 164), the source of music. The *Sangita Ratnakara* says that all three parts of *sangita*—singing, playing of instruments, and dancing—are established in *tala*. Finally, OM is identified with Shiva (p. 72), and the chapter on *tala* in *Sangita Ratnakara* begins with praising both Shiva and *tala* simultaneously.

TRADITION

Upanishad, Smriti, dictionaries.

ETYMOLOGY

pra + √lī + ac → pralaya;

or **pra + laya → pralaya.**

pra* + √*lī ▸ to dissove, to disappear; ***ac*** ▸ suffix to denote location of an action. ***pra*** ▸ eminent, distinguished; ***laya*** ▸ rhythm.

QUOTES

"As it dissolves all *prana*-s, OM is called *pralaya*."

—*Atharva Shikha Upanishad*

"All [mantra-s] arise from OM and certainly dissolve in it."

"*Omkara* is called *pralaya*."

—*Yogi Yajnavalkya Smriti*

"*Pralaya*—the mystic syllable OM. OM, [because] everything arises from it and dissolves into it."

—Apte Sanskrit dictionary

(77)

prasvara

(प्रस्वार = *prasvāra*)

MEANING

"the distinguished sound."

EXPLANATION

The name *prasvara* of OM occurs in the *pratishakhya* of the Rig Veda. The context in the text is the start of a Vedic study session under a guru. The *pratishakhya* describes that the guru should sit towards the north, east, or north-east. If there are one or two students, they should sit to his right; if there are more, they should sit as space permits. The students should then touch his feet and say '*bhoh*'. The guru should then make the distinguished sound 'OM'. This distinguished sound, or *prasvara*, normally has three morae with a high pitch. Or it has four morae with first half having a low pitch, or six morae with double accent. The *pratishakhya* declares OM to be the door to heaven for the guru and the students, the Supreme Brahman, and the beginning of self-study (*svadhyaya*).

The Sanskrit word *svara* (स्वर) means a sound, a vowel, a pitch (accent), or a musical note. The Hindi word for a musical note is *sur* (सुर), which is derived from the Sanskrit *svara*. The word *prasvara* is derived from *svara* which here means a sound. The word becomes *svara* (स्वार), with the first vowel elongated and no change in meaning (words which undergo this transformation are called *prajnadi*). The prefix *pra* means distinguished; for example, a distinguished *acharya* (teacher) is called *pracharya*. Similarly, a distinguished *svara* (sound) is called *prasvara*.

OM is the distinguished sound because it is considered Brahman—it is both the name of Brahman (p. 36) and Brahman itself as *Shabda Brahman* (p. 189).

Prasvara is also a technical term used in the Indian musical tradition. In the *Natya Shastra* of Bharata, *prasvara* refers to the repetition of the eight-beat melody occurring at the end of a quarter as the beginning of the next quarter. Abhinavagupta explains the word *prasvara* as the eminent voicing (*svarana*) of a sound (*shabda*). Coincidentally, this concept of lengthening (repeating) a melody in music is also present in the lengthening of the vowel sound in OM with three morae (p. 28).

TRADITION

Vedic phonetics, commentaries.

ETYMOLOGY

√svar + gha → svara; svara + aṇ → svāra;
pra + svāra → prasvāra.

√svar ▸ to make a sound; ***gha*** ▸ suffix to denote means of an action; ***aṇ*** ▸ suffix with no meaning. ***pra*** ▸ distinguished.

QUOTES

"*Prasvara* has three instants (morae). *Prasvara* [is] that OM sound."

—Rig Veda's *Pratishakhya*, its commentary

(78)

rasa

(रस = *rasa*)

MEANING

"1 essence 2 water 3 sap of plants or nectar 4 Brahman 5 the nine aesthetic sentiments 6 the six flavours."

EXPLANATION

OM is called *rasa* ("essence") in the *Shankhayana Grihya Sutra.* The *Jaiminiya Brahmana* says that OM is the essence of Vedic speech. The *Chandogya Upanishad* describes OM as follows—"Earth is the essence of beings, water is the essence of earth, herbs are the essence of water, the human is the essence of herbs, speech is the essence of the human, the Vedic verse is the essence of speech, the Sama Veda is the essence of Vedic verse, and *udgitha* (OM) is the essence of the Sama Veda." The Upanishad calls OM "the most superior essence of all essences".

Rasa also refers to the six flavours. Since water is considered their basic element, it is also called *rasa.* In the *Mahabharata,* the elders tell the sage Aurva that all *rasa*-s are made of water. The Vedic deities associated with water are Apas ("the waters"), the Rig Veda has several hymns to them. Apas are equated with OM in the popular *sandhya* mantra *om apo jyoti raso'mritam brahma,* which means "OM is the waters, light, nectar, and Brahman."

The life-giving sap of plants is also called *rasa,* and so is nectar. The sap of Soma is called *somarasa,* which is also interpreted as the mystic nectar. In the *Gita,* Krishna says that he nourishes all the plants by becoming the moon, which is *rasatmaka* (consisting of *rasa,* i.e. sap or nectar).

Rasa also denotes Brahman, the source of transcendental bliss. The *Taittiriya Upanishad* says "Brahman is certainly *rasa*" (*raso vai sah*). OM as Brahman (p. 36) is the blissful *rasa*.

Rasa also refers to the nine aesthetic sentiments (*navarasa*)—*shringara* (love), *hasya* (mirth), *karuna* (pathos), *vira* (heroism), *raudra* (anger), *bhayanaka* (fear), *bibhatsa* (abhorrence), *adbhuta* (wonder), and *shanta* (tranquility). Like the three states—*shanta*, *ghora*, and *mudha* (p. 186)—OM represents the nine sentiments.

As stated before, *rasa* refers to the six flavours (*shadrasa*)—*madhura* (sweet), *amla* (sour), *lavana* (salty), *katu* (pungent), *tikta* (bitter), and *kashaya* (astringent). In the *Gita*, Krishna identifies himself with *rasa* in the waters (which can be understood as any of the six flavours) and OM in the Veda-s in the same verse.

TRADITION

Veda, Upanishad, *Grihya Sutra*, commentaries.

ETYMOLOGY

ras + ghañ → rasa.

√***ras*** ▸ to taste; ***ghañ*** ▸ suffix to denote object of an action.

QUOTES

"Now speech is Brahman, and OM is [its] *rasa*. With *rasa*, one pleases this very speech."

—*Jaiminiya Brahmana*

"*Udgitha* (OM) is the *rasa* of all *rasa*-s."

—*Chandogya Upanishad*

"... should be offered in the water with [the recitation of] a *Varuni* verse or *rasa*. *Rasa* is OM—the essence of the Veda-s."

—*Shankhayana Grihya Sutra*, its commentary

(79)
rudra
(रुद्र = *rudra*)

MEANING

"1 that which is instantly understood by the rishi-s **2** that which makes the evildoers cry **3** Agni, the fire god **4** the eleven *rudra*-s **5** Shiva **6** Vishnu **7** Hanuman."

EXPLANATION

The *Atharva Shira Upanishad* mentions the name *rudra* of OM. It says that OM is called so since its nature is understood instantly by *rishi*-s, who are the enlightened (*jnani*-s) as per the *Dipika* commentary. The Upanishad suggests that the *ru* of *rudra* comes from *rishi* while *dra* comes from *druta* ("instantly"). The transformations *ri* → *ru* and *dru* → *dra* can be explained by considering *rudra* in the *prishodaradi* class of words.

As per the *Unadi Sutra*, *rudra* derives from the causative form of √*rud* ("to cry") and the suffix *ra* and accordingly means "one who makes [somebody] cry". Commentaries explain the word as the Supreme Brahman who makes the sinners or those engrossed in worldly existence cry. Both ideas are echoed elsewhere too. In the *Gita*, Krishna—who identifies himself with OM (p. 85)—says that he manifests himself to destroy the evildoers. OM is called *bhavanashana* (p. 104), i.e. the destroyer of worldly existence.

Agni, who is identified with OM (p. 6), is also called *Rudra*. The *Taittiriya Samhita* of the Yajur Veda gives the reason. Once after defeating the *asura*-s, the gods offered the riches they won to Agni to protect them from *asura*-s in the future. Agni desired the riches for himself and fled from them. The gods chased Agni to forcefully take back the riches. Agni cried and so he came to be known as Rudra (from √*rud*, "to cry"). Agni's tears became silver; this is why silver is not offered to fire in a *yajna*.

The word *rudra* also refers to the eleven Vedic gods to whom several Vedic hymns are dedicated. Following the *Unadi Sutra*, a commentary on the *Amara Kosha* explains that *rudra*-s make the *asura*-s cry. OM is identified with many Vedic deities; and with this name it can be identified with the eleven *rudra*-s.

Rudra also refers to Shiva and is one of Vishnu's names in the *Vishnu Sahasranama*. Both are identified with OM (pp. 72, 206). Also, Hanuman is considered the incarnation of Rudra (Shiva)—he is called *rudra-avatara* by Tulsidas in the *Vinay-patrika*.

Commenting on verse 1.114.1 in the Rig Veda, Sayana gives five more etymologies of *rudra* with these meanings—(1) one who makes everybody cry at the time of death (2) destroyer of worldly sorrow (3) propounded by the Upanishad-s (4) giver of knowledge of atman to worshippers (5) destroyer of darkness. These five meanings can be applied to OM also.

TRADITION

Upanishad.

ETYMOLOGY

√rud + ṇi + rak → rudra.

√rud ▸ to cry; ***ṇi*** ▸ causative suffix; ***rak*** ▸ suffix indicating performer of an action.

QUOTES

"Then, why is OM called *rudra*? Because its nature is instantly understood by the rishi-s but not by other devotees."

—*Atharva Shira Upanishad*

(80)
sarvapavana
(सर्वपावन = *sarvapāvana*)

MEANING

"**1** all-purifying **2** Agni, fire."

EXPLANATION

The *Lakshmi Tantra* includes *sarvapavana* ("all-purifying") as a name of OM. *Sarva* means "everything" and *pavana*, from the root √*pu*, means "purifier". The words *pavitra* ("means of purifying") and *pavana* (पवन, "the wind") also come from √*pu*.

OM is considered a purifier in the Yoga tradition. Patanjali's *Yoga Sutra* includes *svadhyaya*, which means both self-study and chanting, as an element of *Kriya Yoga*. The commentary by Vyasa says that *svadhyaya* refers to the chanting of purificatory mantra-s like OM or the study of scriptures dealing with *moksha*. The *Yogi Yajnavalkya Smriti*, which also describes OM as *pavana*, states that the chanting of OM burns sins, and *pranayama* (practised with OM, p. 46) burns impurities.

The name *sarvapavana* also refers to Agni or the fire element. OM is identified with the three fires and Agni as indicated by its names *tridhama* (p. 6) and *rudra* (p. 150). Agni is believed to be the purifier of *sarva*—everything and everybody. A verse that occurs in both the *Skanda Purana* and the *Shiva Purana* goes, "All impure things surely become pure in an instant by coming in contact with fire, which is why he (Agni) is called *pavaka*."

Sarvapavana and similar words are used to describe many deities in Hindu scriptures. In the *Shiva Sahasranama* occurring in the *Linga Purana*, *saravapavana* is one of the names of Shiva.

It is also one of the names of Rama in the *Rama Sahasranama* of the *Ananda Ramayana*. The feminine form of *saravapavana* is *sarvapavani*. Krishna uses the word to describe Parvati in the *Anushasana Parva* of the *Mahabharata*, while Indra uses the word to address Lakshmi in the *Vishnu Purana*. In the *Skanda Purana* and the *Padma Purana*, the river Narmada is described as the purifier of all means of purification (*sarva-pavitra-pavana*). In the *Bhagavata Purana*, Krishna is called the purifier of all worlds (*pavanah sarvalokanam*). In the *Ramayana*, Agastya praises Rama as the purifier of all beings (*pavanah sarvabhutanam*).

As OM is *sarva-pavana*, it is also *patita-pavana*, or the purifier of even the fallen ones. Krishna is called *patita-pavana* in the *Garga Samhita* as he liberated even Putana, who had come to kill him on the orders of Kamsa. *Patita-pavana* is also a popular appellation of Rama; Tulsidas mentions the word as a name of Rama in the *Vinay-patrika*. The devotional song *raghupati raghava raja rama*, popularized by Mahatma Gandhi and enchantingly rendered by Pandit D. V. Paluskar, also addresses Rama as *patita-pavana*.

TRADITION

Tantra.

ETYMOLOGY

sarva + pāvana → sarvapāvana.

sarva ▸ all, everything; ***pāvana*** ▸ purifier.

QUOTES

"The sound OM is called *sarvapavana*."

—*Lakshmi Tantra*

(81)
sarvavid
(सर्वविद् = *sarvavid*)

MEANING

"1 omnipresent 2 omniscient, all-knowing 3 all-obtaining, all-possessing 4 knowledge of everything, complete knowledge."

EXPLANATION

A synonym of OM listed in the *Vaijayanti Kosha* is *sarvavid.* It is a compound of *sarva* ("everything") and *vid,* which can be derived from three different roots which are all spelt *vid.*

(1) The root √*vid sattayam* (विदँ सत्तायाम्) means "to exist" and is the source of the word *vidyamana* ("existent"). With this root, *sarvavid* means "that which exists in everything", or omnipresent. The *Taittiriya Upanishad* says "OM is all this (everything). The names *vibhu* (p. 204) and *vishva* (p. 208) also mean the same.

(2) The root √*vid jnane* (विदँ ज्ञाने) means "to know" and is the source of the word *vidvan* ("one who knows", or learned). With this root, *sarvavid* means "that which knows everything", or omniscient. The *Yogi Yajnavalkya Smriti* says that a name of OM is *sarvajna,* which has the same meaning.

(3) The root √*vid labhe* (विदॢँ लाभे) means "to obtain" or "to possess" and is the source of the word *go-vinda* ("one who posseses cows", i.e. Krishna). With this root, *sarvavid* means "that which obtains or possesses everything". As per the *Gopatha Brahmana,* the word OM derives from √*ap* ("to obtain", p. 30).

Like *vid,* the word *veda* ("Veda-s") can be derived from these three roots and also from √*vid vicharane* (विदँ विचारणे) which means "to contemplate". Therefore, the word *veda* has many meanings like "ever existing", "means of knowing", "means of obtaining [Brahman]", and "means/place of contemplation". All these are applicable to the Veda-s as they are considered to be *apaurusheya,* the repositories of contemplative philosophy, the means of knowledge, and the means of achieving Brahman.

When derived from *√vid jnane,* the word *vid* also means knowledge; it occurs in the last mantra of hymn 1.31 of the Rig Veda and is explained as *jnana* in the commentary by Sayana. The empty suffix *kvip* denotes abstraction (*bhava*) here. *Sarvavid* then means knowledge of everything, or complete knowledge. OM is the name of Brahman, and the *Aitareya Upanishad* says Brahman is *prajnana* ("having eminent knowledge").

The name is used for other divinities too. In the *Atharva Veda,* the auspicious goddess and Indra are called *sarvavid.* Vishnu is similarly called *sarvajna* twice in the *Vishnu Sahasranama.*

TRADITION

Dictionaries.

ETYMOLOGY

sarva + √vid + kvip → sarvavid.

sarva ▸ **1** everything **2** complete; ***√vid*** ▸ **1** to exist **2** to know **3** to attain; ***kvip*** ▸ suffix which undergoes complete elision and denotes the agent of an action or an abstract noun.

QUOTES

"OM is known as *sarvavid.*"

—*Vaijayanti Kosha*

"OM is synonymously known as *sarvajna.*"

—*Yogi Yajnavalkya Smriti*

(82)
sarvavyapi
(सर्वव्यापी = *sarvavyāpī*)

MEANING

"all-pervading."

EXPLANATION

OM is called *sarvavyapi* in several Hindu scriptures and also in the lexicon *Naigama Kosha.* The word *sarva* means "everything", and *vyapi* means "the pervader". The word *vyapi* comes from the root *vi* + √*ap* ("to pervade"), from which the names *vyapta* and *vyapi* in the *Vishnu Sahasranama* are derived. One of the derivations of the word OM itself is from √*ap* (p. 30).

OM is believed to pervade all space, time, and matter. The *Gopatha Brahmana* states that Prajapati created the directions of space, the seasons of time, and all matter (the elements, the worlds, the senses, the sense organs, etc.) from the components of OM. The *Atharva Shira Upanishad* states that OM pervades all realms like oil pervades ground sesame powder, i.e. in an inseparable way. The *Yogi Yajnavalkya Smriti* adds that OM pervades the body, the universe, and all branches of knowledge.

The word *sarvavyapi* occurs thrice in the *Shvetashvatara Upanishad* to describe Brahman. In the first instance, it is said that Brahman pervades everything just like ghee pervades milk. In the second occurrence, the *sarvavyapi* god is called Shiva. This is why *sarvavyapi* is considered to be a name of Shiva. Another similar name of Shiva is *jagadvyapi* ("the pervader of the worlds"); it is one of the 108 names of Shiva explained in the *Shiva Tattva Rahasya* (p. 88).

TRADITION

Upanishad, Smriti, Purana, dictionaries.

ETYMOLOGY

sarva + vi + √āp + ṇini → sarvavyāpī.

sarva ▸ everyone, everything; ***vi* + √*āp*** ▸ to pervade, to permeate; ***ṇini*** ▸ suffix in the sense of "having the nature of".

QUOTES

"Then, why is it called *sarvavyapi*? Since on merely being pronounced it pervades all realms, just like oil pervades a lump of ground sesame, and becomes inseparable after reaching the peaceful state of omnipresence—hence it is called *sarvavyapi*."

—*Atharva Shira Upanishad*

"This syllable *Omkara* is called *sarvavyapi* ... since it exists everywhere, pervading the body, the universe, and all branches of knowledge."

—*Yogi Yajnavalkya Smriti*

"Know the Supreme Brahman to be *pranava*, which is all-pervading and imperishable."

—*Linga Purana*

"The mantra OM is [called] *sarvavyapi*."

—*Naigama Kosha*

(83)

satya

(**सत्य** = ***satya***)

MEANING

"**1** truth **2** true, real **3** beneficial for the noble **4** vital force, food, and the sun **5** that which leads to the goal."

EXPLANATION

In Brahmana and Aranyaka texts, OM is called *satya*, which is a name of OM in Tantra. *Satya* means "true", as in *satya-vachana* ("true words"), as well as "truth", as in *satyameva jayate* ("truth alone is victorious"). OM is called *satya* in both senses in Vedic texts—it is said to be the true syllable as well as the truth.

Satya derives from the word *sat* and the suffix *ya*. *Sat* has many meanings including truth, a wise person, a noble person, existent, excellent, object of worship, resolute, and respectable. The suffix *ya* has the sense of "skilled at" or "beneficial for". *Satya* means "skilled at truth", i.e. truthful, or "beneficial for truth". OM is truthful as it is identified with Rama (p. 38), who never lies. OM is the nourisher of virtues (p. 122), hence it is beneficial for truth, a virtue. Or, *satya* means beneficial for the wise, the noble, the excellent, the venerable, the resolute, and the respectable. OM is *satya* in this sense as it is said to endow such *mahatma*-s with special knowledge (p. 65).

The *Aitareya Aranyaka* gives another meaning of *sattya* (a variant spelling of *satya*)—*sat* means *prana*, *t* means food, and *ya* means the sun. Hence, *sattya* refers to the *trivrit* (triad, p. 190) of vital force, food, and the sun. OM is elsewhere explained as vital force and food (p. 78) or as vital force and the sun (p. 182).

As per Yaska's *Nirukta*, Shakatayana derived *satya* from *sat* and *ya*—from the causative form of √*i* ("to go"). Durgacharya explains *satya* accordingly as "that which leads to the goal". OM as *satya* is the means of liberation, the final goal (*purushartha*). Names of OM like *tara* (p. 170) reflect this idea.

The *Taittiriya Upanishad* describes Brahman as *satya*. As per the *Shabda Ratnavali*, one of Rama's names is *Satya*. Vishnu is called *Satya* thrice in the *Vishnu Sahasranama*, where six other names begin with *satya*. The first verse of the *Bhagavata Purana* ends with "we meditate on the supreme *satya* (Krishna)".

TRADITION

Veda, Tantra.

ETYMOLOGY

sat + yat → satya.

sat ▸ **1** truth **2** wise **3** good, noble **4** existent **5** excellent **6** object of worship or honour **7** resolute **8** respectable; ***yat*** ▸ suffix to denote the sense of "skilled at" or "beneficial to".

QUOTES

"One should respond with OM only. That is certainly *satya*, that the gods know."

—*Shatapatha Brahmana*

"That which is OM is this *satya* syllable."

—*Jaiminiya Brahmana*

"OM—this is truth (*satya*). *Na*—this is non-truth (*anrita*)."

—*Aitareya Aranyaka*

"The sound OM is called *satya*."

—*Bija Varna Abhidhana*

(84)

setu

(सेतु = *setu*)

MEANING

“**1** a ridge or a mound, a barrier [against destruction]
2 a bridge [to cross the worldly ocean]
3 a means of connection [to immortality or Brahman].”

EXPLANATION

In the *Kalika Purana*, OM is called the *setu* of mantra-s. *Setu* is a name of OM as per Tantric texts like *Tantra Sara* (“The essence of Tantra”). The word *setu*, from the root √*si* (“to bind”), literally means something which binds or restrains. A ridge or mound of earth which separates farms is called a *setu*, as it is the boundary which encloses the farms. A dike or a dam is called a *setu* as it restrains the flow of water. A bridge is called a *setu* as it binds (connects) two shores of a water body. The chain of limestone shoals between Rameshwaram island in India and Mannar island in Sri Lanka is called *Rama-setu* (“the bridge of Rama”).

OM is *setu* since, like a mound, it encloses the study of Veda-s and acts as a barrier against destruction of learning. The *Manu Smriti* says that one should always utter OM when starting and ending Vedic study, for Vedic learning trickles away if not started with OM and is destroyed if not ended with OM. Alternatively, OM is identified with the Supreme Brahman which is called *setu* of the worlds for preventing destruction (*sambheda*) in the *Brihad Aranyaka Upanishad*.

As OM is *tara* (p. 170), the means to cross over the worldly ocean, it is akin to a bridge. Hence also it is called *setu*. The metaphor of crossing a water body is also seen in the explanation of *pranava* in the *Shiva Purana* as a boat or a ship (p. 62).

Finally, OM is *setu* as it binds or connects—like a bridge—to immortality, Brahman, or the deity of a mantra. As Brahman itself (p. 36), OM connects the living being with transcendental bliss. In the *Mundaka Upanishad*, the Supreme Brahman is called the *setu* to immortality. As the means of liberation (p. 170), OM connects the atman to Brahman. As the *bija* of a mantra (p. 92), OM is the bridge to the deity of the mantra. For the standalone mantra OM, the *setu* is OM itself as per the *Kalika Purana*. Therefore, it is also the *setu* of the *setu*, like it is the *prana* of the *prana* (p. 67).

In the *Vishnu Sahasranama*, Vishnu is called *jagatah setuh* ("the *setu* for the universe"). This is interpreted in commentaries as a barrier for preventing a breach of *varnashrama* or confusion of *dharma*, or as the spine which binds the moving limbs.

TRADITION

Purana, Tantra.

ETYMOLOGY

√si + tun → setu.

√*si* ▸ to bind; ***tun*** ▸ suffix indicating performer of the action.

QUOTES

"The bridge (binding force) of all mantra-s is OM. And its bridge is known to be OM [itself]."

—*Kalika Purana*

"[The word] *setu* means *pranava* (OM)."

—*Tantra Sara*

(85)

shabda

(शब्द = *śabda*)

MEANING

"1 word 2 speech, any sound."

EXPLANATION

The *Amrita Nada Upanishad* refers to OM as *shabda*. Many texts identify OM with *Shabda Brahman*—the supreme divinity of the grammarians, also called *shabdika*-s ("associated with *shabda*"). The term *Shabda Brahman* is mentioned in many Hindu scriptures including the *Maitri Upanishad*, the *Gita*, various Purana-s (*Bhagavata*, *Agni*, *Vishnu*, and *Linga*), and the *Mahabharata*. The concept is systematically and exquisitely presented in the grammatical and philosophical work *Vakyapadiya* by Bhartrihari. In the very first verse, Bhartrihari says that the imperishable Brahman, without beginning or end, has the nature of *shabda* (the word) and manifests itself as *artha* (the meaning of the word).

Shabda comes from the root √*shabd* ("to make a sound") and most commonly means "a word". The science of grammar is called *shabda-anushasana* ("the instruction of words"). In the context of OM, *shabda* means the distinguished word. OM is the distinguished word just like it is the distinguished sound (p. 146).

Shabda also means human speech or any sound in general. OM is considered the essence of all speech (pp. 94, 148) and the distinguished sound (p. 88). In the *Gita*, Krishna identifies himself with both OM and sound by saying "I am OM in all the Veda-s and sound in the ether."

In Sanskrit, verbs associated with sound are of two types—some are used to convey the expression of *vyakta vak* (intelligible speech) and others convey the expression of *avyakta vak/shabda* (unintelligible speech or sound). As the word OM or human speech, *pranava* is *vyakta vak* or *saguna*. As unintelligible speech and sounds, it is *avyakta shabda/shabda* or *nirguna*. As the generic sound, it is both *saguna* and *nirguna*, as stated earlier (p. 26).

In the *Linga Purana*, Suta identifies *Shabda Brahman* and OM with Shiva. While bowing down to the supreme lord before narrating the Purana, Suta describes Shiva as having the body of *Shabda Brahman* and the form of OM. *Shabda-brahma* is also one of the names of Shiva in the *Shiva Sahasranama* in the *Linga Purana*. In addition, the Purana describes Narasimha also being praised as *shabda-brahma* by the deities.

TRADITION

Upanishad, grammar.

ETYMOLOGY

śabd + ghañ → śabda.

√***śabd*** ▸ to make a sound; ***ghañ*** ▸ suffix to denote abstract noun or object of an action.

QUOTES

"Closing one nostril with a finger and inhaling air with the other, one should hold the fire (i.e., breath) and meditate on *shabda* (OM) alone."

—*Amrita Nada Upanishad*

(86)

shrutipada

(श्रुतिपद = *śrutipada*)

MEANING

" 1 the origin of the Veda-s 2 the origin of musical notes. "

EXPLANATION

Shrutipada is explained as OM in the *Kalanidhi* commentary on the *Sangita Ratnakara*, a musicological text from the thirteenth century. The opening verse of the *Sangita Ratnakara* refers to the self-luminous *shrutipada*, situated in the lotus of the heart. The *Kalanidhi* commentary explains that *shrutipada* means OM as it is the *pada* (origin) of the *shruti*-s (Veda-s). This interpretation is in accordance with the *Gopatha Brahmana*, which describes how Brahma obtained the Veda-s from the components of OM (p. 16).

In the context of music, the word *shruti* refers to the notes of music which are also called *svara*-s. There are twenty-two *shruti*-s, or divisions of the octave, in the Indian musical tradition. These *shruti*-s form the seven *svara*-s, or notes. These notes are described by the eighth century musicological work *Brihaddeshi* as originating from *Nada Brahman* (God as resonance)—"There is no song without *Nada*, there are no musical notes without *Nada*. There is no dance without *Nada*. Therefore, the whole world consists of *Nada*." The concept of *Nada Brahman* enriches the concept of *Shabda Brahman* (p. 189) by incorporating music, which is non-linguistic. *Nada* is closely related to OM, being considered one of its elements (p. 51). As per the *Nada Bindu Upanishad*, the union of Brahman and OM is *Nada*, whereas many other sources identify OM itself as the *Nada Brahman*.

The *Sangita Ratnakara* extols *Nada Brahman* as follows—"We worship that unparalleled and blissful *Nada Brahman* which is the consciousness of all beings and which is manifest in the form of the world. By the worship of *Nada*, the gods Brahma, Vishnu, and Shiva are certainly worshipped, because these three are not different from that (*Nada Brahman*)."

Puranic texts also refer to this association between Brahman and music. In the *Bhagavata Purana*, Narada has a dialogue with Vyasa in which he narrates his past life and how he moves about singing *Harikatha* (the tales of Vishnu). Narada says that his lute is adorned by *Svara Brahman*. As per commentaries, *Svara Brahman* implies that the seven notes themselves are Brahman.

TRADITION

Music, commentaries.

ETYMOLOGY

śruti + pada → śrutipada.

śruti ▸ **1** Veda-s **2** the twenty-two divisions of the octave which make up the seven notes; ***pada*** ▸ place of origin.

QUOTES

"*Shrutipada* means the place of origin of the Veda-s, i.e. OM."

—Commentary on *Sangita Ratnakara*

(87)
shukla
(शुक्ल = *śukla*)

MEANING

"1 that which calls out or exhausts [the body]
2 pure, spotless, white **3** the destination of the mind
4 the abode of Sarasvati."

EXPLANATION

The *Atharva Shira Upanishad* says that OM is called *shukla* as it "calls out" and "exhausts". The two corresponding roots are √*kland* and √*klam*, which have the sound *kla* of *shukla*. The *Dipika* commentary explains "calls out" as OM manifesting or pervading as a sound. It further explains that as OM is pronounced with a high pitch (*udatta*), the greater effort involved exhausts the body when it is chanted. Alternatively, it can be understood that OM exhausts vices or bondage. OM being all-purifying (*sarva-pavana*, p. 152), it purifies the mind by strengthening virtues (*gunajivaka*, p. 122) and exhausting vices. As OM is the means of liberation (p. 170), it exhausts mortal bondage.

The *Yogi Yajnavalkya Smriti* also mentions the name *shukla* of OM, adding that it is called so as it is white (or pure), leads to the pure state, and parches sins. This explanation relates OM to the usual meanings of *shukla* in Sanskrit—pure, spotless, or white. Elsewhere, the Smriti says that OM is white in colour.

A commentary on the *Amara Kosha* derives the word *shukla* from the root √*shuk*, which means "to go" or "to move". The commentary says that *shukla* is where the mind goes (i.e., is attracted). As OM captivates the mind (p. 114), it is called *shukla*.

The feminine word *shukla* (शुक्ला) is a name of Sarasvati, who is described as "fair like the jasmine flower, the moon, the snow, and a necklace of pearls". Hence, the neuter word *shukla* (शुक्ल) can also mean "that which has *shukla* in it", i.e. the dwelling or abode of *shukla* (Sarasvati). The *Nyasa*, a grammatical commentary, explains how mansions having white colour (*shukla*) are also called *shukla*, and a city in which such mansions stand is also called *shukla*. Similarly, *shukla* can be understood as the abode of Sarasvati, the goddess of knowledge. OM is believed to be all-knowing, as it is called *sarvajna* (p. 154).

The word *shukla* has no formal grammatical derivation and is obtained via a *nipatana* (see p. 34) in *Unadi Sutra*.

TRADITION

Upanishad, Smriti.

ETYMOLOGY

From √kland, √klam + ṇic, or √śuk. Or, śuklā + ac → śukla.
√kland ▸ to call out. ***√klam*** ▸ to be exhausted. ***ṇic*** ▸ suffix in causative sense. ***√śuk*** ▸ to go. ***śuklā*** ▸ Sarasvati; ***ac*** ▸ *arśa·ādi* suffix having the sense of "of this" or "in this".

QUOTES

"Why is it called *shukla*? Since on merely being pronounced, it weakens and exhausts [vices]—hence it is called *shukla*."

—*Atharva Shira Upanishad*

"Know OM as *shukla*. ... It is white (pure) by colour, it leads to the clear (pure) state, and it parches (purifies) the three kinds of sins—hence it is called *shukla*."

—*Yogi Yajnavalkya Smriti*

(88)
sukshma
(सूक्ष्म = *sūkṣma*)

MEANING

"1 subtle, fine, minute **2** that which pierces and binds."

EXPLANATION

The name *sukshma* ("subtle") of OM is mentioned in Upanishad and Smriti texts. The *Atharva Shira Upanishad* says that OM is called so as when it is pronounced, it subtly resides in the body of the chanter. The body referred to here is not the physical body but the subtle body, which is also called *sukshma sharira*, or simply *sukshma*. Several Hindu philosophical systems admit the existence of three bodies—(1) the gross body (*sthula sharira*) made of the five elements; (2) the invisible subtle body which comprises the mind, the intellect, the ego, the memory, the five vital forces, and the ten sensory powers; and (3) the causal body (*karana sharira*) which is the sheath of bliss.

The *Shiva Purana* describes OM as *ati-sukshma* ("very subtle" or "infinitesimal") and also *mahartha* ("massive"). How is it that the same OM which is *sarvavyapi* ("all-pervading", p. 156) and *ananta* ("infinite", p. 100) is also *ati-sukshma* ("infinitesimal")? The *Shiva Purana* explains this by comparing OM to the seed of a banyan tree. As a tiny seed conceals in itself a giant banyan tree, the infinitesimal OM conceals infinity in itself.

The word *sukshma* comes from the root √*such* which means "to act maliciously" but has the connotation of piercing and binding. The Sanskrit word for needle, *suchi*, comes from the same root. A needle pierces and also sews or binds together.

In Vedic texts, OM is presented as that which pierces and binds together. The *Jaiminiya Brahmana* of the *Sama Veda* says that just as leaves of a tree are pierced and fastened by a needle, OM pierces and fastens all the worlds. A similar comparison is found in the *Chandogya Upanishad* which says that just as the leaves are pierced and held together by a stalk, OM pierces and holds together all speech. These two similes refer to two contrasting properties of OM: it is subtle and yet pervading as it pierces (pervades) speech and the universe, and holds them together like a needle or a stalk.

TRADITION

Upanishad, Smriti, Purana.

ETYMOLOGY

√sūc + sman → sūkṣma.

√*sūc* ▸ to pierce; ***sman*** ▸ suffix indicating performer of an action.

QUOTES

"Then, why is it called *sukshma*? Since on merely being pronounced, it becomes subtle and resides in bodies [of the reciters] and is in contact with all organs."

—*Atharva Shira Upanishad*

"OM is known as *sukshma.*"

—*Yogi Yajnavalkya Smriti*

"It (OṂ) is extremely infinitesimal and also massive (infinite). It is to be understood as the seed of a banyan tree."

—*Shiva Purana*

(89)

tara

(तार = *tāra*)

MEANING

“**1** the saviour **2** the means of liberation **3** liberation.”

EXPLANATION

OM is called *tara* in many scriptures. The word is used in the title of the *Tarasara Upanishad,* which presents the essence (*sara*) of OM (*tara*). *Tara* comes from the root √*tri* which means to swim or go across, literally (as in crossing a river) or metaphorically (as in crossing the worldly ocean). The verb *tairna* (“to swim”) in Hindi comes from this root, as does the name of the Sikh holy place Tarn Taran (“the means to swim across”). The sense is metaphorical in the name *tara* of OM which means that which liberates, the means of liberation, or the act of liberation.

As OM is considered the Supreme Brahman (p. 36), it is seen as the saviour that can liberate living beings. OM is described as the means of liberation in the *Taittiriya Aranyaka* (p. 182) and the *Taittiriya Upanishad* (p. 31). Finally, OM is understood to be liberation itself; for it is what remains after liberation. OM's name *akshara* (p. 84) also means liberation.

Vishnu is called *tarana* once and *tara* twice in the *Vishnu Sahasranama.* While commenting on the second *tara* name, Adi Shankara says that Vishnu is called *tara* as he enables one to cross the worldly ocean, or because *tara* is OM. *Tara* is also a famous name of Rudra (Shiva); it occurs in the *Shatarudriya* hymn in *Vajasaneyi, Kanva, Taittiriya,* and *Maitrayani* branches of the Yajur Veda as *namah taraya* (“Salutations to *tara*”).

TRADITION

Upanishad, Smriti, Purana, dictionaries.

ETYMOLOGY

√tṝ + ṇic + ac → tāra.

√tṝ ▸ to swim, sail, or go across; ***ṇic*** ▸ suffix in causative sense; ***ac*** ▸ suffix to denote the agent or means of an action, or an abstract noun.

QUOTES

"Since on merely being pronounced it liberates from the great fear of gestation, birth, disease, old age, death, and world; and also protects—hence it (OM) is called *tara.*"

—*Atharva Shira Upanishad*

"OM is known as *tara.* ... When it is meditated upon, it delivers one from the rising tide of all sorrows agitated by the binding ocean of the world; hence it is called *tara.*"

—*Yogi Yajnavalkya Smriti*

"As it (OM) carries them whose mind is engrossed in chanting it across the ocean of the world, it is known as *tara.*"

—*Skanda Purana*

"The minds of all deities were skilled in the constant chanting of *tara* (OM) and Hrillekha (the goddess residing in the hearts of the enlightened)."

—*Devi Bhagavata*

"[The word *tara* means] that which liberates those who chant it from the ocean of the world. Or, that by means of which one is liberated. Or, the suffix *ac* is in the abstract sense."

—*Vachaspatya Kosha*

(90)
traikalya
(त्रैकाल्य = *traikālya*)

MEANING

"the three times—past, present, and future."

EXPLANATION

This name of OM comes from the *Yogi Yajnavalkya Smriti*. OM represents the three times—the past, the present, and the future. This triad is called the time form of OM in the *Maitri Upanishad* (p. 176). Upanishad-s say that not only does OM pervade the three times, but whatever is beyond the three times is also OM.

This name of OM refers to the concept of *kala*, a word used for both time and Supreme Brahman, in Hindu thought. *Kala* is thought to be both temporal and eternal. The divisions of time like day and night, months, seasons, and years as well as past, present, and future are the divisions or temporal aspects of *kala*. *Kala* itself is, however, eternal and indivisible. Both temporal and eternal time are identified with the supreme divinity. The Vedic *Purusha Sukta*—which presents the Supreme Brahman as the cosmic being (*Purusha*)—says that whatever is (the present), whatever was (the past), and whatever will be (the future) is *Purusha* alone. In the *Gita*, Krishna says that he is the eternal *Kala*. This is similar to how OM, the supreme divinity, is seen as the three times and also that which is beyond them.

Kala is often seen as the ultimate cause and controller in Indian philosophy. The poet-philosopher Bhartrihari (5th century CE) vividly describes *Kala* as the string-puller which controls the world by preventing or allowing events, and as the master player which plays a game on the board of the world with living beings as pegs. As if he were witnessing the ruins of a capital city, Bhartrihari says, "I salute *Kala* due to which that delightful city, that great king, that feudal empire, that council of ministers, that bevy of beauties, that arrogant prince, and that band of bards—all of this is now only a memory."

The word *traikalya* also refers to the time of sunrise, noon, and the time of sunset. These are the three times for the daily *sandhya* worship, in which OM is recited many times. The triple *sandhya* is said to destroy all transgressions, just like OM is said to be all-purifying (*sarvapavana*, p. 152). *Traikalya* also means the three phases of origin, continuance, and destruction. The *Maitri Upanishad* says that all entities originate from *kala*, grow with it, and dissolve in it. Just as OM represents the three gods Brahma (progenitor), Vishnu (preserver), and Shiva (destroyer); it also represents the three phases of the cosmic cycle and also the cycle itself. Finally, *traikalya* refers to the three phases of life—childhood, youth, and old age. OM denotes these three phases, and is itself beyond aging as it is ever new (*pranava*, p. 65).

TRADITION

Upanishad, Smriti.

ETYMOLOGY

tri + kāla + ṣyañ → traikālya.

tri ▸ three; ***kāla*** ▸ time; ***ṣyañ*** ▸ suffix with no change in meaning.

QUOTES

"OM is known as *traikalya* due to [it being] the past, the present, and the future."

—*Yogi Yajnavalkya Smriti*

(91)

tridhatu

(त्रिधातु = *tridhātu*)

MEANING

"**1** the three bodily humours—wind, bile, and phlegm

2 having three elements

3 Ganesha—the nourisher of three objectives."

EXPLANATION

This name of OM is associated with Ayurveda, the ancient Indian system of medicine. Ayurveda recognizes three *dhatu*-s (humours) in the body—*vata* (wind), *pitta* (bile), and *kapha* (phlegm). These three are related to the three qualities (*sattva*, *rajas*, and *tamas*), the five elements (earth, water, fire, ether, and wind), and the six flavours (sweet, sour, salty, pungent, bitter, and astringent). As per Ayurveda, the body is healthy when the three humours are present in their natural balance. All illnesses of the body result from an imbalance of any of the three humours. When all three humours are imbalanced, the condition is called *sannipata* ("combined attack") or *trilinga* ("having three signs"). Interestingly, *trilinga* is also a name of OM (p. 178).

OM is called *tridhatu* as its component sounds represent the three life-sustaining humours. Itself, OM is beyond the three humours and the diseases caused by their imbalance. *Tridhatu* is one of the names of Krishna. In the *Shanti Parva* of the *Mahabharata*, Krishna tells Arjuna that the knowers of Ayurveda call him *tridhatu* since life depends on the three humours—humans (and other animals) are sustained by these three and perish when these three wear away.

In general, *dhatu* (literally, "bearer") refers to elements or components. Specifically, it refers to the three humours, the seven body constituents (in Ayurveda), the five gross elements and their five qualities, the five sense organs, metals, and roots of words. In addition to Krishna, OM is also called *tridhatu* in the *Shanti Parva* of the *Mahabharata,* which is explained as having three components—the sounds *a, u,* and *m.*

As per the *Trikanda-shesha* dictionary, the word *tridhatu* refers to Ganesha. Ganesha is *tridhatu* as he bears and nourishes the three human objectives—righteousness, prosperity, and wishes. Thus, the name *tridhatu* identifies OM, also described as the bestower of three objectives (*triprayojana,* p. 184), with Ganesha, the supreme divinity in the Ganapatya tradition. In the *Ganesha Sahasranama* of the *Ganesha Purana,* two names—*panchaksharatma* ("one whose form is OM", p. 50) and *ekakshara-parayana* ("one whose abode is OM")—associate OM with Ganesha. A commentary explains that *ekakshara* is OM (p. 120) and Ganesha is situated in OM.

TRADITION

Smriti, *Mahabharata,* Ayurveda.

ETYMOLOGY

tri + dhātu → tridhātu; tri + √dhā + tun → tridhātu.

tri ▸ three; ***dhātu*** ▸ **1** bodily humour **2** element. ***√dhā*** ▸ to bear; ***tun*** ▸ suffix indicating performer of an action.

QUOTES

"OM is declared to be *tridhatu*—wind (*vata*), bile (*pitta*), and phlegm (*shleshma* or *kapha*)."

—*Yogi Yajnavalkya Smriti*

(92)

trika

(त्रिक = *trika*)

MEANING

"the triad."

EXPLANATION

OM is called *trika* in the Tantra work *Pranatoshini*. The word means "a collection of three", or a triad. OM is called *trika* as it represents many triads. Many of OM's names begin with *tri*, which means "three"; fourteen sections of this book explain such names. While most of these names are found in Smriti-s, especially the *Yogi Yajnavalkya Smriti*, the association of OM with triads goes back to the Upanishad-s. The *Maitri Upanishad* says that the word OM itself is OM's sound-specific form. The *Dipika* commentary explains that the triad of three Vedic accents (high, low, and falling) is implied here. The Upanishad then lists eleven triads as forms of OM—

(1) feminine, masculine, and neuter: gender form (p. 178).
(2) fire, wind, and the sun: luminous form (p. 74).
(3) Brahma, Shiva, and Vishnu: sovereign form (p. 2).
(4) the three fires: mouth form (*trimukha*, p. 6).
(5) the three Veda-s: knowledge form (p. 8).
(6) earth, atmosphere, and heaven: realm form (p. 4).
(7) past, present, and future: time form (p. 172).
(8) *prana*, fire, and the sun: heat form.
(9) food, water, and the moon: growth form.
(10) intellect, mind, and ego: conscious form.
(11) *prana*, *apana*, and *vyana*: vital force form (p. 66).

The Upanishad says that by pronouncing OM, all these eleven triads are mentioned, worshipped, and fixed [in the mind]. The *Dipika* commentary remarks that the entities of the triads are to be associated with OM's three sounds *a*, *u*, and *m* respectively.

In Ayurveda, the word *trika* is used for *triphala*, a potent herbal formula made from three fruits (*phala*-s)—*haritaki* (*Terminalia chebula*), *vibhitaki* (*Terminalia bellirica*), and *amalaki* (*Phyllanthus emblica*)—combined in equal parts. In Ayurvedic texts, *triphala* is said to have the power of destroying *tridosha*, the disorders caused by imbalance of the three *dhatu*-s (wind, bile, and phlegm). As *tridhatu* (p. 174), OM represents the perfect balance of the three humours which is reinstated by *triphala*.

The *Bhagavata Purana* uses the word *trika* for the three fruits of *prapatti* (surrender to the Lord) described as follows—"Just as while eating one gets satisfaction, nourishment, and freedom from hunger with each morsel, one who surrenders obtains the triad of devotion, God-realization, and freedom from passion—all at the same time." OM symbolizes this *prapatti* as per the *Padma Purana*, which interprets the three sounds of OM as Vishnu, Lakshmi, and the being who is their servant (p. 14).

TRADITION

Tantra.

ETYMOLOGY

tri + kan → trika.

tri ▸ three; ***kan*** ▸ suffix denoting a collection.

QUOTES

"The sound OM is called *trika*."

—*Pranatoshini*

(93)
trilinga
(त्रिलिङ्ग = *triliṅga*)

MEANING

"1 the three genders—feminine, masculine, and neuter 2 the three qualities 3 the three types of egoism."

EXPLANATION

This name of OM, found in Smriti texts, is alluded to in the *Maitri Upanishad* which says that the triad of feminine, masculine, and neuter is OM's gender form (p. 176).

Sanskrit has three genders—*stri-linga* (feminine), *pullinga* (masculine), and *napumsaka-linga* (neuter). Most nouns have a fixed gender. Together, the three genders cover all nouns; just like OM is believed to pervade the entire universe. Qualifiers like adjectives do not have a fixed gender in Sanskrit. For example, the qualifier *sundara* is masculine in *sundarah purushah* ("a handome man"), feminine in *sundari nari* ("a beautiful woman"), and neuter in *sundaram chitram* ("a lovely picture"). Such qualifiers are called *trilinga*, as they are found in all three genders. Just like *trilinga* words transcend gender in grammar, the *trilinga* divinity OM transcends gender in nature. In the *Gajendra Moksha* account of the *Bhagavata Purana* (p. 187), Vishnu is similarly described as "neither female, nor neuter, nor male, nor devoid of the three genders." This principle is reflected in how Hinduism allows for worshipping the supreme divinity in any gender—as Shri, Lalita, or Durga (female); as Vishnu, Shiva, Rama, or Krishna (male); as Brahman or OM (neuter); or even as Ardha-narishvara (androgynous).

The *Bhagavata Purana* uses the word *trilinga* to describe Shiva as the lord of the three *guna*-s and to refer to *ahamkara* (egoism) which is of three types—*vaikarika* (from which the five organs each of perception and action plus the mind arise), *taijasa* (which assists the other two), and *bhutadi* (from which the five subtle elements arise). Both meanings are rooted in the Sankhya philosophy and apply to OM, which is also called *triguna* (p. 22).

The word *linga*—which comes from the root √*ling* ("to go" and also "to colour or distinguish")—means that which distinguishes, i.e. a mark or a sign. Gender, quality, and type of egoism are all called *linga* as they distinguish words, actions, and creation.

A mark or sign is also the sense in *shiva-linga*, the *nirakara* (formless, or non-anthropomorphic) emblem of Shiva as opposed to his *sakara* (anthropomorphic) form. The male genitive organ is also called *linga*, but this is not the meaning in the context of *shiva-linga*. Ancient Sanskrit lexicons explain the word *linga* as "a specific form or image (*murti*) of Shiva" without any reference to phallus unlike modern Western dictionaries.

Trilinga ("having three [famous] *shiva-linga*-s") is the ancient name of the Telangana-Andhra Pradesh region.

TRADITION

Upanishad, Smriti, grammar.

ETYMOLOGY

tri + liṅga → triliṅga.

tri ▸ three; ***liṅga*** ▸ **1** gender; **2** quality (*guna*); **3** type of egoism.

QUOTES

"OM is called *trilinga*—feminine, masculine, and neuter."

—*Yogi Yajnavalkya Smriti*

(94)

triprajna

(त्रिप्रज्ञ = *triprajña*)

MEANING

"having threefold cognizance—of dreams, of the world, and of deep sleep."

EXPLANATION

This name of OM in the *Yogi Yajnavalkya Smriti* refers to the threefold cognizance discussed in the *Mandukya Upanishad,* the shortest Upanishad with only twelve verses. The Upanishad says that the same atman has threefold cognizance as follows.

In the awakened state, the atman is said to be *bahihprajna* ("having external cognizance"). The atman in this state is called *vaishvanara* ("of all beings") and is identified with the first sound *a* of OM. *Vaishvanara* is equated with Lakshmana (Rama's closest brother) and Balarama (Krishna's brother) in the *Rama Tapini* (p. 40) and *Gopala Tapini* (p. 12) Upanishad-s respectively. *Vaishvanara* is described as having seven limbs and nineteen 'mouths'. The seven limbs are understood as the head, the eyes, breath, the torso, the genitive organ, the feet, and the mouth. The nineteen 'mouths' are understood as the five sense organs, five action organs, five *prana*-s, and the four components that form the internal organ (mind, intellect, memory, and ego).

In the state of dreaming, the atman is said to be *antahprajna* ("having internal cognizance"). The atman in this state is called *taijasa* ("brilliant") and is identified with the second sound *u* of OM. *Taijasa* is equated with Shatrughna (Rama's youngest brother) and Pradyumna (Krishna's son) in the *Rama Tapini* and

Gopala Tapini Upanishad-s respectively. *Taijasa* is also said to have seven limbs and nineteen mouths.

In the third state of deep sleep, the atman is said to be *prajnana-ghana* or *ghanaprajna* ("having dense cognizance"). The atman in this state is called *prajna* (प्राज्ञ, "well-knowing") and is identified with the third sound *m* of OM. *Prajna* is equated with Bharata (Rama's devoted brother) and Aniruddha (Krishna's grandson) in the *Rama Tapini* and *Gopala Tapini* Upanishad-s respectively. *Prajna* is said to have only one mouth—memory.

These three states correspond to the three sounds of OM. OM itself is the atman which is beyond the three states. The *Mandukya Upanishad* describes the fourth state as that in which the atman has neither internal cognizance, nor external cognizance, nor a combination of both, nor dense cognizance, nor eminent cognizance, nor a lack of cognizance. OM, or the atman in this state, is said to reside in the half mora beyond the three sounds.

TRADITION

Upanishad, Smriti.

ETYMOLOGY

tri + prajñā → triprajña.

tri ▸ three; ***prajñā*** ▸ cognizance, knowledge.

QUOTES

"OM is called *triprajna*. ... It is said to be cognizant of the dreams (*antahprajna*), cognizant of the material world (*bahishprajna*), and cognizant of deep sleep (*ghanaprajna*)."

—*Yogi Yajnavalkya Smriti*

(95)

tripratishthita

(त्रिप्रतिष्ठित = *tripratiṣthita*)

MEANING

"firmly established in three—the liberated atman, the vital force, and the sun."

EXPLANATION

The word *pratishthita* means "firmly established". Several Hindu texts have discussions on where everything is firmly established. A passage in the *Taittiriya Aranyaka* discusses eleven means of liberation of which eight—truth, penance, restraint, tranquility, charity, righteousness, *yajna*, and mental austerity—are praised as that where everything is firmly established. The passage ends with praising OM as the means of attaining *samadhi* (liberation), implying that OM—the most eminent means of liberation—is that where everything is firmly established. But in what is OM itself established? The *Yogi Yajnavalkya Smriti* says that it is firmly established in three entities—the liberated atman, the vital force, and the sun—and so it is called *tripratishthita*.

The liberated atman is described as the fourth state (*turya*), the other three being the awakened state, the dreaming state, and deep sleep. OM is understood as not only the means of liberation, but also the very state of liberation (see *tara*, p. 170). This is how OM is established in *turya*. The *Prashna Upanishad* says that the liberated being is firmly established in the supreme syllable OM. Thus, both OM and the liberated atman are firmly established in each other. The *Mandukya Upanishad* also equates OM with the fourth state of the atman.

OM is said to be firmly established in the vital force (*prana*). Upanishad, Purana, and Yoga texts identify OM with *pranayama* (the yogic control of breath)—*a*, *u*, and *m* being inhalation, holding the breath, and exhalation, respectively (p. 46). The texts say that *pranayama* is filled with OM. Interestingly, the *Prashna Upanishad*, which praises *prana* in several questions, says that everything is established in *prana* just like the spokes are firmly fixed at a wheel's hub.

OM is also described as being firmly established in the sun in Upanishad and Smriti texts. The *Chandogya Upanishad* identifies OM with the golden being in the interior of the sun, which is praised by the Rig Veda and the Sama Veda. This is the reason why *suryantargata* ("existing inside the sun", p. 82) is one of the names of OM in the *Yogi Yajnavalkya Smriti*.

The word *tripratishthita* is used in a mystic verse in the Atharva Veda to describe the brilliant golden sheath inside the city with eight *chakra*-s and nine openings (i.e., the human body). A commentary interprets *tripratishthita* as firmly established in *karma* (actions), *upasana* (worship), and *jnana* (knowledge).

TRADITION

Upanishad, Smriti, Yoga.

ETYMOLOGY

tri + pratiṣṭhita → tripratiṣṭhita.

tri ▸ three; ***pratiṣṭhita*** ▸ situated, located.

QUOTES

"OM is called *tripratishthita*. ... It is established in all three—the atman in the fourth state, the vital force, and the sun."

—*Yogi Yajnavalkya Smriti*

(96)

triprayojana

(त्रिप्रयोजन = *triprayojana*)

MEANING

"having three purposes—*dharma*, *artha*, and *kama*."

EXPLANATION

Triprayojana means having three *prayojana*-s, reasons or purposes of commencement or existence. A Sanskrit maxim says that even an ignorant person does not set out doing anything without aiming for a *prayojana*. As per Kumarila Bhatta, no scripture or action is accepted by anybody till its *prayojana* is established. What then is the *prayojana* or *raison d'être* of OM, which represents the Vedic scriptures (*tribrahma*, p. 8)?

The *Yogi Yajnavalkya Smriti* answers this question by saying that OM is called *triprayojana* as it has three purposes—the attainment of merit (*dharma*), prosperity (*artha*), and sensual pleasure (*kama*). The three together are known as *trivarga* ("the group of three"). The *Garuda Purana* emphasizes the *trivarga* by saying that those whose days pass by without the *trivarga* are not alive, even though they may be breathing.

Various definitions exist for the three purposes in many texts. They are succinctly summarized in the *Niti Vakya Amrita*. As per the text, *dharma* is the means of achieving progress and auspiciousness (or liberation), *artha* is that with which all [other] objects are accomplished, and *kama* is that which grants gratification—abounding in bodily sentiment—to all senses.

Within the *trivarga*, *dharma* is generally seen as a greater goal than *artha*, which in turn is said to be a greater goal than *kama*.

This view is supported by even the *Kama Sutra*, Vatsyayana's treatise on *kama*, which begins with the sentence "Salutations to *dharma*, *artha*, and *kama*". In the *Arthashastra*, Chanakya states that *artha* alone is supreme, for it is the basis of *dharma* and *kama*. In the *Manu Smriti*, Manu summarizes all such opinions and finally gives his own by saying, "the truth is that *trivarga* is superior." Manu's purport is that the balanced aggregate of the three goals, not in opposition to each other, is superior. Manu later says, "One should abandon *artha* and *kama* that are devoid of *dharma*, and even *dharma* that leads to sorrow in future and that is disapproved by people." Several examples of such *dharma* are given in the *Manubhashya*. Donating all of one's property is an act of *dharma* that leads to sorrow in future. *Niyoga*, or a woman having a child with her late husband's brother, is an act of *dharma* that is disapproved by people.

Along with liberation (*moksha*), the three goals form the four objects for humans (*purushartha*-s). The three component sounds of OM represent the *trivarga*, while OM itself represents *moksha* (*tara*, p. 170) which is beyond the *trivarga*.

TRADITION

Smriti.

ETYMOLOGY

tri + prayojana → triprayojana.

tri ▸ three; ***prayojana*** ▸ purpose.

QUOTES

"OM is called *triprayojana*—the triad of *dharma* and *artha* along with *kama* is said to be the purpose."

—*Yogi Yajnavalkya Smriti*

(97)
triravastha
(त्रिरवस्थ = *triravastha*)

MEANING

"having three states—gentle, vehement, and confounding."

EXPLANATION

This name of OM refers to the three states of the elements in *Sankhya* philosophy, as per which the five gross elements (earth, water, fire, wind, and sky) have three states—*shanta* (gentle), *ghora* (vehement), and *mudha* (confounding). Commentaries explain the gentle state as pleasant, vehement as painful, and confounding as confusing. The same element can have a different state for different people or at different times. The sky (empty space) is pleasant for somebody who has come out from a small house; painful for somebody exposed to cold, heat, wind, or rain; and confusing for somebody who has lost their way. The wind is pleasant when it breezes through a window, painful when it blows in the hot summer, and confusing when it is dusty or cold. Fire is pleasant for one shivering with cold, painful for one sweating with heat, and confusing as a conflagration. Water is pleasant in summer, painful in winter, and confusing for a shipwrecked sailor who cannot see the shore. The earth is pleasant when it is abounding with greenery during rain, painful when it is hot during summer, and confounding with its unfamiliar flora and fauna for a lost traveller.

In Yoga philosophy, *shanta*, *ghora*, and *mudha* are the three dispositions of the mind, caused by the dominance of the *sattva*, *rajas*, and *tamas* qualities, respectively. As mentioned under *triguna* (p. 22), these qualities influence everybody and any one dominates the other two, resulting in different dispositions of the mind at different times. A balanced mind is gentle, an angry mind is vehement, and a stupefied mind is confounding.

The three sounds of OM represent the states of the five elements and the dispositions of the mind. As with the three qualities (*sattva*, *rajas*, and *tamas*), OM itself is *avasthatita*, or beyond the states which cause pleasure, pain, and confusion. The words *avasthatita* or *niravastha* ("without any state") are used to refer to OM and the Supreme Brahman in several works.

The eighth canto of the *Bhagavata Purana* contains the account of *Gajendra Moksha*, popular in Vaishnava traditions and immortalized in many sculptures, statues, and paintings. An alligator catches the hold of one leg of an elephant herd leader in a lake. After exhausting all his strength, the elephant prays to Vishnu who rescues him. In his prayer, the elephant addresses Vishnu as OM and also calls him *shanta*, *ghora*, and *mudha*.

TRADITION

Smriti.

ETYMOLOGY

tri + avasthā → triravastha.

tri ▸ three; ***avasthā*** ▸ state.

QUOTES

"OM is considered as having three states—gentle (*shanta*), vehement (*ghora*), and confounding (*mudha*)."

—*Yogi Yajnavalkya Smriti*

"Glory to him who is gentle, vehement, and confounding."

—*Bhagavata Purana*

(98)

tristhana, tryavasthana

(त्रिस्थान, त्र्यवस्थान = *tristhāna, tryavasthāna*)

MEANING

"having three places—the chest, the throat, and the palate."

EXPLANATION

These names of OM, found in the *Yogi Yajnavalkya Smriti*, allude to the three major places of articulation as recognized in the tradition of *Shiksha* (Vedic phonetics). The *Paniniya Shiksha* presents the theory of articulation as follows. The atman perceives objects or concepts with the mind, and then inspires the mind to speak. The mind, in turn, kindles the fire of the body which drives the breath upwards. The breath generates the soft tone as it passes the chest (lungs), the middle tone as it passes the throat, and the shrill tone as it passes the palate, giving rise to sounds (syllables) of various kinds.

These names of OM are associated with a hymn in the fourth book of the Rig Veda which is addressed to five deities—Agni (fire), Surya (sun), Jala (water), Go (speech), and Ghrita (ghee). A mystical verse in the hymn goes—"The bull with four horns, three feet, two heads, and seven hands is bound at three places and roars loudly; the great god has entered the mortals." In the grammar tradition, this verse is interpreted as a description of *Shabda Brahman*, the supreme divinity whose nature is sound, as follows. The great deity or the bull is *Shabda Brahman*; its four horns are parts of speech—nouns, verbs, prefixes, and particles; its three feet are the tenses—past, present, and future; its two heads are the two types of words—eternal (words as concepts) and produced (spoken words); its seven hands are the seven cases (*vibhakti*-s) of grammar; and the three places where it is bound (i.e., formed when spoken) are the places of articulation—the chest, the throat, and the palate. Many sources, including the *Maitri Upanishad* equate OM with the *Shabda Brahman*. Thus OM, and all speech of which it is the essence, resides in the three places of articulation. This is the purport of the names *tristhana* and *tryavasthana*. Note that the Rig Veda verse mentions three places of binding, and the word *avasthana* specifically means a place where something is fastened or steadily situated.

Apart from grammar, some other traditions also acknowledge the concept of *Shabda Brahman* or God as sound. A popular verse that occurs (with minor variations) in Upanishad-s, Purana-s, and the *Mahabharata* says that two Brahman-s are worth knowing—the *Shabda Brahman* and the Supreme Brahman, and one who knows the *Shabda Brahman* reaches the Supreme Brahman.

TRADITION

Smriti, grammar.

ETYMOLOGY

tri + sthāna → tristhāna; tri + avasthāna → tryavasthāna.

tri ▸ three; ***sthāna*** ▸ place [of articulation]. ***avasthāna*** ▸ dwelling, abode, fastening place.

QUOTES

"OM is known as *tryavasthana* due to the heart, the throat, and the palate ... OM is proclaimed as *tristhana* ... One should say (know) the three places as the heart, the throat, and the palate."

—*Yogi Yajnavalkya Smriti*

(99)
trivrit
(त्रिवृत् = *trivṛt*)

MEANING

“1 threefold, composed of three parts
2 that which selects three [sounds].”

EXPLANATION

OM is referred to as *trivrit* in the *Manu Smriti* and the *Bhagavata Purana*. The word *trivrit* can be derived using two roots. The first root is √*vrit* (“to exist”). When derived from this root, *trivrit* means that in which there is existence (*vrit*) of three (*tri*), i.e. triple or threefold. The word is used in this sense many times in the Veda-s. For example, the triple chariot of the Ashvin-s is called *trivrit ratha* in the Rig Veda. The *trivrit stoma* is a method of chanting three triads of Vedic verses. OM is called *trivrit* as it is composed of three sounds (p. 192). Or, as the *Manu Smriti* says, OM is the original threefold Veda, and hence it is *trivrit*. Or, OM is *trivrit* as it represents many triads—three gods, three *loka*-s, three fires, three types of penances, three strides of Vishnu, three qualities, three morae, three places, three times, three establishments, three types of cognizance, three states, three genders, three bodily humours, three purposes, etc. OM is also called *trika* (p. 176), which means threefold or a triad.

Trivrit can also be derived from the root √*vri* (“to choose, to select”), and so it also means “that which selects a triad”. In the *Bhagavata Purana*, Krishna says that he is the *trivrit* OM among all mantra-s. A commentary on the Purana explains that OM is *trivrit* as it chooses or selects the three letters *a*, *u*, and *m*.

TRADITION

Smriti, Purana, commentaries.

ETYMOLOGY

tri + √vṛt + kvip → trivṛt;

or **tri + √vṛ + kvip → trivṛt.**

tri ▸ three; ***√vṛt*** ▸ to be, to exist; ***kvip*** ▸ suffix to denote abstract noun or subject of an action. ***√vṛ*** ▸ to select, to choose.

QUOTES

"The primeval three-syllabled Brahman (i.e. OM), on which the triad of Veda-s rests, is the other mystic *trivrit* (threefold) Veda. He who knows that knows the Veda."

—*Manu Smriti*

"Among the mantra-s, I am the *trivrit* OM."

—Krishna to Uddhava, *Bhagavata Purana*

"One should practise (repeat) with the mind the pure and supreme sound of Brahman which is *trivrit*."

—*Bhagavata Purana*

(100)

tryakshara

(त्र्यक्षर = *tryakṣara*)

MEANING

"**1** having three sounds **2** having three syllables **3** imperishable at all times (in past, present, and future)."

EXPLANATION

The many meanings of the Sanskrit word *akshara* (p. 84) include a sound, a syllable, and a letter. A sound, e.g. a vowel or a consonant, is the basic unit of speech. A syllable is the basic unit of pronunciation containing one vowel sound and zero, one, or more consonant sounds. A letter is the basic unit of writing.

In Upanishad-s and Smriti-s, OM is called *tryakshara*, a name which comes from *tri* ("three") and *akshara* ("sound"). Although OM is a monosyllable, it is called *tryakshara* as it results from three sounds (*a*, *u*, and *m*) coming together by *sandhi*. The names of the three sounds of OM are given in the *Lakshmi Tantra*—*a* is called *dhruva* ("fixed point"), *u* is called *karna* ("oar"), and *m* is called *nabhi* ("central point"). The names seem to suggest that OM represents an individual's transcendental journey with *a* fixing the boat and *u* steering it towards the destination *m* which is the central essence of the universe. OM's name *tara* (p. 170) echoes this idea of liberation.

As the word *akshara* means "a syllable" too, the name *tryakshara* also means "having three syllables". Mantra-s like *aim klim sauh* in Hinduism and *om ah hum* in Buddhism are called *tryakshara* mantra-s. Gayatri is invoked by the name *tryakshara* (त्र्यक्षरा) in a *sandhya* verse as she is identified with OM or because her name consists of three syllables (*ga-ya-tri*). OM is called *tryakshara* because both *omkara* (*om-ka-ra*) and *pranava* (*pra-na-va*), two of its most popular names, have three syllables each. The uniqueness of this name of OM is self-reference: it is an autonym. Just like the English word *pentasyllabic* ("having five syllables") is itself five-syllabled (pen-ta-syl-la-bic), the Sanskrit word *tryakshara* ("having three syllables") is itself three-syllabled (*trya-ksha-ra*) and hence, autological.

In the *Linga Purana*, Shiva is called *tryakshara*. The name is explained in a commentary as imperishable (*akshara*) in the three (*tri*) times—the past, the present, and the future. This meaning applies to OM also, as it is called *anadi* ("beginningless", p. 98), *ananta* ("endless", p. 100), and *traikalya* ("timeless", p. 172).

TRADITION

Upanishad, Smriti.

ETYMOLOGY

tri + akṣara → tryakṣara.

tri ▸ three; ***akṣara*** ▸ **1** sound **2** imperishable.

QUOTES

"OM is *tryakshara*."

—*Maitri Upanishad*

"OM is known as *tryakshara*. It has three sounds—the sound *a*, the sound *u*, and the sound *m*."

—*Yogi Yajnavalkya Smriti*

"The primeval Brahman, which is *tryakshara* (i.e. OM) and on which the three Veda-s rest, is the other hidden threefold Veda."

—*Manu Smriti*

(101)
vaidyuta
(**वैद्युत** = ***vaidyuta***)

MEANING

" 1 the illuminator **2** brilliant, lustrous
3 fire, Agni **4** the sun, Surya."

EXPLANATION

A name of OM is *vaidyuta*, which means the illuminator. The reason as per the *Atharva Shira Upanishad* and its *Dipika* commentary is that OM causes the light of Brahman to manifest in the great darkness of ignorance.

Taken as an adjective, the word *vaidyuta* means "brilliant" or "lustrous"; it is used several times in this sense in the *Taittiriya Aranyaka*. The *Yogi Yajnavalkya Smriti* says that OM is *vaidyuta* since it shines as the aura between the eyebrows and destroys darkness. The reference is to the *ajna chakra*, located between the eyebrows, whose seed sound (*bijamantra*) is OM as per Yoga traditions. While describing *jyotirdhyana* ("meditation on light"), the *Gheranda Samhita*—an important text of hatha yoga—states that the light of OM is situated between the two eyebrows. Or, OM is brilliant and lustrous as it represents the three shining gods Brahma, Vishnu, and Shiva (*tri-daivata*, p. 2).

Vaidyuta can be derived directly from the root *vi* + √*dyut*, or indirectly from the cognate word *vidyut* ("lightning"). And so, *vaidyuta* also means "originating from lightning". Agni is called *vaidyuta* in the *Taittiriya Brahmana*. The Rig Veda says that Agni first manifested himself in the sky as lightning. Therefore, the name *vaidyuta* of OM refers to Agni or fire (p. 6).

As it is the illuminator of the world and extremely lustrous, the sun is also called *vaidyuta.* In the *Mahabharata*, *vaidyuta* is one of the 108 names of Surya narrated by Dhaumya to Yudhishthira in exactly twelve verses (the number twelve represents the twelve Aditya-s identified with Surya). Yudhishthira recites the 108 names to propitiate Surya, who grants him the *akshaya patra* (the inexhaustible source of food). Appropos OM, it is identified with the sun at many places (see *aditya*, p. 94).

TRADITION

Upanishad, Smriti, Yoga.

ETYMOLOGY

vi + √dyut + ṇic + kvip + aṇ[1] → vaidyuta;
or **vidyut + aṇ[2] → vaidyuta.**

vi* + √*dyut ▸ to shine, to flash; ***ṇic*** ▸ suffix in causative sence; ***kvip*** ▸ suffix to denote performer of an action; ***aṇ[1]*** ▸ *prajñādi* suffix with no change in meaning. ***vidyut*** ▸ lightning; ***aṇ[2]*** ▸ suffix denoting “born in”, “originating from”, “belonging to”, etc.

QUOTES

“Then, why is it called *vaidyuta*? Since on merely being pronounced, it makes [Brahman] shine in the massive and great darkness—hence it is called *vaidyuta*.”

—*Atharva Shira Upanishad*

“Know OM as *vaidyuta*. ... For ascetics, it manifests as the luminous aura between the eyebrows, and shines forth destroying [all] darkness; hence it is called *vaidyuta*.”

—*Yogi Yajnavalkya Smriti*

(102)
vartula
(वर्तुल = *vartula*)

MEANING

" 1 circular or spherical **2** revolving, or turning around."

EXPLANATION

The *Bija Varna Abhidhana*, a Tantra work, lists *vartula* among the names of OM. The word comes from the root √*vrit* ("to revolve") and means "circular" or "spherical". OM is described as circular in several Tantra works. In addition, OM is identified with the universe (p. 208), which is spherical as per Hindu cosmology. The astronomical work *Surya Siddhanta* also states that the *brahmanda* (universe) is spherical. It is described as a full sphere in this popular verse praising the guru—

akhanda-mandalakaram vyaptam yena characharam
tatpadam darshitam yena tasmai shrigurave namah

"Salutations to the guru who has shown the entity which pervades the animate and inanimate universe, shaped like a full sphere." Since *pada* means both "an entity" and "a word", the verse can also be explained as "Salutations to the guru who has revealed that word (OM) which pervades the animate and inanimate universe and which is shaped like a full sphere."

Another meaning of *vartula* is something that revolves or turns around. In Sanskrit, a circle or sphere is also called *nistala* ("without a surface"), one of whose meanings is mobile. Since OM stands for the three deities responsible for the creation, sustenance, and destruction of the universe (p. 2), it represents the entire cosmic cycle, or the *brahma-chakra*. The *Shvetashvatara*

Upanishad says that the *brahma-chakra* is being constantly made to turn by the greatness of Brahman. Or, since OM symbolizes the past, the present, and the future (p. 172), it is the ever-revolving, beginningless, and endless *kala-chakra* ("the wheel of time") as described in the *Mahabharata* and the *Sushruta Samhita*.

Since OM is called *pranava* and is said to be circular, the term *pranavakara* (प्रणवाकार), literally "having the shape of OM", means circular or elliptical. In the *Shiva Purana*, the abode of Shiva at Mount Kailasa is described as *pranavakara* and Shiva's chariot, adorned by five *mandala*-s (circular rings), is also called *pranavakara*. The term is used in architectural texts for temple or canopy plans. The canopy above the *garbha-griha* (sanctum sanctorum) of the Ranganathaswamy Temple at Srirangam in Tamil Nadu is called *Pranavakara Vimanam*. It is ellipsoidal in shape. A popular verse refers to the *Pranavakara Vimanam* and says that the lord in the sleeping posture at Srirangam is the illuminator of the meaning of *pranava* (OM).

TRADITION

Tantra.

ETYMOLOGY

√vṛt + ulac → vartula.

√***vṛt*** ▸ to revolve, to turn around (like a wheel); ***ulac*** ▸ suffix to denote subject of an action.

QUOTES

"The sound OM is called *vartula*."

—*Bija Varna Abhidhana*

(103)
vedadi
(वेदादि = *vedādi*)

MEANING

"**1** the beginning of the Veda-s **2** the first among Veda-s **3** the source (cause) of the Veda-s."

EXPLANATION

OM is called *vedadi* in Purana and Tantra works. The word *adi* means "beginning", as in the name *anadi* ("without beginning") of OM (p. 98). *Adi* also means "first"—Valmiki is *adikavi* ("the first poet"), Ramayana is *adikavya* ("the first poem"), and the first book of *Mahabharata* is titled *Adi Parva.* Therefore, *vedadi* means the beginning of the Veda-s or the first Veda—as will be explained under *vedarambha* (p. 200). The *Taittiriya Aranyaka* alludes to these meanings while referring to OM as the *svara* (p. 88) uttered at *vedadi* (the beginning of Vedic mantra-s) and established in *vedanta* (the Upanishad-s).

As *adi* also means "cause" or "origin", *vedadi* translates as "origin of the Veda-s". This is the meaning of *vedadi* as per the *Shiva Purana* and the *Skanda Purana* where the term is used for both Shiva and OM simultaneously. The origin of the three Veda-s from OM is also mentioned in the *Manu Smriti* (p. 9).

Another name of OM is *vedadi-bija* ("the seed which is the origin of the Veda-s"), used in the *Raja Rajeshvari Tantra.* In another Tantra work, the goddess is called *vedadi-mandita* ("adorned with OM"). In the *Rama Tapini Upanishad,* Rama is called *vedadi-rupa* and *omkara.* Haridasa's commentary explains that the *rupa* (form) of OM is seen at the beginning of the Veda-s.

TRADITION

Purana, Tantra.

ETYMOLOGY

veda + ādi → vedādi.

veda ▸ Veda-s; ***ādi*** ▸ **1** beginning **2** first **3** source, cause.

QUOTES

"The mantra known as *pranava* is [called] *vedadi.*"

—*Shiva Purana*

"O dear, the verses of Veda-s arise from me alone ... therefore I am called *vedadi.* The *pranava* denotes me. Due to it being my indicator, it is also called *vedadi.*"

—Shiva to Parvati, *Shiva Purana*

"In front of him, Brahma saw *vedadi* (OM)—from where arose the Veda-s, the origin of everything, with their six limbs."

—*Skanda Purana* on Omkareshvara

"One should meditate with *vedadi* (OM), and thereafter contemplate sequentially on *mandala*-s (orbs) of the sun, the moon, and fire; one above the other."

—*Garuda Purana*

"[The word] *vedadi* means *pranava* (OM)."

—*Brihat Tantra Sara*

"The six-syllable mantra of Shukra (Venus) should be uttered as *vedadi* (OM) followed by *hrim*, the seed *shrim*, and *shukraya*."

—*Rudra Yamala Tantra*

"You are the source of the Veda-s which begin with OM."

—The gods to Brahma, *Kumarasambhava*

(104)
vedarambha

(वेदारम्भ = *vedārambha*)

MEANING

" the beginning of the Veda-s. "

EXPLANATION

The *Amara Kosha* states that the words *omkara* (p. 56) and *pranava* (p. 58) are synonymous. Its *Rasala* commentary explains the words and adds that they are synonyms of *vedarambha*, which translates as "the beginning of the Veda-s". OM is called *vedarambha* as it is recited at the beginning of Vedic mantra-s (p. 130) and Vedic study (p. 17).

Or, OM is called *vedarambha* as the three Veda-s began as OM. A verse in the ninth canto of the *Bhagavata Purana* states that in the *Satya Yuga*, there was only one Veda—OM, and the threefold Veda was revealed to King Pururavas when the *Treta Yuga* started. Shuka narrates the events leading to this as follows. The *apsara* Urvashi came to earth on hearing about the virtues of King Pururavas. The king asked her to stay with him. Urvashi put forward three conditions to which the king agreed. The *apsara* and the king spent many years together. When one of Urvashi's conditions was violated, she left. Pururvas searched for her and found her, now pregnant, on the banks of the river Sarasvati. Pururavas requested her to stay with him, but Urvashi said that the king would be able to stay with her for only one night every year. The king came back a year later when she was with their son. When Pururavas returned to his palace again, he kept thinking about Urvashi the entire night. It was then that the *Satya Yuga* ended and the *Treta Yuga* began, and the three Veda-s revealed themselves in the heart of Pururavas. Following this, the Jatavedas fire arose when the king kindled fire using two *arani*-s (sticks). The king used the knowledge of the three Veda-s to make the Jatavedas fire also threefold—*garahapatya*, *ahavaniya*, and *dakshinagni* (p. 6)—and accepted Jatavedas as his son. Shuka then tells Parikshit that in the *Satya Yuga* there was one Veda—OM, one god—Narayana, one worldly fire, and one *varna* called *hamsa*. The threefold Veda started only in the *Treta Yuga*. Commentaries explain that in the *Satya Yuga* most people were dominated by the quality of *sattva*, while in the *Treta Yuga* they were dominated by *rajas* and so the threefold path of karma appeared. The immense and passionate desire of Pururavas to be with Urvashi reflects the onset of *rajas* as explained in various commentaries on the *Bhagavata Purana*.

Vedarambha is the name of the eleventh of the sixteen *samskara*-s mentioned in the *Vyasa Smriti*. This *samskara* is performed when the study of the Veda-s is started.

TRADITION

Commentaries.

ETYMOLOGY

veda + ārambha → vedārambha.

veda ▸ Veda-s; ***ārambha*** ▸ beginning, commencement.

QUOTES

"*Omkara* ... *pranava* ... two [synonyms] of *vedarambha*."

—Commentary on *Amara Kosha*

"In the beginning, there was only one Veda—OM."

—*Bhagavata Purana*

(105)
vedatma
(वेदात्मा = *vedātmā*)

MEANING

"1 the atman (Self) of the Veda-s
2 enshrined in the Veda-s."

EXPLANATION

OM is called by the name *vedatma* in the *Lakhsmi Tantra*. This name can be interpreted in several ways, owing to the large number of meanings of *atma* (*atman*). As *atman* primarily means the Self, *vedatma* means "the Self of the Veda-s", i.e. Veda itself. The three sounds of OM are considered to be the three Veda-s (p. 8), and hence OM is the one Self of all the three Veda-s.

The word *atman* also means the body or essence. Therefore, another meaning of *vedatma* is that which has the Veda-s as its body or essence, i.e. enshrined in the Veda-s. The word *vedatma* is used in the sense of "declared in the Veda-s" in several Hindu scriptures. In the *Mahabharata*, Bhishma tells Yudhishthira about the three kinds of laws (*vyavahara*-s), of which the second is *vedatma* which refers to laws laid down in the Veda-s. The *Matsya Purana* and the *Linga Purana* say that *yajna* which is *vedatma* is called *shrauta*. As the word OM is proclaimed in the Veda-s as Brahman (p. 24), it is called *vedatma*.

Vedatma is a name of Surya, the sun-god, in the Purana-s. The *Markandeya Purana* eulogizes Surya, who it equates with the Supreme Brahman, as *vedatma* and states that the three Veda-s give warmth at different times according to the position of the sun—the Rig Veda in the morning, the Yajur Veda at noon, and the Sama Veda in the afternoon. In the *Matsya Purana*, Nandi refers to Surya as *vedatma* while describing a method of sun-worship to Narada.

In addition to Surya, the word *vedatma* is used to describe many gods or their forms in Hindu scriptures revered by Vaishnava, Shaiva, and Shakta traditions. In the *Valmiki Ramayana*, Brahma uses the word for Rama. Krishna is referred to as *vedatma* twice in the *Mahabharata*, including in the *Bhishma Stavaraja*, Bhishma's paean to Krishna. Shiva is praised as *vedatma-rupa* and *vedatma-murti* by Brahma in the *Linga Purana* and the *Kurma Purana* respectively. In the *Devi Mahatmya* of the *Kurma Purana*, King Himavan (the Himalaya mountain) praises Devi (Shakti) in 1,008 names and describes her form as *ashesha-vedatmaka*. Elsewhere in the *Kurma Purana*, King Vasumana praises the four-headed Brahma as *vedatma-murti*. OM is identified with each of these gods—with Surya (p. 94), Rama (p. 38), Krishna (p. 12), Shiva (p. 72), Devi (p. 44), and Brahma (p. 48).

TRADITION

Tantra.

ETYMOLOGY

veda + ātman → vedātma.

veda ▸ Veda-s; ***ātman*** ▸ **1** Self, or essence **2** form, body.

QUOTES

"The sound OM is called *vedatma*."

—*Lakshmi Tantra*

(106)
vibhu

(विभु = *vibhu*)

MEANING

"**1** omnipotent, almighty **2** omnipresent **3** manifold **4** atman **5** master **6** great, grand, glorious **7** eternal **8** fixed, firm."

EXPLANATION

The *Yogi Yajnavalkya Smriti* states that OM is known as *vibhu*. The *Gopatha Brahmana* of the Atharva Veda describes OM as *sarva-vibhu* ("almighty"). The primary meaning of *vibhu* is "omnipotent" or "all-powerful". OM is considered the most powerful word in Hinduism. In the *Gita*, Krishna says that of all speech (words), he is the monosyllable OM. OM's name *prabhu* (p. 142), which rhymes with *vibhu*, also means "powerful".

Coming from the root *vi* + √*bhu*, the word *vibhu* has several meanings. One of its oldest meanings is found in Yaska's *Nirukta*, which explains *vibhu* in a mantra from the Rig Veda as "the most spread out", or "the most pervading". OM is said to pervade the entire universe; this omnipresence is alluded to in names like *vishnu* (p. 206) and *sarvavyapi* (p. 156).

Another meaning of *vibhu* is manifold. OM is manifold as it is identified with not only the *nirguna* Brahman but also the supreme divinity of all major *saguna* traditions in Hinduism. In addition to the three sounds of OM being identified with Brahma, Vishnu, and Shiva, OM is separately identified with each one of the three (pp. 48, 206, 72). Interestingly, the word *vibhu* is also used for all three—Brahma, Vishnu, and Shiva. It is also used by Arjuna to describe Krishna in the *Gita*.

The word *vibhu* means the atman; it is used in this sense in popular Ayurveda works like the *Sushruta Samhita* and the *Charaka Samhita*. This meaning is also congruous with OM which is believed to pervade all atman-s, as evidenced by the name *narayana* (p. 132).

Vibhu also means master or lord. OM is *vibhu* as it is identified with the Supreme Brahman (p. 36), the master of the universe.

Vibhu also means grand or magnificent. The word *vaibhava*, derived from *vibhu*, means greatness, grandeur, or glory. The cognate word *vibhuti* refers to great powers. OM is considered the greatest among all mantra-s (p. 131), and so it is no surprise that one of its names means grand or magnificent.

Other meanings of *vibhu* include "eternal" and "fixed". Both of these are applicable to OM. OM is eternal as it is considered imperishable at all times (*tryakshara*, p. 192). OM is also called *dhruva* (p. 112), which means fixed and firm.

TRADITION

Veda, Smriti.

ETYMOLOGY

vi + √bhū + ḍu → vibhu.

vi + √bhū ▸ **1** to be capable **2** to pervade **3** to divide, to become manifold; ***ḍu*** ▸ suffix indicating performer of an action.

QUOTES

"Brahma saw OM, which was *sarva-vibhu* (almighty)."

—*Gopatha Brahmana*

"OM is known as *vibhu*."

—*Yogi Yajnavalkya Smriti*

(107)
vishnu
(*विष्णु = viṣṇu*)

MEANING

"1 Vishnu 2 all-pervading."

EXPLANATION

The *Yogi Yajnavalkya Smriti* lists *vishnu* as a name of OM. Vishnu is identified with OM at several places in Hindu scriptures. The *Vishnu Purana* says that OM is Lord Vishnu, and the *Matsya Purana* says that Vishnu is known as *pranava.* The *Matsya Purana* also describes the sage Markandeya seeing Vishnu as a child on the branch of a banyan tree at the time of *pralaya* (dissolution). When Vishnu reveals himself to Markandeya, the latter says that Vishnu is OM, the saviour.

In addition to being directly identified with each other, OM and Vishnu share many names in common. Many names of OM in this book are also found in the *Vishnu Sahasranama.* The first two names in the hymn are *vishva* ("the universe") and *vishnu* ("the pervader")—both are names of OM. The hymn twice lists *pranava,* the famous name of OM, as a name of Vishnu. Some other names of OM in the *sahasranama* are *satya* ("truth") which occurs thrice; *akshara* ("imperishable"), *aditya* ("of Aditi"), *dhruva* ("motionless"), and *vibhu* ("omnipotent") which occur twice each; and *narayana* ("refuge of humans"), *sukshma* ("minute"), *tara* ("saviour"), and *hamsa* ("swan") which occur once each. Another name of Vishnu in the hymn is *spashtakshara* ("clear syllable"). Commenting on this name, Adi Shankara explains that the clear syllable is the sound OM.

The many common names of OM and Vishnu show the confluence of *nirakara* ("formless") and *sakara* ("with form") Brahman in Hinduism. As it is a sound, OM is formless. As he takes many avatar-s, Vishnu is with a form. OM is the Supreme Brahman of Upanishad-s and the Yoga traditions, while Vishnu is the Supreme Brahman of Vaishnava Purana-s and Vaishnavism. Both are seen as one and have many common names.

As has been explained (p. 10), the word *vishnu* comes from the root √*vish* ("to pervade") and literally means "he who pervades". Vishnu is said to be not bound by space (*desha*), time (*kala*), or matter (*vastu*). Similarly, OM is believed to pervade all space, time, and matter—as evidenced in the names *ananta* (p. 100), *traikalya* (p. 172), and *sarvavyapi* (p. 156) respectively.

TRADITION

Smriti, Purana.

ETYMOLOGY

√viṣ + nu → viṣṇu.

√*viṣ* ▸ to pervade; ***nu*** ▸ suffix indicating the performer of an action.

QUOTES

"OM is known as *vishnu*."

—*Yogi Yajnavalkya Smriti*

"The sound OM is Lord Vishnu."

—*Vishnu Purana*

"Vishnu is considered to be *pranava* (OM)."

"Vishnu said, 'I am the one-syllabled mantra OM.'"

—*Matsya Purana*

(108)
vishva
(विश्व = *viśva*)

MEANING

“**1** Vishnu **2** the world, the universe
3 that which enters [everything], i.e. omnipresent
4 that in which *yogi*-s enter.”

EXPLANATION

Vishva is the first name of Vishnu in the *Vishnu Sahasranama.* Adi Shankara’s brilliant commentary on this name concludes that the word *vishva* means OM, citing many authoritative verses from the Upanishad-s (*Mundaka, Taittiriya, Katha, Prashna, Chandogya, Mandukya*, and *Narayana*), the *Gita*, and the *Manu Smriti* in support. The word *vishva* forms a part of ten more names in the *Vishnu Sahasranama* like *vishvakarma, vishvatma, vishvamurti*, etc.

When used as a pronoun, *vishva* means all or entire. This is why all Vedic deities are commonly referred to as *vishve deva*-s. As a noun, the word refers to “the entire world” (the universe), identified with the Supreme Brahman and OM in several Upanishad-s. The *Mandukya Upanishad* begins with the proclamation “OM—this syllable is all this”, referring to the entire universe which is believed to be pervaded by OM.

Vishva comes from the root √*vish* (विश्, “to enter”)—from which *pravesha* (“entrance”) is derived—and the *unadi* suffix *kvan.* This root is different from √*vish* (विष्, “to pervade”), from which the word *vishnu* derives. Understanding the suffix *kvan* in the usual sense of the agent of the action, *vishva* literally means "that which enters", to be understood as omnipresent (see also *vibhu*, p. 204). Or, as Baladeva Vidyabhushana explains Vishnu's name, *vishva* is that which enters all entities different from itself.

The suffix in *vishva* can also denote the object of entering. Accordingly *vishva* means "where beings enter". This meaning of OM is alluded to in the *Gita*, where Krishna talks about the syllable (*akshara*) which dispassionate ascetics enter (*vishanti*). The *Bhavadipa* commentary states that OM is the syllable being referred to. The *Taittiriya Upanishad*, which unambiguously identifies OM with Brahman (p. 37), describes Brahman as that from where beings arise, that with which these born beings subsist, and that which the beings enter when they depart. Several commentaries interpret this to mean that beings enter Brahman or OM at the time of *pralaya*, or dissolution of the universe. OM is also called *pralaya* (p. 144) for this reason.

TRADITION

Commentaries.

ETYMOLOGY

√viś + kvan → viśva.

√*viś* ▸ to enter, to pervade; ***kvan*** ▸ suffix to denote performer, means, or location of the action.

QUOTES

"The word *vishva* refers to OM."

—Adi Shankara's commentary on *Vishnu Sahasranama*

"The syllable which yogi-s enter ... the syllable, i.e. the indicator named OM."

—*Gita*, its commentary

(109)
om
(ओम् = *om*)

MEANING

"**1** the protector **2** ever-moving **3** the charmer **4** the lover
5 contented **6** the knower **7** the pervader **8** the listener
9 the ruler **10** the entreater **11** the doer **12** the wisher
13 radiant **14** the attainer **15** the embracer
16 the destroyer [of worldly existence] **17** the receiver
18 one that divides itself [into many] **19** ever-growing."

EXPLANATION

In the highly structured and mathematical tradition of Sanskrit grammar, the word OM is derived from the root √*av* and the suffix *m[an]*. This is the only known derivation of the word OM as per grammatical rules codified in Panini's *Ashtadhyayi.*

The root √*av* is special. The *Dhatupatha,* which lists nearly 2,000 roots and their meanings, gives as many as nineteen meanings of √*av*—by far the most for any root. It is a spectacular coincidence that the most celebrated word in Sanskrit is derived by its grammar from its richest root. The step-by-step derivation of OM from √*av* is shown below, where A stands for the *Ashtadhyayi* and US for the *Unadi Sutra.* The sound *av* changes first to *u* and then to *o* in the derivation.

√*av* → *uṇadayo bahulam* (A 3.3.1) →
avateṣṭilopaśca (US 1.128) → *av man* → *av* + *m* →
jvara-tvara-śrivyavi-mavāmupadhāyāśca (A 6.4.20) → *ū* + *m* →
sārva-dhātukārdha-dhātukayoḥ (A 7.3.84) → *o* + *m* → *om.*

Usually, words formed with *unadi* suffixes denote the performer of an action. As a result, the word OM has nineteen meanings corresponding to the different actions meant by √*av*.

(1) As √*av* means "to protect", OM means "the protector" or "that which protects". OM is described as the protector of gods (p. 129) and also of life, vital forces, and living beings (p. 70).

(2) As √*av* means "to move", OM means "that which [constantly] moves". OM is called *vartula* (p. 196), which means "that which revolves".

(3) As √*av* means "to be beautiful", OM means "charming" or "beautiful". One of the names of OM is *divya* (p. 114), which means "charming".

(4) As √*av* means "to love", OM means "the lover". The *Skanda Purana* derives the name *pranava* of OM from *pra* + √*ni* (p. 60), one of whose meanings is "to love".

(5) As √*av* means "to be satisfied", OM means "contended", or that which is satisfied. OM is identified with Shiva (p. 72), who is called *Ashutosha* ("easily satisfied").

(6) As √*av* means "to know", OM means "the knower" or "omniscient". OM has the names *sarvavid* and *sarvajna* (p. 154), which mean omniscient.

(7) As √*av* means "to pervade", OM means "the pervader". Many names of OM like *akshara* (p. 84), *hamsa* (p. 124), *narayana* (p. 132), *sarvavyapi* (p. 156), and *vishnu* (p. 206) mean "the pervader" or "all-pervading". The *Gopatha Brahmana* derives OM from the root √*ap* (p. 30), which also means "to pervade".

(8) As √*av* means "to listen", OM means "the listener". OM is identified with the compassionate Vishnu (p. 206), who listens to the prayers of the living beings.

(9) As √*av* means "to rule", OM means "the ruler". OM is called *prabhu* (p. 142), meaning master or lord (one who rules).

(10) As √*av* means "to entreat", OM means "the entreater". OM is identified with Vishnu (p. 206), who as Vamana asked Bali for land (space) measured by three steps. The three sounds of OM are also explained as the three steps of Vishnu (p. 10).

(11) As √*av* means "to do", OM means "the doer" or "the performer". As the three gods (p. 2), OM performs the functions of creation, sustenance, and destruction of the universe.

(12) As √*av* means "to wish", OM means "one who wishes". OM is identified with Brahman (p. 36) and the *Taittiriya Upanishad* describes how the one Brahman wished to become manifold and created the universe.

(13) As √*av* means "to shine", OM means "radiant". OM is called *vaidyuta* (p. 194) meaning radiant and also *svara* (p. 90) which means self-luminous.

(14) As √*av* means "to attain", OM means "the attainer". The root √*ap*, from which the *Gopatha Brahmana* derives OM, also means "to attain" or "to obtain" (p. 30). OM is also called *sarvavid* (p. 154), one of whose meanings is "all-attaining".

(15) As √*av* means "to embrace", OM means "the embracer". OM is the universal embracer as it is the refuge of all humans and atman-s (p. 132).

(16) As √*av* means "to destroy", OM means "the destroyer". OM is called *bhavanashana* (p. 104), which means "the destroyer of worldly existence". OM is also called *hamsa,* which also means "the destroyer [of sins]".

(17) As √*av* means "to receive", OM means "the receiver". As OM is the one Supreme Brahman (p. 36) called by different names (p. 74), offerings to all deities go to OM. As a popular verse goes, "obeisance to all deities goes to Keshava".

(18) As √*av* means "to divide", OM means "one that divides [itself]". OM, or the Supreme Brahman, (p. 36) divides itself to reside in the heart of all living beings as *antaryami*. This concept of *antaryami* Brahman is expounded in the *Brihad Aranyaka Upanishad*.

(19) As √*av* means "to grow", OM means "ever-growing". OM is called *brahma* (p. 108), which means that which grows or expands.

TRADITION

Grammar, Purana.

ETYMOLOGY

av + man → om.

√***av*** ▸ **1** to protect **2** to move **3** to be lovely or beautiful **4** to love **5** to be satisfied **6** to know **7** to pervade **8** to listen **9** to rule **10** to entreat **11** to do **12** to wish **13** to shine **14** to attain **15** to embrace **16** to destroy **17** to receive **18** to divide **19** to grow; ***man*** ▸ suffix to denote performer of an action.

QUOTES

"Suffix *man* occurs from the root √*av*, and only *m* remains of it. The word *om* means the subject of the verb *av*."

—*Unadi Sutra*, its commentary.

"He is known as OM because of *avana* (an act of √*av*)."

—*Kurma Purana*.

Index

Index of the 84 names

if NOT me then WHO?

M. Ram Murty · V. Kumar Murty

The Mathematical Legacy of Srinivasa Ramanujan

Springer

M. Ram Murty
Department of Mathematics and Statistics
Queen's University
Kingston, Ontario
Canada

V. Kumar Murty
Department of Mathematics
University of Toronto
Toronto, Ontario
Canada

ISBN 978-81-322-0769-6 ISBN 978-81-322-0770-2 (eBook)
DOI 10.1007/978-81-322-0770-2
Springer New Delhi Heidelberg New York Dordrecht London

Library of Congress Control Number: 2012949894

Printed on acid-free paper

Springer is part of Springer Science+Business Media (www.springer.com)

On a height he stood that looked towards greater heights.
Our early approaches to the Infinite
Are sunrise splendours on a marvellous verge
While lingers yet unseen the glorious sun.
What now we see is a shadow of what must come.

Sri Aurobindo, Savitri *1.4*

How I wish I could show you the world through my eyes.

Vivekananda

Preface

22 December 2012 marks the 125th birth anniversary of the Indian mathematician Srinivasa Ramanujan. Being largely self-taught, he emerged from extreme poverty to become one of 20th century's most influential mathematicians. His story is a phenomenal "rags to mathematical riches" story. In his short life, he had a wealth of ideas that have transformed and reshaped 20th century mathematics. These ideas continue to shape mathematics of the 21st century.

This book is meant to be a panoramic view of his essential mathematical contributions. It is not an encyclopedic account of Ramanujan's work. Rather, it is an informal account of some of the major developments that emanated from his work in the 20th and 21st centuries. The twelve essays focus on a subset of his significant papers and show how these papers shaped the course of modern mathematics.

These essays are based on lectures given by the authors over the years at the Chennai Mathematical Institute, Harish-Chandra Research Institute, IISER (Kolkata), IISER (Bhopal), IIT (Powai), IIT (Chennai), Institute for Mathematical Sciences (Chennai), and the Tata Institute for Fundamental Research (Mumbai) as well as Queen's University, the Fields Institute, and the University of Toronto. The lectures were given so that the material is accessible to undergraduates and graduate students. We have striven to not be too technical. At the same time, we tried to convey some depth of the mathematical theories emerging from the work of Ramanujan. Surely, it is impossible to be comprehensive in such a mammoth task. Still, we hope that the reader will see how the vast landscape of Ramanujan's garden has blossomed over the past century.

Toronto, Canada

M. Ram Murty
V. Kumar Murty

Contents

Chapter 1
The Legacy of Srinivasa Ramanujan

Mathematics enjoys the freedom of art and the precision of science. There is freedom of combination of ideas and concepts, but there is also the precision of logic and the ring of truth. It is like a master symphony. The Soviet mathematician, I.R. Shafarevich [186] once remarked that "a superficial glance at mathematics may give an impression that it is a result of separate individual efforts of many scientists scattered about in continents and in ages. However, the inner logic of its development reminds one much more of the work of a single intellect, developing its thought systematically and consistently using the variety of human individualities only as a means. It resembles an orchestra performing a symphony composed by someone. A theme passes from one instrument to another, it is taken up by another and performed with irreproachable precision."

This is no doubt true and yet, the music reaches a crescendo in the hands of certain luminaries. One such luminary was Srinivasa Ramanujan. What is fascinating about Ramanujan is that he was largely self-taught and emerged from extreme poverty to become one of the 20th century's influential mathematicians. His story is a "rags to mathematical riches" story. In the cosmic symphony of mathematics, he played a major role.

The music of Ramanujan emanates both from his life and his work. Born on 22 December 1887 in humble and poor surroundings in the town of Erode situated in present day Tamil Nadu, India, Ramanujan cultivated his love for mathematics singlehandedly and in total isolation. As a child, he was quiet and often to himself. Those that knew him were impressed by his shining large eyes which were his most prominent features. He had a prodigious memory, and at school, he would entertain his friends by reciting the various declensions of Sanskrit roots and by repeating the value of the constant π to any number of decimal places.

At the age of 12, he borrowed a book on trigonometry from an older student and completely mastered its contents. This book was Loney's *Plane Trigonometry* published by Cambridge in 1894 and contains a great deal of information on summation of series, logarithms of complex numbers, calculation of π and Gregory's series. This certainly goes far beyond any modern curriculum of trigonometry taught in our high schools today. But the book that influenced him the most was Carr's *A synopsis*

M.R. Murty, V.K. Murty, *The Mathematical Legacy of Srinivasa Ramanujan*, DOI 10.1007/978-81-322-0770-2_1, © Springer India 2013 *of elementary results in pure and applied mathematics*. This book is a compilation of some 6165 theorems, systematically arranged but with practically no proofs. It is not a remarkable book and was used by students of Carr for their preparation for the Mathematical Tripos, the entrance examination of Cambridge University. But Ramanujan has made the book famous in that he set about demonstrating to himself each of the assertions enunciated therein. To do this, he used a slate, jotting down the formula to be proved, erasing it with his elbow, jotting down some more formulas that led to the proof, then erasing them again with his elbow and jotting down some more formulas. People used to speak about his bruised elbow, and we know how he got it. Thus he worked his way through the book. This experience influenced him profoundly, and his contact with this book marks the beginning of his exploration of the world of mathematics. Carr's synopsis was therefore a great blessing. But unfortunately, Ramanujan took this synopsis as his model for writing, and his famous notebooks consisting of over 4000 formulas are written down in this style without proofs. The intermediate results, the links of the chain, have been erased by the elbow of Ramanujan, and his legacy is simply a set of discoveries, a melody of formulas.

When we look through these formulas discovered by Ramanujan, it is like great music echoing through our consciousness and the music lingers. Each is pregnant with meaning and heralding further exploration. Perhaps it is not so unfortunate that Ramanujan had taken Carr as his model for writing. We all now have work to do. "When the kings are building, the carters have work to do."

Another thing that we learn from the early mathematical development of Ramanujan, is the importance of problem solving in the primary grades. The mathematician and educator, George Pólya, was right when he stated that mathematics cultivates logical and orderly thinking, and a precision for the expression of ideas. So Ramanujan mastered a large tract of college level mathematics simply through problem solving and working through Carr's synopsis.

A year later, in 1903, he secured a seat in the Government College in Kumbakonam. However, his passionate absorption in mathematics led him to neglect his other subjects, and the inevitable happened. He failed the exams at the end of his first year. Four years later, he entered another college in Madras (now called Chennai) but met with the same fate at the end of his first year.

In 1909, at the age of 22, he married Kumari Janaki, and with his new responsibility, it was necessary for him to secure a job. This he succeeded in doing in 1912, when he became a clerk in the Madras Port Trust Office. There his duties were light, and he found time to devote to his mathematical research. Moreover, as luck would have it, the manager of the office, S.N. Aiyar, was a mathematician who took kindly to him and his discoveries. With Aiyar's encouragement, Ramanujan communicated some of his results to several British mathematicians. (For a short biography of S.N. Aiyar and the role he played in Ramanujan's life, we refer the reader to a recent article by Berndt [23].) His first three attempts produced little or no response. But in 1913, he wrote to G.H. Hardy at Trinity College, Cambridge. This was a turning point since Hardy was a renowned expert in analysis and number theory.

We should say here that number theory should not be confused with numerology. There is no mysticism attached to number theory. The only mystifying element is that there are beautiful formulas and there is a logical, mathematical order in the apparent chaotic universe. Number theory is the study of hidden mathematical patterns among numbers. It is called the queen of mathematics because the problems of number theory have given birth to the diverse disciplines of mathematics. Problems are utilized as points of focus of concentration. In themselves, the problems are unimportant. But in the finding of their solution, new concepts arise, and new links and patterns are found with other concepts and disciplines of mathematics. It is the final mosaic that is the end in view and not the esoteric problem, which is used only as a means of motivation.

So when Hardy received the letter, he found himself a little confounded and could not at first decide whether it was written by a crank or a genius. To the letter were attached about 120 theorems of which a representative sample is given by the following 15:

$$1-\frac{3!}{(1!2!)^3}x^2+\frac{6!}{(2!4!)^3}x^4-\cdots$$
$$=\left(1+\frac{x}{1!^3}+\frac{x^2}{2!^3}+\cdots\right)\left(1-\frac{x}{1!^3}+\frac{x^2}{2!^3}-\cdots\right). \tag{1}$$

$$1-5\left(\frac{1}{2}\right)^3+9\left(\frac{1\cdot 3}{2\cdot 4}\right)^3-13\left(\frac{1\cdot 3\cdot 5}{2\cdot 4\cdot 6}\right)^3+\cdots=\frac{2}{\pi}. \tag{2}$$

$$1+9\left(\frac{1}{4}\right)^4+17\left(\frac{1\cdot 5}{4\cdot 8}\right)^4+25\left(\frac{1\cdot 5\cdot 9}{4\cdot 8\cdot 12}\right)^4+\cdots=\frac{2^{3/2}}{\sqrt{\pi}\,\Gamma(3/4)^2}. \tag{3}$$

$$1-5\left(\frac{1}{2}\right)^5+9\left(\frac{1\cdot 3}{2\cdot 4}\right)^5-13\left(\frac{1\cdot 3\cdot 5}{2\cdot 4\cdot 6}\right)^5+\cdots=\frac{2}{\Gamma(3/4)^4}. \tag{4}$$

$$\int_0^\infty \frac{1+(\frac{x}{b+1})^2}{1+(\frac{x}{a})^2}\cdot\frac{1+(\frac{x}{b+2})^2}{1+(\frac{x}{a+1})^2}\cdots dx$$
$$=\frac{\sqrt{\pi}}{2}\frac{\Gamma(a+\frac{1}{2})\Gamma(b+1)\Gamma(b-a+\frac{1}{2})}{\Gamma(a)\Gamma(b+\frac{1}{2})\Gamma(b-a+1)}. \tag{5}$$

$$\int_0^\infty \frac{dx}{(1+x^2)(1+r^2x^2)(1+r^4x^2)\ldots}=\frac{\pi}{2(1+r+r^3+r^6+r^{10}+\cdots)}. \tag{6}$$

If $\alpha\beta=\pi^2$, then

$$\alpha^{-1/4}\left(1+4\alpha\int_0^\infty\frac{xe^{-\alpha x^2}}{e^{2\pi x}-1}dx\right)=\beta^{-1/4}\left(1+4\beta\int_0^\infty\frac{xe^{-\beta x^2}}{e^{2\pi x}-1}dx\right). \tag{7}$$

$$\int_0^a e^{-x^2}\,dx = \frac{1}{2}\sqrt{\pi} - \frac{e^{-a^2}}{2a+}\,\frac{1}{a+}\,\frac{2}{2a+}\,\frac{3}{a+}\,\frac{4}{2a+\cdots}. \tag{8}$$

$$4\int_0^\infty \frac{xe^{-x\sqrt{5}}}{\cosh x}\,dx = \frac{1}{1+}\,\frac{1^2}{1+}\,\frac{1^2}{1+}\,\frac{2^2}{1+}\,\frac{2^2}{1+}\,\frac{3^2}{1+}\,\frac{3^2}{1+\cdots}. \tag{9}$$

$$\text{If}\quad u = \frac{x}{1+}\,\frac{x^5}{1+}\,\frac{x^{10}}{1+}\,\frac{x^{15}}{1+\cdots},\qquad v = \frac{x^{1/5}}{1+}\,\frac{x}{1+}\,\frac{x^2}{1+}\,\frac{x^3}{1+\cdots},$$
$$\text{then}\quad v^5 = u\,\frac{1-2u+4u^2-3u^3+u^4}{1+3u+4u^2+2u^3+u^4}. \tag{10}$$

$$\frac{1}{1+}\,\frac{e^{-2\pi}}{1+}\,\frac{e^{-4\pi}}{1+\cdots} = \left\{\sqrt{\left(\frac{5+\sqrt{5}}{2}\right)} - \frac{\sqrt{5}+1}{2}\right\}e^{2\pi/5}. \tag{11}$$

$$\frac{1}{1+}\,\frac{e^{-2\pi\sqrt{5}}}{1+}\,\frac{e^{-4\pi\sqrt{5}}}{1+\cdots} = \left[\frac{\sqrt{5}}{1+(5^{3/4}(\frac{\sqrt{5}-1}{2})^{5/2}-1)^{1/5}} - \frac{\sqrt{5}+1}{2}\right]e^{2\pi/\sqrt{5}} \tag{12}$$

$$\text{If}\quad F(k) = 1 + \left(\frac{1}{2}\right)^2 k + \left(\frac{1\cdot 3}{2\cdot 4}\right)^2 k^2 + \cdots \quad\text{and}$$
$$F(1-k) = \sqrt{210}F(k),\quad\text{then}$$
$$k = (\sqrt{2}-1)^4(2-\sqrt{3})^2(\sqrt{7}-\sqrt{6})^4(8-3\sqrt{7})^2(\sqrt{10}-3)^4$$
$$\times(4-\sqrt{15})^4(\sqrt{15}-\sqrt{14})^2(6-\sqrt{35})^2. \tag{13}$$

The coefficient of x^n in $(1-2x+2x^4-2x^9+\cdots)^{-1}$ is the integer nearest to

$$\frac{1}{4n}\left(\cosh\pi\sqrt{n} - \frac{\sinh\pi\sqrt{n}}{\pi\sqrt{n}}\right). \tag{14}$$

The number of numbers between A and x which are either squares or sums of two squares is

$$K\int_A^x \frac{dt}{\sqrt{\log t}} + \theta(x), \tag{15}$$

where $K = 0.764\ldots$, and $\theta(x)$ is very small compared with the previous integral.

These fifteen entries from Ramanujan's letter to Hardy give a representative sample of the formulas contained there. The first four belong to the theory of infinite series. The next three are new definite integrals. Formulas (8) to (12) are in the theory of continued fractions. Formula (13) belongs to the theory of complex multiplication and singular moduli. Formula (14) is the first suggestion of Ramanujan's knowledge of the circle method (about which we say more in a later chapter). Finally, (15) belongs to analytic number theory.

Hardy took over two hours to analyse the letter to ascertain whether the author was a crank or a genius. Hardy's reaction is expressed in his own words: "I should like you to begin by trying to reconstruct the immediate reactions of an ordinary professional mathematician who receives a letter like this from an unknown Indian clerk."

"The first question was whether I could recognise anything. I had proved things rather like (7) myself and seemed vaguely familiar with (8). Actually (8) is classical; it is a formula of Laplace first proved properly by Jacobi and (9) occurs in a paper published by Rogers in 1907."

So the conclusion was that Ramanujan had rediscovered all of these theorems amidst the impoverished mathematical background of his rustic surroundings.

Hardy continues, "I thought, that as an expert in definite integrals, I could probably prove (5) and (6) and did so, though with a good deal more trouble than I had expected. … The series formulas (1)–(4) I found much more intriguing and it soon became obvious that Ramanujan must possess much more general theorems and was keeping a great deal up his sleeve. … The formulas (10)–(13) are on a different level and obviously both difficult and deep. An expert in elliptic functions can see at once that (13) is derived somehow from the theory of complex multiplication, but (10)–(12) defeated me completely; I had never seen anything in the least like them before. … The last two formulas stand apart. … The function in (14) is a genuine approximation to the coefficient, though not at all close as Ramanujan imagined and Ramanujan's false statement was one of the most fruitful he ever made, since it ended by leading us to all our joint work on partitions."

Indeed, (14) could only be derived by the circle method, a powerful technique developed later by Hardy and Ramanujan in their work on the partition function. The entry in the letter shows that Ramanujan had already thought about the circle method in India, before he had met Hardy.

It seems that Hardy invited his colleague Littlewood and showed him the letter. They sat with it for three hours, from 9pm to midnight and finally concluded that this indeed was the work of a genius. Hardy [67] wrote later, "A single look at them is enough to show that they could only be written down by a mathematician of the highest class. They must be true, because if they were not true, no one would have had the imagination to invent them."

Soon thereafter, Hardy invited Ramanujan to come to Cambridge, which he felt could provide a better environment in which his mathematical genius could flourish. So Ramanujan sailed for England in March 1914.

Against the background of the first world war, from 1914 to 1917, Hardy and Ramanujan spent time in wonderful mathematical collaboration. Hardy remarks that every day Ramanujan would show him about half a dozen new theorems. These three years saw prodigious mathematical activity by both Hardy and Ramanujan. In that period, Ramanujan wrote over 30 papers, in which were laid the foundations of three fundamental methods in number theory.

The first of them concerns the circle method which, as noted earlier, already has its genesis in Eq. (14) of his first letter to Hardy. This method concerns an ingenious idea for computing the integral of a function by studying its behaviour at rational points and sufficiently small neighborhoods. The method can be developed further and enables one to attack classical unsolved problems such as Goldbach's conjecture, Waring's problem and explicit formulas for the Fourier coefficients of modular forms and modular functions. These problems have defied solution for a long time. Due to Ramanujan's early demise, this work was carried on by Hardy and Littlewood, and today it is called the circle method, or the Hardy–Littlewood method. In their paper on the partition function, Hardy and Ramanujan laid the groundwork of the method. But it was clear that this was a viable technique for attacking many age-old problems. Subsequently, this technique was developed and improved by Hardy and Littlewood and I.M. Vinogradov.

The second major contribution was the normal order method which proved that almost all natural numbers have $\log\log n$ prime factors. These investigations were later developed into the beautiful probabilistic theory of numbers, starting with the work of Turán and culminating in the celebrated Erdös–Kac theorem. Afterwards, it was taken up by Kubilius, who infused finer improvements into the theory. We feel that there is a further direction for these investigations into the domain of Fourier coefficients of modular forms, and we discuss this theme in this monograph. This brings us to the third great contribution of Ramanujan.

In 1916, he wrote a classic paper entitled "On certain arithmetical functions" in which he investigated the Fourier coefficients of various modular forms. There, he noticed patterns of congruences and made three significant conjectures concerning the behaviour of these Fourier coefficients. The most famous of these concerns the Ramanujan τ-function. He conjectured that this function satisfies a multiplicative law and that its growth is controlled by a simple polynomial function. At the time, the conjecture did not have much meaning other than as an esoteric problem in analytic number theory. Indeed, regarding the τ-function, Hardy [67] wrote, "We may seem to be straying into one of the backwaters of mathematics, but the genesis of $\tau(n)$ as a coefficient in so fundamental a function compels us to treat it with respect."

Putting respect aside, the fact is that the function occupies a central place in the pantheon of coefficients of modular forms. So the legacy left by Ramanujan's conjecture is vast and deep. For it slowly transpired that these conjectures had intimate connection with profound aspects of number theory and algebraic geometry.

The first significant step towards the conjectures of Ramanujan was taken by Mordell, who proved the multiplicative law, the first part of Ramanujan's conjectures. But Mordell only treated the case of τ and did not realize that it was prototypical of a spectrum of functions, each in its own right of central importance. This realization came twenty years later, in the work of the German mathematician Erich Hecke (who incidently was also born in the same year as Ramanujan), and the meaning of the multiplicative properties conjectured by Ramanujan was unravelled. This work of Hecke is considered a masterpiece of mathematics.

But the connections to algebraic geometry were deeper still. Indeed, after the pioneering work of Artin and Hasse, Weil formulated in 1949 general conjectures about solutions of systems of equations over finite fields. In the 1950s, it was suspected that the τ-function of Ramanujan enumerates the number of these solutions for a certain system of equations (called a variety). Several Japanese mathematicians constructed the possible candidate, but there were technical problems related to compactification. These problems were resolved in 1974 by a Belgian mathematician Pierre Deligne, who completely settled the conjectures of Ramanujan. In 1976, Deligne was awarded the Fields medal (which is the mathematical analogue of the Nobel prize) for this achievement. This is quite a legacy!

The connection between Ramanujan's conjecture and Weil's conjecture could not be so easily foreseen. Both conjectures reflect elements of the master symphony that Shafarevich spoke about. Indeed, in his retrospective essay on number theory, André Weil wrote [201], "In 1947, in Chicago, I felt bored and depressed, and not knowing what to do, I started reading Gauss's two memoirs on biquadratic residues, which I had never read before. The Gaussian integers occur in the second paper. The first one deals essentially with the number of solutions of equations $ax^4 - by^4 = 1$ in the prime field modulo p, and with the connection between these and certain Gaussian sums. ... then I noticed that similar principles can be applied to all equations of the form $ax^m + by^n + cz^r + \cdots = 0$, and that this implies the truth of the so-called "Riemann hypothesis" for all curves $ax^n + by^n + cz^n = 0$ over finite fields, and also a "generalized Riemann hypothesis" for varieties in projective space with a "diagonal" equation $\sum a_i x_i^n \equiv 0$. This led me in turn to conjectures about varieties over finite fields."

It was only a matter of time before several notable mathematicians realized that Ramanujan's conjecture was really a "Riemann hypothesis" for a certain zeta function of a variety over a finite field and that it would follow from Weil's conjecture. This was the achievement of Pierre Deligne in 1974.

No one could have foreseen such a cosmic connection. Yet, Weil is quite harsh on Hardy and in the same essay [201] wrote "Hardy's remarkable comment is: "We seem to have drifted into one of the backwaters of mathematics." To him it was just another inequality; he found it curious that anyone could get deeply interested in it. In fact, he becomes apologetic and explains that, in spite of the apparent lack of interest of this problem it might still have some features which made it not unworthy of Ramanujan's attention."

The problem with Weil's assessment of Hardy is that it is inaccurate. Hardy's original quotation is that "We may seem to be straying into one of the backwaters of mathematics, but the genesis of $\tau(n)$ as a coefficient in so fundamental a function compels us to treat it with respect." The reader will note that Weil replaced "We may seem" with "We seem" which gives quite a twist to the meaning. Moreover, Hardy does not say we will study it simply because Ramanujan had studied it, but rather that it is the coefficient of a fundamental function, namely $\Delta(z)$ in the theory of modular forms. If Hardy thought that the τ-function was in the backwaters of mathematics, then it would have been unreasonable to give it as a doctoral thesis problem to one of his celebrated students, R.A. Rankin, who created what is now called Rankin's method (also called the Rankin–Selberg method) an analogue of which was instrumental in the resolution of the Weil conjectures. So it is quite presumptuous to make absolute pronouncements on the significance of various mathematical ideas since we never know how ideas are interconnected. And this is part of the legacy.

But this legacy does not end here, and these investigations form just the tip of an iceberg. The central problem of number theory revolves around what is called the reciprocity law. The function of Ramanujan, and Fourier coefficients in general and their congruence properties reflect some aspects of the non-abelian reciprocity law. The theory of modular forms was further generalized by Jacquet and Langlands, and higher-dimensional versions of Ramanujan's conjectures were formulated as part of the Langlands program. Some of these conjectures go beyond the Ramanujan conjecture. Finer distribution conjectures concerning the τ-function inspired by the work of Sato and Tate in the theory of elliptic curves and first enunciated by Serre have now been proved. These results represent Himalayan peaks in the mathematical landscape of the 21st century.

Returning to our narrative of Ramanujan, we find that at the end of his three years work in England, he left behind a tremendous mathematical legacy. In the summer of 1917, he fell ill with what was suspected to be tuberculosis. He never recovered. Nevertheless, he continued to work unabated. Hardy relates an interesting story during the time that Ramanujan was staying in the hospital in Putney. He went to visit him in a taxicab, and as he entered Ramanujan's room, remarked that he had just ridden in a taxicab with number 1729 which seemed to be to him a rather dull number and hoped that this was not the indication of a bad omen. Ramanujan replied that on the contrary it is a very interesting number. It is the smallest number which can be expressed as the sum of two cubes in exactly two different ways:

$$1729 = 1^3 + 12^3 \quad = 10^3 + 9^3.$$

This is not without significance. Recently, a beautiful theorem in the theory of elliptic curves was proved involving this taxicab number. If for each k, there is a squarefree natural number n that can be expressed in at least k different ways as the sum of two cubes, then an outstanding problem in the theory of elliptic curves has an affirmative solution, namely ranks of elliptic curves over $\mathbb{Q}$ tend to infinity.

Ramanujan had great intuition into what was important and central. His facile mind revealed an artistic symbiosis between intellect and inspiration. We are reminded of a statement made by a great Indian sage, Swami Vivekananda, over a century ago. He said: "Just as the intellect is the instrument of knowledge, so is the heart the instrument of inspiration. In a lower state, the heart is a much weaker instrument than the intellect. ... Properly cultivated, the heart can be changed and will go beyond intellect; it will function through inspiration. Man will have to go beyond intellect in the end. The knowledge of man, his powers of perception, of reasoning and intellect and heart, all are busy churning this milk of the world. Out of long churning comes butter ... Men of [cultivated] heart get the butter and the buttermilk is left for the intellectual."

We do not know how Ramanujan discovered his theorems. On this point, Hardy [67] wrote, "It was his insight into algebraical formulas, transformations of infinite series and so forth, that was most amazing. On this side most certainly I have never met his equal, and I can compare him only with Euler or Jacobi. He worked far more than the majority of modern mathematicians, by induction from numerical examples; all his congruence properties of partitions, for example, were discovered in this way. But with his memory, his patience, and his power of calculation he combined a power of generalisation, a feeling for form, a capacity for rapid modification of his hypothesis, that were often really startling, and made him, in his own peculiar field, without a rival in his day."

These comments were made by Hardy in 1936 when he delivered his famous Harvard lectures on the work of Ramanujan. He began them with a rather sentimental tone. "I have to help you," he said, "to form some sort of reasoned estimate of the most romantic figure in the recent history of mathematics ... Ramanujan was, in a way, my discovery. I did not invent him—like other great men, he invented himself—but I was the first really competent person who had a chance to see some of his work, and I can still remember with satisfaction that I could recognize at once what a treasure I had found ... And my association with him is the one romantic incident in my life." These are powerful feelings indeed describing one of the great collaborations of mathematics!

We conclude this introduction by reflecting upon what we call the cultural legacy left behind by Ramanujan. We can do this no better than to relate the feelings expressed by the Nobel laureate, Subramanian Chandrasekhar, at the Ramanujan Centennial Conference in Urbana in 1987. He wrote [31]: "It must have been a day in April 1920, when I was not quite ten years old, when my mother told me of an item in the newspaper of the day that a famous Indian mathematician, Ramanujan by name, had died the preceding day; and she told me further that Ramanujan had gone to England some years earlier, had collaborated with some famous English mathematicians and that he had returned only very recently, and was well known internationally for what he had achieved. Though I had no idea at that time of what kind of a mathematician Ramanujan was, or indeed what scientific achievement meant, I can still recall the gladness I felt at the assurance that one brought up under circumstances similar to my own, could have achieved what I could not grasp. I am sure that others were equally gladdened. I hope that it is not hard for you to imagine what the example of Ramanujan could have provided for young men and women of those times, beginning to look at the world with increasingly different perceptions.

"The fact that Ramanujan's early years were spent in a scientifically sterile atmosphere, that his life in India was not without hardships, that under circumstances that appeared to most Indians as nothing short of miraculous, he had gone to Cambridge, supported by eminent mathematicians and had returned to India with every assurance that he would be considered, in time, as one of the most original mathematicians of the century—these facts were enough—more than enough—for aspiring young Indian students to break their bonds of intellectual confinement and perhaps soar the way that Ramanujan did.

"It may be argued, perhaps with some justice, that this was a sentimental attitude: Ramanujan represents so extreme a fluctuation from the norm that his being born an Indian must be considered to a large extent as accidental. But to the Indians of the time, Ramanujan was not unique in the way we think of him today. He was one of others who had, during that same period, achieved, in their judgement, comparably in science and in other areas of human activity. Gandhi, Nehru, Rabindranath Tagore, J.C. Bose, C.V. Raman, M.N. Saha, S.N. Bose and a host of others, were in the forefront of the then fermenting scene."

In these words of Chandrasekhar, we see the legacy of Ramanujan. For the life of Chandrasekhar was equally full of hardships. Born in the same village surroundings as Ramanujan, he went to study at Cambridge and there as a graduate student discovered the mathematical implications of the theory of relativity in the collapse of certain massive stars. These he predicted degenerate into black holes. The high priests of physics of that time rejected his calculations as meaningless. He had to wait for another thirty years before the theory came into the forefront of modern physics and finally in 1983, he was awarded the Nobel prize in physics as recognition of his work. The life of Subramanian Chandrasekhar itself reveals to some extent the grandeur of the legacy of Ramanujan.

But a scientist belongs to no nation. Many of the mathematicians of distinction that we have met and talked with have all told us that Ramanujan directly or indirectly inspired their mathematical life. This is not surprising. For as we have seen, Ramanujan embodies that marvelous miracle of the human mind to frame concepts and to use formulas and symbols as tools of thought to probe deeper into the mysteries of one's own being. As long as the spirit of science is alive, his legacy will live, and the music will pass from one luminary to another. And all of us who think and work with mathematical ideas are participants in that wonderful symphony.

Chapter 2
The Ramanujan τ-Function

1 Introduction

The 1916 memoir of Ramanujan, innocuously entitled "On certain arithmetic functions", introduced the τ-function. This is an integer-valued function on the natural numbers which, at first, manifested as part of an "error term" in counting the number of ways that a number could be written as a sum of 24 squares. However, Ramanujan realized that it was a function worthy of study in its own right. It would not be an overstatement to say that one of the significant themes of mathematics in the 20th century has emanated from this observation.

The τ-function is defined by the formal identity

$$\sum_{n=1}^{\infty} \tau(n) q^n = q \prod_{n=1}^{\infty} (1 - q^n)^{24}. \tag{1}$$

It is in fact more than a formal identity. If we think of q as a complex number with $|q| < 1$, then taking the logarithm of the infinite product and expanding, we see that it is

$$\log q - 24 \sum_{n=1}^{\infty} \sum_{m=1}^{\infty} \frac{q^{nm}}{m}.$$

Interchanging sums, we see that the double sum is

$$-24 \sum_{m=1}^{\infty} \frac{1}{m} \frac{q^m}{1 - q^m},$$

and this converges for $|q| < 1$. For a complex number z with $\Im(z) > 0$, we see that

$$q = e^{2\pi i z}$$

satisfies $|q| < 1$, and so we may define a function $\Delta(z)$ by the right-hand side of (1). Moreover, we see that $\Delta(z) \neq 0$ as it is given as an absolutely convergent product of non-zero terms.

M.R. Murty, V.K. Murty, *The Mathematical Legacy of Srinivasa Ramanujan*,
DOI 10.1007/978-81-322-0770-2_2, © Springer India 2013

The function $\Delta(z)$ was known to previous authors. If we consider the Eisenstein series

$$E_{2k}(z) = \sum_{(m,n)\neq(0,0)} \frac{1}{(mz+n)^{2k}}$$

where the sum ranges over pairs of integers (m,n) which are not both zero, then there is the identity

$$\Delta(z) = \frac{1}{1728}\left(E_4(z)^3 - E_6(z)^2\right).$$

Dedekind had studied $\Delta(z)$ (and a 24th root of it known as the η-function). The η-function occurs in the transformation properties of the Dedekind sums, and the Δ-function occurs in the theory of the moduli of elliptic curves. It also occurs in the limit formula of Kronecker. However, Ramanujan was the first to realize that the coefficients of the q-expansion give rise to an interesting arithmetic sequence.

2 The τ-Function and Partitions

Writing integers as sums of elements of a distinguished subset is a theme that occupied Ramanujan in many of his works. As we said, the τ-function itself arises in the problem of representing an integer as a sum of 24 squares. Ramanujan also gave considerable attention to the partition problem, namely the number of ways of writing a positive integer as a sum of positive integers. If we denote by $p(n)$ the number of such representations of a positive integer n, then we see that the first few values are given by $p(1)=1$, $p(2)=2$, $p(3)=3$, $p(4)=5$, $p(5)=7$, $p(6)=11$ and so on. If we consider the generating function

$$\sum_{n=1}^{\infty} p(n)q^n$$

then it is easily seen to be equal to

$$\prod_{m=1}^{\infty}\left(1-q^m\right)^{-1}.$$

This bears some superficial resemblance to (1). Indeed, such series had been studied classically by Euler, Jacobi and others. However, it was Ramanujan who began to observe arithmetical properties of the coefficients, such as congruences. For example, he observed that

$$p(5n+4) \equiv 0 \pmod 5$$

and

$$p(7n+5) \equiv 0 \pmod 7.$$

He continued this line of thought to the τ-function itself. We know now that such congruences are based on deep aspects of the theory of modular forms.

While the sequence $\{p(n)\}$ and $\{\tau(n)\}$ share properties such as congruence relations, they are, however, very different in terms of their growth properties. Ramanujan's circle method (described in another chapter) shows that $p(n)$ grows exponentially as a function of n, while as we shall see in this chapter, $\tau(n)$ has a polynomial growth in n.

3 Related Generating Functions

Euler had studied the function

$$\prod_{n=1}^{\infty}(1-q^n) \tag{2}$$

and proved that it is equal to

$$\sum_{n\in\mathbb{Z}}(-1)^n q^{(3n^2+n)/2}.$$

Numbers of the form $n(3n+1)/2$ are called *pentagonal*. This and related q-expansion identities can be expressed in terms of the number of partitions of an integer into other integers satisfying various constraints. For example, Euler's identity can be interpreted as giving an expression for the number of partitions of a number into an even number of unequal parts minus the number of partitions of the same number into an odd number of unequal parts.

We can ask for which integers m there is an $n \in \mathbb{Z}$ such that

$$m = \frac{1}{2}n(3n+1)? \tag{3}$$

We need to have $1+24m$ to be a perfect square, say r^2. Moreover, we need $-1 \pm r$ divisible by 6, and in particular, 6 should not divide r. When these conditions are satisfied, we have

$$n = \frac{1}{6}(-1 \pm r).$$

In particular, given m, there are at most two values of n satisfying (3). Thus, when (2) is written as a power series in q, the coefficients are bounded. Moreover, the number of $m \leq x$ for which (3) has a solution is $\leq \sqrt{2x/3}$. In particular, most of the coefficients are zero, and the series is "lacunary". We can say a little more about which coefficients are nonzero. Indeed, for $1+8m=r^2$ to be satisfied, we need r odd, and

$$r+1=a, \qquad r-1=b$$

for some factorization $8m = ab$. This implies that $r = \frac{1}{2}(a+b)$ and $a = b+2$. In particular, both a and b are even, and $r = b+1$ and $8m = b(b+2)$.

Jacobi studied the third power of (2) and proved that

$$\prod_{n=1}^{\infty}(1-q^n)^3 = \sum_{n=0}^{\infty}(2n+1)q^{n(n+1)/2}. \tag{4}$$

Numbers of the form $n(n+1)/2$ are called *triangular*. Again, it is seen that this is a lacunary series, in the sense that the set of n for which the coefficient of q^n is nonzero has density zero. Note that we have

$$\sum_{n=1}^{\infty}\tau(n)q^n = q\left(\sum_{m\in\mathbb{Z}}(-1)^m q^{(3m^2+m)/2}\right)^{24}$$

and

$$\sum_{n=1}^{\infty}\tau(n)q^n = q\left(\sum_{m=0}^{\infty}(2m+1)q^{m(m+1)/2}\right)^{8}.$$

In particular, one can derive the following formulas for $\tau(n)$:

$$(n-1)\tau(n) = \sum_{1\le|m|\le a_n}\left(n-1-\frac{25m}{2}(3m+1)\right)\tau\left(n-\frac{m}{2}(3m+1)\right)$$

where

$$a_n = \frac{1}{6}(1+(1+24n)^{\frac{1}{2}});$$

$$(n-1)\tau(n) = \sum_{1\le m\le b_n}(-1)^{2m+1}(2m+1)\left(n-1-\frac{9m}{2}(m+1)\right)\tau\left(n-\frac{m}{2}(m+1)\right)$$

where

$$b_n = \frac{1}{2}((1+8n)^{\frac{1}{2}}-1).$$

The first of these is due to Lehmer, and the second to Ramanujan. However, these formulas do not seem to be useful in giving an expression for $\tau(n)$ in terms of elementary functions. They cannot be viewed as 'closed-form' expressions since the range of summation is a function of the argument. However, they do suffice to show that $\tau(n)$ has at most polynomial growth in n.

4 Values of the τ-Function

It is easy to compute the first few values: $\tau(1) = 1$, $\tau(2) = -24$, $\tau(3) = 252$. The following table is copied from [110].

n	$\tau(n)$	n	$\tau(n)$	n	$\tau(n)$
1	1	11	534,612	21	−4,219,488
2	−24	12	−370,944	22	−12,830,688
3	252	13	−577,738	23	18,643,272
4	−1472	14	401,856	24	21,288,960
5	4830	15	1,217,160	25	−25,499,225
6	−6048	16	987,136	26	13,865,712
7	−16744	17	−6,905,934	27	−73,279,080
8	84480	18	2,727,432	28	24,647,168
9	−113,643	19	10,661,420	29	128,406,630
10	−115,920	20	−7,109,760	30	−29,211,840

Looking at this table and others that give more values, many natural questions come to mind. Firstly, we see that the numbers are growing fairly rapidly. However, the growth is not exponential since it was shown by Ramanujan that

$$\left|\tau(n)\right| \ll n^7.$$

He conjectured that

$$\left|\tau(n)\right| \le d(n)n^{11/2}$$

where $d(n)$ denotes the number of positive divisors of n. This is known as the Ramanujan conjecture (actually Hardy called it the Ramanujan hypothesis), and it is now a theorem as we shall explain in another chapter. The only proof of this relies on "reducing" it to a special case of the Weil conjectures and appealing to the proof of these conjectures by Deligne.

It is a classical result that $d(n) = \mathbf{O}(n^\epsilon)$ for any $\epsilon > 0$, and so a weaker version of the Ramanujan conjecture is that for any $\epsilon > 0$,

$$\tau(n) \ll_\epsilon n^{11/2+\epsilon}$$

where the subscript indicates that the implied constant may depend on ϵ.

We might also notice from the table a fact that Ramanujan stated as a conjecture, namely that the τ-function is multiplicative:

$$\tau(mn) = \tau(m)\tau(n) \tag{5}$$

for positive integers m and n that are relatively prime. Moreover, Ramanujan observed that for a fixed prime p, the values of $\tau(p^m)$ satisfy a second-order recurrence relation: for $m \ge 1$, we have

$$\tau\left(p^{m+1}\right) = \tau(p)\tau\left(p^m\right) - p^{11}\tau\left(p^{m-1}\right). \tag{6}$$

p	$\tau(p)$	p	$\tau(p)$	p	$\tau(p)$
2	−24	31	−52,843,168	73	1,463,791,322
3	252	37	−182,213,314	79	38,116,845,680
5	4830	41	308,120,442	83	−29,335,099,668
7	−16744	43	−17,125,708	89	−24,992,917,110
11	534,612	47	2,687,48,496	97	75,013,568,546
13	−577,738	53	−1,596,055,698	101	81,742,959,102
17	−6,905,934	59	−5,189,203,740	103	−225,755,128,648
19	10,661,420	61	6,956,478,662	107	90,241,258,356
23	18,643,272	67	−15,481,826,884	109	73,482,676,310
29	128,406,630	71	9,791,485,272	113	−85,146,862,638

Both of these properties were proved by Mordell within a year of the publication of Ramanujan's paper. These relations imply that all of the values of the τ-function can be determined once they are known at prime arguments. Above is a table of $\tau(p)$ for primes $p \le 113$ (the first 30 primes).

Consider again the values of the τ-function on powers of a prime. Denote by α_p and β_p the complex numbers which are roots of the equation

$$T^2 - \tau(p)T + p^{11} = 0.$$

Then $\tau(p) = \alpha_p + \beta_p$ and $\alpha_p\beta_p = p^{11}$. Let us write

$$\alpha_p = p^{11/2}e^{i\theta_p}.$$

Here θ_p is a complex number, and the Ramanujan conjecture is the assertion that in fact θ_p is real. In any case, we deduce that

$$\tau(p) = 2p^{11/2}\cos(\theta_p).$$

This implies that

$$\tau(p)^2 = 4p^{11}\big(1 - \sin^2(\theta_p)\big).$$

We see from this that we cannot have $\sin(\theta_p) = 0$ as $\tau(p)$ is an integer. Moreover, relation (6) shows that

$$\tau\big(p^2\big) = \tau(p)^2 - p^{11} = \alpha_p^2 + \alpha_p\beta_p + \beta_p^2.$$

More generally, by induction, we can show that

$$\tau\big(p^a\big) = \frac{\alpha_p^{a+1} - \beta_p^{a+1}}{\alpha_p - \beta_p}.$$

Equivalently,

$$\tau\left(p^a\right) = p^{11a/2}\frac{\sin(a+1)\theta_p}{\sin\theta_p}. \tag{7}$$

5 Parity of the τ-Function

A few more calculations will show that $\tau(p)$ seems to be even for all primes p. This is in fact true and can be proved as follows. We have the congruence

$$\left(1-q^n\right)^{24} \equiv \left(1+q^{8n}\right)^3 \pmod 2.$$

Now, by a q-series identity of Jacobi, we have

$$\prod_{n=1}^{\infty}\left(1+q^{8n}\right)^3 = \sum_{m=0}^{\infty} q^{4m^2+4m}.$$

Thus, we deduce that

$$\sum_{n=1}^{\infty}\tau(n)q^n \equiv q\sum_{m=0}^{\infty} q^{4m^2+4m} \equiv \sum_{m=0}^{\infty} q^{(2m+1)^2} \pmod 2.$$

In particular, $\tau(n)$ is odd if and only if $n=(2m+1)^2$, in other words, if and only if n is an odd square. In particular, $\tau(p)$ is even for every prime p.

6 Congruences Satisfied by the τ-Function

The result of the previous paragraph is that

$$\tau(p) \equiv 0 \pmod 2$$

for all primes p. There are many other congruence relations discovered by Ramanujan. Here is a partial list:

(1) $\tau(p) \equiv 1+p^3 \pmod{2^5}$
(2) $\tau(p) \equiv 1+p \pmod 3$
(3) $\tau(p) \equiv p+p^{10} \pmod{5^2}$
(4) $\tau(p) \equiv p+p^4 \pmod 7$
(5) $\tau(p) \equiv 1+p^{11} \pmod{691}$

More congruences were discovered later by other authors including Bambah, Chowla, Gandhi, Swinnerton-Dyer and Wilton.

As mentioned briefly earlier, Ramanujan was also the first to find congruences satisfied by the partition function. Some of these are

(1) $p(5m+4) \equiv 0 \pmod 5$
(2) $p(7m+5) \equiv 0 \pmod 7$
(3) $p(11m+6) \equiv 0 \pmod{11}$

In Chap. 7, we will indicate how such congruences can be proved.

7 Vanishing of the τ-Function

Of the many problems that are open with respect to the τ-function, there is a conjecture of Lehmer [111] that asserts that

$$\tau(p) \neq 0$$

where p is a prime. Equivalently,

$$\tau(n) \neq 0$$

for any $n \geq 1$. In fact, we have the following elementary result of Lehmer.

Proposition 7.1 *Let n_0 denote the least value of n for which $\tau(n) = 0$ (if it exists). Then n_0 is prime.*

Proof The multiplicativity of the τ-function (5) shows that n_0 is a prime power, say $n_0 = p^a$. Suppose that $a > 1$ (in other words, $\tau(p) \neq 0$). Then from (7) we deduce that

$$\sin(a+1)\theta_p = 0$$

and so

$$\theta_p = k\pi/(a+1) \tag{8}$$

for some integer k. The number

$$4(\cos\theta_p)^2 = \tau(p)^2/p^{11}$$

is rational. On the other hand, by (8), it is an algebraic integer. Thus, it is in fact an integer, say m, and it is also clear that $m > 0$. Again, by (8), θ_p is real, and so $|\cos\theta_p| \leq 1$ and so $m \leq 4$. Then

$$\tau(p)^2 = mp^{11}$$

and as $\tau(p)$ is an integer, m must be divisible by p. Putting all of these constraints together, we see that $p = m = 2$ or $p = m = 3$. This implies that

$$\tau(2) = \pm 2^6 \quad \text{or} \quad \tau(3) = \pm 3^6.$$

But neither of these can hold as we see from the tables above: $\tau(2) = -24$ and $\tau(3) = 252$. This completes the proof. □

We also have the following curious result.

Proposition 7.2 *Suppose that the set* $\{n : \tau(n) = 0\}$ *has density zero. Then it is, in fact, empty.*

Proof Suppose that $\tau(n) = 0$ for some n. Then by the previous result, the least such n is a prime number, p (say). It follows that if $n = mp$ with $p \nmid m$, then $\tau(n) = 0$. Thus, the set

$$\{n : \tau(n) = 0\}$$

has density $\geq (p-1)/p^2$, contradicting our hypothesis. □

Using the congruences satisfied by the τ-function, it is possible to show that n_0 (if it exists) must be quite large. Indeed, Lehmer himself observed that if $\tau(p) = 0$, then the congruences imply that

$$p^3 \equiv -1 \pmod{2^5}.$$

Since $p \neq 2$, we also have that

$$p^{16} \equiv 1 \pmod{2^5}.$$

These two congruences together imply that

$$p^2 \equiv 1 \pmod{2^5}$$

from which it follows that

$$p \equiv -1 \pmod{2^5}.$$

Similarly, one finds $p \equiv -1 \pmod{2^5 \cdot 3 \cdot 5^2 \cdot 691}$. This immediately implies that

$$p \geq 2^5 \cdot 3 \cdot 5^2 \cdot 691 - 1 = 1{,}658{,}399.$$

In fact, one can do much better, and it is currently known that $\tau(p) \neq 0$ for $p < 10^{15}$. Of course. Lehmer's conjecture is that it should be nonzero for all p. Recently, this conjecture has been related to the irrationality of coefficients of certain mock modular forms.

There is an even stronger conjecture than that of Lehmer, which has been suggested by Atkin and Serre. For every $\epsilon > 0$, they ask whether

$$|\tau(p)| \gg_\epsilon p^{\frac{9}{2}-\epsilon}?$$

Nothing is known about this conjecture. In terms of the angle θ_p introduced earlier, the above conjecture is equivalent to the assertion that

$$\left|\theta_p - \frac{\pi}{2}\right| \gg_\epsilon \frac{1}{p^{1+\epsilon}}.$$

If we consider $\tau(n)$ rather than $\tau(p)$, it is possible to prove a kind of lower bound. It is shown in [134] that there is an effectively computable absolute constant $c > 0$ such that for all positive integers n for which $\tau(n)$ is *odd*, we have the lower bound

$$\left|\tau(n)\right| \geq (\log n)^c.$$

The condition on the parity of $\tau(n)$ ensures that it is not divisible by the first power of any prime. Thus, the set of n for which the result applies is the so-called squarefull numbers (that is, numbers for which every prime divisor occurs to at least the second power).

It is also interesting to ask for lower bounds that hold infinitely often. Hardy showed that

$$\tau(n) > n^{11/2}$$

holds infinitely often. The best result in this regard is to due to R. Murty [128], who showed that there is an absolute and effective constant $c > 0$ such that

$$\left|\tau(n)\right| > n^{11/2} \exp\{c \log n / \log\log n\}.$$

This result is essentially best possible since we know that

$$d(n) < \exp\left\{c' \log n / \log\log n\right\}$$

and by Ramanujan's conjecture (Deligne's theorem), we have

$$\left|\tau(n)\right| \leq d(n) n^{11/2}.$$

With recent developments on the Sato–Tate conjecture (see Chaps. 10 and 12), these results are valid for any $c < \log 2$. □

8 Divisibility of $\tau(p)$ by p

The many congruences satisfied by the τ-function all have a fixed modulus and varying argument. A different kind of congruence is the one in the title of this section, namely whether

$$\tau(p) \equiv 0 \pmod{p}. \tag{9}$$

Indeed, this does occur, and the first example is $p = 2$ as we have already seen above. The only primes known to satisfy (9) are $p = 2, 3, 5, 7, 2411, 7758337633$.

(This last prime was discovered quite recently [116].) It is not known whether there are infinitely many such primes. Neither is it known that the complement is infinite! In this regard, the situation is similar to that of Wieferich primes.

Heuristic reasoning would suggest that

$$\#\{p \leq x : \tau(p) \equiv 0 \pmod{p}\} \sim \log\log x. \tag{10}$$

However, the function $\log\log x$ grows so slowly that it is computationally difficult to distinguish it from a constant. (For example, $\log\log 10^{15}$ is approximately 3.54.) If (10) were true, we would expect that

$$\sum_{\tau(p)\equiv 0 \pmod{p}} \frac{1}{\log p}$$

converges. However, we do not even know whether

$$\sum_{\tau(p)\equiv 0 \pmod{p}} \frac{1}{p}$$

converges.

Suppose that p is a prime for which (9) holds. Then from the relation

$$\tau\left(p^{a+1}\right) = \tau(p)\tau\left(p^{a}\right) - p^{11}\tau\left(p^{a-1}\right)$$

we see that for all $a \geq 1$,

$$\tau\left(p^{a}\right) \equiv 0 \pmod{p^{a}}.$$

We also note that if $\tau(p) \equiv 0 \pmod{p}$ and $n = pm$ where $(p, m) = 1$, then

$$\left(\tau(n), n\right) \neq 1. \tag{11}$$

If the set of primes for which (9) holds has positive density, then it follows by an elementary sieve argument that the set of n for which (11) holds has density 1. This latter statement can be proved unconditionally. In fact, one knows that

$$\#\{n \leq x : \left(\tau(n), n\right) = 1\} \ll x/\log\log\log x.$$

It is interesting to note that if there are infinitely many primes p such that $\tau(p) = 0$, then for any value of k, there exist infinitely many values of n such that $\tau(n) = \tau(n+1) = \tau(n+2) = \cdots = \tau(n+k) = 0$. This is an easy exercise using the Chinese remainder theorem.

9 Lehmer's Conjecture and Harmonic Weak Maass Forms

Finally, we report on some recent work of Bruinier, Ono and Rhoades [27] that opens another line of investigation for Lehmer's conjecture. We give a brief (and slightly technical) explanation of this new development.

After the study of classical modular forms, it is natural to study the space of weakly holomorphic modular forms which are just meromorphic modular forms whose singularities may only occur at the cusps. These spaces are contained in the larger space of harmonic weak Maass forms which need not be holomorphic but are annihilated by a second-order differential operator. At the cusps, we allow for exponential growth of a special type. To be precise, let

$$\Delta_k := -y^2\left(\frac{\partial^2}{\partial x^2}+\frac{\partial^2}{\partial y^2}\right)+iky\left(\frac{\partial}{\partial x}+i\frac{\partial}{\partial y}\right).$$

Let χ be a Dirichlet character modulo N. A *harmonic weak Maass form of weight k on $\Gamma_0(N)$* with Nebentypus χ is a smooth function on the upper half-plane satisfying the following three conditions:

(1) $$f\left(\frac{az+b}{cz+d}\right)=\chi(d)(cz+d)^k f(z) \quad \text{for all} \begin{pmatrix} a & b \\ c & d \end{pmatrix} \in \Gamma_0(N);$$

(2) $\Delta_k f = 0$;
(3) there is a polynomial $P_f = \sum_{n\le 0} c_f^+(n)q^n \in \mathbb{C}[q^{-1}]$ such that for some fixed $\epsilon > 0$, $f(z) - P_f(z) = O(e^{-\epsilon y})$ as y tends to infinity, with analogous conditions at the other cusps. The polynomial P_f is called the *principal part* of f at the corresponding cusp.

This vector space of harmonic weak Maass forms is denoted $H_k(\Gamma_0(N), \chi)$. One can show that every weight $2-k$ harmonic weak Maass form $f(z)$ has a Fourier expansion at each cusp of the following form:

$$f(z)=\sum_{n\gg -\infty} c_f^+(n)q^n+\sum_{n<0} c_f^-(n)\Gamma\big(k-1, 4\pi|n|y\big)q^n,$$

where $\Gamma(a,x)$ is the incomplete Gamma function given by

$$\Gamma(a,x)=\int_x^\infty t^{a-1}e^{-t}\,dt.$$

The differential operator

$$\xi_w := 2iy^w\overline{\frac{\partial}{\partial \overline{z}}},$$

has the property that

$$\xi_{2-k} : H_{2-k}\big(\Gamma_0(N), \chi\big) \to S_k\big(\Gamma_0(N), \overline{\chi}\big).$$

A straightforward calculation shows that

$$\xi_{2-k}(f) = -(4\pi)^{k-1}\sum_{n=1}^{\infty}\overline{c_f^-(-n)}n^{k-1}q^n.$$

In other words, the coefficients $c_f^-(n)$ are really coefficients of classical cusp forms. Now let $g \in S_k(\Gamma_0(N), \chi)$ be a normalized newform. We say that a harmonic weak Maass form f is *good for* g if the following conditions are satisfied:

(1) The principal part of f at the cusp ∞ belongs to $F_g[q^{-1}]$, where F_g is the number field obtained by adjoining the Fourier coefficients of g to $\mathbb{Q}$;
(2) The principal parts of f at the other cusps of $\Gamma_0(N)$ are constant;
(3) $\xi_{2-k}(f) = g/(g, g)$, where $(\cdot, \cdot)$ denotes the Petersson inner product.

The main theorem of [27] is that if

$$g = \sum_{n=1}^{\infty} c_g(n) q^n \in S_k\big(\Gamma_0(N), \overline{\chi}\big)$$

is a normalized newform and $f \in H_{2-k}(\Gamma_0(N), \chi)$ is good for g, then for any p coprime to N for which $c_g(p) = 0$, we have $c_f^+(n)$ algebraic for any n with $\text{ord}_p(n)$ odd. In other words, the vanishing of the Fourier coefficients of a Hecke eigenform implies the algebraicity of the Fourier coefficients of the corresponding harmonic weak Maass form. The authors in [27] discuss the case for Lehmer's conjecture in this context.

Chapter 3
Ramanujan's Conjecture and ℓ-Adic Representations

Let us recall that Ramanujan's conjecture asserts that for all primes p, we have

$$|\tau(p)| \le 2p^{11/2}.$$

The key to understanding this is the modular nature of $\Delta(z)$. There is an action of the modular group

$$\mathrm{SL}_2(\mathbb{Z}) = \left\{ \begin{pmatrix} a & b \\ c & d \end{pmatrix}, a, b, c, d \in \mathbb{Z},\ ad - bc = 1 \right\}$$

on complex numbers with positive imaginary part, the so-called upper half-plane

$$\mathcal{H} = \{ z \in \mathbb{C} : \Im(z) > 0 \}.$$

The action is given by fractional linear transformations

$$\begin{pmatrix} a & b \\ c & d \end{pmatrix} z = \frac{az + b}{cz + d}.$$

Under this action, Δ has the following transformation property:

$$\Delta(\gamma z) = (cz + d)^{12} \Delta(z).$$

This, and the holomorphy of Δ on $\mathcal{H}$ as well as at the boundary of $\mathcal{H}$, make Δ a modular form. The weight of a modular form is determined by the power of the automorphy factor

$$j(\gamma, z) = (cz + d)$$

that appears in the transformation property. Thus Δ is a modular form of weight 12. The q-expansion

$$\Delta(z) = \sum_{n=1}^{\infty} \tau(n) q^n, \qquad q = e^{2\pi i z}$$

M.R. Murty, V.K. Murty, *The Mathematical Legacy of Srinivasa Ramanujan*,
DOI 10.1007/978-81-322-0770-2_3, © Springer India 2013

is then seen as the Fourier expansion of Δ (at the cusp $i\infty$). The fact that the Fourier expansion has no constant term (that is, the coefficient of q^0 is 0) designates Δ as a cusp form.

Petersson generalized Ramanujan's conjecture to other modular forms which are cusp forms. More precisely, he conjectured that for a cusp form of weight k and having a Fourier expansion

$$f(z) = \sum_{n=1}^{\infty} a_n q^n$$

at the cusp $i\infty$, the coefficients satisfy the inequality

$$|a(p)| \ll_\epsilon p^{(k-1)/2+\epsilon}$$

for any $\epsilon > 0$.

1 The Weil Conjectures

Let X be a smooth projective variety over a finite field $\mathbb{F}$ of q elements. Let us fix an algebraic closure $\overline{\mathbb{F}}$ of $\mathbb{F}$ and for each integer $n \geq 1$, denote by $\mathbb{F}_n$ the unique extension of $\mathbb{F}$ of degree n contained in $\overline{\mathbb{F}}$. The function

$$\zeta(X, T) = \exp\left(\sum_{n=1}^{\infty} |X(\mathbb{F}_n)| \frac{T^n}{n}\right) \tag{12}$$

is called the zeta function of X. For example, if $X = \mathbb{P}^1$ is the projective line, then $|X(\mathbb{F}_n)| = q^n + 1$, and an easy calculation shows that

$$\zeta(\mathbb{P}^1, T) = \frac{1}{(1-T)(1-qT)}.$$

More generally, if $X = \mathbb{P}^n$, writing projective space as a stratified union of affine spaces of smaller dimension, we find that

$$\zeta(\mathbb{P}^n, T) = \frac{1}{(1-T)(1-qT)(1-q^2T)\cdots(1-q^nT)}.$$

Weil made three conjectures about this class of zeta functions. First, he conjectured that it is a rational function of T. More precisely, he conjectured that there are polynomials $P_i(X, T) \in \mathbb{Z}[T]$ for $0 \leq i \leq 2\dim X$ so that

$$\zeta(X, T) = \prod_{i=0}^{2\dim X} P_i(X, T)^{(-1)^{(i+1)}} \tag{13}$$

with $P_0(T) = (1-T)$ and $P_{2\dim X}(T) = (1 - q^{\dim X} T)$.

He also conjectured that the P_i satisfy a functional equation relating $P_i(X, T)$ to $P_{2\dim X-i}(X, (q^{b_i}T^{a_i}))$ where a_i and b_i are integers determined by the topology of X. Finally, and perhaps most strikingly, he conjectured that the polynomials P_i can be factored as

$$P_i(T) = \prod_{j=1}^{2b_i}(1 - \alpha_{i,j}T) \tag{14}$$

and the $\alpha_{i,j}$ are complex numbers satisfying

$$|\alpha_{i,j}| = q^{i/2} \tag{15}$$

for all relevant values of j. This third conjecture is called the Riemann hypothesis for X.

To understand this terminology, we have to rely on another (equivalent) definition of the zeta function. Let us set (see [182]) for a complex number s,

$$\zeta(X, s) = \prod_{P}\left(1 - \frac{1}{N(P)^s}\right)^{-1}$$

where the product is over the closed points P of X, and $N(P)$ is the order of the residue field of P. This is the geometric analogue of the Riemann zeta function. We assume that $\Re(s)$ is sufficiently large so that this product converges. Then, we have the relation

$$\zeta(X, s) = Z\big(X, q^{-s}\big)$$

where q is the cardinality of $\mathbb{F}$. In this case, (15) and (14) show that the zeros of $\zeta(X, s)$ satisfy $\Re(s) = 1/2, 3/2, \ldots, \dim X - \frac{1}{2}$ and the poles satisfy $\Re(s) = 0, 1, \ldots, \dim X$. In the sense that (15) allows us to locate the zeros and poles of $\zeta(X, s)$ on certain vertical lines, it can be said to be an analogue of the Riemann hypothesis.

The original motivation of Weil in proposing his conjectures was to address the problem of counting the number of points on varieties over finite fields. If we logarithmically differentiate relations (12), (13) and (14), we deduce that

$$\big|X(\mathbb{F}_n)\big| = \sum_{i=0}^{2\dim X}\sum_{j=1}^{2b_i}(-1)^i\alpha_{i,j}^n$$

and using (15), this becomes

$$\big|X(\mathbb{F}_n)\big| = q^{(\dim X)n}\big\{1 + \mathbf{O}_X\big(q^{-n/2}\big)\big\}$$

where the constant implicit in the error term depends on X.

2 The Case of Elliptic Curves

Weil himself proved his conjectures in the case that X is a curve (that is $\dim X = 1$). In this case, the expectation is that

$$Z(X,T) = \frac{P(T)}{(1-T)(1-qT)} \tag{16}$$

where $P(T) \in \mathbb{Z}[T]$, and the degree of $P(T)$ should be $2g$ where g is the genus of the curve X.

The case of elliptic curves is of particular interest. Here we have $g = 1$, and so $P(T)$ is a quadratic polynomial. Understanding this case provides insight into Weil's intuition that there should be a relationship between the topology of X and the number of solutions of various congruences (number of points on X).

Over the complex numbers, an elliptic curve E is a one-dimensional torus

$$E(\mathbb{C}) = \mathbb{C}/L. \tag{17}$$

Here $L \subset \mathbb{C}$ is a lattice, in other words, $L \simeq \mathbb{Z} \oplus \mathbb{Z}$. We see that for any $1 \leq n \in \mathbb{Z}$, we have

$$E[n] = \frac{1}{n}L/L \simeq \mathbb{Z}/n\mathbb{Z} \oplus \mathbb{Z}/n\mathbb{Z}$$

where $E[n]$ denotes the set of points R in $E(\mathbb{C})$ satisfying $nR = 0$. The subgroups $E[n]$ form a directed system under the partial ordering on $\mathbb{Z}$ given by divisibility, with natural morphisms

$$E[n] \longrightarrow E[m]$$

whenever $m|n$ given by

$$R \mapsto \frac{n}{m}R.$$

The inverse limit under these maps is then seen to be

$$L \otimes \hat{\mathbb{Z}} \simeq \prod_{\ell} (L \otimes \mathbb{Z}_\ell).$$

In particular, for each prime ℓ, the ℓ-primary component is denoted $T_\ell(E)$ and is called the Tate module of E. We see that as abelian groups

$$T_\ell(E) \simeq L \otimes \mathbb{Z}_\ell \simeq \mathbb{Z}_\ell \oplus \mathbb{Z}_\ell.$$

For elliptic curves over more general fields F, one no longer has the uniformization given by (17). However, the groups $E[n]$ still make sense, as does $T_\ell(E)$. Moreover, if ℓ is different from the characteristic of F, we still have

$$T_\ell(E) \simeq \mathbb{Z}_\ell \oplus \mathbb{Z}_\ell$$

as abelian groups. But if F is not algebraically closed, there is a new structure that emerges. If we choose an algebraic closure $\overline{F}$ of F, then the $E[n]$ and $T_\ell(E)$ are not only abelian groups, but modules for the natural action of $\mathrm{Gal}(\overline{F}/F)$. Thus, we have a representation

$$\mathrm{Gal}(\overline{F}/F) \longrightarrow \mathrm{Aut}_{\mathbb{Z}_\ell}\big(T_\ell(E)\big) \simeq GL_2(\mathbb{Z}_\ell).$$

In particular, if $F = \mathbb{F}$ is a finite field of q elements, we have the Frobenius automorphism $\sigma \in \mathrm{Gal}(\overline{F}/F)$ which is given by

$$\sigma(x) = x^q.$$

For $(\ell, q) = 1$, we thus get a matrix in $GL_2(\mathbb{Z}_\ell)$. If we denote by $P_\ell(T)$ the characteristic polynomial of this matrix, it is a fact that

$$P_\ell(T) = P(T), \tag{18}$$

where $P(T)$ is given by (16). In particular, $P_\ell(T)$ has coefficients in $\mathbb{Z}$ (instead of just $\mathbb{Z}_\ell$) and is independent of ℓ.

If we now consider an elliptic curve E over a number field F, the above constructions still make sense, and we can speak of the Tate module $T_\ell(E)$. We again have the family of Galois representations

$$\mathrm{Gal}(\overline{F}/F) \longrightarrow \mathrm{Aut}_{\mathbb{Z}_\ell}\big(T_\ell(E)\big) \simeq GL_2(\mathbb{Z}_\ell) \tag{19}$$

giving the action of the Galois group on points on E of ℓ-power order.

If v is a prime of F, we may consider the reduction E_v of E modulo v. Naively, this just means that we reduce the coefficients of an equation defining E modulo v. Apart from a finite number of primes v of F, we have that E_v is again an elliptic curve, and it is defined over the residue field $\mathbb{F}$, which is a field of cardinality equal to the norm $\mathbb{N}v$ of v.

As in the previous paragraph, we may consider (now for ℓ not dividing $\mathbb{N}v$), the Tate module $T_\ell(E_v)$. On the other hand, we may consider the original $T_\ell(E)$ but now viewing it as a module restricted to just the decomposition group at v. It is a theorem that under the assumption that E_v is an elliptic curve, the inertia subgroup at v acts trivially on $T_\ell(E)$, and thus it may also be viewed as a module for $\mathrm{Gal}(\overline{\mathbb{F}}/\mathbb{F})$. (The converse of this theorem is also true. Thus, if the inertia subgroup at v acts trivially on $T_\ell(E)$, then the reduction E_v is again an elliptic curve.)

Now we have two modules for $\mathrm{Gal}(\overline{\mathbb{F}}/\mathbb{F})$, namely $T_\ell(E)$ and $T_\ell(E_v)$. It turns out that they are isomorphic. In particular, we may speak of the characteristic polynomial of Frobenius at v acting on $T_\ell(E)$, and it is the same $P_\ell(T) = P(T)$ that we found in (18).

Considering again the global Galois representation (19), we now have a family of ℓ-adic representations which have the property that for any prime v of the number field F at which the inertia subgroup acts trivially, the characteristic polynomial of Frobenius at v makes sense, and if we denote it by $P_\ell(T, v)$, then it is an element of $\mathbb{Z}[T]$ and is independent of ℓ.

Moreover, $P_\ell(T, v)$ is the numerator of the zeta function of an elliptic curve E_v over a finite field. It is thus of the form

$$P_\ell(T, v) = 1 - a_v T + (Nv)T^2$$

where $a_v \in \mathbb{Z}$, and applying the Riemann hypothesis for E_v, it follows that

$$|a_v| \leq 2(Nv)^{\frac{1}{2}}. \tag{20}$$

We may also use this information to construct a formal product

$$\prod_v \left(1 - a_v(Nv)^{-s} + (Nv)^{1-2s}\right)^{-1}.$$

The product only ranges over primes v for which E_v is an elliptic curve. Using estimate (20), we see that the formal product actually converges absolutely for $Re(s) > 3/2$. Up to finitely many factors (namely those at primes v for which E_v is not an elliptic curve), this function is called the L-function associated to E and denoted $L(E, s)$. By analogy with the definition in the first section, the zeta function of E is given by

$$\zeta(E, s) = \zeta(s)\zeta(1 - s)/L(E, s).$$

3 ℓ-Adic Representations

More generally, let us consider a number field F and a family M_ℓ of finite-dimensional $\mathbb{Z}_\ell$ modules which carry an action of $\mathrm{Gal}(\overline{F}/F)$. We say that the representation (or equivalently, the module M_ℓ)

$$\mathrm{Gal}(\overline{F}/F) \longrightarrow \mathrm{Aut}_{\mathbb{Z}_\ell}(M_\ell)$$

is unramified at a prime v of F if the inertia subgroup at v acts trivially. We say that the family $\{M_\ell\}$ is unramified at v if every element M_ℓ of the family is unramified at v. Finally, we say that $\{M_\ell\}$ is a compatible family of ℓ-adic representations if there is a finite set S of primes of F such that for all primes $v \notin S$, the family is unramified at v and for any prime ℓ that is relatively prime to

$$Nv \prod_{w \in S} Nw,$$

the characteristic polynomial $P_\ell(T, v)$ is independent of ℓ and has coefficients in $\mathbb{Z}$.

There are many such families that arise from algebraic geometry. The example of elliptic curves was seen in the previous section. Now the question is whether there is such a family with $F = \mathbb{Q}$ and unramified at all primes, and with the property that for $p \neq \ell$,

$$P_\ell(T, p) = 1 - \tau(p)T + p^{11}T^2.$$

If there were such a representation, then there would be the hope that the Ramanujan conjecture could be put into a context where the Weil conjectures would apply. In that case, it might even be possible to deduce the Ramanujan conjecture from the Weil conjectures.

4 Elliptic Curves and Modular Forms

An example may illustrate what we can expect. Writing

$$q\prod_{n=1}^{\infty}(1-q^n)^{24} = q\prod_{n=1}^{\infty}(1-q^n)^2\prod_{n=1}^{\infty}(1-q^n)^{22}$$

we see that

$$\sum_{n=1}^{\infty}\tau(n)q^n \equiv q\prod_{n=1}^{\infty}(1-q^n)^2\prod_{n=1}^{\infty}(1-q^{11n})^2 \pmod{11}.$$

Using the notation of the chapter on the Ramanujan τ function, the right-hand side of the congruence can be written as $\eta(z)^2\eta(11z)^2$ (where as usual, we are writing $q = e^{2\pi i z}$). Expanding the product, and writing

$$\eta(z)^2\eta(11z)^2 = \sum_{n=1}^{\infty} a_n q^n$$

we have the following table of values:

n	a_n	n	a_n	n	a_n
1	1	6	2	11	−1
2	−2	7	−2	12	−2
3	−1	8	0	13	4
4	2	9	−2	14	4
5	1	10	−2	15	−1

The function $f(z) = \eta(z)^2\eta(11z)^2$ is an example of a modular form. It is a holomorphic function defined for complex numbers z with the property that $\Im(z) > 0$. Moreover, it satisfies a functional equation with respect to certain fractional linear transformation. Namely, if we denote

$$\Gamma_0(N) = \left\{\begin{pmatrix} a & b \\ c & d\end{pmatrix}, a, b, c, d \in \mathbb{Z},\ ad - bc = 1, N|c\right\}$$

then

$$f\left(\frac{az+b}{cz+d}\right) = (cz+d)^2 f(z).$$

Since

$$\frac{d}{dz}\left(\frac{az+b}{cz+d}\right) = (cz+d)^{-2}$$

it follows that $f(z)\,dz$ is invariant under the action of $\Gamma_0(N)$.

Now we define a map

$$\Phi_f : \Gamma_0(N) \longrightarrow \mathbb{C}$$

as follows. Fix a point $z_0 \in \mathbb{C}$ with $\Im(z_0) > 0$. Set

$$\Phi_f(\gamma) = \int_{z_0}^{\gamma z_0} f(z)\,dz.$$

The integral on the right does not depend on z_0. Indeed, we have

$$\int_{z_1}^{\gamma z_1} = \int_{z_1}^{z_0} + \int_{z_0}^{\gamma z_0} + \int_{\gamma z_0}^{\gamma z_1}.$$

By a change of variables and the invariance of $f(z)\,dz$ under the action of γ, we see that

$$\int_{\gamma z_0}^{\gamma z_1} f(z)\,dz = \int_{z_0}^{z_1} f(z)\,dz = -\int_{z_1}^{z_0} f(z)\,dz.$$

Thus,

$$\int_{z_1}^{\gamma z_1} f(z)\,dz = \int_{z_0}^{\gamma z_0} f(z)\,dz.$$

Note also that as the upper half-plane is simply connected, the value of the integral does not depend on the path chosen from z_0 to γz_0.

The map Φ_f is in fact a homomorphism since for $\gamma_1, \gamma_2 \in \Gamma_0(N)$, we have

$$\Phi_f(\gamma_1\gamma_2) = \int_{z_0}^{\gamma_2 z_0} f(z)\,dz + \int_{\gamma_2 z_0}^{\gamma_1\gamma_2 z_0} f(z)\,dz.$$

Again by a change of variables and using the invariance of $f(z)\,dz$ under γ_2, we see that this is equal to

$$\Phi_f(\gamma_1\gamma_2) = \Phi_f(\gamma_1) + \Phi_f(\gamma_2).$$

The elements in $\Gamma_0(N)$ can be classified into three types depending on their trace. Thus an element

$$\gamma = \begin{pmatrix} a & b \\ c & d \end{pmatrix}$$

is called elliptic if $|\operatorname{trace}(\gamma)| = |a + d| < 2$, hyperbolic if $|\operatorname{trace}(\gamma)| > 2$ and parabolic of $|\operatorname{trace}(\gamma)| = 2$.

Proposition 4.1 *If $\gamma \in \Gamma_0(N)$ is elliptic or parabolic, then $\Phi_f(\gamma) = 0$.*

Proof If γ is elliptic, then it has finite order. Since $\Phi_f(1) = 0$, and Φ_f is a homomorphism, it follows that $\Phi_f(\gamma) = 0$ for any element of finite order. If γ is parabolic, then $a + d = \pm 2$. Note that $-I \in \Gamma_0(N)$. Moreover, as it is of order 2, by the comment above, $\Phi_f(-I) = 0$. Hence, multiplying γ by $-I$ if necessary, we may suppose that $a + d = 2$. Suppose first that $c = 0$. Then

$$\gamma = \begin{pmatrix} 1 & r \\ 0 & 1 \end{pmatrix}.$$

Then

$$\Phi_f(\gamma) = \int_{z_0}^{z_0+r} f(z)\, dz.$$

As f is a cusp form, its constant term at the cusp $i\infty$ vanishes, and so

$$\int_{z_0}^{z_0+1} f(z)\, dz = 0.$$

Iterating this, we deduce that $\Phi_f(\gamma) = 0$. Now suppose that $c \neq 0$. As γ is parabolic, it fixes the rational point $(a - 1)/c$. Choose a matrix $\beta \in \mathrm{SL}_2(\mathbb{Z})$ such that β maps this point to $i\infty$. Then

$$\gamma_1 = \beta\gamma\beta^{-1}$$

fixes $i\infty$. We have

$$\int_{z_0}^{\gamma z_0} f(z)\, dz = \int_{z_0}^{\beta^{-1}\gamma_1\beta z_0} f(z)\, dz.$$

The right-hand side is equal to

$$\int_{\beta z_0}^{\gamma_1\beta z_0} \left(f|\beta^{-1}\right)(z)\, dz = \int_{\beta z_0}^{\beta z_0+r} \left(f|\beta^{-1}\right)(z)\, dz.$$

And this is zero as f is a cusp form and the constant term of $f|\beta^{-1}$ vanishes. This proves the result.

Let us set

$$\Lambda_f = \left\{\Phi_f(\gamma) : \gamma \in \Gamma_0(N)\right\}.$$

It is a theorem of Eichler and Shimura that if f has integer Fourier coefficients, then Λ_f is a lattice in $\mathbb{C}$. (In general, if the Fourier coefficients lie in a number field, we would consider a higher-dimensional version of Λ_f which would give rise to a lattice in $\mathbb{C}^g$ for some $g > 1$.)

Using this lattice, one may then consider the torus $\mathbb{C}/\Lambda_f$ which is an elliptic curve. At first, it is a curve defined over the complex numbers. However, the theory of Eichler and Shimura shows that it in fact has a model defined over the rationals $\mathbb{Q}$.

As an example, consider $\Gamma_0(11)$. It is generated by the three elements

$$T = \begin{pmatrix} 1 & 1 \\ 0 & 1 \end{pmatrix}, \qquad V_4 = \begin{pmatrix} 8 & 1 \\ -33 & -4 \end{pmatrix}, \qquad V_6 = \begin{pmatrix} 9 & 1 \\ -55 & -6 \end{pmatrix}.$$

Since T is parabolic, $\Phi_f(T) = 0$. If we set $\omega_1 = \Phi_f(V_4)$ and $\omega_2 = \Phi_f(V_6)$, then Λ_f is the lattice spanned by ω_1 and ω_2. In fact, the corresponding elliptic curve is given by the equation

$$y^2 + y = x^3 - x^2 - 10x - 20$$

and is denoted $X_0(11)$.

As discussed earlier, we have a compatible family of ℓ-adic Galois representations

$$\mathrm{Gal}(\overline{\mathbb{Q}}/\mathbb{Q}) \longrightarrow \mathrm{Aut}_{\mathbb{Z}_\ell}\big(T_\ell\big(X_0(11)\big)\big) \simeq GL_2(\mathbb{Z}_\ell)$$

which are unramified outside 11. Moreover, recall that we have set

$$f(z) = \sum_{n=1}^{\infty} a_n q^n.$$

Then for any prime $p \neq 11$, the characteristic polynomial of the Frobenius automorphism at p is

$$1 - a_p T + pT^2.$$

If we "reduce" the 11-adic representation modulo 11, that is, if we compose it with the natural map

$$GL_2(\mathbb{Z}_{11}) \longrightarrow GL_2(\mathbb{Z}/11\mathbb{Z})$$

then the characteristic polynomial of the Frobenius automorphism at p is

$$1 - \big(a_p \pmod{11}\big)T + \big(p \pmod{11}\big)T^2.$$

Now by the congruence given at the start of this section, it follows that this is the same as

$$1 - \big(\tau(p) \pmod{11}\big)T + \big(p \pmod{11}\big)T^2.$$

It is a theorem of Shimura that the map

$$\mathrm{Gal}(\overline{\mathbb{Q}}/\mathbb{Q}) \longrightarrow GL_2(\mathbb{Z}/11\mathbb{Z})$$

is surjective. It follows from an application of the Chebotarev density theorem that for any residue classes $a, b \in \mathbb{Z}/11\mathbb{Z}$ with $b \neq 0$, we can find infinitely many primes (in fact a positive density set of primes) p for which

$$\tau(p) \equiv a \pmod{11}$$

and

$$p \equiv b \pmod{11}.$$

Thus, there cannot exist any special congruences for the τ function modulo 11.

We see from this that the theory of ℓ-adic representations gives us a tool to "understand" congruences satisfied by the τ function. However, the construction described in this section only gives us a "mod ℓ"-representation and that too, only for one value of ℓ, namely $\ell = 11$. The question now becomes where one should look for the general family of representations.

Since the motivation in this chapter is Ramanujan's conjecture on the size of $\tau(p)$, we have to look for these representations in algebraic geometry. □

5 Geometric Realization of Modular Forms of Higher Weight

We begin by giving a brief description of how modular forms of higher weight occur in the cohomology of certain algebraic varieties. Let Γ denote a subgroup of finite index of $SL_2(\mathbb{Z})$. It acts by fractional linear transformations on the upper half-plane:

$$\begin{pmatrix} a & b \\ c & d \end{pmatrix} \cdot z = \frac{az+b}{cz+d}.$$

Consider now the product $\mathcal{H} \times \mathbb{C}$ of the upper half-plane and the complex line. There is an action of $\Gamma \rtimes \mathbb{Z}^2$ on this product by

$$\left(\begin{pmatrix} a & b \\ c & d \end{pmatrix}, (m,n) \right) \cdot (z, w) = \left(\frac{az+b}{cz+d}, (cz+d)^{-1}(w+mz+n) \right).$$

We consider the quotient $(\Gamma \rtimes \mathbb{Z}^2)\backslash(\mathcal{H} \times \mathbb{C})$. This is in fact an open algebraic surface, and there is a compactification B_Γ of it called the 'universal elliptic curve'. The terminology comes from the fact that it is a fibre variety over the modular curve. The modular curve itself parameterizes elliptic curves with additional structure, and the fibre at a point of the modular curve 'is' the elliptic curve corresponding to that point.

Now, let us consider holomorphic 2-forms on B_Γ. Let f be a holomorphic modular form of weight 3 for Γ and consider the 2-form $f(z)\,dz \wedge dw$ on $\mathcal{H} \times \mathbb{C}$. It is invariant under the action of $\Gamma \rtimes \mathbb{Z}^2$. Indeed, an element

$$\left(\begin{pmatrix} a & b \\ c & d \end{pmatrix}, (m,n) \right)$$

acts on f by

$$f\left(\frac{az+b}{cz+d}\right)d\left(\frac{az+b}{cz+d}\right)\wedge d\left(\frac{w+mz+n}{cz+d}\right)$$

which is

$$(cz+d)^3 f(z)(cz+d)^{-2}\,dz\wedge(cz+d)^{-1}\,dw = f(z)\,dz\wedge dw.$$

Because of this invariance, $f(z)\,dz\wedge dw$ gives rise to a holomorphic 2-form on the quotient and on the surface B_Γ. In fact, it is true that all holomorphic 2-forms on B_Γ can be obtained in this way in the sense that there is an isomorphism of the space of cusp forms on Γ of weight 3 and holomorphic 2-forms on B_Γ.

One can go further and analyze the entire Hodge decomposition of $H^2(B_\Gamma,\mathbb{C})$. We have

$$H^2(B_\Gamma,\mathbb{C}) = H^0(B_\Gamma,\Omega^2)\oplus\overline{H^0(B_\Gamma,\Omega^2)}\oplus H^{1,1}.$$

The above discussion identifies the first two pieces. The third piece, $H^{1,1}$ turns out to consist entirely of rational (and hence, by Lefschetz, algebraic) classes. This is a result of Shioda [191].

In general, in the construction of B_Γ, if we replace $\mathbb{C}$ with $\mathbb{C}^{k-2}$, one gets what is known as a Sato variety $B_\Gamma^{(k)}$. This is a variety of dimension $k-1$, fibred over the modular curve as before. The fibre at a given point of the modular curve is the $(k-2)$nd power of 'the' elliptic curve corresponding to that point. Again, one can show that the space of holomorphic $(k-1)$ forms on $B_\Gamma^{(k)}$ is isomorphic to the complex vector space of weight k cusp forms for Γ. In general, we do not know much about the field of definition of $B_\Gamma^{(k)}$. However, if Γ is a congruence subgroup, then we know from the general theory of Shimura and others that it is defined over a number field.

Now let us restrict our attention to Γ a congruence subgroup, say $\Gamma_0(N)$. All of the discussion above also has an ℓ-adic analogue. In this case, the complex cohomology referred to above is replaced with ℓ-adic cohomology. This theory is a vast generalization of the theory of the Tate module discussed earlier. In fact, the first ℓ-adic homology of an elliptic curve is its ℓ-adic Tate module.

In general, one considers the ℓ-adic cohomology of $B_\Gamma^{(k)}$ (or rather, a model of this variety defined over the rationals), and one finds that $H_\ell^{k-1}(B_\Gamma^{(k)})$ contains a subspace S_ℓ (say) of dimension $2\dim S_k(\Gamma)$. Moreover, $H_\ell^{k-1}(B_\Gamma^{(k)})$ has two important actions on it. Firstly, it is a module for the action of $\mathrm{Gal}(\overline{\mathbb{Q}}/\mathbb{Q})$, and secondly, it is a module for the Hecke algebra, an algebra of operators referred to in an earlier chapter. The subspace S_ℓ is invariant under both of these actions. Diagonalizing the Hecke action, we get a decomposition

$$S_\ell = \oplus_f S_\ell(f)$$

into submodules, where each $S_\ell(f)$ is a rank two module over $K_f[\mathrm{Gal}(\overline{\mathbb{Q}}/\mathbb{Q})]$, and K_f is a certain number field (the field generated by the Fourier coefficients of f).

These are the Galois representations attached to modular forms of higher weight whose existence had been conjectured by Serre and constructed by Deligne [38].

Moreover, the Galois action is unramified outside primes dividing ℓN, and if $p \nmid \ell N$, then the characteristic polynomial of the Frobenius conjugacy class at p is

$$\prod \left(1 - a_f(p)^\sigma T + p^{k-1} T^2\right)$$

the product ranging over embeddings $\sigma : K_f \hookrightarrow \overline{\mathbb{Q}_\ell}$. If we factor the quadratic polynomials above, we get complex numbers $\pi_f(p)^\sigma$ such that

$$a_f(p)^\sigma = \pi_f(p)^\sigma + \overline{\pi_f(p)^\sigma}$$

and

$$\pi_f(p)^\sigma \overline{\pi_f(p)^\sigma} = p^{k-1}.$$

It is the reduction of the variety $B_\Gamma^{(k)}$ that one applies the Weil conjectures to. By the above remark about the characteristic polynomial of Frobenius, we see that when $B_\Gamma^{(k)}$ is seen as a variety over $\mathbb{F}_p$, in the action of Frobenius on $H_\ell^{k-1}(B_\Gamma^{(k)} \times \mathbb{F}_p)$, amongst the eigenvalues of Frobenius will be the $\{\pi_f(p)\}$ and by the Weil conjectures, these numbers are all of complex absolute value $p^{(k-1)/2}$. This is, in brief, how the Ramanujan conjecture is deduced from the Weil conjectures. The reader may find the survey article [91] also helpful.

Chapter 4
The Ramanujan Conjecture from $GL(2)$ to $GL(n)$

1 The Ramanujan Conjectures

In retrospect, one sees a progression of ideas from Ramanujan's work on the τ-function to Hecke's theory of modular forms, and then moving to the representation theoretic perspective, we see this progression linking itself to theories of Harish-Chandra and Langlands. Ramanujan's conjecture now sits as a special case of a more comprehensive conjecture in the Langlands program. The survey article [141] provides an excellent introduction to this chain of ideas, and we recommend this to the reader. But the origins of the chain go back to the 1916 paper of Ramanujan which acted as a catalyst for this development.

In his epic paper of 1916, Ramanujan [162] considered the function

$$\Delta(z) = q\prod_{n=1}^{\infty}(1-q^n)^{24}, \quad q = e^{2\pi i z}.$$

As we have seen, expanding the right-hand side as a power series in q defines the celebrated Ramanujan τ-function:

$$q\prod_{n=1}^{\infty}(1-q^n)^{24} = \sum_{n=1}^{\infty}\tau(n)q^n.$$

In his paper, Ramanujan made three conjectures concerning $\tau(n)$:

(1) $\tau(mn) = \tau(m)\tau(n)$, for $(m,n) = 1$,
(2) for p prime and $a \geq 1$, $\tau(p^{a+1}) = \tau(p)\tau(p^a) - p^{11}\tau(p^{a-1})$,
(3) $|\tau(p)| \leq 2p^{11/2}$.

The first two conjectures were proved a year later by Mordell [126]. His proof was reproduced by Hardy in his 1936 lectures on Ramanujan's work delivered at Harvard University. Almost twenty years after Ramanujan's paper, Hecke [77] published the conceptual framework from which (1) and (2) emerge as special cases of a larger theory, now called Hecke theory. Despite heroic efforts to settle conjecture (3) by such luminaries as Hardy, Kloosterman, Rankin and Selberg, we had to

DOI 10.1007/978-81-322-0770-2_4,

wait until 1974 when Deligne proved it as a consequence of his proof of the Weil conjectures.

We outline the proofs of these conjectures. As mentioned in the introduction to Chap. 3, the essential property of $\Delta(z)$ is that it is a modular form of weight 12 for the full modular group $SL_2(\mathbb{Z})$, which is the group of 2×2 matrices with integer entries and determinant 1. This means that for z in the upper half-plane $\mathfrak{h}$, we have

$$\Delta\left(\frac{az+b}{cz+d}\right) = (cz+d)^{12}\Delta(z) \quad \forall \begin{pmatrix} a & b \\ c & d \end{pmatrix} \in SL_2(\mathbb{Z}). \tag{21}$$

The set of holomorphic functions $f : \mathfrak{h} \to \mathbb{C}$ vanishing at infinity and satisfying the modular relation

$$f\left(\frac{az+b}{cz+d}\right) = (cz+d)^k f(z) \quad \forall \begin{pmatrix} a & b \\ c & d \end{pmatrix} \in SL_2(\mathbb{Z})$$

forms a finite-dimensional vector space S_k over $\mathbb{C}$. Since $-I \in SL_2(\mathbb{Z})$, the modular relation shows that $S_k = 0$ for k odd. For k even, one can show without too much difficulty [183] that $\dim S_2 = 0$ and $\dim S_k = [k/12]$ if $k \not\equiv 2 \pmod{12}$. Thus, S_{12} is one-dimensional and spanned by Δ. In fact, 12 is the first value of k for which $S_k \neq 0$.

Hecke discovered a family of linear transformations T_n of the finite-dimensional vector space S_k. These are now called Hecke operators, though they are nascent in Mordell's work. To describe these, it is convenient to introduce the following notation.

Let $GL_2^+(\mathbb{R})$ denote the group of 2×2 matrices with real entries and positive determinant. It is easy to see that $GL_2^+(\mathbb{R})$ acts on $\mathfrak{h}$ via the usual fractional linear transformations:

$$\gamma z := \frac{az+b}{cz+d}, \quad \gamma = \begin{pmatrix} a & b \\ c & d \end{pmatrix} \in GL_2^+(\mathbb{R}).$$

Given $f \in S_k$, we define the "slash operator" via

$$(f|\gamma)(z) := (\det \gamma)^{k/2}(cz+d)^{-k} f(\gamma z).$$

Thus, $f \in S_k$ if and only if $f|\gamma = f$ for all $\gamma \in SL_2(\mathbb{Z})$.

Hecke observed that $SL_2(\mathbb{Z})$ acts on the set M_n of matrices with integer entries and determinant n. Indeed, with $\Gamma = SL_2(\mathbb{Z})$, we have

$$\Gamma M_n = M_n \Gamma = M_n.$$

Consequently, we can decompose M_n as a disjoint union of Γ-orbits. In fact, a simple application of the division algorithm shows that

$$M_n = \coprod_{ad=n, d>0} \coprod_{b=0}^{d-1} \Gamma \begin{pmatrix} a & b \\ 0 & d \end{pmatrix}.$$

Thus, the finite set of matrices

$$\begin{pmatrix} a & b \\ 0 & d \end{pmatrix}, \quad ad = n, d > 0, \quad 0 \leq b \leq d-1,$$

comprises a complete set of orbit representatives for this action. Hecke defines

$$T_n(f) = n^{k/2-1} \sum_{ad=n, d>0} \sum_{b=0}^{d-1} f \Big| \begin{pmatrix} a & b \\ 0 & d \end{pmatrix}. \tag{22}$$

Since $\Gamma M_n = M_n \Gamma = M_n$, it is easily seen that for any $\gamma \in \Gamma$, we have

$$T_n(f)|\gamma = T_n(f).$$

Noting that $T_n(f)$ also vanishes at infinity whenever f does, shows that $T_n(f) \in S_k$. In other words, for each natural number n, we have a linear transformation $T_n : S_k \to S_k$. These transformations are called Hecke operators. Since

$$\begin{pmatrix} 1 & 1 \\ 0 & 1 \end{pmatrix} \in SL_2(\mathbb{Z}),$$

every $f \in S_k$ has a Fourier expansion

$$f(z) = \sum_{m=1}^{\infty} \lambda_f(m) e^{2\pi i m z}.$$

The expansion starts from 1 since the function is holomorphic and vanishes at infinity. From (22) one can routinely compute the Fourier expansion of $T_n(f)$. Indeed,

$$f \Big| \begin{pmatrix} a & b \\ 0 & d \end{pmatrix} (z) = n^{k/2} d^{-k} \sum_{m=1}^{\infty} \lambda_f(m) e^{2\pi i m (az+b)/d}.$$

Inserting this into the inner sum of (22) and applying the elementary fact

$$\sum_{b=0}^{d-1} e^{2\pi i m b/d} = 0,$$

unless $d|m$, in which case it is d, we obtain that

$$T_n(f) = n^{k-1} \sum_{ad=n, d>0} d^{1-k} \left(\sum_{m=1, d|m}^{\infty} \lambda_f(m) e^{2\pi i m a z/d} \right).$$

Writing $m = dr$, we can re-write the inner sum as

$$\sum_{r=1}^{\infty} \lambda_f(dr) e^{2\pi i r a z}.$$

Collecting the terms with $ra = m$, we see that

$$T_n(f) = n^{k-1} \sum_{m=1}^{\infty} \left(\sum_{ad=n, ar=m} \lambda_f(dr) d^{k-1} \right) e^{2\pi i m z}.$$

The coefficient can be re-written as

$$\sum_{a|n,m} \lambda_f\left(nm/a^2\right)(n/a)^{1-k}$$

so that

$$T_n(f) = \sum_{m=1}^{\infty} \left(\sum_{a|n,m} \lambda_f\left(nm/a^2\right) a^{k-1} \right) e^{2\pi i m z}. \tag{23}$$

In the case of $f = \Delta$, we see immediately that $T_n(\Delta) = c_n \Delta$ since S_{12} is one-dimensional. The constant c_n is computed easily by comparing the first Fourier coefficient of both sides. We obtain

$$T_n(\Delta) = \tau(n)\Delta. \tag{24}$$

If $(m,n) = 1$, then computing the mth Fourier coefficient of the left-hand side of (24) using (23) shows that it is $\tau(mn)$. Comparing this with the mth Fourier coefficient of the right-hand side of (24), we obtain $\tau(mn) = \tau(m)\tau(n)$ whenever $(m,n) = 1$, which is Ramanujan's first conjecture.

The second conjecture also follows directly from (23). Indeed, for p prime,

$$T_p(\Delta) = \tau(p)\Delta$$

so that by comparing the p^ath Fourier coefficient of both sides leads to

$$\tau\left(p^{a+1}\right) + p^{11}\tau\left(p^{a-1}\right) = \tau(p)\tau\left(p^a\right),$$

which is Ramanujan's second conjecture.

The significance of Ramanujan's second conjecture is that the power series

$$\sum_{a=0}^{\infty} \tau\left(p^a\right) x^a$$

is a rational function and can be written as

$$\left(1 - \tau(p)x + p^{11}x^2\right)^{-1}.$$

With regard to the third conjecture, there is a simple argument that leads to the estimate $\tau(p) = O(p^6)$. Though this was first proved by Hardy, his proof was more elaborate. We need only make two observations. The first is that a fundamental domain D for the action of $SL_2(\mathbb{Z})$ on the upper half plane can be taken to be the standard one, namely, $|z| \geq 1$, $|\Re(z)| \leq 1/2$. In other words, every element in the upper half-plane is $SL_2(\mathbb{Z})$-equivalent to some element of D, and no two interior elements of D are $SL_2(\mathbb{Z})$-equivalent. The second observation is that

$$y^{12}\left|\Delta(z)\right|^2, \quad z = x + iy$$

is invariant under the action of $SL_2(\mathbb{Z})$ as is easily checked using the modular transformation for Δ. From the Fourier expansion of $\Delta(z)$ we see that it has exponential decay at infinity, and therefore it is bounded (say by K) in the fundamental domain D. Since

$$\Delta(x+iy) = \sum_{n=1}^{\infty} \tau(n) e^{-2\pi ny} e^{2\pi inx}$$

we can calculate the nth Fourier coefficient by

$$\tau(n)e^{-2\pi ny} = \int_{-1/2}^{1/2} \Delta(x+iy)e^{-2\pi inx}\, dx.$$

Since $|\Delta(z)| \leq K/y^6$, we deduce

$$\left|\tau(n)\right|e^{-2\pi ny} \leq K/y^6.$$

Choosing $y = 1/n$ gives the estimate $\tau(n) = O(n^6)$.

With Ramanujan, we can consider the Dirichlet series

$$L_\Delta(s) := \sum_{n=1}^{\infty} \frac{\tau(n)}{n^s}$$

which by our modest estimate of $\tau(n)$ converges absolutely for $\Re(s) > 7$. By Ramanujan's conjecture (1) and (2), we can write this as an Euler product:

$$\sum_{n=1}^{\infty} \frac{\tau(n)}{n^s} = \prod_p \left(1 - \frac{\tau(p)}{p^s} + \frac{1}{p^{2s-11}}\right)^{-1}.$$

The modular relation (21) implies that

$$\Delta(-1/iy) = y^{12}\Delta(iy)$$

and this can be used to derive an analytic continuation and functional equation for $L_\Delta(s)$. Apparently, this was first done by Wilton in 1928. This is a major theme of Hecke theory developed systematically, again, much later in the 1930s.

Seated in the comfort of the modern era, it is easy for us to be surprised that some obvious developments did not take place earlier or with greater rapidity. We must however understand that much of this work seems to be against the background of two world wars and there was no one giving us the "bigger picture". In his book,

Lang [106] wrote, "Partly because of Hitler and the war, which almost annihilated the German school of mathematics, and partly because of the great success of certain algebraic methods of Artin, Hasse, and Deuring, modular forms and functions were to a large extent ignored by most mathematicians for about thirty years after the 1930s. Eichler, Maass, Petersson and Rankin were the main exceptions."

This was the case with even Hecke theory. Much more is true about the Hecke operators. A straightforward calculation using (23) shows that $T_n T_m = T_m T_n$ for all m, n. It was only in 1939 that Hecke's student, Hans Petersson introduced an inner product on S_k by defining

$$(f, g) = \int_D y^k f(z)\overline{g(z)} \frac{dx\,dy}{y^2}.$$

He was able to show that

$$\big(T_n(f), g\big) = \big(f, T_n(g)\big) \tag{25}$$

so that the T_ns are a commutative family of Hermitian operators. Already in the proof of (25), it was clear that one needed to move to "higher levels" and not just confine oneself to $SL_2(\mathbb{Z})$. Petersson's theorem allowed him to prove that S_k has a basis of eigenfunctions for all of the Hecke operators T_n since (by a familiar theorem of linear algebra) the T_ns could be simultaneously diagonalized.

The theory generalizing the first two conjectures of Ramanujan to other congruence subgroups of $SL_2(\mathbb{Z})$ was slow in maturing. It was only in 1970, when Atkin and Lehner [12] published their fundamental paper that the first part of the theory reached completion.

As for the third conjecture, this had several strands of development. The first strand was largely a development of analytic methods of attack beginning with Kloosterman [98], who, in 1927, applied the circle method and at the same time devised a new way of handling the major arcs, thereby discovering the celebrated Kloosterman sum (about which more will be said below). Kloosterman was able to show that $\tau(p) = O(p^{6-1/8})$ by his method.

In the early 1930s, Salie and Davenport (independently) refined earlier methods and were able to show $\tau(p) = O(p^{6-1/6})$. In the late 1930s, Hardy's doctoral student, R.A. Rankin [169] developed a new method using Eisenstein series that enabled one to get better estimates on $\tau(n)$. This new method came to be known as Rankin's method (or sometimes, the Rankin–Selberg method, since Selberg arrived at it independently). This method (which we will discuss later in this chapter) gives $\tau(p) = O(p^{6-1/5})$.

Yet another analytic method using the theory of Poincaré series was developed by Selberg. This method allows one to get an explicit formula for $\tau(n)$ that involves Kloosterman sums and Bessel functions. Selberg [180] showed that this explicit formula leads to the improved estimate $O(p^{6-1/4})$.

Selberg's work led to many further and fundamental developments, most notable of which is the Selberg trace formula. In a special case, this becomes the Eichler–Selberg trace formula which gives a formula for the trace of the nth Hecke operator acting on the space of cusp forms in terms of class numbers of imaginary quadratic fields. In particular, it relates the Ramanujan τ-function to such sums of class numbers.

Though these methods did not settle Ramanujan's third conjecture, they initiated new and hidden connections with other parts of mathematics. The most spectacular is the 1965 paper of Selberg [180] where he discusses the spectral theory of the Laplace operator and connects it with estimates for $\tau(n)$. In the same paper, he formulates the now celebrated Selberg eigenvalue conjecture of which we shall say more later.

At the end of his paper, Selberg [180] wrote, "It seems most likely that little new may be expected along these lines in the near future, and that a proof of, for instance, the Ramanujan conjecture is more likely to result from future developments in algebraic geometry."

Indeed, if one looks at the Ramanujan conjecture for general Hecke eigenforms, then in 1954, Eichler, Shimura and Igusa solved it for the case $k = 2$ by noting that if we consider

$$\Gamma_0(N) = \left\{ \gamma = \begin{pmatrix} a & b \\ c & d \end{pmatrix} \in SL_2(\mathbb{Z}),\ c \equiv 0 \pmod N \right\}$$

then $\Gamma_0(N)\backslash\mathfrak{h}$, suitably compactified, has the structure of a Riemann surface and consequently, can be identified as the $\mathbb{C}$-locus of a curve. This curve, denoted $X_0(N)$, is called the modular curve of level N and is defined over the integers. One can therefore consider the zeta function of this curve over the finite field of p elements. The "Riemann hypothesis" for this zeta function turns out to be equivalent to the analogue of the Ramanujan conjecture for weight 2 Hecke eigenforms.

In the early 1960s, it was strongly believed that the Ramanujan conjecture would be proved similarly, not from the "Riemann hypothesis" for curves, but rather from considering higher-dimensional varieties and as a consequence of the Weil conjectures. In fact, Eichler, Shimura, Kuga and Ihara constructed a variety that should have worked but did not quite work since it was not compact. Deligne showed how to compactify their variety and finally, resolved Ramanujan's conjecture. This was the geometric attack on Ramanujan's conjecture, described briefly in the previous chapter.

Yet another analytic method connected to representation theory was outlined by Langlands [108]. We sketch this method below. But first, we have to discuss another aspect of the Ramanujan conjecture, and this is the analogue in the context of Maass wave forms.

2 Maass Forms of Weight Zero

The Ramanujan conjecture and its generalization by Petersson opened the way to a better understanding of what it meant in the bigger picture. Surely, Ramanujan knew that this held in greater generality since in his 1916 paper, he formulated it for other modular forms as well. This laid the foundation for a conceptual enlightenment. In the 1960s, Jacquet and Langlands [86] reworked Hecke's theory for general automorphic forms on $GL(2)$. Indeed, once the general notion of an automorphic form on $GL(n)$ was precisely formulated, it soon became clear that classical modular forms comprise only half of the theory of automorphic forms on $GL(2)$. There was another side to the story, and this is the theory of Maass wave forms. The Ramanujan–Petersson conjecture for holomorphic Hecke eigenforms could be extended to cover Maass wave forms also, and more generally to automorphic forms on $GL(n)$. This became known as the Ramanujan conjecture for $GL(n)$ and in this generality represents a major unsolved problem in the general theory today. Its solution would have significant consequences in number theory and related areas.

The conceptual insight gained by reformulating the Ramanujan conjecture for $GL(n)$ in this way led to a larger understanding of another celebrated conjecture, namely, the Selberg eigenvalue conjecture, originally formulated in the context of Maass wave forms. In fact, in the adelic formulation, the Ramanujan conjecture "at the infinite prime" becomes the Selberg eigenvalue conjecture. We review this theory briefly below.

Indeed, if we consider modular forms without the holomorphy condition but insist that our function is an eigenfunction of the non-Euclidean Laplacian

$$\Delta = -y^2\left(\frac{\partial^2}{\partial x^2} + \frac{\partial^2}{\partial y^2}\right)$$

we arrive at the notion of real analytic forms. We may write such a function as a function of the variables x, y, and since $f(z+1) = f(z)$, we have

$$f(x, y) = \sum_n a_n(f, y)e^{2\pi inx}.$$

Suppose that $\Delta f = \lambda f$. This gives us a condition on the coefficients $a_n(f, y)$, namely that they satisfy

$$-y^2\frac{d^2}{dy^2}a_n(f, y) = \left(\lambda - 4\pi^2 n^2 y^2\right)a_n(f, y).$$

This is a Bessel-type differential equation with two solutions. But we only take the one which gives rise to a convergent series above. One can renormalize and show that

$$f(x, y) = a_0(f)y^s + a_0'(f)y^{1-s} + \sum_{n\neq 0} a_n(f)\sqrt{y}K_{ir}\left(2\pi|n|y\right)e^{2\pi inx}$$

where

$$K_{ir}(y) = \frac{1}{2}\int_{-\infty}^{\infty} e^{-y\cosh t - irt}\,dt$$

with $\lambda = 1/4 + r^2$. Maass [117] proved that the series

$$\sum_{n \neq 0} \frac{a_n(f)}{|n|^s}$$

extends to a meromorphic function for all $s \in \mathbb{C}$ analytic everywhere except possibly at $s = 0$ and $s = 1$, and satisfies a functional equation.

The analog of the Ramanujan conjecture in this context is that for any $\epsilon > 0$, $a_n(f) = O(n^\epsilon)$. The Selberg conjecture is that $\lambda \geq 1/4$, or equivalently, r is real and not purely imaginary.

In his 1970 paper, Langlands [108] indicated how the Ramanujan conjecture would follow if a family of L-functions discussed below admit an analytic continuation to a fixed half-plane. At the same time, he interpreted the Selberg conjecture as the Ramanujan conjecture "at infinity" and thus put both conjectures on an equal conceptual footing. (This adelic viewpoint had roots in earlier work of Satake.) We will outline this argument of Langlands below.

At the moment, the best general estimate for $GL(2)$ are due to Kim and Shahidi [97], who showed that $a_n = O(n^{7/64})$, and Kim and Sarnak [95], who showed that $\lambda \geq 0.238$.

3 Upper Bound for Fourier Coefficients and Eigenvalue Estimates

In [108], Langlands also introduced symmetric power L-functions and conjectured that they extend to analytic functions for all values of s. He outlined how this conjecture would lead to a proof of the extended Ramanujan conjecture and the Selberg eigenvalue conjecture. The general theory of symmetric power L-functions has come to play a central role in number theory and representation theory of automorphic forms. We sketch the argument of Langlands below.

We begin with the elementary observation in analytic number theory

$$e^{-1/x} = \frac{1}{2\pi i} \int_{2-i\infty}^{2+i\infty} \Gamma(s) x^s \, ds$$

which is easily demonstrated by contour integration and Stirling's formula. Hence,

$$\sum_{n=1}^{\infty} a_n e^{-n/x} = \frac{1}{2\pi i} \int_{(2)} \Gamma(s) f(s) x^s \, ds$$

where

$$f(s) = \sum_{n=1}^{\infty} a_n / n^s.$$

Now suppose that $a_n \geq 0$ and $f(s)$ is absolutely convergent for $\Re(s) \geq 1+\epsilon$. Moving the line of integration to $\Re(s) = 1+\epsilon$ gives

$$\sum_{n=1}^{\infty} a_n e^{-n/x} = O\left(x^{1+\epsilon}\right).$$

Thus, for any individual term in the sum, we have

$$a_n e^{-n/x} = O\left(x^{1+\epsilon}\right).$$

Choosing $x = n$, we deduce that $a_n = O(n^{1+\epsilon})$.

If we let π be an automorphic representation on $GL(2)$ with local parameters, α_p, β_p, then one can give an intuitive description of the symmetric power L-functions attached to π in the following way.

Consider, with r_m denoting the m-th symmetric power of π,

$$L_m(s) := L(s,\pi,r_m) = \prod_p \prod_{j=1}^{m} \left(1 - \frac{\alpha_p^{m-j}\beta_p^j}{p^s}\right)^{-1}$$

where we are ignoring the finitely many Euler factors that need to be modified corresponding to the ramified factors.

Consider the L-function

$$L(s,\pi,r_m \otimes \overline{r}_m) = \prod_{k \leq 2m, k \text{ odd}} L(s,\pi,r_k).$$

The proof of this identity is equivalent to the trigonometric identity

$$1 + \frac{\sin 3\theta}{\sin\theta} + \frac{\sin 5\theta}{\sin\theta} + \cdots + \frac{\sin(2m-1)\theta}{\sin\theta} = \left(\frac{\sin m\theta}{\sin\theta}\right)^2$$

which is easily proved by induction and left as an exercise for the reader.

Thus, the series $L(s,\pi,r_m \otimes \overline{r}_m)$ is a Dirichlet series with non-negative coefficients. If we now suppose that for each $m \geq 1$, $L(s,\pi,r_m)$ is analytic for $\Re(s) \geq 1+\epsilon$, then its pth coefficient (for p prime) is $O(p^{1+\epsilon})$ by the argument given above. But the pth coefficient is easily calculated to be

$$\left|\sum_{j=1}^{m} \alpha_p^{m-j}\beta_p^j\right|^2.$$

Moreover, $|\alpha_p\beta_p| = 1$, so that if the Ramanujan conjecture is false, one of these has absolute value greater than 1. Without any loss of generality, suppose it is α_p. Then, in the above summation, α_p^m dominates the sum, so we deduce

$$|\alpha_p|^{2m} = O\left(p^{1+\epsilon}\right).$$

Taking $2m$th roots, we obtain

$$\alpha_p = O\big(p^{(1+\epsilon)/2m}\big),$$

and letting m tend to infinity, we obtain $\alpha_p = O(1)$, which is the Ramanujan conjecture.

Using the fact that each of the L-functions $L(s, \pi, r_m)$ satisfies a functional equation, one can improve the estimate using a classical result of Chandrasekharan and Narasimhan [32]. This result says that if $a_n \geq 0$ and $f(s) = \sum_{n=1}^{\infty} a_n/n^s$ is convergent in some half-plane, has analytic continuation for all s except for a pole at $s = 1$ of order k and satisfies a functional equation of the form

$$Q^s \Delta(s) f(s) = w Q^{1-s} \Delta(1-s) f(1-s)$$

where $Q > 0$ and

$$\Delta(s) = \prod_i \Gamma(\alpha_i s + \beta_i)$$

then

$$\sum_{n \leq x} a_n = x P_{k-1}(\log x) + O\big(x^{\frac{2A-1}{2A+1}} \log^{k-1} x\big)$$

where $A = \sum_i \alpha_i$. Taking differences, we deduce that

$$a_n = O\big(n^{\frac{2A-1}{2A+1}} \log^{k-1} n\big).$$

In [129], this result is stated with a typo on page 525. (On lines 3 and 7 of [129], $(2A-1)(2A+1)$ should be $(2A-1)/(2A+1)$ in both instances.) Hardy [67] was aware of this argument, at least for $m = 2$, as is indicated in the tenth of his twelve lectures on Ramanujan's work.

A similar reasoning can be applied to obtain bounds in the Selberg eigenvalue conjecture. If π corresponds to a Maass form with eigenvalue λ, then the Gamma factors in the functional equation of $L(s, \pi, r_m)$ will have the following shape:

$$\Gamma(s, \pi, r_m) = \prod_{j=0}^{m} \Gamma\left(\frac{s - \lambda_j}{2}\right), \quad \lambda_j = i(m - 2j)r, \quad \lambda = \frac{1}{4} + r^2.$$

Using the conjectured analyticity of $L_m(s)$ for all m and this information on the Γ-factor for $L_m(s)$ now gives the Selberg eigenvalue conjecture.

4 Eisenstein Series

It is interesting to note that R.A. Rankin was a doctoral student of G.H. Hardy and had taken up Ramanujan's conjecture for his doctoral thesis in 1933. The thesis was a fundamental advance since it set the stage to what was to become the celebrated Rankin–Selberg method. This method involved an unfolding trick that generalized to the $GL(n)$ setting as was noted by Jacquet, Piatetski-Shapiro and Shalika [87].

We present this method in its simplest setting. The earliest example of a Maass form is given by the Eisenstein series

$$E(z,s)=\pi^{-s}\Gamma(s)\frac{1}{2}\sum_{(m,n)\neq(0,0)}\frac{y^s}{|mz+n|^{2s}}.$$

This series converges for $\Re(s)>1$, and we clearly have

$$E(\gamma z,s)=E(z,s)$$

for all $\gamma\in SL_2(\mathbb{Z})$. In addition, it is easily verified that

$$\Delta E(z,s)=s(1-s)E(z,s)$$

so that $E(z,s)$ is a weight zero Maass form with eigenvalue $s(1-s)$. Since $E(z,s)$ is periodic with period 1, we can derive its Fourier series:

$$E(z,s)=\sum_{r=-\infty}^{\infty}a_r(y,s)e^{2\pi irx}$$

and

$$a_r(y,s)=\int_0^1 E(x+iy,s)e^{-2\pi irx}\,dx.$$

We do the obvious. We insert the series expansion for $E(z,s)$ into the integral and apply Fubini's theorem. First, the contribution to $E(z,s)$ from $m=0$ is

$$\pi^{-s}\Gamma(s)y^s\zeta(2s).$$

This is part of $a_0(y,s)$ but not all of a_0 as we shall see below. Now suppose $m\neq 0$. Since (m,n) and $(-m,-n)$ give the same summand in $E(z,s)$, we may suppose that $m>0$. Thus,

$$a_r(y,s)=\pi^{-s}\Gamma(s)y^s\sum_{m=1}^{\infty}\sum_{n=-\infty}^{\infty}\int_0^1\left[(mx+n)^2+m^2y^2\right]^{-s}e^{-2\pi irx}\,dx.$$

If we put $n=qm+d$ with $0\le d<m$, the sum becomes

$$\sum_{m=1}^{\infty}\sum_{d\bmod m}\int_{-\infty}^{\infty}\left[(mx+d)^2+m^2y^2\right]^{-s}e^{-2\pi irx}\,dx.$$

We change the variable $x = u - d/m$ to get

$$\sum_{m=1}^{\infty} m^{-2s} \int_{-\infty}^{\infty} (u^2 + y^2)^{-s} e^{-2\pi i r u} \left(\sum_{d \bmod m} e^{2\pi i d r/m} \right) du.$$

The innermost sum is zero unless $m|r$ in which case it is m. Thus, the sum becomes

$$\sum_{m|r} m^{1-2s} \int_{-\infty}^{\infty} (u^2 + y^2)^{-s} e^{-2\pi i r u}\, du.$$

If $r = 0$, we get

$$\pi^{-s} \Gamma(s) y^s \zeta(2s-1) \int_{-\infty}^{\infty} (u^2 + y^2)^{-s}\, du$$

which is equal to

$$\pi^{-s} \sqrt{\pi}\, \Gamma(s - 1/2) y^{1-s} \zeta(2s-1).$$

Thus, the constant term (on applying the functional equation for $\zeta(s)$) is equal to

$$a_0(y, s) = \pi^{-s} \Gamma(s) \zeta(2s) y^s + \pi^{s-1} \Gamma(1-s) \zeta(2-2s) y^{1-s}.$$

If $r \neq 0$, then we get

$$a_r(y, s) = 2|r|^{s-1/2} \sigma_{1-2s}(|r|) \sqrt{y} K_{s-1/2}(2\pi |r| y)$$

where

$$\sigma_{1-2s}(r) = \sum_{m|r} m^{1-2s}.$$

One can show that $a_r(y, s) = a_r(y, 1-s)$ and $r^s \sigma_{-2s}(r) = r^{-s} \sigma_{2s}(r)$, from which the functional equation is easily deduced.

5 Eisenstein Series and Non-vanishing of $\zeta(s)$ on $\Re(s) = 1$

We want to indicate a proof of the non-vanishing of $\zeta(s)$ on $\Re(s) = 1$ which uses the theory of Eisenstein series and as a consequence does not use the Euler product of $\zeta(s)$ as most conventional proofs do. The idea was used by Jacquet and Shalika [89] in their general result about the non-vanishing on $\Re(s) = 1$ of automorphic L-functions associated with GL_n.

Recall that

$$E(z, s) = \pi^{-s} \Gamma(s) \frac{1}{2} \sum_{(m,n) \neq (0,0)} \frac{y^s}{|mz + n|^{2s}}.$$

Notice that we may also write this as

$$E(z,s)=\pi^{-s}\Gamma(s)\frac{1}{2}\zeta(2s)\sum_{\gamma\in\Gamma_\infty\backslash\Gamma}\Im(\gamma z)^s$$

where Γ_∞ is the stabilizer of the cusp at infinity.

We have already indicated that

$$\begin{aligned}E(z,s)&=\pi^{-s}\Gamma(s)\zeta(2s)y^s+\pi^{s-1}\Gamma(1-s)\zeta(2-2s)y^{1-s}\\&\quad+\sum_{r\neq 0}|r|^{s-1/2}\sigma_{1-2s}\big(|r|\big)\sqrt{y}K_{s-1/2}\big(2\pi|r|y\big)e^{2\pi irx}\end{aligned}$$

where $\sigma_v(n)=\sum_{d|n}d^v$ and

$$K_s(y)=\frac{1}{2}\int_0^\infty e^{-y(t+t^{-1})/2}t^s\,\frac{dt}{t}.$$

One can prove directly that $K_s(y)=K_{-s}(y)$ and $r^s\sigma_{-2s}(r)=r^s\sigma_{2s}(r)$, which allows us to deduce the functional equation of $E(z,s)$ from its Fourier expansion.

This result lies at the heart of the Langlands–Shahidi method of analytic continuation of Eisenstein series. It is also at the core of the Rankin–Selberg method of analytic continuation discussed in the next section.

Now suppose that $\zeta(1+it_0)=0$ for some t_0 real. Then, $\zeta(1-it_0)=0$ also. We put $s=(1+t_0)/2$ in $E(z,s)$. Then, the constant term vanishes, and we get a Maass cusp form:

$$E\big(z,(1+it_0)/2\big)=4\sqrt{y}\sum_{r=1}^{\infty}r^{it_0/2}\sigma_{-it_0}(r)\cos(2\pi rx)\int_0^\infty e^{-\pi ry(t+t^{-1})}\,\frac{dt}{t^{1-it_0/2}}.$$

Using standard estimates for the integral, one can show that the sum is $O(e^{-cy})$ for some $c>0$. As the constant term of $E(z,(1+it_0)/2)$ is zero, we have a genuine Maass cusp form on our hands.

In particular,

$$\int_0^1 E\big(x+iy,(1+it_0)/2\big)\,dx=0.$$

Multiplying this equation by y^{s-2} and integrating from 0 to ∞, we get

$$\int_0^\infty\int_0^1 E\big(x+iy,(1+it_0)/2\big)y^{s-2}\,dx\,dy=0.$$

Now we use the basic idea that

$$\bigcup_{\gamma\in\Gamma_\infty\backslash\Gamma}\gamma(\Gamma\backslash H)=[0,1]\times[0,\infty],$$

usually referred to as the "unfolding" of the domain of integration. Thus,

$$\sum_{\gamma\in\Gamma_\infty\backslash\Gamma} \int_{\gamma(\Gamma\backslash H)} E\big(z, (1+it_0)/2\big)\Im(z)^s \frac{dx\,dy}{y^2} = 0.$$

As $E(\gamma z, s) = E(z, s)$, we may change variables and get:

$$\begin{aligned} 0 &= \sum_{\gamma\in\Gamma_\infty\backslash\Gamma} \int_{\Gamma\backslash H} E\big(z, (1+it_0)/2\big)\Im(\gamma z)^s \frac{dx\,dy}{y^2} \\ &= \int_{\Gamma\backslash H} E\big(z, (1+it_0)/2\big)E(z, s) \frac{dx\,dy}{y^2} \end{aligned}$$

valid for all $s \in \mathbb{C}$.

From the definition of $E(z, s)$ (or its Fourier expansion) we see that

$$E(z, \bar{s}) = \overline{E(z, s)}.$$

Therefore, putting $s = (1 - it_0)/2$, we get from the penultimate equation:

$$0 = \int_{\Gamma\backslash H} \big|E\big(z, (1+it_0)/2\big)\big|^2 \frac{dx\,dy}{y^2}.$$

Thus, the integrand is identically zero. That is, we have proved that $\zeta(1+it_0) = 0$ implies that

$$E\big(z, (1+it_0)/2\big) \equiv 0.$$

We now show that this is a contradiction. We do this by showing that some Fourier coefficient of $E(z, (1+it_0)/2)$ is non-zero. That is, we need to check

$$\int_0^\infty e^{-\pi r y(u+u^{-1})} \frac{du}{u^{1+it_0}} \neq 0.$$

If we set $u = e^\theta$, we have to show that

$$\int_{-\infty}^\infty e^{-\pi r y(e^\theta+e^{-\theta})-it_0\theta}\, d\theta \neq 0.$$

In other words, it suffices to show that

$$\int_0^\infty e^{-\pi r y(e^\theta+e^{-\theta})} \cos t_0\theta\, d\theta \neq 0.$$

This integral is of the form

$$\int_0^\infty e^{-y(a^\theta+a^{-\theta})} \cos\theta\, d\theta, \quad a > 1.$$

We would like to determine its behaviour as y tends to infinity. To do this, we can apply Laplace's saddle point method: if f has two continuous derivatives, with $f(0)=f'(0)=0$ and $f''(0)>0$, and f is increasing in $[0, A]$, then

$$I(x) := \int_0^A e^{-xf(t)}\,dt \sim \sqrt{\frac{\pi}{2xf''(0)}}$$

as x tends to infinity and provided that $I(x_0)$ exists for some x_0. A slightly generalized version of this says that if g is continuous on $[0, A]$, then

$$\int_0^A g(t)e^{-xf(t)}\,dt \sim g(0)\sqrt{\frac{\pi}{2xf''(0)}}.$$

Now choose $f(t)=a^t+a^{-t}-2$, $g(t)=\cos t$ so that

$$e^{-2x}\int_0^\infty e^{-x(a^\theta+a^{-\theta}-2)}\cos\theta\,d\theta \sim e^{-2x}2\log a\sqrt{\frac{\pi}{x}}$$

from which we see that $E(z,(1+it_0)/2)\not\equiv 0$, as required. This gives the desired contradiction. It is possible to deduce the non-vanishing of the above integrals directly without appealing to Laplace's saddle point method. With some work, it may also be possible to derive a zero-free region for $\zeta(s)$.

6 The Rankin–Selberg L-Function

The unfolding technique employed in the previous section has wider ramifications. It can be used to establish the analytic continuation and functional equation for a large class of L-functions which fall under the umbrella of Rankin–Selberg theory.

Let $F : H \to \mathbb{C}$ be a Γ-invariant function which is of rapid decay (that is, $F(x+iy)=O(y^N)$ for all $N\geq 1$.) Let

$$C(F, y) = \int_0^1 F(x+iy)\,dx, \quad y>0$$

be the constant term of the Fourier expansion. Let

$$L(F, s) = \int_0^\infty C(F, y)y^s\,\frac{dy}{y^2}$$

be the Mellin transform of $C(F, y)$.

Theorem 6.1 *Let $L^*(F,s)=\pi^{-s}\Gamma(s)\zeta(2s)L(F,s)$. Then, $L(F,s)$ has analytic continuation to the whole complex plane, regular everywhere except for a simple pole at $s=1$ with residue equal to*

$$\frac{3}{\pi}\int_{\Gamma\backslash H} F(z)\,dz.$$

The function $L^*(F,s)$ *is regular for all* $s \neq 0, 1$ *and satisfies the functional equation*

$$L^*(F,s) = L^*(F,1-s).$$

Proof The key idea is to use the decomposition described earlier. We have

$$L(F,s) = \int_0^\infty \int_0^1 F(x+iy)y^{s-2}\,dx\,dy.$$

Decomposing the domain of integration as in the "unfolding" technique, this becomes

$$= \sum_{\gamma \in \Gamma_\infty \backslash \Gamma} \int_{\gamma(\Gamma \backslash H)} F(z) y^s \frac{dx\,dy}{y^2}.$$

This can be rewritten as

$$\sum_{\gamma \in \Gamma_\infty \backslash \Gamma} \int_{\Gamma \backslash H} F(\gamma z)\big(\Im(\gamma z)\big)^s \frac{dx\,dy}{y^2} = \sum_{\gamma \in \Gamma_\infty \backslash \Gamma} \int_{\Gamma \backslash H} F(z)\big(\Im(\gamma z)\big)^s \frac{dx\,dy}{y^2}$$

because F is Γ-invariant. Moving the summation inside the integral shows that this is equal to

$$\int_{\Gamma \backslash H} F(z)E(z,s)\frac{dx\,dy}{y^2}.$$

As $E(z,s)$ has analytic continuation and functional equation, we get the same for $L(F,s)$. □

We now give a few examples on how to apply this theorem.

In the special case that f is a cusp form of weight k, we may apply the above result to $F(z) = y^k|f(z)|^2$, which is easily checked to be Γ-invariant.

A straightforward computation shows that the constant term is

$$y^k \sum_{n=1}^\infty |a_n|^2 e^{-4\pi n y}.$$

The Mellin transform of the constant term is

$$\int_0^\infty y^{k+s} \sum_{n=1}^\infty |a_n|^2 e^{-4\pi n y} \frac{dy}{y^2} = (4\pi)^{-s-k+1}\Gamma(s+k-1)\sum_{n=1}^\infty \frac{|a_n|^2}{n^{s+k-1}}.$$

This proves the following:

Theorem 6.2 *Let f be a cusp form of weight k for $SL_2(\mathbb{Z})$. If*

$$f(z) = \sum_{n=1}^{\infty} a_n e^{2\pi i n z}$$

is its Fourier expansion at infinity, then the Dirichlet series

$$\sum_{n=1}^{\infty} \frac{|a_n|^2}{n^s}$$

has a meromorphic continuation to the whole complex plane. In fact, if

$$\psi(s) = \pi^{-2s-k+1} 2^{-2s} \Gamma(s) \Gamma(s+k-1) \zeta(2s) \sum_{n=1}^{\infty} \frac{|a_n|^2}{n^s}$$

then $\psi(s)$ extends to a function which is regular for all $s \in \mathbb{C}$ except at $s = 1$ where it has a simple pole and residue equal to

$$\frac{3}{\pi} \int_{\Gamma \backslash H} y^k |f(z)|^2 \frac{dx\,dy}{y^2} = \frac{3}{\pi}(f, f).$$

Moreover, $\psi(s)$ satisfies the functional equation $\psi(s) = \psi(1-s)$.

If we apply the theorem of Chandrasekharan and Narasimhan [32] mentioned in an earlier section, we deduce that

$$\sum_{n \le x} |a_n|^2 = \frac{3}{\pi}(f, f) x^k + O\left(x^{k-2/5}\right)$$

because twice the sum of the coefficients in the Gamma factors (or equivalently the degree in the sense of Selberg) is equal to 4. By taking a single summand in the sum on the left, we deduce that $a_n = O(n^{k/2-1/5})$. The same technique applied to Maass forms gives us $a_n = O(n^{3/10})$.

If we take f and g to be cusp forms (or even with one of them a cusp form), we consider

$$y^k f(z) \overline{g(z)}$$

which is Γ-invariant. If

$$f(z) = \sum_{n=1}^{\infty} a_n e^{2\pi i n z}$$

and

$$g(z) = \sum_{n=1}^{\infty} b_n e^{2\pi i n z}$$

are the respective Fourier expansions at infinity, then the constant term is easily computed to be equal to

$$y^k \sum_{n=1}^{\infty} a_n \overline{b_n} e^{-4\pi n y}.$$

One could also take forms of different weights k_1 and k_2 and consider

$$y^{(k_1+k_2)/2} f(z)\overline{g(z)}.$$

In the end, applying Theorem 6.1, we deduce that

$$L_{f,g}(s) := \sum_{n=1}^{\infty} \frac{a_n \overline{b_n}}{n^s}$$

admits an analytic continuation to the entire complex plane. If f and g are normalized Hecke eigenforms, then the series has an Euler product. This is essentially a consequence of Ramanujan's identity

$$\sum_{n=0}^{\infty} \left(\frac{z^{n+1}-1}{z-1} \right) \left(\frac{w^{n+1}-1}{w-1} \right) q^n = \frac{1 - zwq^2}{(1-q)(1-zq)(1-wq)(1-zwq)}.$$

A suitably normalized version of this series $L_{f,g}(s)$ (with appropriate Γ-factors, $\zeta(2s)$ and so forth) extends to a function which is regular everywhere except possibly at $s = 1$ where it may have a simple pole with residue equal to

$$\frac{3}{\pi}(f, g).$$

Thus, if f and g are orthogonal to each other, then the normalized series extends to an entire function.

Kronecker's limit formula states that

$$\lim_{s \to 1} \left[E(z, s) - \frac{1}{s-1} \right] = \log(e^{\gamma}/4\pi) - 2\log\left(\sqrt{y}\left|\eta(z)\right|^2\right)$$

where $\eta(z) = q^{1/24} \prod_{n=1}^{\infty} (1 - q^n)$ with $q = e^{2\pi i z}$. If f and g are Hecke eigenforms with π_f, π_g being the associated automorphic representations, the Kronecker limit formula allows us to write down an exact formula for the special value $L(1, \pi_f \otimes \pi_g)$.

7 Poincaré Series for $SL_2(\mathbb{Z})$

The Poincaré series for $SL_2(\mathbb{Z})$ are defined by

$$G_r(z) = \frac{1}{2} \sum_{(c,d)=1} (cz+d)^{-k} e^{2\pi i r \frac{az+b}{cz+d}}$$

where the summation is over all integers c, d with $(c, d) = 1$, and a, b are any integers such that $ad - bc = 1$. Observe that if $r = 0$, this reduces to the classical Eisenstein series $E_k(z)$ (up to a constant). Thus, the Poincaré series are to be viewed as generalizations of Eisenstein series. It is easy to see that the inner summand does not depend on the choice of a solution. Indeed, by the Euclidean algorithm, any other solution for (a, b) has the form $(a + tc, b + td)$, and

$$\frac{(a+tc)z + (b+td)}{cz+d} = \frac{az+b}{cz+d} + t, \quad t \in \mathbb{Z}$$

so that

$$e^{2\pi ir(\frac{az+b}{cz+d}+t)} = e^{2\pi ir(\frac{az+b}{cz+d})}.$$

We can rewrite the series in a more invariant form by setting

$$j(\gamma, z) = cz + d, \quad \gamma = \begin{pmatrix} a & b \\ c & d \end{pmatrix}$$

and then

$$G_r(z) = \sum_{\gamma \in \Gamma_\infty \backslash \Gamma} j(\gamma, z)^{-k} e^{2\pi ir(\gamma z)}.$$

The important thing to note is that $G_r(z)$ is a modular form of weight k. To see this, let $\delta \in \Gamma = SL_2(\mathbb{Z})$. Then,

$$G_r(\delta z) = \sum_{\gamma \in \Gamma_\infty \backslash \Gamma} j(\gamma, \delta z)^{-k} e^{2\pi r(\gamma\delta z)}.$$

Now, we have the so-called cocycle relation

$$j(\gamma\delta, z) = j(\gamma, \delta z) j(\delta, z)$$

as is easily verified, so that

$$j(\gamma, \delta z) = \frac{j(\gamma\delta, z)}{j(\delta, z)}$$

and

$$\begin{aligned} G_r(\delta z) &= j(\delta, z)^k \sum_{\gamma \in \Gamma_\infty \backslash \Gamma} j(\gamma\delta, z)^{-k} e^{2\pi ir(\gamma\delta z)} \\ &= j(\delta, z)^k G_r(z). \end{aligned}$$

Holomorphy is easy to verify using standard tests of complex analysis. In addition, $G_r(i\infty) = 0$ if $r \geq 1$. We conclude that for every $r \geq 1$, $G_r(z)$ is a cusp form of weight k. Thus, Poincaré series give explicit constructions of cusp forms.

For a detailed treatment of this theory, we refer the reader to Rankin's book [171] (especially Chap. 5).

Now let f be any cusp form of weight k. We would like to compute the inner product (f, G_r).

First observe that $e^{2\pi i z} = e^{2\pi i x} \cdot e^{-2\pi y}$ so that

$$\overline{e^{2\pi i z}} = e^{-2\pi i x} \cdot e^{-2\pi y} = e^{-2\pi i (\bar{z})}.$$

Thus,

$$\begin{aligned}
(f, G_r) &= \int_{\Gamma\backslash H} \sum_{\gamma\in\Gamma_\infty\backslash\Gamma} f(z) e^{-2\pi i r \overline{\gamma z}} \overline{(cz+d)}^{-k} y^k \frac{dx\,dy}{y^2} \\
&= \int_{\Gamma\backslash H} \sum_{\Gamma_\infty\backslash\Gamma} (cz+d)^k f(z) e^{-2\pi i r(\overline{\gamma z})} \frac{y^k}{|cz+d|^{2k}} \frac{dx\,dy}{y^2} \\
&= \sum_{\gamma\in\Gamma_\infty\backslash\Gamma} \int_{\Gamma\backslash H} f(\gamma z) \Im(\gamma z)^k e^{-2\pi i r(\overline{\gamma z})} \frac{dx\,dy}{y^2} \\
&= \sum_{\gamma\in\Gamma_\infty\backslash\Gamma} \int_{\gamma(\Gamma\backslash H)} f(z) \Im(z)^k e^{-2\pi i r \bar{z}} \frac{dx\,dy}{y^2} \\
&= \int_0^\infty \int_0^1 f(x+iy) y^k e^{-2\pi i r x} e^{-2\pi r y} \frac{dx\,dy}{y^2}.
\end{aligned}$$

Now from the Fourier expansion of $f(z)$ we have

$$f(z) = \sum_{n=1}^{\infty} a_n e^{2\pi i n x} \cdot e^{-2\pi n y}.$$

We see that the x-integral picks up the rth Fourier coefficient. Thus,

$$(f, G_r) = a_r \int_0^\infty e^{-4\pi r y} y^{k-2}\, dy.$$

By setting $4\pi r y = t$ in the integrand and simplifying, we deduce the following:

Theorem 7.1 *Let f be any cusp form of weight k for Γ. Then,*

$$(f, G_r) = \frac{\Gamma(k-1) a_r}{(4\pi r)^{k-1}}.$$

An important corollary is:

Corollary 7.2 *Every cusp form is a finite linear combination of Poincaré series $G_r(z)$.*

Proof The set of Poincaré series spans a closed subspace in the space of cusp forms. If f is a cusp form not in this space, all of its Fourier coefficients must vanish by the previous theorem. Thus, the orthogonal complement is zero. □

As an example, consider the case $k = 12$. Each of the $G_r(z)$ is a cusp form of weight 12. But any cusp form of weight 12 must be a constant multiple of Δ, Ramanujan's cusp form. Thus,

$$G_r(z) = c_r \Delta(z).$$

What is c_r? By the above theorem,

$$(\Delta, G_r) = \frac{\Gamma(11)\tau(r)}{(4\pi r)^{11}} = c_r(\Delta, \Delta).$$

Hence,

$$\tau(r) = \frac{(4\pi r)^{11}}{10!} \int_{\Gamma\backslash H} y^{12} \Delta(z)\overline{G_r(z)} \frac{dx\,dy}{y^2}$$

which is an interesting formula for the Ramanujan τ-function as an inner product.

8 Fourier Coefficients and Kloosterman Sums

Emanating largely from the work of Petersson [154] in the 1930s and Selberg [179], an explicit formula can be given for the Fourier coefficients of $G_r(z)$. This striking formula involves the Kloosterman sums, and their appearance has opened new connections to the Selberg eigenvalue conjecture as well as applications to classical questions of analytic number theory. We now derive this remarkable formula.

We begin by writing

$$G_r(z) = \sum_{n=1}^{\infty} g_{rn} e^{2\pi i n z}.$$

Then,

$$g_{rn} = \int_0^1 G_r(x) e^{-2\pi i n x}.$$

More precisely, for reasons of convergence, we should consider

$$\int_{i\delta}^{1+i\delta} G_r(z) e^{-2\pi i n z}$$

with $\delta > 0$, but we leave this technical modification to the reader. We have

$$g_{rn} = \frac{1}{2} \sum_{(c,d)=1} \int_0^1 (cx+d)^{-k} e^{2\pi i r\left(\frac{ax+b}{cx+d}\right) - 2\pi i n x}\, dx.$$

Put $cx + d = t$. The argument in the exponential becomes

$$\frac{r}{t}\left(\frac{a}{c}(t-d)+b\right)-\frac{n}{c}(t-d)=\frac{nd+ar}{c}-\frac{nt}{c}-\frac{r}{tc}$$

since $ad - bc = 1$. Thus,

$$g_{rn}=\frac{1}{2}\sum_{c\neq 0}\frac{1}{c}\sum_{\substack{d(\bmod c)\\ ad\equiv 1(\bmod c)}} e^{\frac{2\pi i}{c}(nd+ar)}\int_{-\infty}^{\infty} t^{-k}e^{-\frac{2\pi i}{c}(\frac{r}{t}+nt)}\,dt$$

because

$$\sum_{(c,d)=1}\int_0^1 t^{-k}e^{\frac{2\pi i}{c}(nd+ar-nt)}e^{-\frac{2\pi i r}{t}}\,dt$$

depends only on d (mod c). Writing d as $d_0+(m+1)c$ with varying m, we transform the integral from 0 to 1 into an integral from $-\infty$ to ∞. This integral turns out to be a Bessel function:

$$\int_{-\infty+ci}^{\infty+ci} t^{-k}\exp\left(-\frac{2\pi i}{c}\left(\frac{r}{t}+nt\right)\right)dt=2\pi(n/r)^{(k-1)/2}J_{k-1}(4\pi\sqrt{rn}/c)$$

where

$$J_k(z)=\frac{1}{2\pi i}\int_C t^{-k-1}e^{\frac{z}{2}(t-1/t)}\,dt$$

where C is the unit circle. The sum

$$S(r,n,c):=\sum_{\substack{d(\bmod c)\\ ad\equiv 1(\bmod c)}} e^{\frac{2\pi i}{c}(nd+ar)}$$

is called a Kloosterman sum. Using this notation, we obtain the beautiful formula due to Petersson:

$$g_{rn}=(n/r)^{(k-1)/2}\left\{\delta_{rn}+\pi\sum_{c=1}^{\infty}\frac{S(r,n,c)}{c}J_{k-1}\left(\frac{4\pi\sqrt{rn}}{c}\right)\right\}$$

where δ_{rn} denotes the Kronecker delta function.

We have already noted that the Poincaré series span the space of cusp forms. Thus, to prove the Ramanujan conjecture, it suffices to show that

$$g_{rn}=O\left(n^{\frac{k-1}{2}+\epsilon}\right)$$

for every r. This is tantamount to showing that the expression in parentheses in the above sum is $O(n^{\epsilon})$.

Selberg, using this expression and Weil's estimate for Kloosterman sums:

$$\left|S(r,n,c)\right|\leq d(c)c^{1/2}(r,n,c)^{1/2}$$

as well as the bound

$$J_{k-1}(x) \le A \min\left(x^{k-1}, x^{-1/2}\right)$$

obtained that

$$g_{rn} = O\left(n^{k/2-1/4+\epsilon}\right).$$

Note that this is better than what we obtained earlier by the Rankin–Selberg method. Since the estimate was obtained crudely, Selberg felt that there must be cancellation among the Kloosterman sums. This led him to formulate the following conjecture (which was also arrived at independently by Linnik).

Conjecture (Selberg–Linnik)

$$G(x) := \sum_{c \le x} \frac{S(r,n,c)}{c} = O\left(x^{\epsilon}\right)$$

for $x \ge \gcd(r,n)^{1/2+\epsilon}$ *for any* $\epsilon > 0$.

In his 1965 paper, Selberg stated that this would lead to a proof of the Ramanujan conjecture (for Maass forms as well) but did not indicate a proof. We will indicate below how such a proof can be obtained for the full modular group. The argument is adapted from a paper of R. Murty [129].

Let us first observe that Weil's estimate for Kloosterman sums leads to the estimate

$$G(x) = O\left(x^{1/2} \log x\right)$$

for $(r,n) = 1$. Kuznetsov [102] proved that $G(x) = O(x^{1/6+\epsilon})$, but the O-constant depends on r, n, and so it is not applicable to the estimation of the Fourier coefficients. Let

$$H(x) := \sum_{c \le x} S(r,n,c).$$

By partial summation, the Selberg–Linnik conjecture is equivalent to

$$H(x) = O\left(x^{1+\epsilon}\right).$$

We begin by considering

$$\sum_{c>\sqrt{n}} \frac{S(r,n,c)}{c} J_{k-1}\left(\frac{4\pi\sqrt{rn}}{c}\right)$$
$$= \sum_{c>\sqrt{n}} G(c)\left\{ J_{k-1}\left(\frac{4\pi\sqrt{rn}}{c+1}\right) - J_{k-1}\left(\frac{4\pi\sqrt{rn}}{c}\right)\right\}$$

by partial summation. By the mean value theorem, the expression in parentheses is

$$\frac{4\pi\sqrt{rn}}{c(c+1)} J'_{k-1}(\xi_c)$$

for some $\xi_c \in (4\pi\sqrt{rn}/(c+1), 4\pi\sqrt{rn}/c)$. Using the estimate

$$J'_{k-1}(x) \ll x^{-1/2}$$

we get

$$\sum_{c>\sqrt{rn}} \frac{S(r,n,c)}{c} J_{k-1}\left(\frac{4\pi\sqrt{rn}}{c}\right) \ll n^{1/4} \sum_{c>\sqrt{n}} \frac{|G(c)|}{c^{3/2}} \ll n^{\epsilon}$$

by the Selberg–Linnik conjecture. Thus, we need only consider

$$\sum_{c\leq\sqrt{n}} \frac{S(r,n,c)}{c} J_{k-1}\left(\frac{4\pi\sqrt{rn}}{c}\right).$$

To estimate this, we apply an inductive argument. As there are no cusp forms of weight 10, we have

$$\sum_{c\leq\sqrt{n}} \frac{S(r,n,c)}{c} J_9\left(\frac{4\pi\sqrt{rn}}{c}\right) = O\left(n^{\epsilon}\right).$$

So, if for example, we were trying to establish the conjecture for $k=12$, then it suffices to estimate for $k=10$ the quantity

$$\sum_{c\leq\sqrt{n}} \frac{S(r,n,c)}{c} \left\{ J_{k+1}\left(\frac{4\pi\sqrt{rn}}{c}\right) + J_{k-1}\left(\frac{4\pi\sqrt{rn}}{c}\right)\right\}.$$

By the familiar identity

$$\frac{2kJ_k(x)}{x} = J_{k+1}(x) + J_{k-1}(x)$$

it suffices to estimate

$$\frac{1}{\sqrt{n}} \sum_{c\leq\sqrt{n}} S(r,n,c) J_k\left(\frac{4\pi\sqrt{rn}}{c}\right).$$

Again, by partial summation, we may write this as

$$\frac{1}{\sqrt{n}} \sum_{c\leq\sqrt{n}} H(c) \left\{ J_k\left(\frac{4\pi\sqrt{rn}}{c+1}\right) - J_k\left(\frac{4\pi\sqrt{rn}}{c}\right)\right\}.$$

Again, the expression in the brackets is

$$\frac{4\pi\sqrt{rn}}{c(c+1)}J_k'(\xi_c).$$

Using the estimate

$$J_k'(x) \ll x^{-1/2}$$

as before and the fact that $H(c) = O(c^{1+\epsilon})$, we deduce a final estimate of $O(n^\epsilon)$ as desired. This completes the proof of the fact that the Selberg–Linnik conjecture implies the Ramanujan conjecture (for the full modular group). A similar argument can be applied to higher levels. However, the non-existence of cusp forms of small weight is not guaranteed. In this case, we exploit the fact that we know the Ramanujan conjecture in the weight two case (a result due to Eichler and Shimura).

9 The Kloosterman–Selberg Zeta Function

In order to gain more insight into the Selberg–Linnik conjecture, we will consider (with Selberg [180]) the series

$$Z(r,n,s) = \sum_{c\neq 0} \frac{S(r,n,c)}{|c|^{2s}}.$$

To study this series, Selberg [178] considers the cognate Poincaré series

$$U_n(z,s) = \sum_{\Gamma_\infty\backslash\Gamma} \Im(\gamma z)^s e^{2\pi i n\gamma z}.$$

Clearly, U_n is Γ-invariant. Moreover, if

$$\Delta = -y^2\left(\frac{\partial^2}{\partial x^2} + \frac{\partial^2}{\partial y^2}\right)$$

then

$$\Delta U_n(z,s) = s(1-s)U_n(z,s) + 4\pi n U_n(z,s+1)s.$$

One can show that the Fourier expansion of $U_n(z,s)$ contains $Z(r,n,s)$ in it. This allows us to relate the eigenvalues of Δ with the abscissa of convergence of $Z(r,n,s)$. More precisely,

$$U_n(z,s) = \sum_{m=-\infty}^{\infty} B_n(m,y,s)e^{2\pi i m x}$$

where

$$B_n(m,y,s) = \delta_{nm} y^s e^{-2\pi n y} + \frac{1}{2}\sum_{c\neq 0}\frac{S(m,n,c)}{|c|^{2s}} y^{1-s} \times \int_{-\infty}^{\infty} \exp\left(-2\pi i m y v - \frac{2\pi n}{c^2 y(1-iv)}\right)\frac{dv}{\left(1+v^2\right)^s}.$$

It then turns out that

$$(2\pi\sqrt{nm})^{2s-1}\sum_{c=1}^{\infty}\frac{S(n,m,c)}{|c|^{2s}} = \frac{\sin\pi s}{2}\sum_{j=1}^{\infty}\frac{a_j(n)\overline{a_j(m)}}{\cosh\pi r_j}\Gamma\left(s-\frac{1}{2}+ir_j\right)\Gamma\left(s-\frac{1}{2}-ir_j\right) - \frac{\delta_{nm}}{2\pi}\frac{\Gamma(s)}{\Gamma(1-s)} + \frac{1}{\pi}\int_{-\infty}^{\infty}(n/m)^{ir}\sigma_{2ir}(m)\sigma_{-2ir}(m)\frac{h(r,s)}{|\zeta(1+2ir)|^2}dr$$

where

$$h(r,s) = \frac{\sin\pi s}{2}\Gamma\left(s-\frac{1}{2}+ir\right)\Gamma\left(s-\frac{1}{2}-ir\right)$$

and the $a_j(n)$s are the Fourier coefficients of the Maass form corresponding to the eigenvalue $\lambda_j = 1/4 + r_j^2$. This remarkable formula establishes a striking relationship between the eigenvalues λ_j and the Kloosterman–Selberg zeta function.

10 Rankin–Selberg L-Functions for GL_n

Let $GL_2^+(\mathbb{R})$ be the group of 2×2 matrices with real entries and positive determinant. The upper half-plane can be realized as a symmetric space of $GL_2^+(\mathbb{R})$. More precisely, if Z denotes the subgroup of scalar matrices and $SO(2)$ denotes the special orthogonal group, then the upper half-plane can be realized as the coset space $GL_2^+(\mathbb{R})/ZSO(2)$. Modular forms then can be viewed as functions on $GL_2^+(\mathbb{R})$ that transform appropriately under certain subgroups. Once we view the classical theory from this perspective, it affords a vast generalization. We refer the reader to [36] for details.

For the moment, it will suffice to say that classical Hecke eigenforms correspond to certain representations of $GL_2(\mathbb{A}_{\mathbb{Q}})$ where $\mathbb{A}_{\mathbb{Q}}$ denotes the adele ring of the rational number field. More generally, one can consider cuspidal automorphic representations of $GL_n(\mathbb{A}_Q)$. Such representations π can be decomposed as a restricted tensor product $\pi_\infty \otimes (\otimes' \pi_p)$, and one can associate parameters $\mu_{1,\infty}, \ldots, \mu_{n,\infty}$ to π_∞, and $\alpha_{1,p}, \ldots, \alpha_{n,p}$ called Satake parameters (for all but finitely many primes p). The Ramanujan conjecture for GL_n is the prediction that $|\alpha_{i,p}| = 1$ for all primes p and all $1 \leq i \leq n$. The Selberg eigenvalue conjecture translates into the assertion that $\Re(\mu_{j,\infty}) = 0$ for $1 \leq j \leq n$.

Many of the methods we discussed in the earlier sections can be developed to deal with the higher rank case. We refer the reader to [36] for further details.

With reference to the Rankin–Selberg method, the general theory for GL_n was initiated and developed by Jacquet, Piatetski-Shapiro and Shalika [87], Shahidi [187] and finally completed by Moeglin and Waldspurger [125]. If π_1 and π_2 are cuspidal automorphic representations of GL_m and GL_n of the adele ring over the rationals (say), then the Rankin–Selberg L-function is defined by the Euler product

$$L(s, \pi_1 \otimes \pi_2) = \prod_p L(s, \pi_{1,p} \otimes \pi_{2,p})$$

where for all but finitely many primes p, the Euler factors are given by the formula

$$L(s, \pi_{1,p} \otimes \pi_{2,p}) = \prod_{i,j} \left(1 - \frac{\alpha_{i,p}^{(1)} \alpha_{j,p}^{(2)}}{p^s}\right)^{-1}$$

and

$$L(s, \pi_{r,p}) = \prod_i \left(1 - \frac{\alpha_{i,p}^{(r)}}{p^s}\right)^{-1}$$

for $r = 1, 2$. It is possible to define the Euler factors at all the places so that the final product converges for $\Re(s) > 1$. The completed L-function turns out to be entire unless

$$\pi_2 \simeq \pi_1^v \otimes |\det|^{it}$$

for some real number t, in which case the function is regular everywhere except at $s = 1 - it$ where it has a simple pole.

One can, of course, consider L-functions of higher tensor powers. These L-functions contain finer information about lower rank L-functions, and it would not be an exaggeration to say that the analytic theory is still in formation.

Chapter 5
The Circle Method

1 Introduction

In his early letters to G.H. Hardy, Srinivasa Ramanujan wrote that "the coefficient of x^n in

$$\left(1 - 2x + 2x^4 - \cdots\right)^{-1}$$

is

$$\frac{1}{4n}\left(\cosh \pi\sqrt{n} - \frac{\sinh \pi\sqrt{n}}{\pi\sqrt{n}}\right) + F(\cos \pi\sqrt{n}) + f(\sin \pi\sqrt{n}).$$

I have not written here the forms of F and f as they are very irregular and complicated and their values are very small. Hence, the coefficient is an integer very near to

$$\frac{1}{4n}\left(\cosh \pi\sqrt{n} - \frac{\sinh \pi\sqrt{n}}{\pi\sqrt{n}}\right),$$

and not always the nearest integer, as I hastily wrote to you before." The significance of this passage is that Ramanujan was writing about the explicit determination of the Fourier coefficient of the reciprocal of a modular form of weight $1/2$. We see from this excerpt that he already had some intuition of the circle method even while he was in India and before he met Hardy. Indeed, in his letter, Ramanujan calculated the nth coefficient of the reciprocal of a theta series which is of weight $1/2$. In the case of the partition function, one needs to calculate the nth coefficient of the reciprocal of the Dedekind η-function, which is also a modular form of weight $1/2$. The circle method would become crystallized in their epoch-making paper [71] on the partition function written in 1918. We will make further remarks later on this point.

The idea of the method can be explained very easily. Suppose that we have a set A of numbers and we are interested in counting the number $r_{k,A}(n)$ of ways a natural number n can be written as a sum of k elements in A. It is natural to form

M.R. Murty, V.K. Murty, *The Mathematical Legacy of Srinivasa Ramanujan*,
DOI 10.1007/978-81-322-0770-2_5, © Springer India 2013

the generating function

$$F_A(x) = \sum_{a \in A} x^a$$

and recognize that the coefficient of x^n in the power series expansion of $F_A(x)^k$ is precisely $r_{k,A}(n)$. However, we cannot proceed further unless we have some additional information on the function $F_A(x)$. This is often difficult and in many cases it is unreasonable to expect any further information. If, however, we look at the trigonometric series

$$f_A(\theta) = \sum_{a \in A, a \leq n} e^{2\pi i a \theta},$$

then, by elementary Fourier series, we have

$$r_{k,A}(n) = \int_0^1 f_A(\theta)^k e^{-2\pi i n \theta} \, d\theta.$$

Again, we cannot proceed unless we know something about $f_A(\theta)$. But in this case, we exploit the continuity of f_A and realize that if we know the value of $f_A(a/q)$ for a rational number a/q lying in the unit interval, then we know (by partial summation) the behaviour of $f(\theta)$ in a small neighborhood of a/q. The strategy then is to break up the unit interval (the circle) into "small" intervals around rational numbers (called major arcs) where the behaviour of $f_A(\theta)$ is "known" and a complementary set of intervals (called minor arcs) and expect that the contribution from the major arcs dominates. In other words, one uses an alternate method to deal with the minor arcs to deduce that the contribution is small in comparison with the contribution from major arcs. This often is the difficult part in the application of the method. However, the method is sufficiently powerful that it enables one to make very precise conjectures on the expected behaviour of $r_{k,A}(n)$ in many interesting cases. Indeed, the behaviour of $f(a/q)$ relies on our knowledge of the distribution of the elements of A in residue classes modulo q. For example, in the case that A is the set of prime numbers, $r_{k,A}(n)$ is the number of ways of writing n as a sum of k prime numbers. Then, we have

$$f_A(a/q) = \sum_{p \leq n} e^{2\pi i a p/q} = \sum_{b=0}^{q-1} e^{2\pi i a b/q} \pi(n, q, b),$$

where $\pi(n, q, b)$ is the number of primes $p \equiv b \pmod{q}$ with $p \leq n$. From the theory of classical Dirichlet L-series, one has a great deal of information about $\pi(n, q, b)$, and this information can be injected into the formula above to derive formulas for the number of ways of writing n as a sum of k primes. For instance, in the case of the binary Goldbach problem, the major arc calculation predicts that the number of ways an even number n can be written as a sum of two prime numbers is asymptotic to

$$2C\left(\prod_{p|n,p>2}\frac{p-1}{p-2}\right)\frac{n}{\log^2 n},$$

where C is the "twin prime constant" given by

$$\prod_{p\geq 3}\left(1-\frac{1}{(p-1)^2}\right),$$

and both products are over prime numbers p.

Hardy and Ramanujan developed this strategy to derive an asymptotic formula for the partition function in their epic paper of 1918. After Ramanujan's sudden demise, Hardy and Littlewood developed the method further and applied it to two classical problems, namely, Waring's problem and the Goldbach problem. In this chapter, we will discuss briefly the Hardy–Ramanujan work on the partition function which laid the foundations of the circle method, and then outline how the method can be applied to Waring's problem and the Goldbach problem. In this direction, we take an approach due to Linnik and Hua in our treatment of Waring's problem, where the circle method is needed only at the end. In the case of the Goldbach problem, we essentially follow Hardy and Littlewood in their analysis of the ternary Goldbach problem where they assumed the generalized Riemann hypothesis to get the necessary estimates on the minor arcs.

2 The Partition Function

The function $p(n)$ is the number of ways of partitioning n. For example, the number 4 can be partitioned as $1+1+1+1$, or $1+1+2$, or $2+2$, or $1+3$, or simply 4 so that $p(4)=5$. The reader should note that we do not count the orderings. Thus, the partition $1+1+2$ is the same as $2+1+1$. From the definition it is easy to see that each partition of n can be "factored" as

$$n=k_1+2k_2+3k_3+\cdots+nk_n,$$

where k_i counts the number of times i occurs in the partition. From this observation, we deduce that $p(n)$ has the generating function given by

$$\sum_{n=0}^{\infty}p(n)x^n=\prod_{k=1}^{\infty}(1-x^k)^{-1}.$$

Why is $p(n)$ interesting? Firstly, the function occurs naturally in many places. For instance, if S_n is the symmetric group on n letters, then the conjugacy classes are in one-to-one correspondence with the partitions of n. This observation also leads to an explicit description of the irreducible representations of S_n. Surprisingly, partitions play a fundamental role in the representation theory of general linear groups. They also have a dominant role in combinatorics and theoretical physics.

In 1918, Hardy and Ramanujan discovered, using the circle method, the asymptotic formula

$$p(n) \sim \frac{\exp(\pi\sqrt{2n/3})}{4n\sqrt{3}}$$

as n tends to infinity. In 1937, Rademacher [157] derived the following asymptotic expansion:

$$p(n) = \frac{1}{\pi\sqrt{2}}\sum_{k=1}^{\infty}\sqrt{k}A_k(n)\frac{d}{dn}\left[\frac{\sinh(\frac{\pi}{k}\sqrt{\frac{2}{3}(n-\frac{1}{24})})}{\sqrt{n-\frac{1}{24}}}\right],$$

where

$$A_k(n) = \sum_{0\le m<k;\,(m,k)=1} e^{\pi i[s(m,k)-2nm/k]},$$

and

$$s(b,c) = \frac{1}{4c}\sum_{n=1}^{c-1}\cot\frac{\pi n}{c}\cot\frac{\pi nb}{c}.$$

It seems that Selberg [181] had also arrived at this formula but never published it. He wrote, "In the summer of 1937, I had actually myself been studying number 36 in the Collected Papers of Ramanujan and had arrived at [Rademacher's] formula ... It always seemed strange to me that Hardy and Ramanujan did not end up with this formula ... and I believe firmly that the responsibility for this rests with Hardy."

Recently, Bruinier and Ono [28] discovered a new "exact" formula for $p(n)$. This formula expresses $p(n)$ as a finite sum of special values of a "weak" Maass form evaluated at CM points in the upper half-plane that have discriminant $-24n+1$.

To be precise, let

$$E_2(q) = 1 - 24\sum_{n=1}^{\infty}\sigma(n)q^n, \quad \sigma(n) = \sum_{d|n} d, \quad q = e^{2\pi i z}$$

be the "quasimodular" Eisenstein series of weight two. Let $\eta(z)$ be the classical Dedekind eta function of weight $1/2$. Define

$$f(z) = \frac{E_2(z) - 2E_2(2z) - 3E_2(3z) + 6E_2(6z)}{2\eta(z)^2\eta(2z)^2\eta(3z)^2\eta(6z)^2} = \frac{1}{q} - 10 - 29q - 104q^2 \cdots.$$

One can show that $f(z)$ is a weight -2 meromorphic modular form on $\Gamma_0(6)$. Now let

$$P(z) := -\left(\frac{1}{2\pi i}\frac{d}{dz} + \frac{1}{2\pi y}\right)f(z).$$

This is a weak Maass form of weight zero. It is an eigenfunction of the hyperbolic Laplacian

$$-y^2\left(\frac{\partial^2}{\partial x^2}+\frac{\partial^2}{\partial y^2}\right)$$

with eigenvalue -2. Now consider all positive definite integral binary quadratic forms $Q(x, y) = ax^2 + bxy + cy^2$ with discriminant $b^2 - 4ac = -24n + 1$ and $6|a$. The group $\Gamma_0(6)$ acts on such forms in the obvious way, and we let Q_n be the set of these representatives with $a > 0$, $b \equiv 1 \pmod{12}$. Let

$$\alpha_Q = \frac{-b+\sqrt{1-24n}}{2a}.$$

Then, the theorem of Bruinier and Ono [29] is that

$$p(n) = \frac{1}{24n-1}\sum_{Q\in Q_n} P(\alpha_Q).$$

This formula was announced in early 2011, and upon seeing this, a natural idea that arises is to see if one can derive the Hardy–Ramanujan asymptotic for $p(n)$ from this algebraic formula. This indeed can be done, and the details will appear in a forthcoming paper of M. Dewar and M.R. Murty [42].

As noted by Hardy and Ramanujan, $p(n)$ satisfies the simple recursion formula

$$np(n) = \sum_{h=1}^{n} h \sum_{k\le n/h} p(n-hk). \tag{26}$$

To see this, we simply list all the partitions of n and count up all the numbers in this listing in two ways. The sum of all the numbers is clearly $np(n)$ which represents the left-hand side of (26). On the other hand, for each natural number h with $1 \le h \le n$, we can count how often h occurs in the listing. Indeed, the number of partitions having at least one h is clearly $p(n-h)$. Those having at least two hs is $p(n-2h)$. Thus, the number having exactly one h is

$$p(n-h) - p(n-2h).$$

Thus,

$$\begin{aligned} np(n) &= \sum_{h=1}^{n}\left\{h\big(p(n-h)-p(n-2h)\big)+2h\big(p(n-2h)-p(n-3h)\big)+\cdots\right\} \\ &= \sum_{h=1}^{n} h \sum_{k\le n/h} p(n-hk), \end{aligned}$$

as claimed.

This simple recurrence can be used to derive a weaker result than the Hardy–Ramanujan theorem. In 1942, Erdös [48] indicated how the recursion can actually be used to derive the Hardy–Ramanujan asymptotic formula for $p(n)$. However, he was not able to evaluate the constant $1/4\sqrt{3}$. This was done later by Newman [143] in 1951. Though the proof is elementary, it is by no means simple. We refer the reader to the papers by Erdös and Newman for further details. Here, following Hardy and Ramanujan, we show that the recursion and simple induction can be used to prove that

$$\log p(n) \sim \pi\sqrt{2n/3}. \tag{27}$$

We proceed in two stages. First, we show that

$$p(n) < e^{a\sqrt{n}}, \quad a = \pi\sqrt{2/3}.$$

Second, we show that for every $\epsilon > 0$, there is a constant C_ϵ such that

$$p(n) > \frac{1}{C_\epsilon} e^{(a-\epsilon)\sqrt{n}}.$$

These two inequalities establish (27).

For the first step, we clearly have $p(1) = 1 < e^a$, and we may suppose that $p(m) < e^{a\sqrt{m}}$ has been established for $m < n$. For the recurrence (26), we have

$$np(n) < \sum_{h=1}^{n} \sum_{k=1}^{n/h} h e^{a\sqrt{n-hk}}.$$

We use the elementary inequality

$$(1-x)^u \leq 1 - ux,$$

valid for any $0 < x < 1$ and $u > 0$, to deduce

$$np(n) < \sum_{h=1}^{n} \sum_{k=1}^{n/h} h e^{a\sqrt{n}(1-hk/\sqrt{n})} < e^{a\sqrt{n}} \sum_{k=1}^{n} \sum_{h=1}^{\infty} h e^{-ahk/2\sqrt{n}}.$$

Using the familiar inequality $\sinh x > x$ and

$$\sum_{m=1}^{\infty} m e^{-mx} = \frac{1}{4\sinh^2 \frac{x}{2}} < \frac{1}{x^2},$$

we deduce

$$np(n) < e^{a\sqrt{n}} \sum_{k=1}^{\infty} \frac{4n}{a^2k^2} = \frac{2\pi^2}{3a^2} n e^{a\sqrt{n}},$$

from which the estimate follows. The lower bound is derived similarly.

The central observation in the Hardy–Ramanujan paper is that the generating function

$$\sum_{n=0}^{\infty} p(n)x^n = \prod_{n=1}^{\infty} (1-x^n)^{-1}$$

becomes, upon setting $x = e^{2\pi i\tau}$, related to the Dedekind η-function, which is a modular form of weight $1/2$.

More precisely, if

$$F(x) = \prod_{n=1}^{\infty} (1-x^n)^{-1},$$

setting $x = e^{2\pi i\tau}$, we see that $F(x) = e^{2\pi i\tau/12}/\eta(\tau)$ where

$$\eta(\tau) = q^{1/24} \prod_{n=1}^{\infty} (1-q^n), \quad q = e^{2\pi i\tau},$$

is the Dedekind η-function. Now, η is a modular form of weight $1/2$, and in particular,

$$\eta(-1/\tau) = \sqrt{\tau/i}\,\eta(\tau),$$

so that this translates as

$$F(e^{-2\pi\tau}) = \sqrt{\tau}\, e^{\pi i(1/\tau-\tau)/12} F(e^{-2\pi/\tau}).$$

In other words, if

$$\psi(\tau) = \sqrt{\tau}\exp\left(\frac{\pi}{12}\left(\frac{1}{\tau}-\tau\right)\right),$$

then as τ tends to zero, $e^{-2\pi\tau}$ tends to 1 and $e^{-2\pi/\tau}$ tends to zero, so that $F(e^{-2\pi/\tau})$ tends to 1. Thus, for x sufficiently close to 1, $F(e^{-2\pi\tau})$ is very close to $\psi(\tau)$. It is therefore reasonable to expect that for τ close to zero, $F(e^{-2\pi\tau})$ is approximated by $\psi(\tau)$. By Cauchy's theorem,

$$p(n) = \frac{1}{2\pi i}\int_C \frac{F(x)}{x^{n+1}}\,dx,$$

where C is a circle around $x = 0$ of radius < 1. Equivalently, changing variables, we have

$$p(n) = \int_{-1/2}^{1/2} F(e^{-2\pi\tau})e^{2\pi in\tau}\,d\tau,$$

so that if we insert our approximation for $F(e^{-2\pi\tau})$, we get

$$p(n) \sim \int_{-1/2}^{1/2} \psi(\tau)e^{-2\pi in\tau}\,d\tau.$$

This integral is not too difficult to evaluate and is of "Bessel type." One finds that

$$p(n) \sim \frac{1}{4n\sqrt{3}} e^{a\sqrt{n}}, \quad a = \pi\sqrt{2/3}.$$

Of course, the approximation of $F(e^{2\pi\tau})$ by $\psi(\tau)$ has to be quantified. This is precisely what Hardy and Ramanujan do in their epic paper. The modular transformation property allows one to derive the asymptotic formula for $p(n)$. This is the basic strategy. The details of the paper are not simple. But the idea is.

Shortly after Ramanujan fell ill and returned to India, Hardy and Littlewood recognized the potential of the circle method in treating other problems in number theory. In a series of remarkable papers, they addressed Waring's problem and Goldbach's conjecture. We discuss these in the next two sections as they illustrate the versatility of the method.

3 Waring's Problem

In 1770, Edmund Waring, in his book "Meditationes Algebraicae" made the profound statement (without proof) that *every natural number can be written as a sum of at most four squares, nine cubes, nineteen fourth powers and so on*. More precisely, this observation, called Waring's problem, is stated as follows:

Conjecture (Waring's problem) *For each $k \geq 2$, there exists a positive integer $g = g(k) \geq 2$ such that every natural number n can be written as a sum of $g(k)$ kth powers. That is, for every $n \geq 1$, there exist non-negative integers $x_1, x_2, \ldots, x_g$ such that*

$$n = x_1^k + x_2^k + \cdots + x_g^k.$$

We note here that $g(k)$ is chosen to be the minimal number with the above property. That is, one can find at least one $n \geq 1$ which cannot be written as a sum of $(g(k) - 1)$ kth powers.

In 1909, Hilbert [80] proved that Waring's observation is true. However, his proof only showed that $g(k)$ exists but gave no method to effectively find it or bound it. Thus, we are led to the following questions.

(1) Can we find a precise formula for $g(k)$ for all k?
(2) Can we find a formula for $g(k)$ that works for *sufficiently large values of* k?
(3) Can we determine the asymptotics, lower bounds or upper bounds for $g(k)$?

In 1772, J.A. Euler, the son of L. Euler, conjectured [52] that

$$g(k) = 2^k + \left[\frac{3^k}{2^k}\right] - 2.$$

In 1936, Pillai [156] showed that Euler's conjecture is true, provided that

$$2^k\left\{\left(\frac{3}{2}\right)^k\right\}+\left[\left(\frac{3}{2}\right)^k\right]\leq 2^k.$$

By the work of Mahler [119] in 1956, it is known that there can be at most finitely many values of k for which the above inequality does not hold. It is conjectured that the above inequality holds for all k.

By the celebrated theorem of Lagrange, $g(2) = 4$. In 1909, Wieferich [202] showed $g(3) = 9$. A gap in his proof was filled in later by Kempner [92] in 1919. The fact that $g(4) = 19$ is a recent theorem of Balasubramanian, Deshouillers and Dress [14, 15]. Earlier, Chen showed in 1964 that $g(5) = 37$, and Pillai [155] in 1940 proved that $g(6) = 73$. There are still many open problems in the theory. For instance, it is conjectured that every sufficiently large number can be written as the sum of four cubes.

It is possible to prove the existence of $g(k)$ by using elementary methods. This was first done by Linnik in 1943 using fundamental ideas of Schnirelmann. In this chapter, we outline Linnik's elementary solution of Waring's problem combined with a theorem of Hua on exponential sums. Then, we indicate how to use the circle method to derive an asymptotic formula for the function $r_{g,k}(n)$, the number of ways of writing n as a sum of g kth powers. In this way, the circle method comes in only at the end to enable us to derive the asymptotic formula for the number of such representations.

3.1 Schnirelmann Density

Let $A \subseteq \mathbb{N}$, and for every $n \geq 1$, let $A(n) = \#\{a \in A : a \leq n\}$. We define the *Schnirelmann density* of A, denoted $\delta(A)$ to be

$$\delta(A) := \inf_{n\geq 1} \frac{A(n)}{n}.$$

We observe that $A(n) \geq \delta(A)n$ for all $n \geq 1$. We also observe that $0 \leq \delta(A) \leq 1$ and $\delta(A) = 1$ if and only if $A = \mathbb{N}$.

The Schnirelmann density is different from the *asymptotic density* $\sigma(A)$ defined as

$$\sigma(A) = \lim_{n\to\infty} \frac{A(n)}{n}.$$

While $\sigma(A)$ measures the asymptotic behaviour of $\frac{A(n)}{n}$ for arbitrarily large values of n, the Schnirelmann density $\delta(A)$ is affected by the first few values of n. For example, if $\mathbb{E}$ and $\mathbb{O}$ denote the set of even and odd natural numbers respectively, then $\delta(\mathbb{E}) = 0$ and $\delta(\mathbb{O}) = 1/2$. On the other hand, $\sigma(\mathbb{E}) = \sigma(\mathbb{O}) = 1/2$.

Given two sets A and B of integers, let $A+B$ denote the sumset of A and B, that is, $A+B=\{a+b : a \in A, b \in B\}$. If A and B are subsets of $\mathbb{N}$, let $A \oplus B$ denote the sumset of $A \cup \{0\}$ and $B \cup \{0\}$. That is,

$$A \oplus B := A \cup \{0\} + B \cup \{0\}.$$

The following remarkable theorem was proved by Schnirelmann in 1936:

Theorem 3.1 (Schnirelmann, 1936) *For any two subsets A and B of $\mathbb{N}$,*

$$\delta(A \oplus B) \geq \delta(A) + \delta(B) - \delta(A)\delta(B).$$

Proof Suppose that $A(n) = r$ and the elements $a_i \leq n$ of A are ordered as $1 \leq a_1 < a_2 < a_3 < \cdots < a_r \leq n$. Let

$$B_1 := \{b \in B : b < a_1\},$$

$$B_i := \{b \in B : a_{i-1} + b < a_i\} \quad \text{if } 2 \leq i \leq r$$

and

$$B_{r+1} := \{b \in B : a_r + b \leq n\}.$$

Observe that the sets $\{a_1, a_2, \ldots, a_r\}$ and $A + B_i$ for $1 \leq i \leq r+1$ are disjoint subsets of $(A \oplus B)$, and each element in these sets is $\leq n$. For notational convenience, let us define $B(0) = 0$. We have

$$\begin{aligned}(A \oplus B)(n) &\geq A(n) + \sum_{i=1}^{r+1} \#B_i \\ &\geq A(n) + B(a_1 - 1) + \sum_{i=2}^{r} B(a_i - a_{i-1} - 1) + B(n - a_r).\end{aligned}$$

Combining the above inequality with the property that $B(n) \geq \delta(B)n$, we get that for every $n \geq 1$,

$$\begin{aligned}(A \oplus B)(n) &\geq A(n) + \delta(B)\left\{(a_1 - 1) + \sum_{i=2}^{r}(a_i - a_{i-1} - 1) + (n - a_r)\right\} \\ &= A(n) + \delta(B)(n - r) \\ &= A(n) + \delta(B)\big(n - A(n)\big) \\ &= A(n)\big(1 - \delta(B)\big) + \delta(B)n \\ &\geq \delta(A)n\big(1 - \delta(B)\big) + \delta(B)n \\ &= n\big(\delta(A) + \delta(B) - \delta(A)\delta(B)\big).\end{aligned}$$

This proves the theorem. □

A more general version of Schnirelmann's theorem can be stated as follows:

Theorem 3.2 *For* $A_1, A_2, \ldots, A_t \subseteq \mathbb{N}$,

$$\delta\left(\bigoplus_{i=1}^{t} A_i\right) \geq 1 - \prod_{i=1}^{t}\big(1 - \delta(A_i)\big).$$

Proof We have already proved this theorem for $t = 2$. A simple inductive exercise proves it for all $t \geq 2$. □

For any $m \in \mathbb{N}$ and $A \subseteq \mathbb{N}$, we denote

$$mA := \bigoplus_{i=1}^{m} A.$$

Lemma 3.3 *If* $\delta(B) > 1/2$ *for some* $B \subseteq \mathbb{N}$, *then* $\delta(2B) = 1$. *In other words,* $2B = \mathbb{N}$.

Proof Let $n \in \mathbb{N}$. We will show that $n \in 2B$. If $n \in B$, then we are done. If $n \notin B$, let $B_n = \{b \in B : b < n\}$ and $B_n' = \{n - b : b \in B_n\}$. Clearly, $\#B_n = \#B_n' = B(n)$, and $B_n \cup B_n' \subseteq \{1, 2, \ldots, n\}$. Thus, $\#(B_n \cup B_n') \leq n$.

Since $\delta(B) > 1/2$, we get

$$\#B_n = B(n) = \#B_n' > \frac{n}{2}.$$

Let us assume that B_n and B_n' are disjoint. This implies $n < \#(B_n \cup B_n')$, which contradicts the fact that $\#(B_n \cup B_n') \leq n$. Hence, our assumption is false, and B_n and B_n' are not disjoint. In other words, there exist $b_1, b_2 < n \in B$ such that $b_1 = n - b_2$, that is, $b_1 + b_2 = n$. This proves that $n \in 2B$.

This proves the lemma. □

The following theorem of Schnirelmann connects the concept of Schnirelmann density with Waring's problem:

Theorem 3.4 *If* A *is a subset of* $\mathbb{N}$ *such that* $\delta(A) > 0$, *then there exists* $m \in \mathbb{N}$ *such that* $\delta(mA) = 1$.

Proof If $\delta(A) = 1$, we are done. If not, we have $0 < \delta(A) < 1$. Since $0 < 1 - \delta(A) < 1$, we may choose t large enough so that

$$\big(1 - \delta(A)\big)^t < \frac{1}{2}.$$

By Theorem 3.2, we see that

$$\delta(tA) \geq 1 - \big(1 - \delta(A)\big)^t > \frac{1}{2}.$$

Theorem 3.4 follows as a quick application of Lemma 3.3. □

In 1942, Mann [120] proved that Schnirelmann's theorem can be refined to show that $\delta(A \oplus B) \geq \min(\delta(A) + \delta(B), 1)$.

3.2 Schnirelmann Density and Waring's Problem

Schnirelmann introduced these ideas to attack Goldbach's conjecture and indeed, using elementary sieve methods, showed that there is a constant c_0 such that every number can be written as a sum of at most c_0 primes. Many mathematicians have successively improved upon this constant c_0, and at the moment, $c_0 = 7$, a result due to Ramaré [168]. By the same methods, one can show that every even number is the sum of at most six prime numbers. It is remarkable how far such an elementary method can be pushed.

In 1943, Linnik applied Schnirelmann's method to attack Waring's problem. We discuss this now.

Let $k \geq 2$ and $A_k = \{x^k; x \in \mathbb{N}\}$. We observe that

$$\frac{1}{n} \leq \frac{A_k(n)}{n} \leq \frac{n^{1/k}}{n} \quad \text{for every } n \geq 1.$$

Now,

$$\delta(A_k) \leq \sigma(A_k) \leq \lim_{n\to\infty} \frac{n^{1/k}}{n} = 0.$$

Thus, $\delta(A_k) = 0$. In view of Theorem 3.4 of Schnirelmann, if we could show that $\delta(mA_k) > 0$ for some $m \geq 2$, then for some $g = g(k) \geq 1$, $\bigoplus_{i=1}^{g} A_k = \mathbb{N}$. This would solve Waring's problem.

For positive integers g and m, let $r_{g,k}(m)$ denote the number of non-negative integral solutions of the equation $x_1^k + x_2^k + \cdots + x_g^k = m$. Observe that if this equation holds, then $0 \leq x_i \leq m^{1/k}$ for each $1 \leq i \leq g$. Thus,

$$r_{g,k}(m) \leq \left(m^{1/k} + 1\right)^g \ll_g m^{g/k}.$$

The following theorem of Linnik, which we will prove in the next section, shows that we can find some g for which the above estimate for $r_{g,k}(m)$ can be sharpened.

Theorem 3.5 *For any $k \in \mathbb{N}$, there exist $g \in \mathbb{N}$ and a constant $c(k)$ depending only on k such that for all $m \geq 1$,*

$$r_{g,k}(m) \leq c(k) m^{\frac{g}{k} - 1}.$$

With the help of Linnik's theorem, we prove the following theorem:

Theorem 3.6 *For any $k \in \mathbb{N}$, there exists $g \in \mathbb{N}$ such that $\delta(gA_k) > 0$.*

Proof By Theorem 3.5, there exists $g \in \mathbb{N}$ such that

$$\sum_{\substack{m=0 \\ r_{g,k}(m)\neq 0}}^{n} r_{g,k}(m) \leq \sum_{\substack{m=0 \\ r_{g,k}(m)\neq 0}}^{n} c(k)m^{\frac{g}{k}-1} \leq c(k)n^{\frac{g}{k}-1} \sum_{\substack{m=0 \\ r_{g,k}(m)\neq 0}}^{n} 1. \tag{28}$$

We also observe that for each $1 \leq i \leq g$, if

$$0 \leq x_i \leq \frac{n^{1/k}}{g^{1/k}},$$

then,

$$\sum_{i=1}^{g} x_i^k \leq n.$$

Thus,

$$\sum_{\substack{x_1,x_2,\ldots,x_g \\ 0\leq x_i \leq \frac{n^{1/k}}{g^{1/k}}}} 1 \leq \sum_{\substack{m=0 \\ r_{g,k}(m)\neq 0}}^{n} r_{g,k}(m). \tag{29}$$

Observe that

$$\sum_{\substack{x_1,x_2,\ldots,x_g \\ 0\leq x_i \leq \frac{n^{1/k}}{g^{1/k}}}} 1 = \left(\left[\frac{n^{1/k}}{g^{1/k}}\right]+1\right)^g \geq \left(\frac{n^{1/k}}{g^{1/k}}\right)^g$$

and

$$\sum_{\substack{m=0 \\ r_{g,k}(m)\neq 0}}^{n} 1 = (gA_k)(n).$$

Combining these observations with the inequalities in (28) and (29), we get

$$\left(\frac{n^{1/k}}{g^{1/k}}\right)^g \leq c(k)n^{\frac{g}{k}-1}(gA_k)(n) \quad \text{for every } n \geq 1.$$

This implies that there exists a positive constant $C(k) > 0$ such that for every $n \geq 1$,

$$(gA_k)(n) \geq C(k)n.$$

Hence, $\delta(gA_k) > 0$. □

Thus, Linnik's theorem solves Waring's problem. In the next section, we prove Linnik's theorem.

3.3 Proof of Linnik's Theorem

We start this section with a basic lemma on linear equations.

Lemma 3.7 *For a positive integer n, let $q(n)$ denote the number of integer solutions (x_1, x_2, y_1, y_2) of the equation*

$$x_1 y_1 + x_2 y_2 = n \tag{30}$$

such that $|x_i| \le X$ and $|y_i| \le Y$. Then

$$q(0) \ll (XY)^{3/2}$$

and

$$q(n) \ll \left(XY \sum_{d|n} \frac{1}{d} \right) \quad \text{for } n \ge 1.$$

Proof We first consider the case where $n = 0$. Clearly, x_1, x_2 and y_1 can take at most $2X + 1$, $2X + 1$ and $2Y + 1$ values respectively. Once these are chosen, y_2 can take at most one value. Thus,

$$q(0) \le (2X + 1)^2 (2Y + 1) \ll X^2 Y.$$

Similarly, $q(0) \ll XY^2$. Thus,

$$q(0) \ll \min\{X^2 Y, XY^2\} \ll \sqrt{X^2 Y.XY^2} \ll (XY)^{3/2}.$$

We can do better when $n \ne 0$. We assume, without loss of generality, that $X \le Y$. Let $q_1(n)$ be the number of integer solutions to $x_1 y_1 + x_2 y_2 = n$ such that $|x_2| \le |x_1| \le X$ and $|y_i| \le Y$. This ensures that $x_1 \ne 0$. Otherwise, we would get $x_2 = 0$, which implies that $n = 0$.

Let us start by fixing x_1 and x_2 and assume that $(x_1, x_2) = 1$. Given a particular solution (y_1', y_2'), all solutions of Eq. (30) are of the form

$$y_1 = y_1' + t x_2, \qquad y_2 = y_2' - t x_1, \quad t \in \mathbb{Z}.$$

We observe that

$$|t| = \frac{|y_2' - y_2|}{|x_1|} \le \frac{2Y}{|x_1|}.$$

We conclude

$$q_1(n) \le \sum_{1 \le |x_1| \le X} \sum_{|x_2| \le |x_1|} \left(2\frac{2Y}{|x_1|} + 1 \right) \le 5Y \sum_{1 \le |x_1| \le X} \frac{2|x_1| + 1}{|x_1|} \ll XY.$$

Thus, Eq. (30) has $\ll XY$ integer solutions.

If $(x_1, x_2) = d > 1$, Eq. (30) has an integer solution, provided that $d|n$. In this case, we take

$$x_1' - \frac{x_1}{d}, \qquad x_2' = \frac{x_2}{d}.$$

From above, the number of integer solutions to the equation

$$x_1' y_1 + x_2' y_2 = \frac{n}{d}$$

is $\ll XY/d$. Finally, we conclude that

$$q(n) \ll XY \sum_{d|n} \frac{1}{d}.$$

□

From the above lemma we deduce the following:

Lemma 3.8 *Let $f(x)$ be a polynomial of degree 2 with integer coefficients, say, $f(x) = c_2 x^2 + c_1 x + c_0$ with $c_2 = \mathcal{O}(1)$, $c_1 = \mathcal{O}(P)$ and $c_0 = \mathcal{O}(P^2)$. The number of solutions in the variables x_i and y_i such that $0 \leq x_i, y_i \leq P$ for $1 \leq i \leq 4$ to the equation*

$$f(x_1) + f(x_2) + f(x_3) + f(x_4) = f(y_1) + f(y_2) + f(y_3) + f(y_4) \qquad (31)$$

is $\ll P^6$.

Proof We observe that

$$f(x_i) - f(y_i) = (x_i - y_i)\big[c_2(x_i + y_i) + c_1\big].$$

We put $z_i = x_i - y_i$ and $w_i = c_2(x_i + y_i) + c_1$.

The number of solutions of Eq. (31) is less than or equal to the number of solutions of the equation

$$z_1 w_1 + z_2 w_2 = -z_3 w_3 - z_4 w_4,$$

where $z_i \ll P$ and $w_i \ll P$. By Lemma 3.7, we see that for a fixed $n \geq 0$, the number $q(n)$ of solutions of $z_1 w_1 + z_2 w_2 = n$ is

$$\ll P^3 \quad \text{if } n = 0$$

and

$$\ll P^2 \sum_{d|n} \frac{1}{d} \quad \text{if } n \geq 1.$$

Thus, the number of solutions of the equation

$$z_1 w_1 + z_2 w_2 = -z_3 w_3 - z_4 w_4,$$

where $z_i \ll P$ and $w_i \ll P$, is

$$\begin{aligned}\sum_{|n|\ll P^2} q(n)^2 &\ll P^6 + \sum_{1\le n\le cP^2}\left(P^2\sum_{d|n}\frac{1}{d}\right)^2\\ &\ll P^6 + P^4 \sum_{1\le n\le cP^2}\sum_{\substack{d_1|n\\ d_2|n}}\frac{1}{d_1d_2}\\ &\ll P^6 + P^4 \sum_{\substack{1\le d_1\le cP^2\\ 1\le d_2\le cP^2}}\frac{1}{d_1d_2}\frac{P^2}{[d_1,d_2]}\\ &\ll P^6 + P^6 \sum_{\substack{1\le d_1\le cP^2\\ 1\le d_2\le cP^2}}\frac{(d_1,d_2)}{(d_1d_2)^2}\\ &\ll P^6 + P^6\sum_{d_1=1}^{\infty}\sum_{d_2=1}^{\infty}\frac{1}{(d_1d_2)^{3/2}} \ll P^6,\end{aligned}$$

where in the penultimate step, we used the elementary observation that $(d_1, d_2)^2 \le d_1d_2$. This proves the lemma. □

Let us note that the proof of this lemma shows that the number of integer solutions of the equation

$$n_1h_1 + n_2h_2 = -n_3h_3 - n_4h_4$$

with $|n_i| \le X$ and $0 < |h_i| \le Y < X$ is $\ll (XY)^3$.

As a precursor to Linnik's theorem, we now prove the following theorem, due to Hua [83].

Theorem 3.9 *Let $k \ge 2$, and $f(x)$ be a polynomial of degree k with integer coefficients, say,*

$$f(x) = c_kx^k + c_{k-1}x^{k-1} + \cdots + c_1x + c_0$$

such that

$$c_k = \mathcal{O}(1),\ c_{k-1} = \mathcal{O}(P),\ \ldots,\ c_1 = \mathcal{O}\big(P^{k-1}\big),\ c_0 = \mathcal{O}\big(P^k\big).$$

Then

$$\int_0^1 \left|\sum_{x=0}^{P} e^{2\pi i f(x)\alpha}\right|^{8^{k-1}} d\alpha = \mathcal{O}\big(P^{8^{k-1}-k}\big). \tag{32}$$

Proof Let us start with $k = 2$. Observe that

$$\int_0^1 \left| \sum_{x=0}^{P} e^{2\pi i f(x)\alpha} \right|^8 d\alpha = \int_0^1 \left(\sum_{x=0}^{P} e^{2\pi i f(x)\alpha} \right)^4 \left(\sum_{x=0}^{P} e^{-2\pi i f(x)\alpha} \right)^4 d\alpha.$$

Thus, the integral in question is equal to the number of solutions to Eq. (31), which is $\ll P^6$ by Lemma 3.8. This proves the lemma for $k = 2$. We now proceed by mathematical induction and assume that Eq. (32) holds when we replace k by $k - 1$.

Observe that

$$\begin{aligned} \left| \sum_{x=0}^{P} e^{2\pi i f(x)\alpha} \right|^2 &= \sum_{x_1=0}^{P} \sum_{x_2=0}^{P} e^{2\pi i (f(x_1) - f(x_2))\alpha} \\ &= \sum_{x=0}^{P} e^{-2\pi i f(x)\alpha} \sum_{h=-x}^{P-x} e^{2\pi i f(x+h)\alpha} \\ &= P + 1 + \sum_{h \neq 0}{}' \sum_{x}{}' e^{2\pi i (f(x+h) - f(x))\alpha}, \end{aligned}$$

where the dash on top of the summations refers to all those integers h lying between $-P$ and P and those integers x such that both $x + h$ and x lie between 0 and P. Now,

$$f(x+h) - f(x) = \sum_{j=0}^{k} c_j \left((x+h)^j - x^j \right) = \sum_{j=0}^{k} c_j \sum_{i=0}^{j-1} \binom{j}{i} x^i h^{j-i}.$$

Thus, $f(x+h) - f(x) = h\phi(x, h)$, where $\phi(x, h)$ is a polynomial in h of degree at most $k - 1$. Let us define

$$a_h = \sum_{x}{}' e^{2\pi i h \phi(x,h)\alpha}.$$

Then, we have

$$\left| \sum_{x=0}^{P} e^{2\pi i f(x)\alpha} \right|^2 = P + 1 + \sum_{h \neq 0}{}' a_h.$$

Raising both sides by the power 8^{k-2}, we have

$$\left| \sum_{x=0}^{P} e^{2\pi i f(x)\alpha} \right|^{2.8^{k-2}} = \left(P + 1 + \sum_{h \neq 0}{}' a_h \right)^{8^{k-2}} \ll P^{8^{k-2}} + \left| \sum_{h \neq 0}{}' a_h \right|^{8^{k-2}}.$$

If

$$\left| \sum_{h \neq 0}{}' a_h \right| \leq P,$$

then

$$\left|\sum_{x=0}^{P} e^{2\pi i f(x)\alpha}\right|^{2.8^{k-2}} \ll P^{8^{k-2}}.$$

Hence,

$$\int_0^1 \left|\sum_{x=0}^{P} e^{2\pi i f(x)\alpha}\right|^{8^{k-1}} d\alpha \ll P^{4.8^{k-2}} \ll P^{8^{k-1}-k},$$

since $4.8^{k-2} \geq k$ for all $k \geq 2$. This proves the theorem, provided that $|\sum'_{h\neq 0} a_h| \leq P$.

Suppose now that

$$\left|\sum_{h\neq 0}' a_h\right| \geq P.$$

Then,

$$\left|P+1+\sum_{h\neq 0}' a_h\right|^{8^{k-2}} \ll \left|\sum_{0<|h|\leq P}' a_h\right|^{8^{k-2}}.$$

Applying the Cauchy–Schwarz inequality, we have

$$\left|\sum_{h\neq 0}' a_h\right|^{8^{k-2}} = \left(\left|\sum_{h\neq 0}' a_h\right|^2\right)^{2^{3(k-2)-1}} \ll \left(P\left(\sum_{h\neq 0}' |a_h|^2\right)\right)^{2^{3(k-2)-1}}.$$

Since

$$P^{2^{3(k-2)-1}+2^{3(k-2)-2}+\cdots+1} \sum_{h\neq 0}' |a_h|^{8^{k-2}} = P^{2^{3(k-2)}-1} \sum_{h\neq 0}' |a_h|^{8^{k-2}},$$

a repeated application of the Cauchy–Schwarz inequality leads to an upper bound of the form

$$\left|\sum_{h\neq 0}' a_h\right|^{8^{k-2}} \ll P^{2^{3(k-2)}-1} \sum_{h\neq 0}' |a_h|^{8^{k-2}}. \tag{33}$$

This is also immediate from an application of Hölder's inequality. So, putting it all together,

$$\begin{aligned}\left|\sum_{x=0}^{P} e^{2\pi i f(x)\alpha}\right|^{2.8^{k-2}} &= \left|P+1+\sum_{h\neq 0}' a_h\right|^{8^{k-2}} \\ &\ll \left|\sum_{0<|h|\leq P}' a_h\right|^{8^{k-2}} \ll P^{2^{3(k-2)}-1} \sum_{h\neq 0}' |a_h|^{8^{k-2}}.\end{aligned}$$

By raising Eq. (33) to the fourth power, we immediately deduce

$$\int_0^1 \left| \sum_{x=0}^{P} e^{2\pi i f(x)\alpha} \right|^{8^{k-1}} d\alpha \ll P^{4(8^{k-2}-1)} \int_0^1 \left(\sum_{h \neq 0}{}' |a_h|^{8^{k-2}} \right)^4 d\alpha. \tag{34}$$

We write

$$\left| \sum_{x=0}^{P}{}' e^{2\pi i h\phi(x,h)\alpha} \right|^{8^{k-2}} = \sum_n A(n) e^{2\pi i h n\alpha},$$

where

$$n \ll \max_{0 \le x \le P} \left|\phi(x,h)\right| \ll P^{k-1}.$$

This gives us

$$\begin{aligned} \left|A(n)\right| &= \left| \int_0^1 \left| \sum_{x=0}^{P}{}' e^{2\pi i \phi(x,h)\alpha} \right|^{8^{k-2}} e^{-2\pi i n\alpha} d\alpha \right| \\ &\le \int_0^1 \left| \sum_{x=0}^{P}{}' e^{2\pi i \phi(x,h)\alpha} \right|^{8^{k-2}} d\alpha, \end{aligned}$$

which by induction hypothesis is

$$\ll P^{8^{k-2}-(k-1)}.$$

Thus, by Eq. (34) and the above, we get

$$\begin{aligned} &\int_0^1 \left| \sum_{x=0}^{P}{}' e^{2\pi i f(x)\alpha} \right|^{8^{k-1}} d\alpha \\ &\ll P^{4(8^{k-2}-1)} \int_0^1 \left(\sum_{h \neq 0}{}' |a_h|^{8^{k-2}} \right)^4 d\alpha \\ &\ll P^{4(8^{k-2}-1)} \sum_{\substack{n_1,n_2,n_3,n_4 \\ h_1,h_2,h_3,h_4 \\ n_i \ll P^{k-1} \\ 0<|h_i|\le P \\ n_1h_1+n_2h_2=-n_3h_3-n_4h_4}} A(n_1)A(n_2)A(n_3)A(n_4) \\ &\ll P^{4(8^{k-2}-1)} P^{3k} P^{4.8^{k-2}-4(k-1)} \\ &\ll P^{8^{k-1}-k}. \end{aligned}$$

This proves the theorem. □

Remark 3.1 Note that in all the above inequalities, the implied constants only depend on k.

The following corollary clearly follows from the above theorem.

Corollary 3.10 *For any $k \geq 1$, there exists $g \geq 1$ such that*

$$\int_0^1 \left| \sum_{x=0}^{P} e^{2\pi i x^k \alpha} \right|^g d\alpha \leq c(k) P^{g-k},$$

where $c(k)$ is a constant depending on k. In fact, we can take $g = 8^{k-1}$.

We are now ready to prove Theorem 3.5.

Let $k \geq 1$ and g be as in Corollary 3.10. We have

$$\left(\sum_{x=0}^{P} e^{2\pi i x^k \alpha} \right)^g = \sum_{x_1, x_2, \ldots, x_g = 0}^{P} e^{2\pi i (x_1^k + x_2^k + \cdots + x_g^k)\alpha}$$
$$= \sum_{m \geq 0} c_m e^{2\pi i m \alpha},$$

where

$$c_m = r_{g,k}(m) = \left| \int_0^1 \left(\sum_{x=0}^{P} e^{2\pi i x^k \alpha} \right)^g e^{-2\pi i m \alpha} \, d\alpha \right|.$$

By Corollary 3.10, we deduce

$$c_m \leq \int_0^1 \left| \sum_{x=0}^{P} e^{2\pi i x^k \alpha} \right|^g d\alpha \leq c(k) P^{g-k}.$$

Choosing

$$P = \left[m^{\frac{1}{k}} \right],$$

we get

$$r_{g,k}(m) \leq c(k) m^{\frac{g}{k} - 1},$$

which proves Theorem 3.5.

It is possible to derive an asymptotic formula using the circle method for the number of such representations, provided that g is large enough. Essentially, all the ingredients have been proved above with one exception, and this is the celebrated Weyl's inequality for exponential sums. Using an ingenious differencing technique, Weyl derived non-trivial estimates for exponential sums of the form

$$S := \sum_{n \leq x} e^{2\pi i \alpha P(n)},$$

where $P(n)$ is a polynomial. The idea is simple to explain. For $P(n)$ a monic linear polynomial in n, the sum is a geometric series and can easily be summed. The estimate depends on how close α is to an integer. When $P(n)$ is quadratic, then considering $|S|^2$, we get an exponential sum

$$\sum_{n,m\le x} e^{2\pi i\alpha(P(n)-P(m))}.$$

Using the technique that already appeared in Hua's theorem, we can reduce this to the linear case and derive a non-trivial estimate for S. It is now clear that a delicate inductive process will lead to non-trivial estimates for S when P is any monic polynomial of arbitrary degree. Such an estimate was employed by Hardy and Littlewood in their treatment of Waring's problem. They were able to derive an asymptotic formula for $r_{g,k}(n)$ when $g \ge 2^k + 1$. More precisely, they showed that

$$r_{g,k}(n) = \frac{\Gamma(1+1/k)^g}{\Gamma(g/k)} n^{g/k-1}\mathfrak{S}(n) + o\big(n^{g/k-1}\big),$$

where

$$\mathfrak{S}(n) = \sum_{q=1}^{\infty} T_q(n),$$

and

$$T_q(n) = \sum_{\substack{a=1\\(a,q)=1}}^{q} q^{-g}\left(\sum_{r=1}^{q} e^{2\pi i a r^k/q}\right)^g e^{-2\pi i a n/q}.$$

The series $\mathfrak{S}(n)$ is called the *singular series* and measures the "local obstruction" to the problem of counting the number of solutions. Remarkably, $T_q(n)$ is a multiplicative function of q, and one can write the series as an infinite product from which its positivity can easily be inferred. We refer the reader to two excellent surveys on the topic for further study [47] and [197]. As can be seen from the last reference, there is still ongoing research in the development of the method.

4 Goldbach's Conjecture

In 1742, C. Goldbach conjectured that every even number greater than 2 can be written as a sum of two prime numbers. Consequently, this predicts that every odd number > 5 can be written as a sum of three primes. The binary Goldbach conjecture is still open. However, the Goldbach conjecture for odd numbers is now a theorem due to Vinogradov. His theorem is a good illustration of how one may combine elementary methods with sieve techniques to prove deep theorems. It was originally proved by Hardy and Littlewood by applying the circle method and using the generalized Riemann hypothesis. We indicate how this was done below. It is not our intention here to give an exhaustive treatment of the method. Rather, we shall illustrate its use in the ternary Goldbach problem.

The idea can be explained as follows. Let

$$f(\theta, n) := \sum_{p \le n} e(p\theta), \qquad e(t) = e^{2\pi i t},$$

where the summation is over prime numbers. Let $r(n)$ be the number of ways of writing n as a sum of three primes. Then, clearly,

$$r(n) = \int_0^1 f^3(\theta, n) e(-n\theta)\, d\theta.$$

As explained earlier, we need to have some information on $f(\theta, n)$. When θ is a rational number, say, $\theta = a/q$, we may relate the function to primes in arithmetic progressions as follows:

$$f\left(\frac{a}{q}, n\right) = \sum_{(b,q)=1} e(ba/q)\pi(n, q, b) + O(\log q)$$

since there are at most $O(\log q)$ prime divisors of q. By the generalized Riemann hypothesis,

$$\pi(n, q, b) = \frac{\mathrm{li}(n)}{\phi(q)} + O\big(n^{1/2} \log qn\big),$$

where

$$\mathrm{li}(n) = \int_2^n \frac{dt}{\log t}.$$

Now, the sum

$$\sum_{\substack{b=1 \\ (b,q)=1}}^{q} e(ba/q)$$

is a Ramanujan sum and, as a is coprime to q, is equal to $\mu(q)$ where μ denotes the Möbius function.

Inserting this into the above expression for $f(a/q, n)$ gives

$$f\left(\frac{a}{q}, n\right) = \frac{\mu(q)}{\phi(q)} \mathrm{li}(n) + O\big(q n^{1/2} \log qn\big).$$

Thus, the GRH provides us a good approximation of $f(\theta, n)$ when $\theta = a/q$ and q is not too large. Since the function $f(\theta, n)$ is a continuous function of θ, one may apply partial summation to deduce its behaviour in a suitable neighborhood of a/q. Thus the strategy in the circle method is to decompose the interval into "major arcs" suitably controlled and the set of "minor arcs," which is just the complementary set. I.M. Vinogradov, in his proof of the ternary Goldbach Conjecture, used the elementary sieve of Eratosthenes to estimate $f(\theta, n)$ for θ belonging to a "minor arc." Putting those two estimates together, he was able to obtain the desired asymptotic formula for $r(n)$. The use of the GRH can be replaced by the Siegel–Walfisz theorem, which is what Vinogradov did, and thus, the whole derivation can be made unconditional. As we indicate below, the method breaks down for the binary Goldbach problem.

4.1 Basic Lemmas

We recall, for the benefit of the reader, two elementary results that will be used repeatedly in the proof below. The first is a classical lemma of Dirichlet: given any positive real number θ and a rational $Q > 1$, there exist $(a, q) = 1$ with $q \leq Q$ so that

$$|q\theta - a| \leq \frac{1}{Q}.$$

Indeed, consider the $Q + 1$ numbers $\{n\theta\}$, $0 \leq m \leq Q$. If we subdivide the unit interval into Q equal parts each of length $1/Q$, we see that two of these numbers must lie in the same subinterval. Thus,

$$\left|\{m_1\theta\} - \{m_2\theta\}\right| \leq \frac{1}{Q}$$

for $m_1 \neq m_2 \leq Q$. Hence,

$$\left|(m_1 - m_2)\theta - \big([m_1\theta] - [m_2\theta]\big)\right| \leq \frac{1}{Q}.$$

Setting $q = m_1 - m_2$ and $a = [m_1\theta] - [m_2\theta]$ gives the result.

The second elementary result is Abel's lemma. If

$$B(m) = \sum_{j \leq m} b_j,$$

then,

$$\begin{aligned}
\sum_{j \leq m} a_j b_j &= \sum_{j \leq m} a_j \big(B(j) - B(j-1)\big) \\
&= \sum_{j \leq m} a_j B(j) - \sum_{j \leq m-1} a_{j+1} B(j) \\
&= \sum_{j \leq m} (a_j - a_{j+1}) B(j) + a_m B(m).
\end{aligned}$$

Let us also recall the continuous version of partial summation:

$$\sum_{j\leq m} f(j)b_j = B(m)f(m) - \int_1^m B(t)f'(t)\,dt.$$

4.2 Major Arcs

As indicated in the previous sections, we have

$$r(n) = \int_0^1 f^3(\theta,n)e(-n\theta)\,d\theta.$$

Since the integrand has period 1, we have

$$r(n) = \int_{\frac{-1}{Q}}^{1-\frac{1}{Q}} f^3(\theta,n)e(-n\theta)\,d\theta$$

for any $Q > 0$.

Now let $(a,q) = 1$, $a \leq q$, $q \leq \log^c n$, $Q = n/(\log^c n)$, where c is a constant to be chosen.

Define $I(a,q)$ as the set of points θ such that

$$\left|\theta - \frac{a}{q}\right| \leq \frac{1}{Q}.$$

Observe that no two distinct intervals $I(a,q)$ overlap for if $\theta \in I(a,q)$ and $I(a',q')$, then because $aq' \neq a'q$, we have

$$\frac{1}{qq'} \leq \left|\frac{a}{q} - \frac{a'}{q}\right| = \left|\left(\frac{a}{q} - \theta\right) + \left(\theta - \frac{a'}{q'}\right)\right| \leq \frac{2}{Q},$$

which implies $Q \leq 2qq' \leq 2\log^{2c} n$, a contradiction for n large enough. The major arcs are by the definition

$$\mathfrak{M} = \bigcup_{q\leq \log^c n}\ \bigcup_{(a,q)=1} I(a,q).$$

The minor arcs are $[0, 1]\backslash\mathfrak{M}$, or more accurately

$$\mathfrak{m} = \left[\frac{-1}{Q}, 1 - \frac{1}{Q}\right]\backslash\mathfrak{M}.$$

We then have

$$r(n) = \int_{\mathfrak{M}} f^3(\theta,n)e(-n\theta)\,d\theta + \int_{\mathfrak{m}} f^3(\theta,n)e(-n\theta)\,d\theta,$$

and we analyze each of these intervals separately.

4.3 Application of Partial Summation

Let us begin with the observation that for any trigonometric sum of the form

$$S(\theta, n) = \sum_{m \le n} a_m e(m\theta),$$

we have by partial summation

$$S(\theta_1 + \theta_2, n) = S(\theta_1, n) e(\theta_2 n) - 2\pi i \theta_2 \int_0^n S(\theta_1, u) e(\theta u)\, du.$$

Applying this to $f(\theta, n)$ gives

$$f(\theta_1 + \theta_2, n) = e(\theta_2 n) f(\theta_1, n) - 2\pi i \theta_2 \int_0^n f(\theta_1, u) e(\theta_2 u)\, du.$$

We also introduce the function

$$g(\theta, n) = \sum_{m \le n} \frac{1}{\log m} e(m\theta)$$

and find

$$g(\theta_1 + \theta_2, n) = e(\theta_2 n) g(\theta_1, n) - 2\pi i \theta_2 \int_0^n g(\theta_1, u) e(\theta_2 u)\, du.$$

4.4 Primes in Arithmetic Progressions

Applying the Siegel–Walfisz theorem, we find when $\theta = a/q$,

$$f\left(\frac{a}{q}, n\right) = \frac{\mu(q)}{\phi(q)} \mathrm{li}(n) + O\left(\frac{n}{\log^A n}\right),$$

where we have used the fact that

$$\mu(q) = \sum_{\substack{b=1 \\ (b,q)=1}}^{q} e(ba/q),$$

a familiar Ramanujan sum. Let us observe that

$$\begin{aligned} g(0, n) = \sum_{m \le n} \frac{1}{\log m} &= \int_2^n \frac{dt}{\log t} + O\left(\frac{1}{\log n}\right) \\ &= \mathrm{li}(n) + O\left(\frac{1}{\log n}\right). \end{aligned}$$

Thus,

$$f\left(\frac{a}{q}, n\right) = \frac{\mu(q)}{\phi(q)} g(0, n) + O\left(\frac{n}{\log^A n}\right).$$

By partial summation,

$$f\left(\frac{a}{q} + y, n\right) = e(yn) f\left(\frac{a}{q}, n\right) - 2\pi i y \int_0^n f\left(\frac{a}{q}, u\right) e(yu)\, du$$

and

$$g(y, n) = e(yn) g(0, n) - 2\pi i y \int_0^n g(0, u) e(yu)\, du,$$

so that

$$\begin{aligned}
&\left| f\left(\frac{a}{q} + y, n\right) - \frac{\mu(q)}{\phi(q)} g(y, u) \right| \\
&\quad \le \frac{n}{\log^A n} + 2\pi |y| \int_0^n \left| f\left(\frac{a}{q}, u\right) - \frac{\mu(q)}{\phi(q)} g(0, u) \right| du \\
&\quad \ll \frac{n}{\log^A n} \quad \text{if } |y| \le \frac{\log^A n}{n}.
\end{aligned}$$

Since

$$\left|z^3 - w^3\right| = |z - w| \left|z^2 + w^2 + zw\right|,$$

we immediately deduce

$$\left| f^3\left(\frac{a}{q} + y, n\right) - \frac{\mu(q)}{\phi(q)^3} g^3(y, n) \right| \le \frac{3n^3}{\log^A n} \qquad (*)$$

for $|y| \le (\log^A n)/n$.

4.5 The Singular Series

We can now write down the main term of the asymptotic formula. Let us put

$$J(a, q) := \int_{I(a,q)} f^3(\theta, n) e(-n\theta)\, d\theta$$

and

$$J_1 = \int_{-1/Q}^{1/Q} g^3(y, n) e(-ny)\, dy,$$

so that the inequality of the previous section leads to

$$\left| J(a,q) - \frac{\mu(q)}{\phi^3(q)} J_1 e\left(-\frac{na}{q}\right)\right| \le \frac{3n^3}{\log^A n}\frac{\log^c n}{n} \le \frac{3n^2}{\log^{A-c} n}. \qquad (**)$$

We can choose A as large as we please. If we put

$$\rho(n) = \sum_{m_1+m_2+m_3=n, m_i\ge 2} (\log m_1)^{-1}(\log m_2)^{-1}(\log m_3)^{-1},$$

then

$$\rho(n) = \int_{-1/2}^{1/2} g^3(y,n) e(-ny)\, dy.$$

Let us note that

$$\frac{1}{3}\frac{n^2}{\log^3 n} \le \rho(n) \le n^2,$$

as is easily verified. Moreover,

$$\left|\sum_{m\le n} e(my)\right| \ll \frac{1}{|y|}$$

as is also easily deduced since the sum is a geometric series. Thus, by Abel's lemma,

$$g(y,n) = \sum_{m\le n} \frac{e(my)}{\log m} \ll \frac{1}{|y|}.$$

Thus,

$$\left|\int_{1/Q}^{1/2} g^3(y,n)e(-ny)\, dy\right| \ll Q^2 \ll \frac{n^2}{\log^{2c} n}.$$

A similar estimate holds for the integral over the range $[-\frac{1}{2}, -\frac{1}{Q}]$. Thus, by $(**)$,

$$\rho(n) = \int_{-1/Q}^{1/Q} g^3(y,n)e(-ny)\, dy + O\left(\frac{n^2}{\log^{2c} n}\right).$$

Hence, from $(*)$ we immediately see that

$$\left| J(a,q) - \frac{\mu(q)}{\phi^3(q)}\rho(n) e\left(-\frac{na}{q}\right)\right| \ll \frac{n^2}{\log^{A-c} n}.$$

We denote the Ramanujan sum

$$c_q(n) = \sum_{\substack{a=1 \\ (a,q)=1}}^{q} e\left(-\frac{na}{q}\right),$$

so that

$$\left| \sum_{q \le \log^c n} \sum_{(a,q)=1} J(a,q) - \rho(n) \sum_{q \le \log^c n} \frac{\mu(q)}{\phi^3(q)} c_q(n) \right|$$
$$\ll \frac{n^2}{\log^{A-c} n} \log^{2c} n \ll \frac{n^2}{\log^{A-3c} n}.$$

Thus,

$$\int_{\mathfrak{M}} f^3(\theta, n) e(-\theta n)\, d\theta = \rho(n) \sum_{q \le \log^c n} \frac{\mu(q)}{\phi^3(n)} c_q(n) + O\left(\frac{n^2}{\log^{A-3c} n} \right),$$

and the sum on the right-hand side is called the *singular series*. It is not difficult to see that

$$\sum_{q \le \log^c n} \frac{\mu(q)}{\phi^3(q)} c_q(n) = \sum_{q=1}^{\infty} \frac{\mu(q)}{\phi^3(q)} c_q(n) + O\left(\frac{1}{\log^c n} \right),$$

and using the fact that $c_q(n)$ is multiplicative, we find that the series is

$$\prod_p \left(1 - \frac{c_p(n)}{(p-1)^3} \right).$$

When n is odd, this series is

$$2 \prod_{p>2} \left(1 - \frac{c_p(n)}{(p-1)^3} \right) \ge 2 \prod_{p>2} \left(1 - \frac{1}{(p-1)^2} \right) \ge 2 \prod_{m=1}^{\infty} \left(1 - \frac{1}{m^2} \right) = 1.$$

Thus, in particular, the series is not zero. If we can show

$$\left| \int_{\mathfrak{m}} f^3(\theta, n) e(-n\theta)\, d\theta \right| \ll \frac{n^2}{\log^4 n},$$

we can conclude that

$$r(n) = \rho(n) \prod_p \left(1 - \frac{c_p(n)}{(p-1)^3} \right) + O\left(\frac{n^2}{\log^4 n} \right)$$

and that

$$r(n) \gg \frac{n^2}{\log^3 n},$$

completing the proof.

4.6 The Minor Arcs Estimate Using GRH

We begin by noting that

$$\left|\int_{\mathfrak{m}} f^3(\theta,n)e(-n\theta)\,d\theta\right| \le \sup_{\theta\in\mathfrak{m}} \left|f(\theta,n)\right| \int_0^1 \left|f^2(\theta,n)\right| d\theta \le \pi(n) \sup_{\theta\in\mathfrak{m}} \left|f(\theta,n)\right|$$

by Parseval's formula. Following Hardy and Littlewood, we want to indicate how the generalized Riemann hypothesis (GRH) can be used to supply such an estimate in a quick way.

Let us observe that (as before)

$$\begin{aligned} f\left(\frac{a}{q},n\right) &= \sum_{p\le n} e(pa/q) \\ &= \sum_{(b,q)=1} e(ba/q)\pi(n,q,b) \\ &= \frac{\mu(q)}{\phi(q)}\operatorname{li}(n) + \sum_{(b,q)=1} e(ba/q)E(n,q,b), \end{aligned}$$

where

$$E(n,q,b) = \pi(n,q,b) - \frac{\operatorname{li}(n)}{\phi(q)}.$$

Now,

$$E(n,q,b) = \frac{1}{\phi(q)} \sum_{\chi\ne\chi_0} \overline{\chi}(b)\pi(n,\chi),$$

where the sum is over non-trivial characters $\chi \pmod q$. Thus,

$$\sum_{(b,q)=1} e(ba/q)E(n,q,b) = \frac{1}{\phi(q)} \sum_{\chi\ne\chi_0} \chi(a)\tau(\overline{\chi})\pi(n,\chi),$$

where $\tau(\chi)$ denotes the Gauss sum attached to χ. The GRH is equivalent to the estimate

$$\left|\pi(n,\chi)\right| \ll n^{1/2}\log qn,$$

so that we get

$$f\left(\frac{a}{q},n\right) = \frac{\mu(q)}{\phi(q)}\operatorname{li}(n) + O\big(q^{1/2}n^{1/2}\log qn\big).$$

With these remarks, we may proceed to estimate $f(\theta,n)$ when θ is an element of the minor arcs. We observe that Dirichlet's lemma gives that there are q, a such that

$|q\theta - a| \le 1/Q$. As $\theta \in \mathfrak{m}$, we must have $q \ge \log^c n$. Thus,

$$\left|\theta - \frac{a}{q}\right| \le \frac{1}{qQ} \le \frac{1}{n}.$$

Let $y = \theta - a/q$. Then, by partial summation,

$$f(\theta, n) = f\left(\frac{a}{q} + y, n\right) = e(yn) f\left(\frac{a}{q}, n\right) - 2\pi i y \int_0^n f\left(\frac{a}{q}, u\right) e(yu)\, du,$$

so that

$$\left|f(\theta, n)\right| \ll \frac{n}{\log^{c-1} n}.$$

Choosing c sufficiently large gives us the desired estimate for the minor arcs.

The elimination of the use of GRH by Vinogradov emanates from two simple ideas. The first is an estimate for a trigonometric sum. The second is a clever application of the sieve of Eratosthenes. Combining both of these ideas, Vinogradov showed that the estimate of the function $f(\theta, n)$ on the minor arcs can be deduced without GRH. We refer the reader to [197] for details.

The binary Goldbach problem seems to lie at a deeper level. One can derive the expected main term by analyzing the major arcs as we have done in the ternary Goldbach problem. However, the minor arc estimates are not good enough to yield the desired result. Clearly, a new idea needs to be injected into the method.

These two examples, showing how Waring's problem and the ternary Goldbach problem can be attacked using the circle method, should illustrate the power and scope of the method introduced by Hardy and Ramanujan in their foundational paper giving the asymptotics of the partition function. The method is still a sophisticated tool in additive analytic number theory and very much the focus of current research.

Chapter 6
Ramanujan and Transcendence

1 Nesterenko's Theorems

Although Ramanujan did not work in transcendental number theory, his intuition in the theory of q-series, singular moduli, and the theory of quasi-modular forms played a pivotal role in its development. Indeed, his celebrated paper of 1916 entitled "On certain arithmetical functions" is notable for its wealth of ideas, not only for its enunciation of the Ramanujan conjecture regarding the τ-function, but also for its emphasis on Eisenstein series and the differential equations satisfied by them. More precisely, Ramanujan considers the functions

$$P(q) = 1 - 24\sum_{n=1}^{\infty} \sigma_1(n)q^n,$$

$$Q(q) = 1 + 240\sum_{n=1}^{\infty} \sigma_3(n)q^n,$$

$$R(q) = 1 - 504\sum_{n=1}^{\infty} \sigma_5(n)q^n,$$

where

$$\sigma_k(n) = \sum_{d|n} d^k.$$

These functions are connected to the classical Eisenstein series $E_2(z)$, $E_4(z)$, $E_6(z)$ via the equations

$$E_2(z) = P\big(e^{2\pi iz}\big), \qquad E_4(z) = Q\big(e^{2\pi iz}\big), \qquad E_6(z) = R\big(e^{2\pi iz}\big)$$

with $z \in \mathbb{C}$ and $\Im(z) > 0$. E_4 and E_6 are modular forms of weight 4 and 6 respectively, whereas E_2 is a quasi-modular form of weight 2. It is known [207] that the

M.R. Murty, V.K. Murty, *The Mathematical Legacy of Srinivasa Ramanujan*,
DOI 10.1007/978-81-322-0770-2_6,

algebra of quasi-modular forms is closed under the differential operator $D = qd/dq$ and is generated by E_2, E_4, and E_6.

In his 1916 paper, Ramanujan shows that

$$DP = \frac{1}{12}(P^2 - Q), \qquad DQ = \frac{1}{3}(PQ - R), \qquad DR = \frac{1}{2}(PR - Q^2).$$

These equations played a central role in the remarkable theorem of Nesterenko [142] concerning the special values of these functions.

Theorem 1.1 (Nesterenko, 1996) *For any complex number q with $0 < |q| < 1$, the set*

$$\{q, P(q), Q(q), R(q)\}$$

contains at least three numbers algebraically independent over $\mathbb{Q}$.

As Ramanujan was aware, the functions P, Q, R are related to many interesting elliptic and modular functions. This allows one to relate the above theorem to several specific constants. For instance, if we take $q = e^{-2\pi}$, then one can show that

$$P(e^{-2\pi}) = \frac{3}{\pi}, \qquad Q(e^{-2\pi}) = \frac{3\Gamma(1/4)^8}{(2\pi)^6}, \qquad R(e^{-2\pi}) = 0.$$

Thus, Nesterenko's theorem implies the following:

Corollary 1.2 *The numbers π, e^π, and $\Gamma(1/4)$ are algebraically independent over $\mathbb{Q}$.*

More generally, let $\wp(z)$ be the Weierstrass $\wp$-function with invariants g_2, g_3. Let the corresponding lattice be generated by ω_1, ω_2 and denote by η_1, η_2 the associated quasi-periods. We suppose that $z = \omega_2/\omega_1$ with $\Im(z) > 0$. By the theory of elliptic functions (see Chap. 4 of [107]), we have upon setting $q = e^{2\pi i z}$,

$$P(q) = \frac{3\omega_1\eta_1}{\pi^2}, \qquad Q(q) = \frac{3}{4}\left(\frac{\omega_1}{\pi}\right)^4 g_2, \qquad R(q) = \frac{27}{8}\left(\frac{\omega_1}{\pi}\right)^6 g_3.$$

These formulas imply that $P(q), Q(q), R(q)$ belong to the field $\mathbb{Q}(g_2, g_3, \omega_1/\pi, \eta_1/\pi)$. From Nesterenko's theorem, we have

Corollary 1.3 *Let $\wp(z)$ be the Weierstrass $\wp$-function with algebraic invariants g_2, g_3. Then the numbers*

$$e^{2\pi i(\omega_2/\omega_1)}, \quad \omega_1/\pi, \quad \eta_1/\pi$$

are algebraically independent over $\mathbb{Q}$.

If the elliptic curve associated with $\wp(z)$ has complex multiplication, we deduce the following:

Corollary 1.4 *Let $\wp(z)$ be the Weierstrass $\wp$-function with algebraic invariants g_2, g_3 and whose associated elliptic curve has complex multiplication by the imaginary quadratic field k. If ω is any period of $\wp(z)$, and η is the corresponding quasi-period and $z \in k$ with $\Im(z) \neq 0$, then both sets*

$$\{\pi, \omega, e^{2\pi i z}\} \quad \textit{and} \quad \{\omega, \eta, e^{2\pi i z}\}$$

are algebraically independent over $\mathbb{Q}$.

Indeed, in the case of complex multiplication, ω_2, η_2 are algebraic over the field $\mathbb{Q}(\omega_1, \eta_1)$ (see Chap. 3 of [122]). Using the Legendre relation

$$\omega_2\eta_1 - \omega_1\eta_2 = 2\pi i,$$

we deduce that η_1 is algebraic over $\mathbb{Q}(\omega_1, \pi)$ and that π is algebraic over $\mathbb{Q}(\omega_1, \eta_1)$. This leads to the above corollary.

For any natural number d, there exists a Weierstrass $\wp$-function with algebraic invariants and complex multiplication by $\mathbb{Q}(\sqrt{-d})$. Thus, the previous corollary implies the following:

Corollary 1.5 *For any natural number d, the numbers*

$$\pi, \quad e^{\pi\sqrt{d}}$$

are algebraically independent over $\mathbb{Q}$.

In fact, a stronger result can be deduced from the above. Using the Chowla–Selberg formula [34] and its relation to the theory of elliptic curves [61], we find the following:

Corollary 1.6 *For any imaginary quadratic field with discriminant $-D$ and quadratic character ϵ, the numbers*

$$\pi, \quad e^{\pi\sqrt{D}}, \quad \prod_{a=1}^{D} \Gamma(a/D)^{\epsilon(a)}$$

are algebraically independent over $\mathbb{Q}$.

In the special case that $D = 3$, we deduce, from the corollary upon using the functional equation $\Gamma(z)\Gamma(1-z) = \pi/\sin\pi z$ with $z = 1/3$, the following:

Corollary 1.7 *The numbers π, $e^{\pi\sqrt{3}}$, and $\Gamma(1/3)$ are algebraically independent.*

2 Special Values of the Γ-Function at CM Points

It is, in fact, possible to deduce further transcendence results from Nesterenko's theorem, in the context of Ramanujan's work. In 1915, Ramanujan [158] wrote a paper evaluating the product

$$\prod_{n=0}^{\infty}\left(1+\left(\frac{x}{a+nd}\right)^3\right).$$

In this paper, we find some elegant formulas of the following kind:

$$\prod_{n=1}^{\infty}\left(1+\left(\frac{2\alpha}{\alpha+n}\right)^3\right)=\frac{\Gamma(1+\alpha)^3\sinh(\pi\alpha\sqrt{3})}{\Gamma(1+3\alpha)\pi\alpha\sqrt{3}}$$

and

$$\prod_{n=1}^{\infty}\left(1+\left(\frac{2\alpha+1}{\alpha+n}\right)^3\right)=\frac{\Gamma(1+\alpha)^3\cosh(\pi(\frac{1}{2}+\alpha)\sqrt{3})}{\Gamma(2+3\alpha)\pi}.$$

If we put $\alpha=0$ in the second formula, we deduce the strikingly beautiful evaluation

$$\prod_{n=1}^{\infty}\left(1+\frac{1}{n^3}\right)=\frac{\cosh(\pi\sqrt{3}/2)}{\pi}, \tag{35}$$

which is transcendental by Nesterenko's theorem. One would expect these products to be transcendental for every rational α, but this deduction can only be made (at present) for a limited number of rational values of α like $\alpha=1/3, 1/4$, or $1/6$. Other products appear in Chaps. 13 and 14 of Ramanujan's notebooks. For instance, in [159] we find

$$\prod_{n=1}^{\infty}\left(1+\left(\frac{x}{\alpha+n}\right)^2\right)=\frac{|\Gamma(\alpha)|^2}{|\Gamma(\alpha+ix)|^2}. \tag{36}$$

Since

$$\frac{\sin\pi z}{\pi z}=\prod_{n=1}^{\infty}\left(1-\frac{z^2}{n^2}\right),$$

we immediately deduce from Ramanujan's formula (36) and Nesterenko's theorem the following:

Theorem 2.1 *Let $a+b\sqrt{-D}$ with $a\in\mathbb{Z}$ and $b\in\mathbb{Q}$ be a CM point. Then, $\Gamma(a+b\sqrt{-D})$ is transcendental. In particular, $\Gamma(ix)$ is transcendental for every non-zero rational x.*

We refer to the forthcoming paper [138] for more applications of these ideas in the context of infinite products.

3 Special Values of Jacobi's Theta Series

In Part V of Bruce Berndt's epic series on Ramanujan's notebooks, we find Chapt. 35 dedicated to special values of the theta functions (in Ramanujan's notation)

$$\varphi(q) = \sum_{-\infty}^{\infty} q^{n^2}$$

and

$$\psi(q) = \sum_{n=0}^{\infty} q^{n(n+1)/2}.$$

From the Jacobi triple product identity it is not hard to see that these series can be written as infinite products. More precisely, we have [44]

$$\varphi(q) = \frac{\eta(q^2)^5}{\eta(q)^2\eta(q^4)}$$

and

$$\psi(q) = \frac{\eta(q^4)^2}{\eta(q^2)},$$

where η denotes the Dedekind η-function.

In his notebooks, Ramanujan evaluated many special values of φ and ψ. All of his results are related to either $\varphi(e^{-\pi x})$ or $\psi(e^{-\pi x})$ for certain rational values of x. The striking feature of his evaluations, tabulated on p. 325 of [20], is that the first group ((i)–(x)) of values of $\varphi(q)$ are algebraic multiples of

$$a = \frac{\pi^{1/4}}{\Gamma(3/4)},$$

whereas the second group of values of $\psi(q)$ are algebraic multiples of $ae^{r\pi/32}$ where r is a natural number.

The chapter in [20] provides no theoretical explanation for these formulas. Nor does it give any reason why only $\pi^{1/4}$, $\Gamma(3/4)$, and e^{π} appear as the transcendental quantities. This fact could have only been deduced from the work of Nesterenko.

We indicate briefly the theoretical rationale for these results. The detailed calculations will be given in a forthcoming paper. For the moment, suffice it to say that the 24th power of $\varphi(q)$ or $\psi(q)$ allows us to express it in terms of Ramanujan's Δ-function. This, in turn, can be expressed in terms of $E_4(z)$ and $E_6(z)$, and then Nesterenko's work can be invoked.

4 The Rogers–Ramanujan Continued Fraction

The Rogers–Ramanujan continued fraction is

$$F(q) = \cfrac{q^{1/5}}{1 + \cfrac{q}{1 + \cfrac{q^2}{1 + \ddots}}}.$$

Its genesis is rooted in the celebrated Rogers–Ramanujan identities. These are remarkable identities expressed by the following equations:

$$G(q) := \sum_{m=0}^{\infty} \frac{q^{m^2}}{(1-q)(1-q^2)\cdots(1-q^m)} = \prod_{m=1}^{\infty} \left(1-q^{5m+1}\right)^{-1}\left(1-q^{5m+4}\right)^{-1},$$

$$H(q) := \sum_{m=0}^{\infty} \frac{q^{m(m+1)}}{(1-q)(1-q^2)\cdots(1-q^m)} = \prod_{m=1}^{\infty} \left(1-q^{5m+2}\right)^{-1}\left(1-q^{5m+3}\right)^{-1}.$$

The main feature of these identities is their striking beauty and simplicity. In 1936, Selberg [178] found generalizations of these identities. Closer examination of these identities reveals hidden modular connections.

The Rogers–Ramanujan identities have an exotic history. Apparently, they were first discovered by Rogers [175] in 1894. It seems that he was a gifted mathematician whose work was largely ignored. For instance, he discovered Hölder's inequality before Hölder did (see p. 100 of [67]). The identities were re-discovered by Ramanujan in 1913, before he had come to England. However, he had no proof and knew he had none. Since no one in Hardy's circle of mathematicians could prove them, they were stated without proof in the second volume of MacMahon's book on combinatorial analysis. In 1917, Ramanujan was looking through some old volumes of the Proceedings of the London Mathematical Society and stumbled on the 1894 paper of Rogers. Hardy wrote, "I can remember very well his surprise, and the admiration which he expressed for Rogers's work. A correspondence followed in the course of which Rogers was led to a considerable simplification of his original proof." Around the same time, Schur [177] rediscovered these identities and published two combinatorial proofs. In 1919, Ramanujan [163] published another (more analytic) proof.

In his 1894 paper, Rogers [175] proved that

$$q^{-1/5}F(q) = \frac{H(q)}{G(q)}.$$

Using the Rogers–Ramanujan identities, the right-hand side can be written as

$$\prod_{n=1}^{\infty} \left(1-q^n\right)^{\chi_5(n)},$$

where $\chi_5(n)$ is the non-trivial quadratic character (mod 5) given by the Legendre symbol $(5/n)$. If we put $q = e^{2\pi i z}$, then writing the right-hand side in terms of theta functions, one can show that in fact, $F(e^{2\pi i z})$ is a modular function for $\Gamma(5)$ (see, for example, [43]).

The stage is now set to apply Nesterenko's theorems to $F(q)$. These were derived by Duverney, Ke. Nishioka, Ku. Nishioka, and Shiokawa [44]. The explicit relationship of this function to modular functions is given by the following equation:

$$\frac{1}{F(q)} = F(q) + 1 + q^{2/5}\frac{\eta(q^{1/5})}{\eta(q^5)},$$

where η is the Dedekind η-function. In [44], it was shown that Nesterenko's theorem implies the following:

Theorem 4.1 *$F(\alpha)$ is transcendental for any algebraic α with $0 < |\alpha| < 1$.*

In Ramanujan's letters to Hardy, we find several explicit evaluations of F. For instance, in his first letter, Ramanujan wrote

$$F\left(e^{-2\pi}\right) = \sqrt{\frac{5+\sqrt{5}}{2}} - \frac{1+\sqrt{5}}{2}.$$

He further wrote that $F(e^{-\pi\sqrt{n}})$ can be determined exactly for any natural number n. From the modular perspective, this is now clear since F being a modular function means that it is a rational function in $j(z)$ and $j(5z)$, where j is the j-function. Ramanujan was evaluating the function F at CM points in the upper half-plane, and for such values, the j-function assumes algebraic values by a classical theorem of Schneider (see, for example, [135]).

5 Nesterenko's Conjectures

Nesterenko conjectures that if $z \in \mathbb{C}$, $\Im(z) > 0$, and $q = e^{2\pi i z}$, then the following is true. If the set

$$\{z, q, P(q), Q(q), R(q)\}$$

contains at most three algebraically independent numbers over $\mathbb{Q}$, then z lies in an imaginary quadratic field, and the numbers

$$q, P(q), Q(q)$$

are algebraically independent.

The work of Nesterenko allows us to study transcendental values of modular forms at algebraic arguments. An example of this is illustrated by the following theorem proved by Gun, Murty, and Rath [64]. To state the theorem, we say that two modular forms f, g are equivalent if there are two natural numbers k_1, k_2 such that $f^{k_2} = \lambda g^{k_1}$, with λ algebraic.

Theorem 5.1 *Let α be a non-CM point in the upper half-plane. Let S_α be the set of non-zero modular forms with algebraic coefficients, of arbitrary weight for the full modular group, for which $f(\alpha)$ is algebraic. Then up to equivalence, S_α has at most one element.*

If we assume Nesterenko's conjecture, then there is no exception, and the set S_α is empty.

6 Special Values of the Riemann Zeta Function and q-Analogues

In Entry 21(i) of Chap. 14 in Ramanujan's second notebook, we find the following remarkable formula. If α, β are positive numbers such that $\alpha\beta = \pi^2$, and if r is a positive integer, then

$$\begin{aligned}(4\alpha)^{-r}&\left(\frac{1}{2}\zeta(2r+1)+\sum_{m=1}^{\infty}\frac{1}{m^{2r+1}(e^{2m\alpha}-1)}\right)\\ &-(-4\beta)^{-r}\left(\frac{1}{2}\zeta(2r+1)+\sum_{m=1}^{\infty}\frac{1}{m^{2r+1}(e^{2m\beta}-1)}\right)\\ &=-\sum_{k=0}^{r+1}\frac{(-1)^k B_{2k}B_{2r+2-2k}\alpha^{r+1-k}\beta^k}{(2k)!(2r+2-2k)!},\end{aligned}$$

where the B_js are the Bernoulli numbers. (See pp. 275–276 of [19].) Apart from its intrinsic beauty, this formula is interesting for a variety of reasons. We know that the special value of the Riemann zeta function $\zeta(s)$ for $s = 2k$ is a rational multiple of π^{2k}. If $s = 2k+1$ is odd, the transcendence of $\zeta(2k+1)$ has not been established. Ramanujan's formula expresses these values as a rational multiple of π^{2k+1} plus an additional term which can be interpreted as an Eichler integral. The transcendence of this Eichler integral is studied in a recent paper of Gun, Murty, and Rath [65]. We elaborate on this below.

Apparently, the formula also appears in Ramanujan's lost notebooks, and from this we can surmise that it was discovered before Ramanujan's arrival in England in 1914. In [22], Berndt relates that several mathematicians re-discovered special cases of this formula, the most notable being Emil Grosswald [62], who extended its range of applicability to the upper half-plane. For instance, in the special case $r = 1$, we get

$$\zeta(3) + 2\sum_{n=1}^{\infty}\frac{1}{n^3(e^{2\pi n}-1)} = \frac{7\pi^3}{180}.$$

Thus, at least one of the terms on the left-hand side is transcendental! Similarly, one can deduce that at least one of

$$\zeta(4k+3), \quad \sum_{n=1}^{\infty} \frac{1}{n^{4k+3}(e^{2\pi n}-1)}$$

is transcendental for every integer $k \geq 0$. These identities suggest we consider the function

$$F_k(z) = \sum_{n=1}^{\infty} \sigma_{-k}(n) e^{2\pi i n z}.$$

One can re-write this as

$$-\zeta(k) - \sum_{n=1}^{\infty} \frac{1}{n^k(e^{2\pi i n z}-1)}.$$

For odd negative values of $k \leq -3$, $F_k(z)$ is essentially the Eisenstein series $E_{1-k}(z)$ (apart from the constant term) of weight $1-k$ for the full modular group. For odd positive values of k, one can view $F_k(z)$ as an Eichler integral, which is obtained by integrating a classical modular form. Indeed, noting that

$$\sigma_{-k}(n) = n^{-k} \sigma_k(n),$$

we may re-write $F_k(z)$ as

$$\sum_{n=1}^{\infty} \frac{\sigma_k(n)}{n^k} e^{2\pi i n z}.$$

It is now clear that $F_k(z)$ can be obtained by successive integrations of the classical Eisenstein series minus its constant term. $F_k(z)$ is not quite a modular form, and it seems natural to study what happens to it under modular transformations. Thus, for any given $k \geq 4$, we can look at

$$F_{2k+1}(z) - z^{2k} F_{2k+1}(-1/z)$$

and study the special values of this function at algebraic points. The reason for doing this is clear since this expression is, by the Ramanujan–Grosswald formula,

$$\frac{1}{2}\zeta(2k+1)\left(z^{2k}-1\right) + \frac{(2\pi i)^{2k+1}}{2z} \sum_{j=0}^{k+1} z^{2k+2-2j} \frac{B_{2j} B_{2k+2-2j}}{(2j)!(2k+2-2j)!}.$$

If for some value of z which is not a $2k$th root of unity, we have a zero of the polynomial appearing in the summation, we can then write $\zeta(2k+1)$ as a difference of two Eichler integrals. Indeed, the zeros of the polynomial

$$R_{2k+1}(z) = \sum_{j=0}^{k+1} z^{2k+2-2j} \frac{B_{2j} B_{2k+2-2j}}{(2j)!(2k+2-2j)!},$$

called the Ramanujan polynomial (of degree $2k+2$) by the authors in [137], has been studied by Murty, Smyth, and Wang. For $k \geq 4$, they showed that all the zeros of $R_{2k+1}(z)$ are simple and lie on the unit circle, apart from four real roots. Moreover, the only possible roots of unity which are zeros of $R_{2k+1}(z)$ are $\pm i$ (which happens if and only if k is even) and $\pm\rho, \pm\rho^2$ with $\rho = e^{2\pi i/3}$ (which happens if and only if 3 divides k). As a consequence, they deduce that for $k \geq 4$, there is an algebraic α with $|\alpha| = 1$ which is not a $2k$th root of unity so that

$$\zeta(2k+1) = \frac{2}{\alpha^{2k} - 1} \big(F_{2k+1}(\alpha) - \alpha^{2k} F_{2k+1}(-1/\alpha) \big).$$

The authors in [65] were led to consider the function

$$G_{2k+1}(z) = \frac{1}{z^{2k} - 1} \big(F_{2k+1}(z) - z^{2k} F_{2k+1}(-1/z) \big)$$

since a special value of this function is $\zeta(2k+1)$. They prove the following:

Theorem 6.1 *The set*

$$\left\{ G_{2k+1}(z) : \Im(z) > 0, z \in \overline{\mathbb{Q}}, z^{2k} \neq 1 \right\}$$

contains at most one algebraic number.

It is clear from these results that Eichler integrals will play a prominent role in our understanding of the special values of $\zeta(2k+1)$.

Apéry's surprising result that $\zeta(3)$ is irrational proved in 1977 seemed to be an isolated result. All attempts to generalize it to $\zeta(5)$ and more generally to $\zeta(2k+1)$ met with limited success. Only recently did Rivoal [173] succeed in showing that infinitely many of $\zeta(2k+1)$ are irrational. For instance, we now know that the dimension of the vector space spanned by the values $\zeta(3), \zeta(5), \ldots, \zeta(2a+1)$ is greater than $c \log a$ for some positive constant c. These results emanate from a subtle study of hypergeometric series along with an irrationality criterion of Nesterenko. The theory of q-series and its interconnection to the theory of modular forms and mock modular forms seem to suggest a new paradigm for research in this context. Indeed, new light is shed on the irrationality questions by studying the q-analogues of the Riemann zeta function. This analog is not unrelated to the functions P, Q, R of Ramanujan. It seems natural to define the q-Riemann zeta functions

$$\zeta_q(s) = \sum_{n=1}^{\infty} \frac{n^{s-1} q^n}{1 - q^n}$$

and try to study irrationality and transcendence of these values for specializations of q and s. There are good theoretical reasons for doing so. Indeed, $\zeta_q(2), \zeta_q(4), \zeta_q(6)$ are essentially the same as Ramanujan's P, Q, R respectively. Nesterenko's theorem gives us precise information on transcendence of these values, that is, $\zeta_q(s)$ when s is even, since from the theory of modular forms, $\zeta_q(2k)$ is a polynomial in $\zeta_q(4)$ and $\zeta_q(6)$ for $k \geq 2$. What exactly is the situation with $\zeta_q(2k+1)$?

Recently, Rivoal and others have obtained interesting results in this direction. For instance, Krattenthaler, Rivoal, and Zudilin [101] have shown that the $\mathbb{Q}$-vector space spanned by the values $\zeta_q(1), \zeta_q(3), \ldots, \zeta_q(a)$ has dimension at least $c_1\sqrt{a}$ for some positive constant c_1, provided that q is different from ± 1 and a is an odd integer.

The irrationality of $\zeta_q(1)$ with q algebraic is connected with the study of the q-exponential function and the q-logarithm. The general philosophy of transition from the world of natural numbers to the world of q-numbers is to relate n with $q^n - 1$. Thus, the analog of the q-exponential function is

$$e_q(x) := 1 + \sum_{n=1}^{\infty} \frac{x^n}{(q^n-1)(q^{n-1}-1)\cdots(q-1)},$$

and the q-logarithm is

$$\ell_q(x) := \sum_{n=1}^{\infty} \frac{x^n}{q^n - 1}.$$

It is not difficult to show that

$$e_q(x) = \prod_{n=1}^{\infty} \left(1 + \frac{x}{q^n}\right)$$

and

$$\ell_q(x) = \sum_{n=1}^{\infty} \frac{x}{q^n - x}.$$

One can relate the value of $\zeta_q(1)$ to the special value of a q-logarithm. Even for the q-exponential function, one needs the strength of Nesterenko's theorem to assert that $e_q(1)$ is transcendental for algebraic values of q with $|q| > 1$. It will be interesting to study and develop transcendental number theory to the domain of its q-analogs.

From these results it is clear that this "quantum" world seems to lie deeper than the world of natural numbers. This line of investigation may ultimately shed new light on our understanding of the special values of the Riemann zeta function at odd arguments.

Chapter 7
Arithmetic of the Partition Function

Ramanujan's work on the partition function can be divided into two parts. The first part deals with its arithmetic properties, congruences and identities, now called the Rogers–Ramanujan identities. The second deals with his joint work with Hardy on its asymptotic behaviour, for which the elaborate circle method was developed. Since we discussed the latter method in an earlier chapter, we focus here on the arithmetic side of the partition function. As will be evident, elliptic functions and the modern theory of ℓ-adic representations play a major role in the exposition.

1 Ramanujan's Congruences

Recall that a *partition* of a natural number n is the decomposition of n as a finite number of natural numbers. For example, the five partitions of 4 are given by

$$4 = 3 + 1 = 2 + 2 = 2 + 1 + 1 = 1 + 1 + 1 + 1,$$

so we may think of the summands as being arranged in decreasing order. To the partition $n = \lambda_1 + \lambda_2 + \cdots + \lambda_r$ with $\lambda_1 \geq \lambda_2 \geq \cdots \geq \lambda_r$ we may associate a diagram (often called the Young diagram) which has r rows and in the jth row, we place λ_j empty boxes. The number of partitions of n will be denoted by $p(n)$.

At the time of Ramanujan, very little was known about the arithmetic nature of $p(n)$. Even today, though we have a better understanding, there are still many unanswered questions regarding it. For instance, it is still unknown if $p(n)$ is even "half" the time. More precisely, is it true that

$$\lim_{x \to \infty} \frac{\#\{n \leq x : p(n) \text{ even}\}}{x} = \frac{1}{2}?$$

The conjecture is "yes". Looking at values of $p(n)$, one would guess that perhaps $p(n)$ is "random" and no special residue class is favored. Yet, Ramanujan found some surprising congruences:

$$p(5n + 4) \equiv 0 \pmod 5,$$

M.R. Murty, V.K. Murty, *The Mathematical Legacy of Srinivasa Ramanujan*,
DOI 10.1007/978-81-322-0770-2_7, © Springer India 2013

$$p(7n+5) \equiv 0 \pmod 7,$$
$$p(11n+6) \equiv 0 \pmod{11}.$$

Surprisingly, one needs the theory of elliptic functions to prove these results. In paper 30 of his Collected Papers, these results were published posthumously in 1921 in Mathematische Zeitschrift, prepared for the journal by G.H. Hardy and based on an unpublished manuscript of Ramanujan.

What is interesting in Ramanujan's paper is that he actually proves more general results and the congruences stated above are corollaries of these general results. However, here we will follow an exposition of Berndt [21] that gives a simplified treatment.

As in Ramanujan [165], we have the Eisenstein series

$$P = 1 - 24\sum_{n=1}^{\infty} \frac{nq^n}{1-q^n},$$

$$Q = 1 + 240\sum_{n=1}^{\infty} \frac{n^3q^n}{1-q^n},$$

$$R = 1 - 504\sum_{n=1}^{\infty} \frac{n^5q^n}{1-q^n}.$$

If D denotes the differential operator qd/dq, then these Eisenstein series satisfy

$$DP = \frac{P^2-Q}{12}, \qquad DQ = \frac{PQ-R}{3}, \qquad DR = \frac{PR-Q^2}{2},$$

as was shown by Ramanujan in his celebrated paper [161] of 1916.

The easiest way of establishing the validity of these differential equations is as follows. If we let $q = e^{2\pi iz}$, then Q and R are modular forms of weight 4 and 6 respectively. P is not a modular form but a quasi-modular form and has the following transformation law. Let $E_2(z) = P(e^{2\pi iz})$ and $G_2(z) = 2\zeta(2)E_2(z)$. Then, we have

$$G_2(z+1) = G_2(z+1), \qquad G_2(-1/z) = z^2G_2(z) - 2\pi iz.$$

Then, it is straightforward to check that

$$DP - (P^2 - Q)/12$$

is a modular form of weight 4 which vanishes at infinity. Consequently, it is a cusp form of weight 4. But there are no non-trivial cusp forms of weight 4, and so this is identically zero. The other differential equations are established similarly.

In addition to this, we have the well-known discriminant relation

$$\frac{Q^3-R^2}{1728} = \Delta(q) = q\prod_{n=1}^{\infty}(1-q^n)^{24}.$$

Following Ramanujan's notation, we will denote by J any q-series with integer coefficients and emphasize that J is not necessarily the same at each occurrence. Since we are interested in congruences, this is a useful device (similar to the big 'O' notation of Landau). We begin with the simplest congruence.

Theorem 1.1

$$p(5m+4) \equiv 0 \pmod{5}.$$

Proof Using our notation, we have

$$Q = 1 + 5J, \qquad R = P + 5J,$$

the latter coming from $n^5 \equiv n \pmod{5}$, which is a special case of Fermat's little theorem. We have

$$Q^3 - R^2 = Q(1+5J)^2 - (P+5J)^2 = Q - P^2 + 5J.$$

From the differential equations satisfied by P we see that this is

$$= -12DP + 5J = 3DP + 5J.$$

On the other hand,

$$Q^3 - R^2 = 1728q \prod_{n=1}^{\infty} (1-q^n)^{24} = 3q \prod_{n=1}^{\infty} \frac{(1-q^n)^{25}}{(1-q^n)} + 5J.$$

Using the fact that

$$\left(1-q^n\right)^{25} = 1 - q^{25n} + 5J,$$

we deduce that

$$Q^3 - R^2 = 3q \left(\sum_{n=0}^{\infty} p(n) q^n \right) \prod_{n=1}^{\infty} (1 - q^{25n}) + 5J.$$

Combining this with our earlier formula for $Q^3 - P^2$, we obtain

$$3DP = 3q \left(\sum_{n=0}^{\infty} p(n) q^n \right) \prod_{n=1}^{\infty} \left(1 - q^{25n}\right) \pmod{5}. \tag{37}$$

To deduce the desired result, we need only make the observation that if J is any integral q-series given by

$$J = \sum_{n=0}^{\infty} a(n) q^n,$$

then

$$DJ = \sum_{n=1}^{\infty} na(n)q^n,$$

so that the nth coefficient is always divisible by n. In (37), we have

$$DP \prod_{n=1}^{\infty} (1 - q^{25n})^{-1} \equiv q \sum_{n=0}^{\infty} p(n)q^n \pmod 5,$$

and we compare the coefficients of q^{5m} on both sides of the congruence to deduce the desired result. Indeed, since all the coefficients of q^{5m} of DP are divisible by 5, the same is true of the product on the left-hand side which is an integral q-series. So the same must be true of the right-hand side. But the coefficient of q^{5m} on the right-hand side is precisely $p(5m - 1)$. □

The other congruences are obtained similarly. One needs to use some further identities of the following kind.

Since the q-series of any modular form of weight ≥ 4 and level 1 can be written as a polynomial in Q and R, it is not surprising that we also have

$$Q^2 = 1 + 480 \sum_{n=1}^{\infty} \frac{n^7 q^n}{1 - q^n}, \tag{38}$$

$$QR = 1 - 264 \sum_{n=1}^{\infty} \frac{n^9 q^n}{1 - q^n},$$

and

$$441Q^3 + 250R^2 = 691 + 65520 \sum_{n=1}^{\infty} \frac{n^{11} q^n}{1 - q^n},$$

the right-hand sides being the q-series of Eisenstein series of weight 8, 10, and 12 respectively.

The congruences for 7 and 11 are progressively harder. For the congruence modulo 7, only the identity for Q^2 is needed. For the congruence modulo 11, the other two identities are essential. We proceed with the easier case and follow [21] in our discussion filling in some details.

Theorem 1.2

$$p(7m + 5) \equiv 0 \pmod 7.$$

Proof In our notation, we have

$$R = 1 + 7J,$$

and using Fermat's little theorem (with $p = 7$), from (38) we have

$$Q^2 = P + 7J.$$

Hence, modulo 7, we have

$$\begin{aligned}(Q^3 - R^2)^2 &\equiv (PQ - 1)^2 \equiv P^2Q^2 - 2PQ + 1 \\ &\equiv P^3 - 2PQ + 1 \equiv P(P^2 - Q) - PQ + R.\end{aligned}$$

Using the differential equations satisfied by P, Q, R, we obtain that

$$(Q^3 - R^2)^2 \equiv 5P(DP) - 3DQ \pmod 7.$$

This is the same as (modulo 7)

$$6DP^2 - 3DQ.$$

On the other hand,

$$(Q^3 - R^2)^2 = q^2 \prod_{n=1}^{\infty} (1 - q^n)^{48} = q^2 \prod_{n=1}^{\infty} \frac{(1 - q^n)^{49}}{(1 - q^n)}.$$

Reducing this modulo 7, we obtain

$$(Q^3 - R^2)^2 \equiv q^2 \left(\sum_{n=0}^{\infty} p(n) q^n \right) \prod_{n=1}^{\infty} (1 - q^{49n}) \pmod 7.$$

Combining this with our earlier congruence, we obtain

$$q^2 \sum_{n=0}^{\infty} p(n) q^n \equiv \prod_{n=1}^{\infty} (1 - q^{49n})^{-1} \left(6q \frac{dP^2}{dq} - 3q \frac{dQ}{dq} \right) \pmod 7.$$

Noting again that for any q-series J with integer coefficients, the nth coefficient of DJ is always divisible by n, we need only compare the coefficients of q^{7n} of both sides of this congruence to deduce the desired result. □

The key point to note here is that all of these congruences are emanating from Bernoulli numbers appearing in the appropriate Eisenstein series. This again connects naturally to the theory of ℓ-adic representations and the Serre–Swinnerton-Dyer theory of congruences.

2 Higher Congruences

Based on very scanty numerical evidence, Ramanujan formulated a more general conjecture [164] modulo powers of primes 5, 7, and 11. In 1930, Chowla [33] and

Gupta (independently) found a counterexample to his conjecture modulo 7^3, so that some correction was needed. The precise version is given by the following:

Theorem 2.1 *Let* p *be* 5, 7, *or* 11, *and let* $\delta_{p,k}$ *be the multiplicative inverse of* 24 (mod p^k). *Then,*

(1) $p(5^k m + \delta_{5,k}) \equiv 0 \pmod{5^k}$;
(2) $p(7^k m + \delta_{7,k}) \equiv 0 \pmod{7^{[k/2]+1}}$;
(3) $p(11^k m + \delta_{11,k}) \equiv 0 \pmod{11^k}$.

In 1938, Watson [199] proved (1) and (2). Atkin [11] proved (3) in 1967. What do these proofs involve? What are the conceptual reasons behind them? Folsom, Kent, and Ono [53] used the theory of ℓ-adic modular forms to give a conceptual explanation of these congruences. We refer the reader to this paper for further details.

3 Dyson's Ranks and Cranks

In 1944, Dyson made an important observation to give combinatorial explanations for these congruences. If $(\lambda_1, \ldots, \lambda_r)$ is a partition λ of n (denoted $\lambda \vdash n$), he defined the *length* of λ, denoted $\ell(\lambda)$, to be r and the *rank* of λ, denoted $r(\lambda)$, to be $\lambda_1 - \ell(\lambda)$. For instance, the partition of 4 given by (2, 1, 1) has length 3 and rank -1. Dyson considered the functions

$$R(n, m, M) = \#\{\lambda \vdash n : r(\lambda) \equiv m \pmod{M}\}.$$

He conjectured that

$$p(5n+4) = 5R(5n+4, m, 5)$$

for every $0 \le m \le 4$ and

$$p(7n+5) = 7R(7n+5, m, 7)$$

for every $0 \le m \le 6$. In 1954, using the theory of modular functions, Atkin and Swinnerton-Dyer [13] proved Dyson's conjecture. Unfortunately, Dyson's rank function did not apply to Ramanujan's congruence modulo 11. So he was motivated to conjecture that there is another function, which he called the "crank" function, that would explain combinatorially Ramanujan's congruence (mod 11). In 1988, Andrews and Garvan [8, 56] found Dyson's "crank" function. It is defined as follows. Given a partition λ of n, let $o(\lambda)$ be the number of 1s in λ, and $\mu(\lambda)$ be the number of parts larger than $o(\lambda)$. The *crank* of λ, denoted $c(\lambda)$, is given by λ_1 if $o(\lambda) = 0$ and $\mu(\lambda) - o(\lambda)$ otherwise. It turns out that the crank function gives a combinatorial explanation for Ramanujan's congruences (mod 5) and (mod 7) also. Indeed, define

$$S(n, m, M) = \#\{\lambda \vdash n : c(\lambda) \equiv m \pmod{M}\}.$$

Theorem 3.1

(1) *For each* $0 \le m \le 4$,

$$p(5n+4) = 5S(5n+4, m, 5).$$

(2) *For each* $0 \le m \le 6$,

$$p(7n+5) = 7S(7n+5, m, 7).$$

(3) *For each* $0 \le m \le 10$,

$$p(11n+6) = 11S(11n+6, m, 11).$$

There has been further work of Garvan, Kim, and Stanton [57] in this context. Ramanujan expected that there are no such simple congruences for primes greater than 11. In searching for a theoretical explanation for Ramanujan's intuition, Ahlgren and Boylan [3] in 2003 proved the following theorem.

Theorem 3.2 *If ℓ is a prime and $0 \le \beta < \ell$ for which*

$$p(\ell n + \beta) \equiv 0 \pmod{\ell}$$

for every $n \ge 1$, then

$$(\ell, \beta) \in \{(5,4), (7,5), (11,6)\}.$$

A nice exposition is given in [151]. Thus, Ramanujan's congruences for 5, 7, and 11 are the only "simple" congruences for $p(n)$.

Atkin, Klover, Lovejoy, and Ono have done further work extending this result to prime powers. Surprisingly, these extensions involve modular forms of half-integral weight. More precisely, let

$$F(z) = \eta(24z)^{19} = \sum_{n=1}^{\infty} a(n)q^n = q^{19} - 19q^{43} + 152q^{67} + \cdots,$$

$$G(z) = \eta(24z)^{23} = \sum_{n=1}^{\infty} b(n)q^n = q^{23} - 23q^{47} + 230q^{71} + \cdots.$$

If χ_{12} is the quadratic character given by the Kronecker symbol $(12/\cdot)$, then F is a cusp form of weight 19/2 for $\Gamma_0(576)$ and character χ_{12}. G is a modular form of weight 23/2 for the same group and character. We then have

$$p(5^j n + \delta_{5,j}) \equiv 3^{j-1}5^j a(24n+19) \pmod{5^{j+1}}$$

for j odd and

$$p(5^j n + \delta_{5,j}) \equiv 3^{j-1}5^j b(24n+23) \pmod{5^{j+1}},$$

for j even. These results open a new line of research.

4 Parity Questions

The question of determining the parity of the partition function $p(n)$ was raised by Ramanujan (see [24]), but to date, has not been satisfactorily answered. In 1959, Kolberg [100] proved that $p(n)$ is even infinitely often and odd infinitely often. Since his proof is elementary and short, we give it here. We begin with Euler's pentagonal number theorem:

$$\prod_{n=1}^{\infty}(1-q^n)=\sum_{n=-\infty}^{\infty}(-1)^n q^{n(3n+1)/2}.$$

Since

$$\prod_{n=1}^{\infty}(1-q^n)^{-1}=\sum_{n=0}^{\infty}p(n)q^n,$$

we deduce the recursion (Euler's identity) for $n \geq 1$,

$$p(n)-p(n-1)-p(n-2)+p(n-5)+\cdots=0,$$

where the general term is given by

$$(-1)^k p\big(n-k(3k\pm 1)/2\big).$$

If $p(n)$ is even for all $n \geq a$, then with $n=a(3a-1)/2$, the above identity gives

$$p\big(a(3a-1)/2\big)-p\big(a(3a-1)/2-1\big)-\cdots \pm p(2a-1) \mp p(0)=0,$$

giving a contradiction. Hence $p(n)$ takes odd values infinitely often.

A similar argument works for even values. Indeed, suppose that $p(n)$ is odd for all $n \geq b$. Taking $n=b(3b+1)/2$ in Euler's identity, we again deduce a contradiction since the left-hand side has an odd number of odd terms.

A mild variation of this argument using Euler's identity leads to the following result. For any given $M>1$ and r arbitrary, there are infinitely many n such that $p(n) \not\equiv r \pmod{M}$. A general conjecture was formulated by M. Newman. Newman's conjecture [144] predicts that for any given r and M, there are infinitely many n such that $p(n) \equiv r \pmod{M}$. In his paper, Kolberg uses Ramanujan's congruences to prove some special cases of this conjecture. Namely, he shows that each of the congruences $p(n) \equiv 0 \pmod{10}$, $p(n) \equiv 5 \pmod{10}$, $p(n) \equiv 0 \pmod{14}$, and $p(n) \equiv 7 \pmod{14}$ has infinitely many solutions.

One can try to derive some quantitative results in this context. The Parkin–Shanks [153]conjecture predicts that $p(n)$ is even "half" the time. As stated earlier, this is still open. There are partial results in this direction. In [148], the authors refine the Kolberg argument and essentially using the pigeonhole principle show that

$$\#\big\{n \leq x : p(n) \text{ even}\big\} \gg \sqrt{x}.$$

They also count the number of $n \le x$ for which $p(n)$ is odd. But in this case, they get slightly weaker results of the form $\gg x^{1/2-\epsilon}$ for any $\epsilon > 0$. This was recently improved by Ahlgren [2] and Ahlgren and Boylan [4]. In [3], Ahlgren and Boylan show that Newman's conjecture is true for every prime modulus M, with the possible exception of $M = 3$. In addition, they obtain some quantitative results in this direction.

Subbarao [192] proposed the following generalization. If A, B are integers with $0 \le B < A$, there are infinitely many n for which $p(An + B)$ is even and infinitely many n for which $p(An + B)$ is odd. Over the decades, several special cases of this conjecture were established. For instance, Hirschhorn and Subbarao [81] proved the conjecture for $A = 16$.

Subbarao's conjecture is practically proved. The "odd" part remains open. More precisely, in a beautiful paper, using the theory of modular forms, Ono [150] has shown that there are infinitely many n such that $p(An + B)$ is even. If for some n_0, we have that $p(An_0 + B)$ is odd, then there are infinitely many n such that $p(An + B)$ is odd. Nicolas, Ruzsa, Sarkozy, and Serre [148] have shown that the number of $n \le x$ such that $p(An + B)$ is even is $\gg \sqrt{x}$. In the odd case, Ahlgren [2] has shown that the number of $n \le x$ for which $p(An + B)$ is odd is $\gg \sqrt{x}/\log x$. Recently, some small improvements on these results were obtained by Ahlgren.

There are other arithmetic questions one may ask concerning $p(n)$. We refer the reader to an excellent survey by Adhikari and Mukhopadhay [1] for related questions on this theme. Clearly, there is more work to be done, and what emerges from these recent developments is the ubiquitous modular connection in these problems.

Chapter 8
Some Nonlinear Identities for Divisor Functions

1 A Quadratic Relation Amongst Divisor Functions

Let $\sigma_s(n)$ denote the sum of the sth powers of the divisors of n. Also, set

$$\sigma_s(0) = \frac{1}{2}\zeta(-s)$$

where as usual $\zeta(s)$ denotes the Riemann zeta function. In his fundamental paper "On Certain Arithmetical Functions", Ramanujan showed that there is a quadratic relation involving $\sigma_s(n)$.

We have

$$\sum_{j\le x} \sigma_r(j) = \sum_{j\le x} \sum_{dt=j} d^r.$$

Interchanging the summation, the right-hand side is seen to be

$$\sum_{d\le x} d^r[x/d] = x\sum_{d\le x} d^{r-1} + O\Big(\sum_{d\le x} d^r\Big) = O\big(x^{r+1}\big).$$

On the other hand, we could also write this as

$$\sum_{t\le x} \sum_{d\le x/t} d^r \sim \sum_{t\le x} \frac{1}{r+1}(x/t)^{r+1}.$$

The right-hand side is seen to be

$$\sim \frac{1}{r+1}x^{r+1}\zeta(r+1).$$

The same method will allow us to treat

$$\sum_{j\le x} \sigma_r(j)(x-j)^s$$

and for integers $x = n$, we find that it is

$$\sim \frac{\Gamma(r+1)\Gamma(s+1)}{\Gamma(r+s+2)}\zeta(r+1)n^{r+s+1}$$

provided that $r > 0$ and $s \ge 0$.

M.R. Murty, V.K. Murty, *The Mathematical Legacy of Srinivasa Ramanujan*,
DOI 10.1007/978-81-322-0770-2_8, © Springer India 2013

Now let us set

$$\Sigma_{r,s}(n) = \sigma_r(0)\sigma_s(n) + \cdots + \sigma_r(n)\sigma_s(0).$$

Then, using the fact that

$$n^s < \sigma_s(n) < n^s\left(1^{-s} + 2^{-s} + \cdots\right) = n^s\zeta(s)$$

it follows that for $r > 0$ and $s \geq 0$,

$$\liminf \frac{\Sigma_{r,s}(n)}{n^{r+s+1}} \geq \frac{\Gamma(r+1)\Gamma(s+1)}{\Gamma(r+s+2)}\zeta(r+1)$$

and for $r > 0$ and $s > 1$,

$$\limsup \frac{\Sigma_{r,s}(n)}{n^{r+s+1}} \leq \frac{\Gamma(r+1)\Gamma(s+1)}{\Gamma(r+s+2)}\zeta(r+1)\zeta(s).$$

Ramanujan proves that whenever r and s are positive odd integers,

$$\Sigma_{r,s}(n) = \frac{\Gamma(r+1)\Gamma(s+1)}{\Gamma(r+s+2)} \frac{\zeta(r+1)\zeta(s+1)}{\zeta(r+s+2)}\sigma_{r+s+1}(n) + \frac{\zeta(1-r)+\zeta(1-s)}{r+s} n\sigma_{r+s-1}(n) + O\left(n^{\frac{2}{3}(r+s+1)}\right).$$

Moreover, he shows that in a finite number of cases, there is no error term. In other words, the O-term above can be removed, and one has an exact identity. The values of (r, s) for which this occurs are given in the table below.

r	s
1	1
1	3
1	5
1	7
1	11
3	3
3	5
3	9
5	7

In particular, the case $r = 1$ and $s = 3$ gives the identity

$$\sigma_1(1)\sigma_3(n) + \sigma_1(3)\sigma_3(n-1) + \sigma_1(5)\sigma_3(n-2) + \cdots + \sigma_1(2n+1)\sigma_3(0)$$
$$= \frac{1}{240}\sigma_5(2n+1).$$

2 Quadratic Relations Amongst Eisenstein Series

Since the Fourier coefficients of Eisenstein series are given in terms of the functions $\sigma_k(n)$, the relations of the previous section may be interpreted as quadratic relations satisfied by Eisenstein series. Using the fact that the space of modular forms of level

1 and weight k is one-dimensional for $4 \le k \le 10$ and for $k = 14$, one gets the following relations:

$$E_8(z) = E_4(z)^2,$$
$$E_{10}(z) = E_4(z)E_6(z),$$
$$E_{12}(z) - E_8(z)E_4(z) = -\frac{428000}{691}\Delta(z)$$

and

$$E_{12}(z) - E_6(z)^2 = \frac{762048}{691}\Delta(z).$$

All of these identities can be expressed as relations between the functions $\sigma_k(n)$ for various values of k and $\tau(n)$.

Ghate [59] has classified all monomial relations between Eisenstein series.

3 A Formula for the τ-Function

Building on the ideas of the previous section, we can also ask for relations between Eisenstein series and cusp forms. There is, of course, the relation

$$1728\Delta(z) = E_4(z)^3 - E_6(z)^2.$$

We have the Fourier expansion

$$E_k(z) = 1 - \frac{4k}{B_k}\sum_{n\ge 1}\sigma_{k-1}(n)q^n.$$

In particular,

$$E_4(z) = 1 + 240\sum_{n\ge 1}\sigma_3(n)q^n$$

and

$$E_6(z) = 1 - 504\sum_{n\ge 1}\sigma_5(n)q^n.$$

This leads to a nonlinear relation for $\tau(n)$ in terms of generalized divisor functions.

Starting from Lahiri [104], several authors have investigated the possibility of quadratic relations between Eisenstein series and cusp forms. These relations arise by studying the effect of certain differential operators on the space of modular forms. In particular, we will discuss three formulas for the τ-function in terms of divisor functions.

The first of these is due to Niebur [149].

Theorem 3.1 *For $n \ge 1$, we have*

$$\tau(n) = n^4\sigma(n) - 24\sum_{k=1}^{n-1}(35k^4 - 52k^3n + 18k^2n^2)\sigma(k)\sigma(n-k).$$

Proof Set

$$f(z) = -\log\Delta(z) = -2\pi i z + 24\sum_{n=1}^{\infty}\frac{\sigma(n)e(nz)}{n}.$$

Now define

$$F(z) = 18\big(f^{(3)}(z)\big)^2 + f'(z)f^{(5)}(z) - 16f^{(2)}(z)f^{(4)}(z).$$

Then $F(z) = F(z+1)$. Moreover, the first Fourier coefficient is $2^9 \cdot 3 \cdot \pi^6$. Hence, if we show that $F(-1/z) = z^{12}F(z)$, it will follow that

$$F(z) = 2^9 \cdot 3 \cdot \pi^6 \Delta(z).$$

The definition of f implies that

$$f(-1/z) = -\log z^{12} + f(z).$$

Differentiating this repeatedly, we get the identities

$$\begin{aligned}
f'(-1/z) &= -12z + z^2 f'(z),\\
f^{(2)}(-1/z) &= -12z^2 + 2z^3 f'(z) + z^4 f^{(2)}(z),\\
f^{(3)}(-1/z) &= -24z^3 + 6z^4 f'(z) + 6z^5 f^{(2)}(z) + z^6 f^{(3)}(z),\\
f^{(4)}(-1/z) &= -72z^4 + 24z^5 f'(z) + 36z^6 f^{(2)}(z) + 12z^7 f^{(3)}(z) + z^8 f^{(4)}(z),\\
f^{(5)}(-1/z) &= -288z^5 + 120z^6 f'(z) + 240z^7 f^{(2)}(z) + 120z^8 f^{(3)}(z)\\
&\quad + 20z^9 f^{(4)}(z) + z^{10} f^{(5)}(z).
\end{aligned}$$

Using these equations, we find that

$$H(z) = f^{(4)}(z) + f'(z)f^{(3)}(z) - \frac{3}{2}\big(f^{(2)}(z)\big)^2$$

is a cusp form of weight 4 for $SL_2(\mathbb{Z})$ and hence must be identically zero. On the other hand, we have

$$F(-1/z) = z^{12}F(z) - 12z^{11}H'(z) - 48z^{10}H(z)$$

and so

$$F(-1/z) = z^{12}F(z)$$

as required. □

4 Derivatives of Modular Forms

Let f be a modular form of weight k for a group Γ. In particular, we have

$$f\left(\frac{az+b}{cz+d}\right) = (cz+d)^k f(z)$$

for elements

$$\begin{pmatrix} a & b \\ c & d \end{pmatrix} \in \Gamma. \tag{39}$$

Differentiating this gives

$$(ad - bc)(cz + d)^{-2} f'\left(\frac{az + b}{cz + d}\right) = kc(cz + d)^{k-1} f(z) + (cz + d)^k f'(z)$$

and for $ad - bc = 1$, this is

$$f'\left(\frac{az + b}{cz + d}\right) = (cz + d)^{k+1}\big(kcf(z) + (cz + d) f'(z)\big).$$

Thus we see that differentiation in general destroys the modular property.

Define the differential operator

$$D = \frac{1}{2\pi i}\frac{d}{dz}.$$

Maass proposed the operator

$$\delta_k = \frac{1}{2\pi i}\frac{k}{2iy} + D = \frac{1}{2\pi i}\left(\frac{k}{2iy} + \frac{d}{dz}\right)$$

where $z = x + iy$. This operator, when applied to a holomorphic modular form, preserves the modular transformation property but not the holomorphy. Maass [118] proved that if f is a holomorphic modular form of weight k, then $\delta_k f$ is a real-analytic modular form of weight $k + 2$. More generally, he considered iterates of this operator, namely

$$\delta_k^{(r)} = \left(\frac{1}{2\pi i}\right)^r \left(\frac{k + 2r - 2}{2iy} + \frac{d}{dz}\right)\left(\frac{k + 2r - 4}{2iy} + \frac{d}{dz}\right) \cdots \left(\frac{k}{2iy} + \frac{d}{dz}\right)$$

and showed that it takes holomorphic modular forms of weight k to real-analytic modular forms of weight $k + 2r$.

A large number of nonlinear identities can be produced by computing the effect of the Maass operator on Eisenstein series.

In 1956, Rankin [170] proposed a differential operator on pairs of modular forms that preserves holomorphy. Let f be a modular form of weight k, and g a modular form of weight ℓ, both for the same subgroup Γ of $SL_2(\mathbb{Z})$. Now consider the operator

$$[f, g]_n = \sum_{r=0}^{n} (-1)^r \binom{k + n - 1}{n - r}\binom{\ell + n - 1}{r} D^r f D^{n-r} g.$$

In particular,

$$[f, g]_1 = kf Dg - \ell(Df)g.$$

If both f and g are modular for Γ (of weight k and ℓ respectively), then for

$$\begin{pmatrix} a & b \\ c & d \end{pmatrix} \in \Gamma \tag{40}$$

we have

$$[f,g]_1\left(\frac{az+b}{cz+d}\right)=\frac{1}{2\pi i}(cz+d)^{\ell+k}\big(kf(z)g'(z)-\ell g(z)f'(z)\big) \tag{41}$$

and this is

$$[f,g]_1\left(\frac{az+b}{cz+d}\right)=(cz+d)^{\ell+k+2}[f,g]_1(z).$$

In general, it is a result of Cohen (building on work of Rankin) that $[f,g]_n$ is a modular form of weight $k+\ell+2n$ for the same subgroup Γ. Moreover, if $n\geq 1$, it is a cusp form.

5 Differential Operators and Nonlinear Identities

Many examples of Maass derivatives and Rankin–Cohen brackets have been computed. Such calculations usually result in a nonlinear identity involving Fourier coefficients of Eisenstein series and cusp forms.

Formally, for a series

$$g(z)=\sum_{n=0}^{\infty}a(n)e^{2\pi inz}$$

we have

$$\delta_k^{(r)}g(z)=\sum_{n=0}^{\infty}b(n)e^{2\pi inz}$$

where

$$b(n)=\sum_{j=0}^{r}\binom{r}{j}\frac{\Gamma(k+r)}{\Gamma(k+r-j)}(-4\pi y)^{-j}n^{r-j}.$$

Using this and some general results of Shimura [189, 190], it is shown by Lanphier [109] that

$$\delta_4E_4\cdot\delta_4E_4=\frac{2}{9}\delta_8^{(2)}E_8-\frac{320}{3}\Delta.$$

Taking the projection of both sides to their holomorphic parts, the identity

$$\sum_{m=0}^{n}m\sigma_3(m)(n-m)\sigma_3(n-m)=\frac{2}{9}n^2\sigma_7(n)-\frac{320}{3}\tau(n)$$

is obtained. Rearranging gives the identity

$$\tau(n)=n^2\sigma_7(n)-540\sum_{m=1}^{n-1}m(n-m)\sigma_3(m)\sigma_3(n-m).$$

On the other hand, consider the Rankin–Cohen bracket $[E_4, E_6]_1$, which is a cusp form of weight 12 for the full modular group. Thus, it is a multiple of Δ. Unpacking this gives the relation

$$4E_4DE_6 - 6E_6DE_4 = -3456\Delta. \tag{42}$$

Also, we have the relation

$$E_{10} = E_4E_6.$$

This comes from the fact that the space of modular forms of weight $k \in [4, 10]$ is one-dimensional. Differentiating the above relation gives

$$DE_{10} = E_6DE_4 + E_4DE_6.$$

Inserting this into (42) gives the identity

$$\tau(n) = -\frac{11}{24}n\sigma_9(n) + \frac{35}{24}n\sigma_5(n) + 350\sum_{m=1}^{n-1}(n-m)\sigma_3(m)\sigma_5(n-m).$$

Ramakrishnan and Sahu [167] show how one can obtain all of the results of [109] using Rankin–Cohen brackets in place of the Maass operators and holomorphic projection.

6 Quasi-modular Forms

The Eisenstein series $E_2(z)$ (which is P in Ramanujan's notation) is not quite a modular form. It satisfies the transformation property

$$E_2\left(\frac{az+b}{cz+d}\right) = (cz+d)^2E_2(z) + \frac{12c(cz+d)}{2\pi i}$$

for any

$$\begin{pmatrix} a & b \\ c & d \end{pmatrix} \in SL_2(\mathbb{Z}).$$

More generally, Kaneko and Zagier [90] introduced the notion of a quasi-modular form to capture this behaviour.

Let k and s denote two non-negative integers. A holomorphic function f on the extended upper half-plane (that is, the upper half-plane together with the cusps) is called a quasi-modular form of weight k and depth s if there are holomorphic functions $Q_0(f), \ldots, Q_s(f)$ with the property that for any

$$\begin{pmatrix} a & b \\ c & d \end{pmatrix} \in \Gamma$$

we have

$$f\left(\frac{az+b}{cz+d}\right) = (cz+d)^k\sum_{i=0}^{s}Q_i(f)(z)\left(\frac{c}{cz+d}\right)^i.$$

Thus, E_2 is a quasi-modular form for $SL_2(\mathbb{Z})$ of weight 2 and depth 1.

By applying the identity element in the above, we see that a quasi-modular form f satisfies

$$f = Q_0(f).$$

Moreover, quasi-modular forms have Fourier expansions as they are periodic. This can be seen by applying the element

$$\begin{pmatrix} 1 & 1 \\ 0 & 1 \end{pmatrix} \in SL_2(Z)$$

to a quasi-modular form f giving the relation

$$f(z+1) = Q_0(f)(z) = f(z).$$

Denote by $\tilde{M}_k^{\leq s}$ the space of quasi-modular forms of weight k and depth s for the full modular group. The operator D preserves quasi-modular forms, and in fact

$$D : \tilde{M}_k^{\leq s} \longrightarrow \tilde{M}_{k+2}^{\leq s+1}.$$

Moreover, it is a fact that $s \leq k/2$. At the moment, the only examples of quasi-modular forms that we have are E_2 and derivatives of modular forms. It is a fact that all quasi-modular forms for the full modular group can be obtained in this way. In particular,

$$\tilde{M}_k^{\leq k/2} = \bigoplus_{i=0}^{k/2-1} D^i M_{k-2i} \oplus \mathbb{C} D^{k/2-1} E_2.$$

The functions $Q_i(f)$ in the definition of the quasi-modularity property are themselves quasi-modular forms by a result of Martin and Royer [121], Lemma 19. In fact, $Q_0(f) = f$ and $Q_i(f) \in \tilde{M}_{k-2i}^{\leq s-i}$.

The definition of the Rankin–Cohen bracket can be extended to the space of quasi-modular forms. In particular, Ramanujan's differential equation

$$DE_2 = -\frac{1}{12}\left(E_4 - E_2^2\right)$$

is a consequence of

$$[E_2, \Delta]_1 = \Delta E_4.$$

The relation

$$[E_2, E_2]_4 = -48\Delta$$

gives the Niebur identity

$$\tau(n) = n^4\sigma(n) - 24\sum_{a=1}^{n-1}(35a^4 - 52a^3n + 18a^2n^2)\sigma(a)\sigma(n-a).$$

Moreover, the relation

$$[E_4, DE_4]_1 = 960\Delta$$

gives the van der Pol identity

$$\tau(n) = n^2\sigma_3(n) + 60\sum_{a=1}^{n-1} a(9a - 5n)\sigma_3(a)\sigma_3(n-a).$$

7 Non-linear Congruences and Their Interpretation

Earlier, we saw that congruences satisfied by the τ-function that related it to various of the σ_k functions could be interpreted in terms of Galois representations. More specifically, the reducibility modulo a prime ℓ of the ℓ-adic representation attached to Δ resulted in a congruence for $\tau(p)$ modulo ℓ for (almost all) primes p.

In the case of non-linear relations, it is also possible to derive congruences by reducing modulo a prime that occurs in the support of the coefficients. For example, the van der Pol identity gives the congruence

$$\tau(n) \equiv n^2\sigma_3(n) \pmod{\ell}$$

for $\ell = 2, 3, 5$ (the primes dividing 60). In particular,

$$\tau(p) \equiv p^2\sigma_3(p) \pmod{\ell}$$

and it is this latter congruence that we seek to “explain”.

If we consider the ring of (mod ℓ) Galois representations associated to modular forms, it has an algebra structure under $\otimes$ product. If this algebra is finitely presented, then the set of relations will generate all possible quadratic (and higher-order) relations between the representations and hence also their characters.

Chapter 9
Mock Theta Functions and Mock Modular Forms

1 Historical Introduction

In his last letter to Hardy, written three months before his death in 1920, Ramanujan describes the beginnings of a new theory of what he called "mock theta functions." He gave no precise definition of these objects. Rather, he listed seventeen examples and a qualitative description of their key properties, namely, that these functions have asymptotic expansions at every rational point similar to classical theta functions, but that there was no single theta function whose asymptotic expansion agrees at all rational points with that of the mock theta function.

Since Ramanujan's letter, many mathematicians like G.N. Watson (who had in his possession the famed "lost" notebook), A. Selberg, and G.E. Andrews studied the examples Ramanujan had given and gave rigorous proofs of some of the statements he had made. New excitement emerged in the 1970s when Andrews [7] found Ramanujan's lost notebook among the papers of Watson and attempted to prove some of these conjectures.

Indeed, in 1988, Hickerson (see [78, 79]) proved many of these conjectures. However, no unifying theory emerged from these papers. It was only in 2002, when S. Zwegers completed his doctoral thesis under D. Zagier, that we find in his thesis an intrinsic characterization of mock theta functions. Later, Bringmann and Ono used this theory to resolve several open problems in combinatorics and the theory of q-series.

Before we proceed, it may be useful to direct the reader to the lucid Séminaire Bourbaki survey of Zagier [206] in which he writes "Ramanujan used the word 'theta function' where we would say 'modular form' today, so that 'mock theta functions' meant something like 'mock modular forms'." More precisely, a mock theta function is a mock modular form of weight $1/2$.

All of the seventeen examples of Ramanujan are of the form

$$\sum_{n=0}^{\infty} A_n(q),$$

M.R. Murty, V.K. Murty, *The Mathematical Legacy of Srinivasa Ramanujan*,
DOI 10.1007/978-81-322-0770-2_9, © Springer India 2013

where $A_n(q)$ is in $\mathbb{Q}(q)$, and for all $n \geq 1$, $A_{n+1}(q)/A_n(q) = R(q, q^n)$ for some fixed rational function $R(q, r) \in \mathbb{Q}(q, r)$. Such series are called q-hypergeometric series.

2 Ramanujan's Examples

What exactly was contained in Ramanujan's letter? What were his seventeen examples? Ramanujan divides his examples into three groups, four of "order 3", ten of "order 5" and three of "order" 7, though he gave no definition of what he meant by the word "order". Here are some examples:

$$f(q) = \sum_{n=0}^{\infty} \frac{q^{n^2}}{(1+q)^2 \cdots (1+q^n)^2},$$

$$\phi(q) = \sum_{n=0}^{\infty} \frac{(-q)^{n^2}}{(1+q^2)(1+q^4)\cdots(1+q^{2n})},$$

$$\psi(q) = \sum_{n=1}^{\infty} \frac{(-q)^{n^2}}{(1+q)(1+q^3)\cdots(1+q^{2n-1})}.$$

There is some structural similarity of these functions to those appearing in the Rogers–Ramanujan identities. However, these functions are more complex. Ramanujan states without proof that

$$2\phi(q) - f(q) = f(q) + 4\psi(q) = \frac{1 - 2q + 2q^4 - 2q^9 + \cdots}{(1+q)(1+q^2)(1+q^3)\cdots},$$

where the expression on the right-hand side is easily seen to be a modular form of weight $1/2$ (up to a factor of $q^{-1/24}$). From this example we see there are linear relations among the mock theta functions like $\phi = f + 2\psi$. The space spanned by them contains a subspace of ordinary modular forms, and after multiplying by a suitable power of q, we get modular behaviour. The other mock theta functions in Ramanujan's list have similar properties.

With all of these examples the following features emerge. If $H(q) \in \mathbb{Z}[[q]]$ is one of Ramanujan's mock theta functions, then $H(q)$ acquires some modular transformation property after the following steps: (i) multiply $H(q)$ by a suitable power of q; (ii) change q to $e^{2\pi i\tau}$ and set $h(\tau) = e^{2\pi i\lambda\tau} H(e^{2\pi i\tau})$; (iii) add a simple (but non-holomorphic) correction term so that the corrected function has modular properties.

3 The Work of Zwegers

In 2001, Zwegers (see [206]), in his doctoral thesis, discovered the relation between non-holomorphic modular forms, Lerch sums and indefinite theta series. Zwegers discovered that mock theta functions are really the "holomorphic parts" of real analytic modular forms of weight 1/2. This allowed one to define higher weight "mock theta functions", now called mock modular forms. Thus, a *mock modular form* is the holomorphic part of a weak Maass form, and there is a simple algebro-analytic description of these objects.

To motivate our discussion, we begin with the Fourier expansion of the Eisenstein series of weight k,

$$E_k(z) = 1 - \frac{4k}{B_k}\sum_{n\geq 1}\sigma_{k-1}(n)q^n,$$

and the observation that the infinite sum can be rewritten as

$$\sum_{d\geq 1} d^{k-1}\sum_{m\geq 1} q^{md} = \sum_{d\geq 1} d^{k-1}\frac{q^d}{1-q^d}.$$

A more complicated sum that bears some superficial resemblance to this is

$$\sum_{n\in\mathbb{Z}}(-1)^n\frac{q^{n(3n+1)/2}}{(1+q^n)}.$$

This function occurs in Ramanujan's "lost notebook".

Following Zwegers (and the exposition by Zagier), consider the function of two complex variables

$$\mu(u,v) = \mu(u,v,\tau) = \frac{a^{\frac{1}{2}}}{\theta(v)}\sum_{n\in\mathbb{Z}}\frac{(-b)^n q^{n(n+1)/2}}{1-aq^n},$$

where $q = e^{2\pi i\tau}$, $a = e^{2\pi iu}$ and $b = e^{2\pi iv}$, and $\theta(v)$ is the function

$$\theta(v) = \sqrt{b}q^{1/8}\sum_{m\in\mathbb{Z}}(-1)^m b^m q^{m(m+1)/2},$$

which by the Jacobi identity is

$$\theta(v) = \sqrt{b}q^{1/8}\prod_{n=1}^{\infty}(1-qn)\big(1-bq^n\big)\big(1-b^{-1}q^{n-1}\big).$$

Zwegers defines a function $R(z;\tau)$ with $z,\tau\in\mathbb{C}$ and τ having positive imaginary part, such that the function

$$\mu(u,v,\tau) - R(u-v,\tau)$$

is a Jacobi form. Now using the principle that specializing the elliptic variable in a Jacobi form to a "torsion point" results in a usual modular form (up to a multiple of a power of q), one gets a modular description of mock theta functions.

In particular, the function denoted $f(q)$ in the previous section (which Ramanujan called a mock theta function of order 3) satisfies the identity

$$\prod_{n=1}^{\infty}\big(1-q^n\big)f(q) = \sum_{n\in\mathbb{Z}}(-1)^n\frac{q^{n(3n+1)/2}}{(1+q^n)},$$

and Zwegers shows that if we set

$$R(\tau) = \sum_{n\equiv 1 \bmod 6} \operatorname{sgn}(n)\beta\big(n^2 y/6\big)q^{-n^2/24}$$

where

$$\beta(x) = \int_x^\infty u^{-\frac{1}{2}} e^{-\pi u},$$

then

$$q^{-1/24} f(q) + R(\tau)$$

transforms like a modular form of weight $1/2$ for the principal congruence subgroup $\Gamma(2)$ of level 2.

4 The Space of Mock Modular Forms

With Zweger's theory in hand, Zagier defines the space $\mathcal{M}_k$ of mock modular forms in the following way. It will contain the space $M_k^!$ of weakly holomorphic modular forms of weight k. These are holomorphic functions on the upper half-plane that transform like modular forms of weight k (under the action of a group Γ) and which may have a pole (of finite order) at each cusp. Then $\mathcal{M}_k$ is an extension that fits into an exact sequence

$$0 \longrightarrow M_k^! \longrightarrow \mathcal{M}_k \longrightarrow M_{2-k} \longrightarrow 0$$

where the first map is inclusion, and the second map to the space M_{2-k} of modular forms of weight $2-k$ (the so-called 'shadow map') is defined as follows. Given a modular form $g \in M_{2-k}$, define the transform

$$g^*(z) = (i/2)^{k-1} \int_{-\overline{z}}^{\infty} (w+z)^{-k}\overline{g(-\overline{w})}\, dw.$$

This is essentially an Eichler integral. Then the 'shadow' of $h \in \mathcal{M}_k$ is the unique element $g \in M_{2-k}$ for which $h + g^*$ transforms like a modular form of weight k for a certain subgroup of $SL_2(\mathbb{R})$. (The shadow mapping is reminiscent of Serre duality. See also the last section in Chap. 2.)

Neither the existence nor the uniqueness of g is evident from this description. However, there is an alternate description that will make this clear. Denote by M_k the space of real analytic functions f that transform under Γ by

$$f\left(\frac{az+b}{cz+d}\right) = \rho(\gamma)(cz+d)^k f(z)$$

with a character ρ of Γ. Define $\widehat{M_k}$ to be the elements $f \in M_k$ for which $(\Im z)^k \partial F/\partial \overline{z}$ is anti-holomorphic, that is

$$\frac{\partial}{\partial z}\left((\Im z)^k \frac{\partial F}{\partial \overline{z}}\right) = 0.$$

The elements of $\widehat{M_k}$ are called harmonic weak Maass forms. They are non-holomorphic modular forms which are eigenfunctions of the Laplacian with eigenvalue $k(2-k)/4$ and having at most exponential growth at the cusps.

5 Some Applications

With the formulation of the concept of a mock modular form, many arithmetic applications have been developed. Some of these have to do with congruences satisfied by the partition function. Others have to do with central critical values of L-functions. We briefly describe the latter as formulated by Bruinier and Ono [26].

The work of Waldspurger established a relation between the Fourier coefficients of half-integral weight modular forms and central critical values of quadratic twists of the L-functions associated to integral weight modular forms, with the two forms in question being connected by the Shimura correspondence. In the case of Maass forms, work of Katok and Sarnak related Fourier coefficients of Maass forms of weight $1/2$ to line integrals of certain Maass cusp forms. Bruinier and Ono consider the analogues of these results for harmonic weak Maass forms that are not weakly holomorphic modular forms (in other words, whose shadow is nonzero). Such forms have a Fourier expansion of the form

$$f_g(z) = \sum_{n \gg -\infty} c^+(n)q^n + \sum_{n<0} c^-(n)W(2\pi n v)q^n$$

where

$$W(x) = W_k(x) = \Gamma\big(1-k, 2|x|\big)$$

is the incomplete Gamma function. The first sum is referred to as the holomorphic part of f, and the second sum as the non-holomorphic part.

Now consider a normalized eigenform $G(z)$ of weight 2 for $\Gamma_0(p)$ with the property that the sign of the functional equation in its L-function is -1. By Kohnen's theory (which is an explicit form of the Shimura correspondence), there is a newform g of weight $3/2$ for $\Gamma_0(4p)$ in Kohnen's plus space which lifts to G under the Shimura correspondence. Then, Bruinier and Ono prove that there is a weight $1/2$ harmonic weak Maass form f_g (say) on $\Gamma_0(4p)$ with the following property. If we write the Fourier expansion as

$$f_g(z) = \sum_{n \gg -\infty} c_g^+(n)q^n + \sum_{n<0} c_g^-(n)W(2\pi n v)q^n,$$

then for negative fundamental discriminants D for which $(\frac{D}{p}) = 1$, we have the Waldspurger-type formula

$$L(G, \chi_D, 1) = 8\pi^2 \|G\|^2 \|g\|^2 \sqrt{\frac{|D|}{N}} c_g^-(D)^2,$$

where $\|\cdot\|$ denotes the Petersson norm. Moreover, they show that for positive fundamental discriminants D for which $(\frac{D}{p}) = 1$, we have that the derivative $L'(G, \chi_D, 1) = 0$ if and only if $c_g^+(D)$ is algebraic.

Finally, they make interesting conjectures about the number of transcendental Fourier coefficients and the number of non-zero Fourier coefficients.

All of this opens a new world of mathematics. The reader will profit much by reading the excellent survey by Ono [152] to get a glimpse of more wonders. It is thus fitting to close this informal discussion with some prophetic words of Freeman Dyson [45]: "The mock theta functions give us tantalizing hints of a grand synthesis still to be discovered. Somehow it should be possible to build them into a coherent group-theoretical structure, analogous to the structure of modular forms which Hecke built around the old theta functions of Jacobi. This remains a challenge for the future." With these recent advances, Dyson's dream may soon be realized.

Chapter 10
Prime Numbers and Highly Composite Numbers

1 The Divisor Functions

The structural properties of natural numbers and their detailed study forms a significant chapter in analytic number theory. In his memoir on highly composite numbers, Ramanujan initiated an important method to study general arithmetic functions. This method has become a dominant theme in current research. Surprisingly, these studies take us into allied areas of transcendental number theory and an intimate study of the Riemann zeta function.

Ramanujan's memoir of 1915 dealing with highly composite numbers begins with the divisor function $d(n)$ which is the number of divisors of n. It is easy to see that if

$$n = p_1^{a_1} p_2^{a_2} \cdots p_k^{a_k}$$

is the unique factorization of n as a product of distinct prime powers, then

$$d(n) = (a_1 + 1)(a_2 + 1) \cdots (a_k + 1).$$

There are many ways one can try to understand the nature of such a function. For example, one can try to understand the *average order* by studying

$$\sum_{n \le x} d(n).$$

This was done by Dirichlet who proved that

$$\sum_{n \le x} d(n) = x \log x + (2\gamma - 1)x + O(x^{1/2}),$$

where γ is Euler's constant. Thus, on average, $d(n)$ behaves like $\log n$. The celebrated Dirichlet divisor problem is to find the infimum of all θ such that

$$\sum_{n \le x} d(n) = x \log x + (2\gamma - 1)x + O(x^{\theta}). \tag{43}$$

It is conjectured that this infimum is $1/4$. After Dirichlet, Voronoi proved in 1904 that $\theta \le 1/3$. In 1916, Hardy showed that $\theta \ge 1/4$. After a succession of powerful

DOI 10.1007/978-81-322-0770-2_10, © Springer India 2013

and ingenious methods in the theory of exponential sums, the current record is $\theta \leq 131/416$ due to Martin Huxley in 2003.

One can also study "moments" of the divisor function

$$\sum_{n\leq x} d^k(n)$$

and try to obtain asymptotics for this. This approach was initiated by Ramanujan. For example, he proved that

$$\sum_{n\leq x} d^2(n) = Ax\log^3 x + Bx\log^2 x + Cx\log x + Dx + O\big(x^{3/5+\epsilon}\big),$$

for any $\epsilon > 0$. He noted that the error term can be improved to $O(x^{1/2+\epsilon})$ on the Riemann hypothesis. This should be compared with a result of Ingham [84], who proved in 1927 that

$$\sum_{n\leq x} d(n)d(n+\lambda) \sim \frac{6}{\pi^2}\sigma_{-1}(\lambda)x\log^2 x$$

as x tends to infinity. In other words, $d(n)$ and $d(n+\lambda)$ $(\lambda \neq 0)$ have little "correlation" since this is significantly of lower order by a factor of $\log x$ if $\lambda \neq 0$. More generally, he obtains on the Riemann hypothesis that

$$\sum_{n\leq x} d^k(n) = xP_k(\log x) + O\big(x^{1/2+\epsilon}\big),$$

where $P_k(t)$ is a polynomial of degree $2^k - 1$. In this context, Ramanujan studies the Dirichlet series

$$\sum_{n=1}^{\infty} \frac{d^2(n)}{n^s}$$

and more generally

$$\sum_{n=1}^{\infty} \frac{\sigma_a(n)\sigma_b(n)}{n^s},$$

where $\sigma_a(n) = \sum_{d|n} d^a$ are the generalized divisor functions. This is a precursor to the general construction of a Rankin–Selberg convolution in the theory of automorphic L-functions. Indeed, Ramanujan proves that

$$\sum_{n=1}^{\infty} \frac{\sigma_a(n)\sigma_b(n)}{n^s} = \frac{\zeta(s)\zeta(s-a)\zeta(s-b)\zeta(s-a-b)}{\zeta(2s-a-b)} \tag{44}$$

and, moreover, that

$$\sum_{n=1}^{\infty} \frac{\sigma_a(n)\sigma_b(n)\chi(n)}{n^s} = \frac{L(s,\chi)L(s-a,\chi)L(s-b,\chi)L(s-a-b,\chi)}{L(2s-a-b,\chi^2)}$$

where χ is the non-trivial Dirichlet character (mod 4). Both of these equations are based on a simple power series identity noted by Ramanujan, namely

$$\sum_{n=0}^{\infty}(1+z+z^2+\cdots+z^n)(1+w+w^2+\cdots+w^n)q^n$$
$$=\frac{1-zwq^2}{(1-q)(1-zq)(1-wq)(1-zwq)}.$$

Estermann [51] considered the more general Dirichlet series

$$\sum_{n=1}^{\infty}\frac{d_k(n)^r}{n^s},$$

where $d_k(n)$ is the number of ways of writing n as a product of k natural numbers. In this context, several cognate sums appear, and they are of two types. The first is of "Rankin–Selberg" type, and the second seems to be of "modular type" at least in a majority of cases. An example of the first type is the sum

$$\sum_{n\le x} d(n)d(n+\lambda),$$

mentioned above, and more generally

$$\sum_{n\le x}\sigma_a(n)\sigma_b(n+\lambda),$$

both of which were studied by Ingham in [84], who derived asymptotic formulas for them. Indeed, their asymptotic behaviour had been conjectured by Ramanujan in his 1915 paper. The second type involves

$$\sum_{j<n}\sigma_a(j)\sigma_b(n-j).$$

These convolutions can be evaluated explicitly in terms of Fourier coefficients of modular forms when a, b are odd and ≥ 3. In fact, Ramanujan showed that the above sum is asymptotic to

$$\frac{\Gamma(a+1)\Gamma(b+1)\zeta(a+1)\zeta(b+1)}{\Gamma(a+b+2)\zeta(a+b+2)}\sigma_{a+b+1}(n)$$

and conjectured that the same must hold for other values of a, b. According to Bruce Berndt's commentary, in 1979, Grosjean [60] disproved this conjecture, but the paper seems lodged in a journal that is not so easily accessible. However, in 1957, Halberstam [66] seems to have also disproved the conjecture using the circle method and estimates for Kloosterman sums. (There is also a later work by Motohashi [127] related to this problem.) Halberstam proves that there are additional terms to the asymptotic formula and when a and b are both odd, these terms disappear.

If at least one of a, b is even, there seem to be no explicit formulas of the type Ramanujan derived. One only has asymptotic formulas. A theoretical explanation of why such formulas are missing would be welcome since there is no apparent modular connection and would perhaps open a new area of research.

2 Ramanujan and the Prime Number Theorem

Ingham [85] noted that Ramanujan's identity (44) implies the non-vanishing of $\zeta(s)$ on $\Re(s) = 1$. It is well known that this is equivalent to the prime number theorem, which asserts that the number of primes $p \le x$, denoted $\pi(x)$ satisfies the asymptotic law

$$\pi(x) \sim \frac{x}{\log x}$$

as $x \to \infty$. This was proved by Hadamard and de la Vallée Poussin (independently) in 1896. Using an analogue of (44) for L-series, Ingham [85] noticed we also get non-vanishing of Dirichlet L-series on $\Re(s) = 1$, a fact which is equivalent to the prime number theorem for arithmetic progressions. This says that if $\pi(x, q, a)$ is the number of primes $p \le x$ which are congruent to $a \pmod q$, with $(a, q) = 1$, we have the asymptotic

$$\pi(x, q, a) \sim \frac{x}{\varphi(q) \log x},$$

where φ denotes Euler's function.

As noted by Riemann in his celebrated paper of 1860, the function

$$\operatorname{li} x := \lim_{\epsilon \to 0} \left(\int_0^{1-\epsilon} \frac{dt}{\log t} + \int_{1+\epsilon}^{x} \frac{dt}{\log t} \right)$$

is a better approximation to $\pi(x)$ than $x/\log x$ in the sense that the effective version of the prime number theorem of Hadamard and de la Vallée Poussin can be stated as

$$\pi(x) = \operatorname{li} x + O\left(x e^{-c\sqrt{\log x}}\right)$$

for some constant $c > 0$. Elaborate techniques in the theory of exponential sums have only led to modest improvements of this result. By a 1958 result of Korobov and Richert, we know that

$$\pi(x) = \operatorname{li} x + O\left(x^{-c_1 (\log x)^{2/3}}\right)$$

for some positive constant $c_1 > 0$. There has not been any further improvement. Any result of the form

$$\pi(x) = \operatorname{li} x + O\left(x^{\theta}\right)$$

with $\theta < 1$ is equivalent to the assertion that $\zeta(s) \neq 0$ for $\Re(s) > \theta$. Thus, if we are allowed to take any $\theta > 1/2$, this is equivalent to the Riemann hypothesis. An excellent exposition of the relationship between exponential sums, zero-free regions of $\zeta(s)$ and error terms in the prime number theorem can be found in [198]. In [16], Balasubramanian and Ramachandra show that a suitable extension of (44) immediately leads to the prime number theorem for arithmetic progressions with error terms.

In his first letter to G.H. Hardy sent on 16 January 1913, Ramanujan wrote, "I have found a function which exactly represents the number of primes less than x, 'exactly' in the sense that the difference between the function and the actual number of primes is generally 0 or some finite value even when x becomes infinite. I have got the function in the form of infinite series and have expressed it in two ways:

(1) in terms of Bernoulli numbers ...
(2) as a definite integral ..."

In his second letter, Ramanujan gave a third expression for $\pi(x)$.

These assertions can be given the following form. Using the notation of Hardy [67], let

$$J(x) = \int_0^\infty \frac{(\log x)^t \, dt}{t\zeta(t+1)\Gamma(t+1)},$$

$$G(x) = \frac{4}{\pi} \sum_{k=1}^{\infty} \frac{k}{(2k-1)B_{2k}} \left(\frac{\log x}{2\pi}\right)^{2k-1},$$

$$R(x) = \sum_{k=1}^{\infty} \frac{\mu(k)}{k} \int_c^{x^{1/k}} \frac{dt}{\log t},$$

"where $c = 1.45136380\ldots$ nearly" to quote from Ramanujan's second letter of 27 February 1913.

The last series, $R(x)$, appears for the first time in Riemann's 1860 paper, which Ramanujan could not have read. The series $G(x)$ is related to one discovered by Gram. But the series $J(x)$ was due to Ramanujan. Hardy [67] is of the opinion that Ramanujan discovered all these series for $\pi(x)$ independently.

Ramanujan's assertions imply that if $F(x)$ is any of these three functions,

$$\pi(x) - F(x) = O(1). \tag{45}$$

In his essay on Ramanujan's work on prime numbers, Hardy [67] proceeds to show how (45) is false. Indeed, one can show that

$$J(x) = R(x) + o(1)$$

and

$$G(x) = R(x) + o(1),$$

so that one need only study the validity of

$$\pi(x) = R(x) + O(1).$$

From this would follow

$$\pi(x) = \mathrm{li}\, x + O\left(x^{1/2+\epsilon}\right)$$

for any $\epsilon > 0$, an assertion already noted to be equivalent to the Riemann hypothesis. However, the result also implies, as indicated by Hardy [67],

$$\pi(x) = \mathrm{li}\, x - \frac{1}{2} \mathrm{li}\, x^{1/2} + O\left(x^{1/3+\epsilon}\right)$$

for any $\epsilon > 0$. In particular, this implies

$$\pi(x) - \operatorname{li} x \to -\infty \tag{46}$$

as $x \to \infty$. But in 1914, Littlewood showed that

$$\pi(x) - \operatorname{li} x = \Omega_{\pm}\left(\frac{x^{1/2}\log\log\log x}{\log x}\right).$$

This means that there are positive constants c_1, c_2 such that

$$\pi(x) - \operatorname{li} x > c_1 \frac{x^{1/2}\log\log\log x}{\log x}$$

for infinitely many x tending to infinity and

$$\pi(x) - \operatorname{li} x < -c_2 \frac{x^{1/2}\log\log\log x}{\log x}$$

for infinitely many x tending to infinity. Thus, (46) is false.

In his letters, Ramanujan also made interesting assertions about what we now call "prime number races." In his first letter, he wrote "The difference between the number of prime numbers of the form $4n-1$ and which are less than x, and those of the form $4n+1$ less than x, is infinite when x becomes infinite." In other words, if we denote by $\pi_a(x)$ the number of primes $p \le x$ with $p \equiv a \pmod 4$, with $a = 1, 3$, then Ramanujan's assertion is that

$$\pi_3(x) - \pi_1(x) \to \infty \tag{47}$$

as x tends to infinity. Now from the prime number theorem for arithmetic progressions we have

$$\pi_1(x) \sim \pi_3(x) \sim \frac{1}{2}\operatorname{li} x$$

as x tends to infinity. It is surprising that Hardy does not discuss this in his book since (47) was shown to be false by Littlewood [112] in 1914.

The theme of "prime number races" is a topic of current research. In the 1960s, Knapowski and Turan [99] wrote a series of papers developing a new branch of number theory called comparative prime number theory to tackle such questions.

However, the study of $\pi_3(x) - \pi_1(x)$ goes back to Tchebycheff [195] in 1853, who made two assertions. Let

$$\Delta(x) = \pi_3(x) - \pi_1(x).$$

(1) Then, there exists an infinite sequence of real numbers $\{x_r\}$ tending to infinity such that

$$\lim_{r\to\infty} \frac{\Delta(x_r)\log x_r}{\sqrt{x_r}} = 1;$$

(2) define the function

$$f(\sigma) = \sum_p (-1)^{(p-1)/2} e^{-\sigma p},$$

where the sum is over prime numbers. Then, as $\sigma \to 0^+$, the function $f(\sigma)$ tends to $-\infty$.

The reader will note that in the summation in (2), primes congruent to 1 (mod 4) are weighted with a + sign and primes congruent to 3 (mod 4) are weighted with a − sign. Ramanujan's assertion can be seen as a variation on assertion (2) of Tchebycheff. Naively, the assertion says that there are "more" primes congruent to 3 (mod 4) than there are primes congruent to 1 (mod 4). As mentioned earlier, Littlewood showed in 1918 that

$$\pi_3(x) - \pi_1(x) = \Omega_{\pm}\left(\frac{x^{1/2}\log\log\log x}{\log x}\right),$$

so that Tchebycheff's assertion (1) is true. In fact, the limit 1 can be replaced by any real number, and the assertion is true. Regarding (2), Hardy and Littlewood [68] show that if χ is the non-trivial character (mod 4) and

$$L(s,\chi) = \sum_{n=1}^{\infty} \frac{\chi(n)}{n^s}$$

satisfies the analog of the Riemann hypothesis, then there exists an $H > 0$ such that

$$\sum_p (-1)^{(p-1)/2} e^{-\sigma p} < -\frac{H}{\sqrt{\sigma}\log(1/\sigma)}$$

for all sufficiently small values of σ. Thus, (2) follows on the Riemann hypothesis for $L(s,\chi)$.

On the other hand, Landau [105] showed that if $L(s,\chi)$ does not satisfy the Riemann hypothesis, then

$$-\infty = \liminf_{\sigma\to 0^+} f(\sigma) \quad \text{and} \quad \limsup_{\sigma\to 0^+} f(\sigma) = +\infty.$$

Thus, the function in (2) has no limit as $\sigma \to 0^+$ if the Riemann hypothesis for $L(s,\chi)$ is false. Put in another way, (2) implies the Riemann hypothesis for $L(s,\chi)$.

The more general problem of studying

$$\pi(x,q,a_1) - \pi(x,q,a_2)$$

has been explored in detail in a series of papers by Knapowski and Turan [99].

In his letter of February 1913, Ramanujan wrote that

$$\pi(x,q,a_1) - \pi(x,q,a_2) \to \infty$$

for the triples $(q;a_1,a_2) = (4;3,1), (6;5,1), (8;3,1)$ and $(12;5,1)$. Of course, all of these assertions are false, but they hint at the fact that Ramanujan gave some thought to such oscillation questions in India, before his journey to England in 1914.

3 Highly Composite Numbers

What is perhaps surprising about the "Twelve Lectures" is the arrangement of topics of Hardy's lectures, as well as the omissions. The first four of the lectures are devoted to classical analytic number theory. But Ramanujan's paper on highly composite numbers finds no discussion.

A number n is said to by *highly composite* if $d(m) < d(n)$ whenever $m < n$. His paper discussing highly composite numbers is over sixty pages and signals a general method by which to study other arithmetical functions.

To understand Ramanujan's work in this context, we review some history of results concerning the divisor function. It is elementary to show that

$$d(n) = O\left(n^{\epsilon}\right)$$

for any $\epsilon > 0$ (see, for example, [131]). Using the prime number theorem, Wigert [203] proved in 1907 that for any $\epsilon > 0$,

$$d(n) < 2^{(1+\epsilon)\log n/\log\log n} \tag{48}$$

for all n sufficiently large and that

$$d(n) > 2^{(1-\epsilon)\log n/\log\log n} \tag{49}$$

for infinitely many n. This result determines the maximal order of the divisor function. Ramanujan proved (48) and (49) independently without using the prime number theorem. In fact, he proved the stronger assertion that the maximal order of $\log d(n)$ is

$$(\log 2)\,\mathrm{li}(\log n) + O\left((\log n)\exp(-c\sqrt{\log n})\right)$$

for some positive constant $c > 0$. The essential idea is as follows.

Let

$$\theta(x) = \sum_{p \le x} \log p,$$

where the sum is over primes $p \le x$. Suppose that N has k distinct prime factors. Then, it is easy to show that

$$d(N) < \frac{[(\theta(p_k) + \log N)/k]^k}{(\log p_1)\cdots(\log p_k)},$$

where p_j denotes the jth prime number. Now partial summation shows that

$$\pi(x)\log x - \theta(x) = \int_2^x \frac{\pi(t)\,dt}{t}. \tag{50}$$

If we have the prime number theorem, then it is easy to deduce

$$\theta(p_k) \sim p_k \sim k\log k.$$

But one can deduce $\theta(p_k) \sim k\log k$ from (50), and this is essentially Ramanujan's idea (see also Robin [174]).

As noted by Nicolas [146], Ramanujan's method also determines the maximal order of $r(n)$, the number of ways of writing n as a sum of two squares. One finds that $r(n)$ has the same maximal order as the divisor function. Nicolas [147] points out that this result is given incorrectly on p. 270 of the classic textbook by Hardy and Wright [72].

In his paper, Ramanujan introduces the notion of a "superior highly composite number." N is said to be a *superior highly composite number* if for some $\epsilon > 0$, we have

$$\frac{d(m)}{m^{\epsilon}} \leq \frac{d(N)}{N^{\epsilon}}$$

for all $m < N$. Since

$$d(m) \leq (m/N)^{\epsilon} d(N) < d(N)$$

for all $m < N$, we see that a superior highly composite number is also highly composite.

Ramanujan gave a complete classification of highly composite numbers and superior highly composite numbers. Surprisingly, there is an interesting connection to transcendental number theory that we explain in the next section.

4 Relation to the Six Exponential Conjecture

Define

$$\mathcal{E} = \left\{ \frac{\log(1 + 1/k)}{\log p},\ \ p \text{ prime}, k \geq 1, k \geq \mathbb{Z} \right\}.$$

If $\epsilon \notin \mathcal{E}$, then the maximum of $d(n)/n^{\epsilon}$ is attained at only one integer N_{ϵ}, and we have

$$N_{\epsilon} = \prod_{P} p^{\alpha_p}, \quad \alpha_p = \left[1/\left(p^{\epsilon} - 1\right)\right].$$

By the six exponentials theorem explained below and proved by Siegel, we know that for real λ and three distinct primes p, q, r, the numbers

$$p^{\lambda}, q^{\lambda}, r^{\lambda}$$

cannot all be rational unless λ is an integer. This implies that three elements of $\mathcal{E}$ cannot be equal.

The six exponentials theorem is easy to explain. Suppose that x_1, x_2 are linearly independent over $\mathbb{Q}$ and y_1, y_2, y_3 are linearly independent over $\mathbb{Q}$. Then, at least one of the six exponentials $e^{x_i y_j}$, $1 \leq i \leq 2$ and $1 \leq j \leq 3$, is transcendental. It is conjectured that one can take y_1, y_2 linearly independent over $\mathbb{Q}$ and at least one of the four exponentials $e^{x_i y_j}$ with $1 \leq i, j \leq 2$ is transcendental.

Now suppose that three elements of $\mathcal{E}$ are equal. Then we have

$$\lambda = \frac{\log(1 + 1/k_p)}{\log p} = \frac{\log(1 + 1/k_q)}{\log q} = \frac{\log(1 + 1/k_r)}{\log r}$$

for three distinct primes p, q, r and positive integers k_p, k_q, k_r. Then,

$$p^{\lambda} = 1 + \frac{1}{k_p}, \quad q^{\lambda} = 1 + \frac{1}{k_q}, \quad r^{\lambda} = 1 + \frac{1}{k_r}$$

are all rational. If λ is irrational, this contradicts the six exponentials theorem since we may take $x_1 = 1$, $x_2 = \lambda$ and $y_1 = \log p$, $y_2 = \log q$, $y_3 = \log r$ in the theorem. Therefore, λ is rational. But $p^\lambda = 1 + 1/k_p$ being rational implies that λ must be a positive integer. Now,

$$\lambda = \frac{\log(1 + 1/k_p)}{\log p} \leq \frac{\log 2}{\log p},$$

and hence $p^\lambda \leq 2$, which means $p = 2$ and $\lambda = 1$. The same applies for q and r, a contradiction, since p, q, r are distinct.

The connection to the six exponentials theorem was made by Alaoglu and Erdös [6]. The four exponential conjecture would imply that all elements of $\mathcal{E}$ are distinct. If true, this would mean that $d(n)/n^\epsilon$ attains its maximum at two integers. If false, the maximum would be attained at four integers for some ϵ. As Nicolas [147] points out, this was overlooked by Ramanujan.

5 Counting Highly Composite Numbers

Ramanujan devoted a section of his paper to the study of $Q(x)$, the number of highly composite numbers $\leq x$. Since $d(2n) > d(n)$, we see that between x and $2x$, there is always a highly composite number. Indeed, taking the largest highly composite number v in the interval $[1, x]$, we have $d(v) > d(n)$ for all $n \leq x$, $n \neq v$. Now $2v \in [x, 2x]$ and $d(2v) > d(v)$, so that $Q(x) > \log x$. In his paper, Ramanujan [160] showed that

$$\lim_{x \to \infty} \frac{Q(x)}{\log x} = +\infty.$$

Clearly, the determination of $Q(x)$ was of significant interest to Ramanujan. In their joint paper [70], Hardy and Ramanujan wrote "The problem of determining the number $Q(x)$ of highly composite numbers not exceeding x appears to be one of extreme difficulty. It is still uncertain whether or not the order of $Q(x)$ is greater than that of any power of $\log x$."

Several mathematicians afterwards took up this problem. In 1944, P. Erdös showed that for some $c_1 > 1$, $Q(x) > (\log x)^{c_1}$. The new ingredient was Hoheisel's theorem [82]:

$$\pi\left(x + x^\delta\right) - \pi(x) \geq \frac{x^\delta}{\log x}. \tag{51}$$

Hoheisel's result has since been improved, but the connection to the distribution of primes in short intervals is important. One expects that (51) is true with any $\delta > 0$. The Riemann hypothesis would imply that any $\delta > 1/2$ is permissible.

In 1971, Nicolas [145] proved that there is a constant c_2 such that

$$Q(x) \leq (\log x)^{c_2}.$$

This resolves one of the questions raised by Hardy and Ramanujan. The order of $Q(x)$ is not greater than any power of $\log x$.

Here again, Nicolas [145] used a result from transcendental number theory to prove the theorem. More precisely, he used Feldman's theorem: let

$$\theta = \frac{\log(3/2)}{\log 2}.$$

There exists a κ such that for all integers $u, v \geq 1$, we have

$$|v\theta - u| \geq v^{-\kappa}.$$

The question of determining optimal values of c_1, c_2 remains open. Nicolas remarks that if we assume two conjectures, namely that (51) holds for any $\delta > 0$ and that for all $\eta > 0$, there exists a constant $B(\eta) = B$ such that for all $u, v, w \in \mathbb{Z}$, we have

$$|u \log 5 + v \log 3 + w \log 2| \geq B\big((|u|+1)(|v|+1)\big)^{-1-\eta},$$

then writing $Q(x) = (\log x)^{c(x)}$, we have

$$\limsup_{x\to\infty} c(x) = \frac{\log 30}{\log 16} = 1.227\ldots.$$

Unconditionally, we have

$$1.136 \leq c_1 \leq c_2 \leq 1.71.$$

All of these results are based on our knowledge of Diophantine approximations of $(\log(3/2)/\log 2)$.

6 Maximal Order of Divisor Functions and Other Arithmetic Functions

In his paper on highly composite numbers, Ramanujan studied related arithmetical functions like the generalized divisor functions $d_k(n)$ counting the number of ways of writing n as a product of k numbers. He also studied the generalized divisor sum functions $\sigma_s(n)$, the sum of the sth powers of the positive divisors of n. However, these were not published. In fact, sections 53 to 75 of his paper on highly composite numbers were expunged in the final publication since the London Mathematical Society was having financial difficulties. Indeed, in the first edition of Ramanujan's collected papers, the editors wrote, "The paper, as long as it is, is not complete. The London Mathematical Society was in some financial difficulty at the time and Ramanujan suppressed part of what he had written, in order to save expense" (see p. 238 of [145]). Fortunately, the suppressed part has been preserved and has since been published in the first volume of the Ramanujan journal [166]. The sections of the unpublished part of [160] were in a box of G.N. Watson's papers kept at Trinity College Library and accidentally discovered by G.E. Andrews along with the now famous "Lost Notebook" of Ramanujan.

One would wonder at this strange excision of a complete manuscript by the London Mathematical Society. Nicolas and Robin in [166] wrote, "Hardy did not much like highly composite numbers. In the preface to the "Collected Works" he writes that "The long memoir [160] represents work, perhaps, in a backwater of mathematics," but a few lines later, he does recognize that "it shews very clearly Ramanujan's extraordinary mastery over the algebra of inequalities." One of us can remember Freeman Dyson in Urbana (in 1987), saying that when he was a research student of Hardy, he wanted to do research on highly composite numbers, but Hardy dissuaded him as he thought the subject was not sufficiently interesting or important." This explains to some extent why the topic did not find a place in Hardy's twelve lectures [67]. This is the second occasion in which Hardy used the phrase "backwater of mathematics" referring to some aspect of Ramanujan's work.

In his unpublished sections of [160], Ramanujan extended the notion of a highly composite number to other arithmetical functions such as $r_{2k}(n)$, the number of ways of writing n as a sum of $2k$ squares. He also studied the maximal order of $r_Q(n)$, the number of ways of writing n as $Q(x, y)$ with Q being a positive definite binary quadratic form. As noted above, he considered maximal orders of $d_k(n)$ and $\sigma_s(n)$.

For example, the notion of a superior highly composite number extended to the study of $\sigma(n)$ is a number n such that

$$\frac{\sigma(m)}{m} < \frac{\sigma(n)}{n}$$

for all $m < n$. Such numbers are now called *superabundant numbers*. *Colossally superabundant numbers* are numbers n for which there is a positive $\epsilon > 0$ such that

$$\frac{\sigma(n)}{n^{1+\epsilon}} \geq \frac{\sigma(m)}{m^{1+\epsilon}}$$

for all $m > 1$. It turns out that the set of colossal superabundant numbers is infinite and is a subset of the superabundant numbers [6]. The study of these numbers was initiated by Ramanujan [166] in the suppressed portion of [160].

One particular result here requires special mention. The maximal order of $\sigma_{-1}(n) = \sigma(n)/n$ is $e^{\gamma} \log\log n$, where γ is Euler's constant. From formula (382) of Ramanujan's paper [166] it follows under the Riemann hypothesis that for n_0 sufficiently large,

$$\sigma(n) \leq e^{\gamma} n \log\log n.$$

Robin [174] shows that if this inequality holds for all $n > 5040$, then the Riemann hypothesis follows. Lagarias [103] showed that the Riemann hypothesis is equivalent to

$$\sigma(n) \leq H_n + e^{H_n} \log H_n,$$

where $H_n = \sum_{j \leq n} 1/j$. This particular reformulation finds a place in logic, where it was used to show that the Riemann hypothesis is "Diophantine." In fact, this equivalence of the Riemann hypothesis is intimately connected with the study of highly composite numbers.

7 Maximal Orders of Fourier Coefficients of Cusp Forms

As a consequence of Deligne's work [39], we know that

$$\left|\tau(n)\right| \leq n^{11/2} d(n),$$

and more generally, if $\lambda_f(n)$ is the nth Fourier coefficient of a normalized Hecke eigenform f of weight k, then

$$\left|\lambda_f(n)\right| \leq n^{(k-1)/2} d(n).$$

One would like to determine the maximal order of $\tau(n)$ and generally $\lambda_f(n)$. In other words, are these inequalities sharp? From our earlier discussion about the maximal order of $d(n)$ we see that the above implies

$$\lambda_f(n) = O\left(n^{(k-1)/2} \exp\left(\frac{c \log n}{\log\log n}\right)\right)$$

for some positive constant c. For the full modular group, the reader will recall that normalized Hecke eigenforms have real coefficients, and so, the question of whether these coefficients get very close to the given bound above is the question of its maximal order. R. Murty [128] showed that

$$\lambda_f(n) = \Omega_{\pm}\left(n^{(k-1)/2} \exp\left(\frac{c \log n}{\log\log n}\right)\right)$$

for some $c > 0$. For this purpose, he needed to use analytic properties of symmetric power L-functions attached to the automorphic representation associated to f. With recent progress on the Sato–Tate conjecture, it is likely that new ideas can be injected into the further study of such oscillation results. Indeed, the maximal order of $\tau(n)$ can now be determined explicitly, and one can show that the optimal value of c in the above result is $c = \log 2$.

Chapter 11
Probabilistic Number Theory

1 The Normal Order Method

In their fundamental paper of 1917, Hardy and Ramanujan [69] introduced the concept of "normal order" of an arithmetical function. To be precise, this means the following. Given an arithmetical function $g(n)$ and an increasing function $\phi(n)$, we say that $g(n)$ has *normal order* $\phi(n)$ if for any $\epsilon > 0$, the number of $n \le x$ such that

$$\left| g(n) - \phi(n) \right| > \epsilon\phi(n) \tag{52}$$

is $o(x)$ as $x \to \infty$. In other words, for almost all natural numbers n (in the sense of natural density), we have

$$(1 - \epsilon)\phi(n) < g(n) < (1 + \epsilon)\phi(n).$$

Some arithmetical functions like the divisor function, for example, may not possess a normal order. But other functions like $\omega(n)$, defined as the number of distinct prime factors of n, do have a normal order. In fact, the main result of [69] is that the normal order of $\omega(n)$ is $\log\log n$.

The paper of Hardy and Ramanujan laid the foundations of a new subject called probabilistic number theory. Since then, the subject expanded into a major discipline at the hands of P. Erdös, M. Kac, J. Kubilius and P.D.T.A. Elliott, to name a few. In fact, by 1972, the subject became so enormous that Elliott wrote a two-volume treatise explaining the developments since the time of the Hardy–Ramanujan paper. In the recent past, there have been further developments especially to the study of Fourier coefficients of modular forms. We summarize these at the end of this chapter.

In their seminal paper, Hardy and Ramanujan make use of Brun's sieve to prove that $\omega(n)$ has normal order $\log\log n$. In 1934, Turan [196] showed how one can derive the Hardy–Ramanujan theorem without Brun's sieve and using what can be viewed as Tchebycheff's inequality. Apparently, this paper of Turan was part of his doctoral thesis written under the direction of L. Féjer, and it seems that Turan was unaware of Tchebycheff's inequality or probability theory. As the proof is quite simple, we reproduce it here.

M.R. Murty, V.K. Murty, *The Mathematical Legacy of Srinivasa Ramanujan*,

DOI 10.1007/978-81-322-0770-2_11,

It is fairly straightforward to show that

$$\sum_{n\le x}\omega(n) = x\log\log x + O(x)$$

and

$$\sum_{n\le x}\omega^2(n) = x(\log\log x)^2 + O(x\log\log x).$$

Putting these two together, we get

$$\sum_{n\le x}\big(\omega(n) - \log\log n\big)^2 = O(x\log\log x).$$

Thus, for any function θ with $\theta(n)\to\infty$ as $n\to\infty$, we have the number of $n\le x$ for which $|\omega(n)-\log\log n| > \theta(n)(\log\log n)^{1/2}$ is $O(x/\theta(x))$, which is $o(x)$.

One can actually sharpen this and create a sieve method. This was done in [113] and [115] and expanded to a combinatorial setting in [114]. The method therefore has immense potential and applications beyond number theory.

2 The Erdös–Kac Theorem

It is interesting that Hardy and Ramanujan chose the word "normal" to describe (52) since, as it transpired later on, there is an intimate connection to the normal distribution in probability theory. To elaborate, let $\theta(n)$ be any function tending to infinity as n tends to infinity. Hardy and Ramanujan proved that the number of $n\le x$ such that

$$\big|\omega(n) - \log\log n\big| > \theta(n)(\log\log n)^{1/2} \tag{53}$$

is $o(x)$

In 1940, Erdös and Kac [49] proved a sharper result. Namely, they showed that if

$$N(x) = \#\left\{n\le x : \alpha \le \frac{\omega(n)-\log\log n}{\sqrt{\log\log n}} \le \beta\right\},$$

then

$$\lim_{x\to\infty}\frac{N(x)}{x} = \frac{1}{\sqrt{2\pi}}\int_\alpha^\beta e^{-t^2/2}\,dt.$$

Thus, the distribution of values of $\omega(n)$ has an intimate connection to the normal distribution.

Erdös and Kac [49] proved a more general theorem. To explain this, we recall some definitions. An arithmetical function f is called *additive* if $f(mn) = f(m)+f(n)$ for all coprime m,n. An additive function is called *strongly additive* if $f(p^a) = f(p)$ for p prime and all natural numbers a. If f is a strongly additive function satisfying $|f(p)| \leq 1$ for all primes p, let

$$A_n = \sum_{p \leq n} \frac{f(p)}{p}$$

and

$$B_n = \left(\sum_{p \leq n} \frac{f^2(p)}{p} \right)^{1/2}.$$

Let

$$N_f(x) = \# \left\{ n \leq x : \alpha \leq \frac{f(n) - A_n}{B_n} \leq \beta \right\}.$$

Then,

$$\lim_{x \to \infty} \frac{N_f(x)}{x} = \frac{1}{\sqrt{2\pi}} \int_\alpha^\beta e^{-t^2/2}\, dt.$$

Later, Kubilius and Shapiro (independently) (see Theorem 12.2 of [46]) generalized the Erdös–Kac theorem by eliminating the condition that $|f(p)| \leq 1$ and replacing it with the condition that for each $\epsilon > 0$,

$$\lim_{n \to \infty} \frac{1}{B_n^2} \sum_{p \leq n; |f(p)| > \epsilon B_n} \frac{f(p)^2}{p} = 0.$$

It turns out that the same conclusion now holds.

3 The Hardy–Ramanujan-Type Theorem for the τ-Function

The theorem of Deligne connecting the theory of ℓ-adic representations to Fourier coefficients of Hecke eigenforms opened the door for obtaining many new results regarding the arithmetical nature of these coefficients. In particular, one can now study the number of prime factors of $\tau(p)$ and other arithmetical functions arising from modular forms. Unfortunately, to establish these results, some form of a quasi-Riemann hypothesis needs to be assumed for the non-abelian Artin L-series associated to the ℓ-adic representation. We explain why.

More precisely, this theorem says that if $G_{\mathbb{Q}}$ is the absolute Galois group of $\overline{\mathbb{Q}}$ over $\mathbb{Q}$, then there exists an ℓ-adic representation

$$\rho_\ell : G_{\mathbb{Q}} \to GL_2(\mathbb{Z}_\ell),$$

where $\mathbb{Z}_\ell$ denotes the ring of ℓ-adic integers such that if σ_p denotes the Frobenius automorphism, then

$$\operatorname{tr}\big(\rho_\ell(\sigma_p)\big) = \tau(p), \quad \det \rho_\ell(\sigma_p) = p^{11}, \quad p \neq \ell.$$

In particular, if we want to study the distribution of values of $\tau(p)$ modulo ℓ^n, then this means that we can study the finite Galois extension K_{ℓ^n} and the representation,

$$\rho_{\ell,n} : \mathrm{Gal}(K_{\ell^n}/\mathbb{Q}) \to GL_2\big(\mathbb{Z}/\ell^n\mathbb{Z}\big).$$

Ribet has analyzed the image of this representation. It consists of matrices whose determinant is an 11th power (mod ℓ^n).

Using this representation, the study of $\tau(p)$ (mod ℓ) is reduced to the study of the distribution of the Frobenius automorphism in $\mathrm{Gal}(K_\ell/\mathbb{Q})$. But this distribution is given by the Chebotarev density theorem. Assuming the GRH allows us to use an effective version of this theorem to control error terms that arise in the analysis. It turns out that the full strength of the GRH is not essential in such theorems. Rather, a quasi-GRH, which assumes a zero-free region for the zeta functions in some fixed half-plane to the left of $\Re(s) = 1$ is sufficient for our purpose.

In [132], assuming a quasi-GRH, we showed that

$$\sum_{p \le x}{}' \big(\omega\big(\tau(p)\big) - \log\log p\big)^2 = O\big(\pi(x)\log\log x\big),$$

where the dash on the summation indicates we sum over primes p for which $\tau(p) \ne 0$. Under the same hypothesis, we proved that

$$\sum_{n \le x}{}' \left(\omega\big(\tau(n)\big) - \frac{1}{2}(\log\log n)^2\right)^2 \ll x(\log\log x)^3(\log\log\log\log x).$$

In particular, for any $\epsilon > 0$, we have

$$\big|\omega\big(\tau(p)\big) - \log\log p\big| < (\log\log p)^{1/2+\epsilon}$$

for all but $o(x/\log x)$ primes $p \le x$.

There is nothing particular about $\tau(p)$ or $\tau(n)$. One can establish similar results for Fourier coefficients of normalized Hecke eigenforms of arbitrary weight and level. These results can be viewed as the modular analogues of the classical theorem of Hardy and Ramanujan.

In [133], we extended these results and showed that

$$\#\left\{p \le x, \tau(p) \ne 0 : \alpha \le \frac{\omega(\tau(p)) - \log\log p}{(\log\log p)^{1/2}} \le \beta\right\} \sim \pi(x)\Phi(\alpha, \beta),$$

where

$$\Phi(\alpha, \beta) = \frac{1}{\sqrt{2\pi}} \int_\alpha^\beta e^{-t^2/2}\,dt.$$

Also,

$$\#\left\{n \le x : \alpha \le \frac{\omega(\tau(n)) - \frac{1}{2}(\log\log n)^2}{(\log\log n)^{3/2}/\sqrt{3}} \le \beta\right\} \sim x\Phi(\alpha, \beta),$$

with both theorems using a quasi-GRH.

Of course, analogous results hold for Fourier coefficients of any Hecke eigenform with rational integer coefficients.

4 Non-abelian Generalizations of the Hardy–Ramanujan Theorem

The methods used to derive modular analogues of the Hardy–Ramanujan theorem extend to the study of other arithmetical functions which are not necessarily Fourier coefficients of modular forms or functions related to an ℓ-adic representation. Indeed, if we have a multiplicative function f such that the set of primes p for which $\ell | f(p)$ can be described by Chebotarev conditions, then one can apply similar methods to derive analogous results.

A good example is the case where $f(n) = \phi(n)$, Euler's ϕ-function. In this setting, one can study $\omega(f(p))$ which is the same as the study of $\omega(p-1)$, and one can also study $\omega(\phi(n))$. This was first done by the authors in [132]. Independently and later, Erdös and Pomerance [50] proved that the number of $n \leq x$ for which

$$\alpha \leq \frac{\omega(\phi(n)) - \frac{1}{2}(\log\log n)^2}{(\log\log n)^{3/2}/\sqrt{3}} \leq \beta$$

is asymptotically $x\Phi(\alpha, \beta)$. Here the use of the quasi-GRH is not needed, and one can use the Bombieri–Vinogradov theorem to make the result unconditional.

For the method to work, it is not even essential to have a multiplicative function. To study the divisibility of any sequence of numbers, it is possible to apply these techniques as long as one can relate it again to the Chebotarev density theorem. We give one such example of this type of theorem.

Let a be a natural number which is not equal to ± 1 or a perfect square. A classical conjecture of Artin predicts that a is a primitive root (mod p) for infinitely many primes p. This problem is still open though some spectacular progress has been made in the recent past. In this context, it is natural to study $f_a(p)$, the order of a mod p. Let $f_a(n)$ be the order of a (mod n) with n coprime to a. Under the quasi-GRH, M. Ram Murty and his student F. Saidak [136] showed that the number of primes $p \leq x$ for which

$$\alpha \leq \frac{\omega(f_a(p)) - \log\log p}{\sqrt{\log\log p}} \leq \beta$$

is asymptotic to $\pi(x)\Phi(\alpha, \beta)$. Similarly, under the same hypothesis, the number of $n \leq x$ for which

$$\alpha \leq \frac{\omega(f_a(n)) - \frac{1}{2}(\log\log n)^2}{(\log\log n)^{3/2}/\sqrt{3}} \leq \beta$$

is asymptotic to $x\Phi(\alpha, \beta)$ as x tends to infinity.

Clearly, the normal order method is a powerful method to analyze the arithmetic structure of complicated arithmetical functions. Its potential has not yet been fully exhausted.

Chapter 12
The Sato–Tate Conjecture for the Ramanujan τ-Function

1 Introduction

It was Serre [185] who first conjectured that the Sato–Tate distribution holds for the Ramanujan τ-function. More precisely, he conjectured that the numbers

$$\frac{\tau(p)}{2p^{11/2}},$$

as one ranges over primes p, are equidistributed in the interval $[-1,1]$ with respect to the Sato–Tate measure

$$\frac{2}{\pi}\sqrt{1-x^2}\,dx.$$

In fact, Serre expected that an analogous result should hold for the Fourier coefficients of any normalized Hecke eigenform not of CM type. This was recently proved by Barnet-Lamb, Geraghty, Harris and Taylor [18]. In particular, this applies to Hecke eigenforms of weight 2 not of CM type. By the celebrated modularity conjecture, we know that elliptic curves correspond to Hecke eigenforms of weight 2 with integer Fourier coefficients. Consequently, the "angles of Frobenius" for elliptic curves not of CM type are distributed with respect to the Sato–Tate measure. This was originally proved for elliptic curves with non-integral j-invariant in [35], but the condition was removed in the most recent work [18].

In this chapter, we give an outline of the proof of this theorem. Since the prerequisites are formidable, we aim only for conceptual clarity and arrange the main ideas for the appreciation and understanding of the reader. We also indicate how one can generalize the theorem so as to introduce additional constraints on the primes, such as primes in a fixed arithmetic progression. In particular, for any interval I in $[-1,1]$, we will show that for a given natural number q and a coprime to q, the density of primes $p \equiv a \pmod q$ with $\tau(p)/2p^{11/2} \in I$ is

$$\frac{2}{\pi\varphi(q)}\int_I \sqrt{1-x^2}\,dx.$$

M.R. Murty, V.K. Murty, *The Mathematical Legacy of Srinivasa Ramanujan*,
DOI 10.1007/978-81-322-0770-2_12,

We begin with a historical description of the original conjecture by Sato and Tate in the context of elliptic curves.

Consider the elliptic curve E defined by the equation

$$y^2 = x^3 + ax + b, \quad a, b \in \mathbb{Z}.$$

Let $\Delta = -16(4a^3 + 27b^2)$. As discussed in greater generality in Chap. 3, for each prime p with $(p, \Delta) = 1$, we may consider the congruence

$$y^2 \equiv x^3 + ax + b \pmod{p}$$

and count the number N_p of solutions (x, y). This quantity was first studied by Emil Artin [10] in his 1924 doctoral thesis in which he conjectured that

$$|N_p - p| \leq 2\sqrt{p} \tag{54}$$

for all such primes. In many ways, his study was motivated by the classical Riemann hypothesis. To understand the nature of zeta functions in general, Artin defined the analogue of the Dedekind zeta function in the setting of a function field over a finite field. In the case of a quadratic extension of $\mathbb{F}_p(x)$ defined by

$$y^2 = x^3 + ax + b,$$

the analogue of the Riemann hypothesis for the function field zeta function turns out to be equivalent to (54). In his thesis, Artin verified his conjecture for many small primes p but could not prove it. In February 1933, Hasse [74] proved the conjecture using techniques from algebraic geometry. One could say that understanding this function field analogue of the Riemann hypothesis was an important step in the annals of mathematics. The reader is referred to the historical document [54] for further discussions of this.

Artin's thesis was seminal in many ways. First, it opened up the study of algebraic geometry over finite fields and connected it to the study of exponential sums that occur in classical analytic number theory. Second, it inspired Weil [201] to formulate in 1949 general conjectures that led Grothendieck [63] to chart out a visionary program in algebraic geometry ultimately leading to a resolution of the Weil conjectures in the fundamental work of Deligne [39] in 1974.

Around 1960, Mikio Sato and John Tate [193] (independently) asked about the distribution of the numbers

$$\frac{N_p - p}{\sqrt{p}}$$

in the interval $[-2, 2]$ as p tends to infinity. For example, is it reasonable to expect that these numbers are uniformly distributed in the interval? In other words, is it true that for any interval $[a, b] \subseteq [-2, 2]$, we have

$$\lim_{x\to\infty} \frac{\#\{p \leq x : (N_p - p)/\sqrt{p} \in [a, b]\}}{\#\{p \leq x\}} = b - a?$$

This question is the genesis of the Sato–Tate conjecture. Numerical evidence seemed to suggest otherwise. More precisely, Sato and Tate were led to predict that for a "generic" elliptic curve E, the following is true. If we write

$$(N_p - p)/\sqrt{p} = 2\cos\theta_p, \quad 0 \leq \theta_p \leq \pi,$$

and $[\alpha, \beta] \subseteq [0, \pi]$, then, their conjecture says

$$\lim_{x\to\infty} \frac{\#\{p \leq x : \theta_p \in [\alpha, \beta]\}}{\#\{p \leq x\}} = \frac{2}{\pi}\int_\alpha^\beta \sin^2\theta \, d\theta = \frac{\beta - \alpha}{\pi} - \frac{1}{2\pi}(\sin 2\beta - \sin 2\alpha).$$

The conjecture of Tate [193] on algebraic cycles also provided conceptual evidence for this. Here, "generic" means that the elliptic curve should be without complex multiplication (see [107] for details). In other words, E is said to be without complex multiplication (or without CM) if $\operatorname{End} E = \mathbb{Z}$. If the elliptic curve has complex multiplication, then the (essentially) uniform distribution law for the angles was worked out by Deuring [41] building on earlier work of Hecke [75, 76].

One can formulate a more general conjecture. Let E be an elliptic curve defined over a number field K. For each place v of K where E has good reduction, we may consider the group of points of E mod v. Its cardinality (including the identity element) can be written as

$$Nv + 1 - a_v,$$

where Nv denotes the norm of v, and a_v is an integer satisfying Hasse's inequality $|a_v| \leq 2(Nv)^{1/2}$. As before, one can therefore write

$$a_v = 2N(v)^{1/2}\cos\theta_v,$$

where $\theta_v(E) := \theta_v$ satisfies $0 \leq \theta_v \leq \pi$. The Sato–Tate conjecture now is a statement about how the angles θ_v are distributed in the interval $[0, \pi]$ as v varies. When E has complex multiplication (CM), the distribution law is known and again follows from the classical work of Deuring on Hecke L-series (see [139] for details). In the non-CM case, one expects that the angles are uniformly distributed with respect to the measure

$$\mu_{ST} := \frac{2}{\pi}\left(\sin^2\theta\right) d\theta.$$

On 18 March 2006, Taylor [194] (see also [35]) published a proof of this conjecture when E has at least one prime of multiplicative reduction. He was building on his earlier work with Clozel, Harris and Shepherd-Barron (see Carayol's Séminaire Bourbaki article [30]).

Inspired by the Sato–Tate conjecture for elliptic curves, Serre [185] extended the conjecture for Fourier coefficients of normalized Hecke eigenforms. We review his formalism below and in the next sections give an axiomatic exposition that allows for an application of results by Barnet-Lamb, Geraghty, Harris and Taylor [18] as well as results pertaining to Hilbert modular forms by Barnet-Lamb, Gee and Geraghty [17]. These new developments all prove special cases of the following hypothesis.

Potential automorphy hypothesis $H_K(S,T,\pi)$ Let K be an algebraic number field, and π a cuspidal automorphic representation of $GL_2(\mathcal{A}_K)$ not of CM type. Let S be a finite set of primes of K, and T a finite set of odd positive integers. Then, there exists a finite Galois extension $K_{S,T}$ over K unramified at S with $\mathrm{Sym}^m(\pi)$ automorphic over $K_{S,T}$ for all $m \in T$.

Our first result is a hybrid Chebotarev–Sato–Tate theorem.

Theorem 1.1 *Let K be an algebraic number field. Let π be a cuspidal automorphic representation of $GL_2(\mathbb{A}_K)$, which is not of CM type, M/K a finite solvable Galois extension with $G = \mathrm{Gal}(M/K)$, and C a conjugacy class of G. For every odd number m, assume hypothesis $H_K(S,T,\pi)$ where S is the set of primes of K that ramify in M and T is either $\{m\}$ or $\{1,m\}$. Then the density of prime ideals $\mathfrak{p}$ for which the Artin symbol $\sigma_\mathfrak{p} \in C$ and the angle $\theta_\mathfrak{p} \in [\alpha,\beta]$ with $0 \le \alpha \le \beta \le \pi$ is*

$$\frac{2|C|}{\pi|G|}\int_\alpha^\beta \sin^2\theta\, d\theta.$$

By the work of [18], the potential automorphy hypothesis is now a theorem in the case of classical normalized Hecke eigenforms not of CM type. In particular, we have the following corollary:

Corollary 1.2 *Let f be a normalized Hecke eigenform of weight k and arbitrary level, which is not of CM type. Write the pth Fourier coefficient of f as $a_p(f) = 2p^{(k-1)/2}\cos\theta_p(f)$. Let q be a natural number, and a an integer with $(a,q)=1$. For $0 \le \alpha \le \beta \le \pi$, the density of primes p for which $\theta_p(f) \in [\alpha,\beta]$ and $p \equiv a \pmod q$ is*

$$\frac{2}{\pi\varphi(q)}\int_\alpha^\beta \sin^2\theta\, d\theta.$$

It is evident that by similar arguments, one can handle the joint distribution of angles of any finite set of Hecke eigenforms, provided that there is at most one eigenform in the set without CM.

One can also study the joint distribution of angles of a finite collection of pairwise non-isogenous elliptic curves. This looks like a difficult question, and Harris has recently announced some progress in this direction.

Though our treatment is informal, the background needed for a total understanding is quite formidable spanning representation theory, arithmetic algebraic geometry, analytic and algebraic number theory. Still, we hope that the presentation given here will enable the non-expert to see how the proof is put together and appreciate the interplay of ideas.

Recently, "friendly" exposés of the Sato–Tate conjecture have appeared in various places. The papers by Mazur [123, 124] are a good place to begin for the totally uninitiated reader. Here, our goal is more mathematical. We hope to give (without proofs) the main mathematical ingredients that enter into such equidistribution questions so that the reader may have a conceptual understanding of the results. Because of the celebrated modularity conjecture (now proved by Wiles [204] and others [25]), one can deduce the original conjecture of Sato and Tate, at least in the case that E is defined over the rational number field. In the general number field case, it is still open whether the a_vs can be viewed as coming from automorphic representations as predicted by Langlands. Thus, one can view the Sato–Tate conjecture for elliptic curves as a special case of a more general statement concerning distribution of eigenvalues of Hecke operators or in the general case, of Satake parameters. (See [36] for more details.) One can formulate a function field analogue of the Sato–Tate conjecture, and this has been proved in various contexts. Let K be a rational function field in one variable over a finite field $\mathbb{F}$, and let E denote an elliptic curve over K with nonconstant j-invariant. Let Y denote the projective line over $\mathbb{F}$ and consider the Néron model $\mathcal{E} \longrightarrow Y$. This is a smooth group scheme whose general fibre is E and outside of a finite set S of points $y \in Y$, the fibre $\mathcal{E}_y$ at y is an elliptic curve (the "reduction" of E modulo the residue field corresponding to y). Thus, as an elliptic curve over a finite field, the zeta function of $\mathcal{E}_y$ is of the form

$$\frac{(1-\alpha_y T)(1-\overline{\alpha_y} T)}{(1-T)(1-q^{\deg y} T)}.$$

Here $\alpha_y = q^{(\deg y)/2} e^{i\theta(y)}$ where $0 \leq \theta(y) \leq \pi$. Let $\mathbb{F}_n$ denote the unique extension of $\mathbb{F}$ of degree n. Then, the Sato–Tate conjecture in this context says that as $n \longrightarrow \infty$, we have

$$\#\{y \in Y(\mathbb{F}_n) : \alpha \leq \theta_y \leq \beta\} \sim \left(\int_\alpha^\beta \frac{2}{\pi} \sin^2\theta \, d\theta\right) \left|Y(\mathbb{F}_n)\right|.$$

This was proved by Yoshida in [205] and in a different way by K. Murty in [139]. Very general theorems of Sato–Tate type (in which the base Y is replaced by an arbitrary variety and $\mathcal{E}$ by families of ℓ-adic sheaves) are proved in Deligne [40], Sect. 3.5.

2 Weyl's Criterion

We will begin with a general discussion of the classical setting for uniform distribution. A sequence of real numbers $\{x_n\}$ is called *uniformly distributed* (modulo 1) if for any pair of real numbers α, β with $0 \leq \alpha < \beta < 1$, we have

$$\#\{n \leq N : x_n \in (\alpha, \beta)\} \sim (\beta - \alpha)N$$

as N tends to infinity.

Theorem 2.1 (Weyl's Criterion) *The sequence* $\{x_n\}$ *is uniformly distributed* mod 1 *if and only if for all* $m \geq 1$,

$$\sum_{n \leq N} e^{2\pi i m x_n} = o(N)$$

as N tends to infinity.

Proof (Sketch) First suppose that the sequence is uniformly distributed. We will show the condition is necessary. Let us observe that any continuous function f can be approximated by a linear combination of step functions so that for any given $\epsilon > 0$, we have

$$\sup_{x \in [0,1]} \left| f(x) - \sum_i c_i \chi_{I_i}(x) \right| \leq \epsilon,$$

where χ_I denotes the characteristic function of an interval I. Then,

$$\sum_{n \leq N} f(x_n) = \sum_i c_i \left(\sum_{n \leq N} \chi_{I_i}(x_n) \right) + O(\epsilon N).$$

By hypothesis,

$$\sum_{n \leq N} \chi_{I_i}(x_n) = \mu(I_i)N + o(N),$$

where $\mu(I)$ denotes the measure of an interval I. Now the sum

$$\sum_i c_i \mu(I_i)$$

is a Riemann sum, and as our ϵ gets smaller, the sum converges to the integral

$$\int_0^1 f(x)\, dx.$$

Thus,

$$\frac{1}{N} \sum_{n \leq N} f(x_n) \to \int_0^1 f(x)\, dx.$$

In particular, we can apply this to $\cos mx$ and $\sin mx$ to deduce the required result.

For the converse, we approximate $\chi_I(x)$ by trigonometric polynomials (which can be done by the Stone–Weierstrass theorem). In fact, one can be more precise. For any positive integer K, there are trigonometric polynomials $m(x)$ and $M(x)$ of degree $\leq K$ such that

$$m(x) \leq \chi_I(x) \leq M(x)$$

with

$$m(x) = \sum_{|m| \le K} a_m e^{2\pi i m x}, \qquad M(x) = \sum_{|m| \le K} b_m e^{2\pi i m x}$$

with

$$a_0 = b_0 = \mu(I) + O(1/K).$$

Therefore,

$$\#\{n \le N : x_n \in I\} = \sum_{n \le N} \chi_I(x_n) = \mu(I)N + o(N),$$

as required. □

Theorem 2.1 says that to establish uniform distribution of the angles θ_v, we need to study the exponential sums

$$\sum_{N(v) \le x} e^{2\pi i m \theta_v}.$$

Weyl's theorem is the classical theorem regarding equidistribution for the group $\mathbb{R}/\mathbb{Z}$. Serre [185] extended the Weyl criterion for arbitrary compact groups and formulated an L-series formalism related to it. We review this in Sect. 4. In the next section, we review a classical Tauberian theorem that will be essential to our discussion.

3 Wiener–Ikehara Tauberian Theorem

Theorem 3.1 *Let $f(s) = \sum_{n=1}^{\infty} a_n/n^s$ with $a_n \ge 0$ and $g(s) = \sum_{n=1}^{\infty} b_n/n^s$ be two Dirichlet series with $|b_n| \le a_n$ for all n. Assume that $f(s)$ and $g(s)$ extend analytically to $\Re(s) \ge 1$ except possibly at $s = 1$ where they have a simple pole with residues R and r (which may be zero) respectively. Then*

$$\sum_{n \le x} b_n \sim rx$$

as x tends to infinity.

The classical application of this theorem is the deduction of the prime number theorem. Let

$$f(s) = -\frac{\zeta'}{\zeta}(s) = \sum_{n=1}^{\infty} \frac{\Lambda(n)}{n^s}$$

where $\Lambda(n) = \log p$ when $n = p^a$ for some prime p and zero otherwise. Taking $g(s) = f(s)$ in the above theorem allows us to deduce the prime number theorem

$$\sum_{n \le x} \Lambda(n) \sim x$$

using the well-known fact that the Riemann zeta function does not vanish on $\Re(s) = 1$.

In a fundamental paper written in 1970, Langlands [108] outlined an approach to the Sato–Tate conjecture using the theory of automorphic forms. (It is possible that some of these ideas may have had roots in the earlier work of Sato and Tate.) To simplify matters and notation, we will give only a rough outline of this approach.

Firstly, Langlands suggested the automorphic viewpoint. Thus, the conjecture of Sato–Tate was applicable in a larger context of modular forms, or more generally, to automorphic forms on $GL(2)$. For example, one could take the celebrated Ramanujan τ-function attached to the unique newform of weight 12 and level 1, and write

$$\tau(p) = 2p^{11/2} \cos \theta_p.$$

One expects the same Sato–Tate distribution for these angles θ_p as well.

Here is a brief description of the strategy of Langlands [108]. For each natural number m, put

$$L_m(s) = \prod_v \prod_{j=0}^{m} \left(1 - \frac{\alpha_v^{m-j} \beta_v^j}{N v^s}\right)^{-1}$$

where $\alpha_v = e^{i\theta_v}$ and $\beta_v = e^{-i\theta_v}$. Langlands indicated that the theory of automorphic forms predicts that each $L_m(s)$ should extend to an entire function. In fact, if each $L_m(s)$ extends analytically for $\Re(s) \ge 1$ and does not vanish there, then by the Tauberian theorem, we deduce for $m \ge 1$,

$$\sum_{Nv \le x} \frac{\sin(m+1)\theta_v}{\sin \theta_v} = o\big(\pi(x)\big)$$

as $x \to \infty$. Having this for each m, we will show in the next section that the Sato–Tate conjecture follows. Kumar Murty [139] showed that the non-vanishing hypothesis can be dispensed with because a very elegant argument extending the classical one of Hadamard and de la Vallée Poussin allows one to show non-vanishing from having analytic continuation to $\Re(s) \ge 1$.

In the case F is the rational number field, it is now a theorem due to Wiles and others that $L_1(s)$ is essentially the L-function attached by Hecke to a classical cusp form of weight 2. Thus, in this particular case, the Langlands conjecture is established. The non-vanishing of $L_1(s)$ on $\Re(s) = 1$ is a result due to Rankin. For $m = 2$, Rankin–Selberg theory allows one to deduce that $L_2(s)$ extends to an entire function for $\Re(s) \ge 1$. The continuation of $L_2(s)$ to the entire complex plane was established by Shimura [188] in the case $F = \mathbb{Q}$ and in the general case by

Gelbart and Jacquet [58]. In very recent work, Kim and Shahidi [96] showed that $L_3(s)$ extends to an entire function, and later, Kim showed the same for $L_4(s)$. For the cases $5 \leq m \leq 9$, Kim and Shahidi have shown that $L_m(s)$ extends to a meromorphic function for all $s \in \mathbb{C}$ which is regular for $\Re(s) \geq 1$, except in the case of $m = 9$ where $L_9(s)$ may have a pole at $s = 1$. If $L_9(s)$ were to have a pole at $s = 1$, then the Sato–Tate conjecture would be false, as we will indicate below. Thus, we can go in the reverse direction. The truth of the Sato–Tate conjecture now established implies that $L_9(s)$ does not have a pole at $s = 1$.

4 Weyl's Theorem for Compact Groups

Serre [185] gave the following reformulation of the Weyl criterion for uniform distribution in the context of a compact group. Let G be a compact group, and X its space of conjugacy classes. Let μ denote its normalized Haar measure. A sequence of elements $\{x_n\}$ with $x_n \in X$ is said to be uniformly distributed in X if for every continuous function f, we have

$$\sum_{n \leq N} f(x_n) \sim N \int_X f \, d\mu$$

as N tends to infinity.

Theorem 4.1 (Weyl's criterion for compact groups) *Let G be a compact group with Haar measure μ. A sequence $\{x_n\}$ is uniformly distributed in G if and only if*

$$\sum_{n \leq N} \chi(x_n) = o(N)$$

for every irreducible character χ of G.

The classical case in Theorem 2.1 corresponds to $G = \mathbb{R}/\mathbb{Z}$ because in this case, the irreducible characters are given by $x \mapsto e^{2\pi i m x}$.

Serre gave an interesting reformulation of this criterion in the context of L-functions. Let F be a field and for each place v of F, and let $x_v \in G$. For each irreducible representation $\rho : G \to GL_n(\mathbb{C})$, we let

$$L(s, \rho) = \prod_v \det\bigl(I - \rho(x_v) N v^{-s}\bigr)^{-1}.$$

Theorem 4.2 (Serre) *Suppose that for each irreducible non-trivial representation ρ of G, the L-function $L(s, \rho)$ extends to an analytic function for $\Re(s) \geq 1$. Then, the sequence $\{x_v\}$ is uniformly distributed in X if and only if $L(s, \rho)$ does not vanish on $\Re(s) = 1$ for all irreducible ρ.*

In the context of the Sato–Tate conjecture, one considers the group $SU(2,\mathbb{C})$ where the conjugacy classes are parameterized by

$$X_\theta = \begin{pmatrix} e^{i\theta} & 0 \\ 0 & e^{-i\theta} \end{pmatrix}, \qquad 0 \le \theta \le \pi.$$

The image of the Haar measure in the space of conjugacy classes of $SU(2,\mathbb{C})$ is known to be

$$\frac{2}{\pi}\sin^2\theta\, d\theta.$$

The irreducible representations of $SU(2,\mathbb{C})$ are the symmetric power representations ρ_m of the standard representation ρ_1 of $SU(2,\mathbb{C})$ into $GL(2,\mathbb{C})$. We find that $L(s,\rho_m)$ as defined above by Serre coincide with $L_m(s)$ defined in Sect. 3.

Since tr $\rho_m(X_\theta) = \sin(m+1)\theta/\sin\theta$, the Sato–Tate conjecture is equivalent to the assertion

$$\sum_{N(v)\le x} \frac{\sin(m+1)\theta_v}{\sin\theta_v} = o\big(\pi_F(x)\big)$$

for each natural number m. So far, this has been established only for $m \le 8$ by the work of Kim and Shahidi [96].

5 Symmetric Power L-Series of Elliptic Curves

Let K be an algebraic number field. Let E be an elliptic curve defined over K. Let S be the (finite) set of places where E has bad reduction. For each finite place $v \notin S$ of K, we know that the number of points on E mod v is given by

$$N(v) + 1 - a_v,$$

where a_v is an integer satisfying Hasse's inequality $|a_v| \le 2N(v)^{1/2}$. As in Chap. 3, for each prime ℓ, the action of $\mathrm{Gal}(\overline{K}/K)$ on the ℓ-adic Tate module gives rise to an ℓ-adic representation

$$\rho := \rho_\ell : \mathrm{Gal}(\overline{K}/K) \to GL_2(\mathbb{Q}_\ell)$$

which is integral, that is, the characteristic polynomial of $\rho_\ell(F_v)$ (where F_v denotes the Frobenius automorphism at $v \notin S$) has integer coefficients, independent of ℓ. In fact, this characteristic polynomial is $X^2 - a_v X + N(v)$. Let us write $\alpha_v N(v)^{1/2}$, $\beta_v N(v)^{1/2}$ for the two roots of the quadratic polynomial

$$X^2 - a_v X + N(v).$$

The (partial) mth symmetric power L-function is defined as

$$L_S(s, \mathrm{Sym}^m \rho) := \prod_{v\notin S}\prod_{j=0}^{m}\big(1 - \alpha_v^j \beta_v^{m-j} N(v)^{-s}\big)^{-1}.$$

Clearly, the product converges absolutely for $\Re(s) > 1$.

In 1970, Langlands [108] suggested the existence of an automorphic representation π_m attached to $GL_{m+1}(\mathbb{A}_K)$, where $\mathbb{A}_K$ denotes the adele ring of K, such that $L_S(s, \pi_m) = L_S(s, \mathrm{Sym}^m(\rho))$ where $L_S(s, \pi_m)$ is the automorphic L-function attached to π_m with the Euler factors corresponding to the places $v \in S$ removed. In fact, it is conjectured that one can define the local factors for $v \in S$ in such a way that the completed L-function, $L(s, \mathrm{Sym}^m(\rho))$ (which we shall abbreviate as $L_m(s)$), satisfies a functional equation relating s to $1 - s$. (See, for example, [37] for details.)

If the Langlands conjecture about the existence of π_m is true, then by the theory of automorphic representations, one immediately has analytic continuation of $L_S(s, \mathrm{Sym}^m(\rho))$ to the entire complex plane. and by the result of K. Murty [139], the non-vanishing on the line $\Re(s) = 1$ follows, and the Sato–Tate conjecture follows. The non-vanishing of the L-function on the line $\Re(s) = 1$ can also be deduced from a celebrated result of Jacquet and Shalika [88], who showed that for any automorphic representation π, we have $L(s, \pi) \neq 0$ for $\Re(s) = 1$. So, what is known about the analytic continuation of $L_S(s, \mathrm{Sym}^m(\rho))$? For $m = 1$, this is the (partial) Hasse–Weil L-series attached to the elliptic curve E. It is possible to define the Euler factors at places in S as well, so that the completed L-function conjecturally admits an analytic continuation to the entire complex plane and satisfies a suitable functional equation. In the case $K = \mathbb{Q}$, the Taniyama conjecture, proved by Wiles (in the semistable case) [204] and by Breuil, Conrad, Diamond and Taylor (in the general case) [25], asserts that there is a classical cusp form f of weight 2 and level N (the conductor of E) such that the Hecke L-series $L(s, f)$ attached to f agrees with $L_1(s - 1/2)$. If π_f is the automorphic representation associated to f, then, in the context of the Langlands program, we have $L(s, \pi_f) = L_1(s)$. The series $L_1(s)$ is essentially the L-function attached to ρ, coming from the action of $\mathrm{Gal}(\overline{K}/K)$ on the Tate module.

More generally, $L_m(s)$ is essentially the L-function attached to the representation $\mathrm{Sym}^m(\rho)$, which comes from the action of $\mathrm{Gal}(\overline{K}/K)$. As alluded to above, one expects the existence of an automorphic representation π_m attached to $GL_{m+1}(\mathbb{A}_K)$ satisfying $L(s, \pi_m) = L_m(s)$. This expectation is far from being realized, though important advances have been made in this direction.

What Taylor proves is not the automorphy of $L_m(s)$ but rather its "potential automorphy." This fact, combined with other results in the analytic theory of automorphic L-functions, leads to the Sato–Tate conjecture. This result of "potential automorphy" builds on a massive collection of earlier work that can be traced back to the celebrated conjecture of Serre.

Serre [184] formulated a general conjecture about representations

$$\rho : \mathrm{Gal}(\overline{\mathbb{Q}}/\mathbb{Q}) \to GL_2(\mathbb{F})$$

with $\mathbb{F}$ a finite field, which are odd and absolutely irreducible. More precisely, he predicted that such representations arise from classical modular forms. Serre [184] showed that his conjecture implies the Taniyama conjecture. On the other hand, Frey [55] had a remarkable insight which was completed and made more precise by Ribet [172], who showed that the Taniyama conjecture implies Fermat's last theorem. Thus, Serre's conjecture offered a new approach to Fermat. Wiles [204] proved an important case of Serre's conjecture that was enough to deduce that of Taniyama. This work led to further developments. Most recently, Chandrashekhar Khare [93] proved the level 1 case of the Serre conjecture. In very recent work, Khare and Wintenberger [94] have settled the general case for which they were awarded the Cole Prize by the American Mathematical Society in 2011. This last development not only gives a new proof of Fermat's last theorem, but it also implies the strong Artin conjecture [9] for two-dimensional Galois representations of odd conductor.

In his recent papers, Taylor [194] made substantial progress towards this conjecture. If K is a totally real field and m is odd, he showed that there is a finite, totally real Galois extension L/K such that $(\mathrm{Sym}^m\,\rho)$ restricted to L is automorphic over L. One can choose an L that works simultaneously for any finite set of odd numbers. One can also choose it to be unramified at any finite set of places. Once this theorem is in hand, Taylor uses standard results from the theory of automorphic L-functions to deduce the Sato–Tate conjecture. We will give an outline of this deduction below.

The key result is the potential automorphy property of the symmetric power of a cuspidal automorphic representation, now established for a large class of such representations.

First, let us review some essential theorems from the theory of automorphic L-functions. We refer the reader to [130] for details, definitions and additional references to the literature. More precisely, we highlight pages 119 and 215 of [9] for the exact definitions of the notions of base change and automorphic induction. Here are the key theorems we will need.

First is the theorem of base change and automorphic induction, due to Arthur and Clozel [9]. This says the following. Suppose that L/K is a cyclic extension and π, Π are cuspidal representations of $GL_n(\mathbb{A}_K)$ and $GL_n(\mathbb{A}_L)$ respectively. Then, the base change of π, denoted $B(\pi)$, and the automorphic induction $I(\Pi)$ of Π exist.

The second fact we need is a celebrated theorem of Jacquet and Shalika [88], which states that for any unitary cuspidal automorphic representation π of $GL_n(\mathbb{A}_K)$, we have $L(1+it,\pi)\neq 0$.

The third fact needed is a non-vanishing theorem due to Shahidi [187]. This states that the Rankin–Selberg L-function $L(s,\pi_1\times\pi_2)$ does not vanish on the line $\Re(s)=1$ whenever π_1 and π_2 are unitary cuspidal automorphic representations.

A fourth fact needed is the Artin reciprocity law which states that every abelian Artin L-function of any Galois extension of K is a Hecke L-function and corresponds to a cuspidal automorphic representation of $GL_1(\mathbb{A}_K)$.

6 An Outline of the Proof of the Sato–Tate Conjecture

Here is a brief outline of the proofs in [17], [18] and [194] of the Sato–Tate conjecture. Their main theorem is: let K be a totally real field, and E/K an elliptic curve with multiplicative reduction at some prime. For any odd number m, there is a finite, totally real Galois extension L/K such that $\mathrm{Sym}^m\,\rho$ becomes automorphic over L. In other words, $(\mathrm{Sym}^m\,\rho)|_L$ is automorphic over L. (One can also choose an L that will work simultaneously for any finite set of *odd* positive numbers.)

From this result they deduce the Sato–Tate conjecture in three steps. Here is an outline.

Step 1: For any intermediate field $K \subset F \subset L$ with L/F solvable, $\mathrm{Sym}^m\,\rho$ is automorphic over F. In other words, $(\mathrm{Sym}^m\,\rho)|_F$ is automorphic over F for every F with L/F solvable.

This is proved in his earlier paper [73].

Essentially, it applies the Arthur–Clozel theory of base change, the key idea being that the base change lift of $\mathrm{Sym}^m\,\rho$ to L, which exists by Taylor's main theorem, is Galois invariant and so must be the base change lift of an automorphic representation π_F for every intermediate F with L/F solvable. This is because one can find a chain

$$F = F_0 \subset F_1 \subset F_2 \subset \cdots \subset F_m = L$$

of extensions so that F_{i+1}/F_i is cyclic for $0 \le i \le m-1$ and apply the Arthur–Clozel theorem for automorphic induction successively, in stages, to each of the cyclic extensions $F_m/F_{m-1}, \ldots, F_1/F_0$. We refer the reader to [9] for precise details concerning automorphic induction.

Step 2: Let $G = \mathrm{Gal}(L/K)$. Now apply Brauer induction to write

$$1 = \sum_i a_i \,\mathrm{Ind}_{H_i}^G\, \psi_i$$

with a_i integers and ψ_i one-dimensional characters of nilpotent subgroups H_i of G. Then,

$$L\big(s, (\mathrm{Sym}^m\,\rho) \otimes 1\big) = \prod_i L\big(s, (\mathrm{Sym}^m\,\rho) \otimes \mathrm{Ind}_{H_i}^G\, \psi_i\big)^{a_i}.$$

By Frobenius reciprocity,

$$\big(\mathrm{Sym}^m\,\rho\big) \otimes \mathrm{Ind}_{H_i}^G\, \psi_i = \mathrm{Ind}_{H_i}^G\big(\big(\mathrm{Sym}^m\,\rho\big)\big|_{L^{H_i}} \otimes \psi_i\big).$$

By Step 1, $(\mathrm{Sym}^m\,\rho)|_{L^{H_i}}$ is automorphic over L^{H_i}. By Artin reciprocity, ψ_i is a Hecke character χ_i of L^{H_i}. Thus, $(\mathrm{Sym}^m\,\rho)|_{L^{H_i}} \otimes \psi_i$ is automorphic over L^{H_i}. By invariance of L-series under induction, we deduce

$$L\big(s, \mathrm{Sym}^m\,\rho\big) = \prod_i L\big(s, \big(\mathrm{Sym}^m\,\rho\big)\big|_{L^{H_i}} \otimes \chi_i\big)^{a_i},$$

and the product on the right-hand side, being a product of automorphic L-functions by Step 1, represents a meromorphic function of s. In this way, one derives the meromorphic continuation of the *odd* symmetric power L-functions attached to E.

Step 3: If we apply the Jacquet–Shalika theorem which assures us that there are no poles on $\Re(s) = 1$ for a cuspidal automorphic L-function $L(s, \pi)$, as well as the non-vanishing of $L(s, \pi)$ on $\Re(s) = 1$ for any automorphic representation π, we obtain from the above product the analytic continuation and non-vanishing on $\Re(s) = 1$ of $L(s, \mathrm{Sym}^m \rho)$ for m odd. To treat m even, one uses induction and the identity

$$\mathrm{Sym}^{m-1} \rho \oplus \mathrm{Sym}^{m+1} \rho = \mathrm{Sym}^m \rho \otimes \mathrm{Sym}^1 \rho,$$

which is essentially the trigonometric identity

$$\frac{\sin m\theta}{\sin\theta} + \frac{\sin(m+2)\theta}{\sin\theta} = \left(\frac{\sin(m+1)\theta}{\sin\theta}\right)\left(\frac{\sin 2\theta}{\sin\theta}\right)$$

(or the Clebsch–Gordon branching rule for SL_2). Thus,

$$L\big(s, \mathrm{Sym}^{m-1} \rho\big)L\big(s, \mathrm{Sym}^{m+1} \rho\big) = L\big(s, \big(\mathrm{Sym}^m \rho\big) \otimes \mathrm{Sym}^1 \rho\big).$$

Now apply Step 1 with the two odd numbers $1, m$ to get the base change to L of both $\mathrm{Sym}^m \rho$ and $\mathrm{Sym}^1 \rho$ automorphic. By the same Brauer induction trick of Step 2 applied to the right-hand side, one deduces that the right-hand side has a meromorphic continuation for all complex s. To get analytic continuation to $\Re(s) = 1$, one needs to apply Shahidi's results on the non-vanishing of Rankin–Selberg L-functions which appear on the right-hand side. Poles on the line $\Re(s) = 1$ can also be ruled out by the same theory. This completes the proof.

In many respects, this is the elliptic analogue of Brauer's theorem of the meromorphy of Artin L-series. As can be seen, the non-vanishing of the L-series on the line $\Re(s) = 1$ is essential in the proof. This was ensured by an application of theorems of Jacquet, Shalika and Shahidi. The Jacquet–Shalika theorem and the Shahidi theorem rely on the theory of Eisenstein series (à la Langlands). There are other ways of establishing non-vanishing of the L-series concerned without using the theory of Eisenstein series. Indeed, if one is willing to admit Rankin–Selberg theory and existence and analyticity of these L-functions, then classical non-vanishing techniques (of the type used by Hadamard and de la Vallée Poussin) actually work. This method is outlined in a recent paper of Sarnak [176].

7 A Chebotarev–Sato–Tate Theorem and Generalizations

In this section, we indicate the proof of Theorem 1.1. Before doing so, we discuss some natural generalizations of the Sato–Tate conjecture that one can consider. We indicate briefly what can actually be proved. Firstly, we can take two non-isogenous elliptic curves and consider the joint distribution of the angles. For instance, if E_1 and E_2 are non-isogenous elliptic curves, both without CM, defined over $\mathbb{Q}$, and $\theta_p(E_1)$ and $\theta_p(E_2)$ are the angles respectively, it is reasonable to expect that the distribution of the pair of angles $(\theta_p(E_1), \theta_p(E_2))$ is given by the product distribution

$$\frac{4}{\pi^2}\sin^2\theta_1 \sin^2\theta_2\, d\theta_1\, d\theta_2.$$

More generally, one can consider two distinct non-CM automorphic representations and discuss their joint distribution. One would, of course, expect a similar distribution in the general case.

To prove such an assertion, we can use the formalism of Serre [185]. Using the formalism of [185], it is not difficult to show that this involves the study of certain L-series. Indeed, if both curves are non-CM and have associated Galois representations ρ_1 and ρ_2 respectively, then one needs to show that the L-series

$$L\big(s, \mathrm{Sym}^{m_1}(\rho_1) \otimes \mathrm{Sym}^{m_2}(\rho_2)\big)$$

extends to $\Re(s) \geq 1$ and does not vanish there. This looks like a difficult question to answer with the present state of knowledge. However, Harris has recently announced some progress in this direction.

If however, one of the curves has CM and corresponds to a Hecke character ψ, then one needs to study the L-series

$$L\big(s, \psi^{m_1} \otimes \mathrm{Sym}^{m_2}(\rho_2)\big)$$

and establish analytic continuation and non-vanishing in the region $\Re(s) \geq 1$. This can be done since only Hecke characters intervene, and these can be base-changed to any field by a well-known theorem of Weil [200]. It is also clear that one can take any number of CM elliptic curves and derive a similar theorem for the same reasons.

Proof of Theorem 1.1 By standard Tauberian theory, as discussed in [185], we need to show that for any irreducible representation τ of $G = \mathrm{Gal}(M/K)$, the L-function

$$L\big(s, \tau \otimes \mathrm{Sym}^m \pi\big)$$

is analytic and non-vanishing in the region $\Re(s) \geq 1$. Using Brauer induction, we write

$$\tau = \sum_i c_i \, \mathrm{Ind}_{H_i}^G \phi_i,$$

where c_i are integers, and ϕ_i is an abelian character of H_i, with H_i certain nilpotent subgroups of G. By our hypothesis, we can choose L so that L and M are disjoint and for any odd m, $\mathrm{Sym}^m \pi$ is automorphic over L. In particular, $\mathrm{Gal}(LM/L) = G$ and

$$L\big(s, \mathrm{Sym}^m \pi \otimes \tau\big) = \prod_i L\big(s, \mathrm{Sym}^m \pi \otimes \mathrm{Ind}_{H_i}^G \phi_i\big)^{c_i}.$$

Since we are viewing G as the Galois group of LM/L, we can re-write this, by Frobenius reciprocity, as

$$\prod_i L\big(s, \big(\mathrm{Ind}_{H_i}^G \big(\mathrm{Sym}^m \pi\big)\big|_{(LM)^{H_i}} \otimes \psi_i\big)\big)^{c_i},$$

where ψ_i is the Hecke character corresponding to ϕ_i via Artin reciprocity. As $(\mathrm{Sym}^m \rho)|_L$ is automorphic by our hypothesis, $(\mathrm{Sym}^m \pi)|_{LM}$ is automorphic by the theory of base change applied to the solvable extension LM/L. As in Step 1 of Taylor's theorem, we deduce that $(\mathrm{Sym}^m \pi)|_{(LM)^{H_i}}$ is automorphic over $(LM)^{H_i}$ by an application of the Arthur–Clozel theory. Since ψ_i is a Hecke character, we deduce that

$$\big(\mathrm{Sym}^m \pi\big)\big|_{(LM)^{H_i}} \otimes \psi_i$$

is automorphic over $(LM)^{H_i}$. Consequently, by the invariance of L-series under induction, we deduce that

$$L\big(s, \mathrm{Ind}_{H_i}^G \big(\big(\mathrm{Sym}^m \pi\big)\big|_{(LM)^{H_i}} \otimes \psi_i\big)\big)$$

is automorphic. Thus, it is analytic and non-vanishing for $\Re(s) \geq 1$. This proves that

$$L\big(s, \big(\mathrm{Sym}^m \pi\big) \otimes \chi\big)$$

extends to an analytic function for $\Re(s) \geq 1$ and does not vanish there. This proves the required assertion for m odd. For m even, we proceed as before, by induction to obtain the desired result. This completes the proof of Theorem 1.1. □

8 Concluding Remarks

We conclude this section with an alternate argument in the case that M/K is a nilpotent Galois extension which is simpler. In future variations, this alternate argument may be useful.

By standard Tauberian theory, as discussed in [185], we need to show that for any irreducible representation τ of $\mathrm{Gal}(\overline{K}/K)$, with nilpotent image, the L-function

$$L\big(s, \tau \otimes \mathrm{Sym}^m \pi\big)$$

is analytic and non-vanishing in the region $\Re(s) \geq 1$. Since any irreducible representation of a finite nilpotent group is induced from an abelian character χ of a subgroup H, so

$$\tau \otimes \mathrm{Sym}^m(\pi) = \mathrm{Ind}_H^G\big(\chi \otimes \mathrm{Sym}^m(\pi)|_{L^H}\big).$$

By Arthur–Clozel, $\chi \otimes \mathrm{Sym}^m(\pi)|_{L^H}$ is automorphic. We now complete the proof as before. It is clear from the preceding arguments that if one had the automorphic induction of Hecke characters, the proof would go through for any Galois setting and not just in the nilpotent or solvable setting. Future advances in the Langlands program should translate into general theorems of Chebotarev–Sato–Tate type.

Just as in the classical case of the prime number theorem, one can ask about what error terms we may expect. It may be too early here to make statements that arise from the recent progress on potential automorphy. One would need more precise information about these fields $K_{S,T}$ before such error terms can be written down.

There is an interesting conjecture due to Akiyama and Tanigawa [5] predicting that for any $\epsilon > 0$,

$$\frac{\#\{p \leq x : \theta_p \in [\alpha, \beta]\}}{\#\{p \leq x\}} = \frac{2}{\pi} \int_\alpha^\beta \sin^2 \theta \, d\theta + O\big(x^{-1/2+\epsilon}\big). \tag{55}$$

But this was already proved by Kumar Murty [140] in 1985 assuming that the $L_m(s)$ satisfy the analogue of the Riemann hypothesis. In fact, this result makes explicit the dependence of the error term on the length of the interval $[\alpha, \beta]$. One can also go in the reverse direction. Assertion (55) is already a sufficiently strong conjecture, and one can use standard methods to deduce that it implies that every $L_m(s)$ satisfies the analogue of the Riemann hypothesis for $m \geq 1$.

ERRATUM

Erratum to: The Ramanujan τ-Function

**Erratum to: M.R. Murty, V.K. Murty, *The Mathematical Legacy of Srinivasa Ramanujan*, pp. 11–23,
DOI 10.1007/978-81-322-0770-2_2,**

Page 17: The third displayed equation should be a congruence (mod 2). It is clearer if we note $(1 - q^n)^{24} \equiv (1 - q^{8n})^3 \pmod 2$ and observe that

$$\prod_{n=1}^{\infty} \left(1 - q^{8n}\right)^3 = \sum_{m=0}^{\infty} (-1)^m (2m+1) q^{4m^2+4m} \equiv q^{4m^2+4m} \pmod 2.$$

The online version of the original chapter can be found at doi: 10.1007/978-81-322-0770-2_2.

References

1. S.D. Adhikari, A. Mukhopadhyay, Partition function congruences: some flowers and seeds from "Ramanujan's garden". Expo. Math. **19**, 193–201 (2001)
2. S. Ahlgren, Distribution of parity of the partition function in arithmetic progressions. Indag. Math. (N.S.) **10**(2), 173–181 (1999)
3. S. Ahlgren, M. Boylan, Arithmetic properties of the partition function. Invent. Math. **153**(3), 487–502 (2003)
4. S. Ahlgren, M. Boylan, Odd coefficients of weakly holomorphic modular forms. Math. Res. Lett. **15**(3), 409–418 (2008)
5. S. Akiyama, Y. Tanigawa, Calculation of values of L-functions associated to elliptic curves. Math. Comp. **68**(227), 1201–1231 (1999)
6. L. Alaoglu, P. Erdös, On highly composite and similar numbers. Trans. Am. Math. Soc. **58**, 448–469 (1944)
7. G.E. Andrews, An introduction to Ramanujan's "lost" notebook. Am. Math. Mon. **86**, 89–108 (1979)
8. G.E. Andrews, F. Garvan, Dyson's crank of a partition. Bull. Am. Math. Soc. **18**, 167–171 (1988)
9. J. Arthur, L. Clozel, *Simple Algebras, Base Change and the Advanced Theory of the Trace Formula*. Annals of Mathematics Studies, vol. 120 (Princeton University Press, Princeton, 1989)
10. E. Artin, Quadratische Körper im Gebiete der Höheren kongruenzen, I, II. Math. Z. **19**, 153–246 (1924)
11. A.O.L. Atkin, Proof of a conjecture of Ramanujan. Glasg. Math. J. **8**, 14–32 (1967)
12. A.O.L. Atkin, J. Lehner, Hecke operators on $\Gamma_0(m)$. Math. Ann. **185**, 134–160 (1970)
13. A.O.L. Atkin, H.P.F. Swinnerton-Dyer, Some properties of partitions. Proc. Lond. Math. Soc. **4**, 84–106 (1954)
14. R. Balasubramanian, J.-M. Deshouillers, F. Dress, Problème de Waring pour les bicarrés, I, Schéma de la solution. C. R. Acad. Sci. Paris Sér. I Math. **303**(4), 85–88 (1986)
15. R. Balasubramanian, J.-M. Deshouillers, F. Dress, Problème de Waring pour les bicarrés, II, Résultats axillaires pour le théorème asymptotique. C. R. Acad. Sci. Paris Sér. I Math. **303**(5), 161–163 (1986)
16. R. Balasubramanian, K. Ramachandra, The place of an identity of Ramanujan in prime number theory. Proc. Indian Acad. Sci. **83A**(4), 156–165 (1976)
17. T. Barnet-Lamb, D. Geraghty, T. Gee, The Sato–Tate conjecture for Hilbert modular forms. J. Am. Math. Soc. **24**(2), 411–469 (2011)
18. T. Barnet-Lamb, D. Geraghty, M. Harris, R. Taylor, A family of Calabi–Yau varieties and potential automorphy, II. Publ. Res. Inst. Math. **47**, 29–98 (2011)
19. B.C. Berndt, *Ramanujan's Notebooks, Part II* (Springer, Berlin, 1989)

M.R. Murty, V.K. Murty, *The Mathematical Legacy of Srinivasa Ramanujan*,
DOI 10.1007/978-81-322-0770-2, © Springer India 2013

20. B.C. Berndt, *Ramanujan's Notebooks, Part V* (Springer, Berlin, 1998)
21. B.C. Berndt, Ramanujan's congruences for the partition function modulo 5, 7 and 11. Int. J. Number Theory **3**(3), 349–354 (2007)
22. B.C. Berndt, Ramanujan reaches his hand from his grave to snatch your theorems from you. Asia Pac. Math. Newsl. **1**(2), 8–13 (2011)
23. B.C. Berndt, The chief-accountant and mathematical friend of Ramanujan, S. Narayana Aiyar. Am. Math. Mon. **118**(9), 767–776 (2011)
24. R. Blecksmith, J. Brillhart, I. Gerst, Parity results for certain partition functions and identities similar to theta function identities. Math. Comp. **48**(177), 29–38 (1987)
25. C. Breuil, B. Conrad, F. Diamond, R. Taylor, On the modularity of elliptic curves over $\mathbb{Q}$: wild 3-adic exercises. J. Am. Math. Soc. **14**(4), 843–939 (2001)
26. J. Bruinier, K. Ono, Heegner divisors, L-functions and harmonic weak Maass forms. Ann. of Math. **172**, 2135–2181 (2010)
27. J. Bruinier, K. Ono, R. Rhoades, Differential operators for harmonic weak Maass forms and the vanishing of Hecke eigenvalues. Math. Ann. **342**(3), 673–693 (2008)
28. J.H. Bruinier, K. Ono, An algebraic formula for the partition function (in press)
29. J.H. Bruinier, K. Ono, Algebraic formulas for the coefficients of half-integral weight harmonic weak Maass forms (in press)
30. H. Carayol, La conjecture de Sato–Tate (d'après Clozel, Harris, Shepherd-Barron, Taylor), Sem. Bourbaki **59**(977) (2006–2007)
31. S. Chandrasekhar, On Ramanujan, in *Ramanujan Revisited*, ed. by G.E. Andrews, et al. (Academic Press, San Diego, 1988)
32. K. Chandrasekharan, R. Narasimhan, Functional equations with multiple gamma factors and the average order of arithmetical functions. Ann. of Math. **76**(2), 93–136 (1962)
33. S. Chowla, Congruence properties of partitions. J. Lond. Math. Soc. **9**, 247 (1934)
34. S. Chowla, A. Selberg, On Epstein's zeta function. J. Reine Angew. Math. **227**, 86–110 (1967)
35. L. Clozel, M. Harris, R. Taylor, Automorphy of some ℓ-adic lifts of automorphic mod ℓ Galois representations. Publ. Math. IHES **108**(1), 1–182 (2008)
36. J. Cogdell, H. Kim, M.R. Murty, *Lectures on Automorphic L-functions* (Am. Math. Soc., Providence, 2004)
37. J. Cogdell, P. Michel, On the complex moments of symmetric power L-functions at $s = 1$. Int. Math. Res. Not. **31**, 1561–1617 (2004)
38. P. Deligne, Formes modulaires et représentations ℓ-adiques, in *Séminaire Bourbaki, Exposé 355*. Lecture Notes in Mathematics, vol. 179 (Springer, Berlin, 1971)
39. P. Deligne, La conjecture de Weil, I. Publ. Math. IHES **43**, 273–307 (1974)
40. P. Deligne, La conjecture de Weil, II. Publ. Math. IHES **52**, 138–252 (1980)
41. M. Deuring, Die Typen der Multiplikatorenringe elliptischer Funktionenkörper. Abh. Math. Zem. Hansischen Univ. **14**, 197–272 (1941)
42. M. Dewar, M.R. Murty, A derivation of the Hardy–Ramanujan formula from an arithmetic formula. Proc. Amer. Math. Soc. (in press)
43. W. Duke, Continued fractions and modular functions. Bull. Am. Math. Soc. **42**(2), 137–162 (2005)
44. D. Duverney, K. Nishioka, K. Nishioka, I. Shiokawa, Transcendence of Jacobi's theta series and related results, in *Number Theory*, Eger, 1996 (de Gruyter, Berlin, 1998), pp. 157–168
45. F. Dyson, A walk through Ramanujan's garden, in *Ramanujan Revisited* (Academic Press, Boston, 1988), pp. 7–28
46. P.D.T.A. Elliott, *Probabilistic Number Theory, I, II* (Springer, New York, 1980)
47. W.J. Ellison, Waring's problem. Am. Math. Mon. **78**, 10–36 (1971)
48. P. Erdös, On an elementary proof of some asymptotic formulas in the theory of partitions. Ann. of Math. **43**(2), 437–450 (1942)
49. P. Erdös, M. Kac, The Gaussian law of errors in the theory of additive number theoretic functions. Am. J. Math. **62**(1), 738–742 (1940)

50. P. Erdös, C. Pomerance, On the normal number of prime factors of $\phi(n)$. Rocky Mt. J. Math. **15**, 343–352 (1985)
51. T. Estermann, On the representation of a number as the sum of two products. Proc. Lond. Math. Soc. **31**(2), 123–133 (1930)
52. L. Euler, *Opera Postuma*, vol. 1, (1862), pp. 203–204
53. A. Folsom, Z.A. Kent, K. Ono, ℓ-adic properties of the partition function. Adv. Math. **229**, 1586–1609 (2012)
54. G. Frei, P. Roquette, *Emil Artin and Helmut Hasse, Die Korrespondenz 1923–1934* (Universitätsverlag, Göttingen, 2008)
55. G. Frey, Links between solutions of $A - B = C$ and elliptic curves. Lect. Notes Math. **1380**, 31–62 (1989)
56. F. Garvan, New combinatorial interpretations of Ramanujan's partition congruences mod 5, 7, and 11. Trans. Am. Math. Soc. **305**, 47–77 (1988)
57. F. Garvan, D. Kim, D. Stanton, Cranks and t-cores. Invent. Math. **101**, 1–17 (1990)
58. S. Gelbart, H. Jacquet, A relation between automorphic forms on $GL(2)$ and $GL(3)$. Proc. Natl. Acad. Sci. USA **73**, 3348–3350 (1976)
59. E. Ghate, On monomial relations between Eisenstein series. J. Ramanujan Math. Soc. **15**(2), 71–79 (2000)
60. C.C. Grosjean, Disproving a conjecture about an asymptotic formula of Ramanujan involving the divisor sums. Simon Stevin **53**, 39–70 (1979)
61. B. Gross, On an identity of Chowla and Selberg. J. Number Theory **11**(3), 344–348 (1979). S. Chowla Anniversary issue
62. E. Grosswald, Die Werte der Riemannschen Zetafunktion an ungeranden Argumentstellen. Nachr. Akad. Wiss., Gottinger Math.-Phys. Kl. **2**, 9–13 (1970)
63. A. Grothendieck, The cohomology theory of abstract algebraic varieties. Proc. Int. Congr. Math. Edinburgh, 103–118 (1958)
64. S. Gun, M.R. Murty, P. Rath, Algebraic independence of values of modular forms. Int. J. Number Theory **7**, 1065–1074 (2011)
65. S. Gun, M.R. Murty, P. Rath, Transcendental values of certain Eichler integrals. Bull. Lond. Math. Soc. **43**(5), 939–952 (2011)
66. H. Halberstam, An asymptotic formula in the theory of numbers. Trans. Am. Math. Soc. **84**, 338–351 (1957)
67. G.H. Hardy, *Ramanujan: Twelve Lectures on Subjects Suggested by his Life and Work*, 3rd edn. (Chelsea, New York, 1978)
68. G.H. Hardy, J.E. Littlewood, Contributions to the theory of the Riemann zeta function and the distribution of primes. Acta Math. **41**, 119–196 (1918)
69. G.H. Hardy, S. Ramanujan, The normal number of prime factors of a number n. Q. J. Math. **48**, 76–92 (1917)
70. G.H. Hardy, S. Ramanujan, Asymptotic formulae for the distribution of integers of various types. Proc. Lond. Math. Soc. **16**(2), 112–132 (1917)
71. G.H. Hardy, S. Ramanujan, Asymptotic formulae in combinatory analysis. Proc. Lond. Math. Soc. **17**(2), 75–115 (1918)
72. G.H. Hardy, E.W. Wright, *Introduction to the Theory of Numbers*, 5th edn. (Oxford University Press, London, 1979)
73. M. Harris, N. Shepherd-Barron, R. Taylor, A family of Calabi–Yau varieties and potential automorphy. Preprint available at www.math.harvard.edu/~rtaylor
74. H. Hasse, Beweis des Analogons der Riemannschen Vermutung für die Artinschen und F.K. Shmidtschen Kongruenzzetafunktionen in gewissen zykischen Fällen, Vorläufige Mitteilung. Nachr. Ges. Wiss. Göttingen I. Math.-Phys. Kl. Fachgr. I Math. **42**, 253–262 (1933)
75. E. Hecke, Eine neue Art von Zetafunktionen und ihre Beziehungen zur Verteilung der Primzalhen, I. Math. Z. **1**, 357–376 (1918)
76. E. Hecke, Eine neue Art von Zetafunktionen und ihre Beziehungen zur Verteilung der Primzahlen, II. Math. Z. **6**, 11–51 (1920)

77. E. Hecke, Die primzahlen in der theorie der elliptischen modulfunktionen, in *Mathematische Werke*, Paper 32 (Vandenhoeck & Ruprecht, Gortingen, 1983), p. 577
78. D.R. Hickerson, A proof of the mock theta conjectures. Invent. Math. **94**, 639–660 (1988)
79. D.R. Hickerson, On the seventh order mock theta functions. Invent. Math. **94**, 661–677 (1988)
80. D. Hilbert, Beweis für die Darstellbarkeit der ganzen Zahlen durn eine feste Anzahl n-ter Potenzen (Waringsches Problem). Math. Ann. **67**, 281–300 (1909)
81. M.D. Hirschhorn, M.V. Subbarao, On the parity of $p(n)$. Acta Arith. **50**(4), 351–355 (1988)
82. G. Hoheisel, Primzahlproblem in der Analysis. Berlin Math. Ges. Sitzungsber, 550–558 (1930)
83. L.K. Hua, *Introduction to Number Theory* (Springer, Berlin, 1982)
84. A.E. Ingham, Some asymptotic formulae in the theory of numbers. Journal of the London Mathematical Society, 202–208 (1927)
85. A.E. Ingham, A note on Riemann's ζ-function and Dirichlet's L-functions. J. Lond. Math. Soc. **5**, 107–112 (1930)
86. H. Jacquet, R.P. Langlands, *Automorphic Forms on GL*(2). Lecture Notes in Mathematics, vol. 114 (Springer, Berlin, 1970)
87. H. Jacquet, I.I. Piatetski-Shapiro, J. Shalika, Rankin–Selberg convolutions. Am. J. Math. **105**, 367–464 (1983)
88. H. Jacquet, J. Shalika, A non-vanishing theorem for zeta functions of GL_n. Invent. Math. **38**(1), 1–16 (1976/77)
89. H. Jacquet, J. Shalika, On Euler products and the classification of automorphic representations I. Am. J. Math. **103**, 499–558 (1981)
90. M. Kaneko, D. Zagier, A generalized Jacobi theta function and quasimodular forms, in *The Moduli Space of Curves*. Progress in Mathematics, vol. 129 (Birkhäuser, Boston, 1995), pp. 165–172
91. N. Katz, An overview of Deligne's proof of the Riemann hypothesis for varieties over finite fields. Proc. Symp. Pure Math. **28**, 275–305 (1976)
92. A. Kempner, Bemerkungen zum Waringschen Problem. Math. Ann. **72**(3), 387–399 (1912)
93. C. Khare, Serre's modularity conjecture: the level one case. Duke Math. J. **134**(3), 557–589 (2006)
94. C. Khare, J.-P. Wintenberger, Serre's modularity conjecture, I and II. Invent. Math. **178**(3), 485–504 (2009) (and 505–586)
95. H. Kim, P. Sarnak, Refined estimates towards the Ramanujan and Selberg conjectures in the appendix to functoriality for the exterior square of GL_4 and the symmetric fourth of GL_2. J. Am. Math. Soc. **16**(1), 139–183 (2003)
96. H. Kim, F. Shahidi, Functorial products for $GL_2 \times GL_3$ and functorial symmetric cube for GL_2. C. R. Acad. Sci. Paris Sér. I Math. **331**(8), 599–604 (2000)
97. H. Kim, F. Shahidi, Functorial products for $GL_2 \times GL_3$ and the symmetric cube for GL_2. Ann. of Math. (2) **155**(3), 837–893 (2002).
98. H.D. Kloosterman, Asymptotische Formeln für die Fourierkoeffizienten ganzer Modulformen. Abh. Math. Semin. Univ. Hamb. **5**, 338–352 (1927)
99. S. Knapowski, P. Turan, Comparative prime number theory, I–VIII. Acta Math. Hung. **13**, 299–364 (1962)
100. O. Kölberg, Note on the parity of the partition function. Math. Scand. **7**, 377–378 (1959)
101. C. Krattenthaler, T. Rivoal, W. Zudilin, Séries hypergéométriques basiques, q analogues des valeurs de la fonction zeta et séries d'Eisenstein. J. Inst. Math. Juissieu **5**(1), 53–79 (2006)
102. N.V. Kuznetsov, The Petersson conjecture for cusp forms of weight zero and the Linnik conjecture: sums of Kloosterman sums. Mat. Sb. (N.S.) **111(153)**(3), 334–383 (1980), 479 (in Russian)
103. J. Lagarias, An elementary problem equivalent to the Riemann hypothesis. Am. Math. Mon. **109**, 534–543 (2002)
104. D.B. Lahiri, On Ramanujan's function $\tau(n)$ and the divisor function $\sigma_k(n)$, I. Bull. Calcutta Math. Soc. **38**, 193–206 (1946). II, **39**, 33–52 (1947)

105. E. Landau, Über einige ältere Vermutungen und Behauptungen in der Primzahltheorie. Math. Zeit. **1**, 1–24 (1918) (and 213–219)
106. S. Lang, *Introduction to Modular Forms* (Springer, Berlin, 1976)
107. S. Lang, *Elliptic Functions*, 2nd edn. (Springer, New York, 1987)
108. R. Langlands, Problems in the theory of automorphic forms, in *Lectures in Modern Analysis and Applications*, ed. by R. Dudley, Springer Lecture Notes in Mathematics, vol. 170 (1970), pp. 18–86
109. D. Lanphier, Maass operators and van der Pol-type identities for Ramanujan's tau function. Acta Arith. **113**, 157–167 (2004)
110. D.H. Lehmer, Ramanujan's function $\tau(n)$. Duke Math. J. **10**, 483–492 (1943)
111. D.H. Lehmer, The vanishing of Ramanujan's function $\tau(n)$. Duke Math. J. **14**, 429–433 (1947)
112. J.E. Littlewood, Distribution des nombres premiers. C. R. Acad. Sci. Paris **158**, 1869–1872 (1914)
113. Y.R. Liu, M.R. Murty, The Turán sieve method and some of its applications. J. Ramanujan Math. Soc. **14**(1), 21–35 (1999)
114. Y.R. Liu, M.R. Murty, Sieve methods in combinatorics. J. Comb. Theory, Ser. A **111**(1), 1–23 (2005)
115. Y.R. Liu, M.R. Murty, A weighted Turán sieve method. J. Number Theory **116**(1), 1–20 (2006)
116. N. Lygeros, O. Rozier, A new solution to the equation $\tau(p) \equiv 0 \pmod{p}$. J. Integer Seq. **13**(7) (2010). Article 10.7.4, 11 pp
117. H. Maass, Über eine neue Art von nichtanalytischen automorphen Funktionen und die Bestimmung Dirichletscher Reihen durch Funktionalgleichungen. Math. Ann. **121**, 141–182 (1944)
118. H. Maass, *Siegel Modular Forms and Dirichlet Series*. Lecture Notes in Mathematics, vol. 216 (Springer, Berlin, 1971)
119. K. Mahler, On the fractional parts of the powers of a rational number II. Mathematika **4**, 122–124 (1957)
120. H.B. Mann, A proof of the fundamental theorem on the density of sums of sets of positive integers. Ann. of Math. **43**(3), 523–527 (1942)
121. F. Martin, E. Royer, Formes modulaires et périodes, in *Formes modulaires et transcendance*, Sémin. Congr., vol. 12 (Soc. Math. France, Paris, 2005), pp. 1–17
122. D.W. Masser, *Elliptic Functions and Transcendence*. Lecture Notes in Mathematics, vol. 437 (Springer, Berlin, 1975)
123. B. Mazur, Controlling our errors. Nature **443**, 38–40 (2006)
124. B. Mazur, Finding meaning in error terms. Bull. Am. Math. Soc. **45**, 185–228 (2008)
125. C. Moeglin, J.-L. Waldspurger, Le spectre résiduel de $GL(n)$. Ann. Sci. Éc. Norm. Super. (4) **22**, 605–674 (1989)
126. L.J. Mordell, On Ramanujan's empirical expansions of modular functions. Proc. Camb. Philos. Soc. **19**, 117–124 (1920)
127. Y. Motohashi, The binary additive divisor problem. Ann. Sci. Éc. Norm. Super. **27**, 529–572 (1994)
128. M.R. Murty, Oscillations of Fourier coefficients of modular forms. Math. Ann. **262**, 431–446 (1983)
129. M.R. Murty, On the estimation of eigenvalues of Hecke operators. Rocky Mt. J. Math. **15**(2), 521–533 (1985)
130. M.R. Murty, Recent developments in the Langlands program. C. R. Math. Rep. Sci. Canada **24**(2), 33–54 (2002)
131. M.R. Murty, *Problems in Analytic Number Theory*, 2nd edn. (Springer, New York, 2005)
132. M.R. Murty, V.K. Murty, Prime divisors of Fourier coefficients of modular forms. Duke Math. J. **51**, 57–76 (1984)
133. M.R. Murty, V.K. Murty, An analogue of the Erdös–Kac theorem for Fourier coefficients of modular forms. Indian J. Pure Appl. Math. **15**, 1090–1101 (1984)

134. M.R. Murty, V.K. Murty, T.N. Shorey, Odd values of the Ramanujan τ-function. Bull. Soc. Math. Fr. **115**(3), 391–395 (1987)
135. M.R. Murty, P. Rath, Introduction to transcendental number theory (in press)
136. M.R. Murty, F. Saidak, Non-abelian generalizations of the Erdös–Kac theorem. Can. J. Math. **56**(2), 356–372 (2004)
137. M.R. Murty, C. Smyth, R. Wang, Zeros of Ramanujan polynomials. J. Ramanujan Math. Soc. **26**, 107–125 (2011)
138. M.R. Murty, C. Weatherby, Special values of the gamma function at CM points. Int. J. Number Theory (in press)
139. V.K. Murty, On the Sato–Tate conjecture, in *Number Theory Related to Fermat's Last Theorem*. Cambridge, MA, 1981. Progress in Mathematics, vol. 26 (Birkhäuser, Boston, 1982), pp. 195–205
140. V.K. Murty, Explicit formulae and the Lang–Trotter conjecture. Rocky Mt. J. Math. **15**(2), 535–551 (1985)
141. V.K. Murty, Ramanujan and Harish-Chandra. Math. Intell. **15**(2), 33–39 (1993)
142. Yu.V. Nesterenko, Algebraic independence for values of Ramanujan functions, in *Introduction to Algebraic Independence Theory*. Lecture Notes in Math., vol. 1752 (Springer, Berlin, 2001), pp. 27–46
143. D.J. Newman, Evaluation of the constant in the formula for the number of partitions of n. Am. J. Math. **73**(3), 599–601 (1951)
144. M. Newman, Periodicity modulo m and divisibility properties of the partition function. Trans. Am. Math. Soc. **97**(2), 225–236 (1960)
145. J.L. Nicolas, Répartition des nombres hautement composés de Ramanujan. Can. J. Math. **23**, 116–130 (1971)
146. J.L. Nicolas, Grandes valeurs des fonctions arithmétiques. Sém. Delange-Pisot-Poitou, Paris, no. G20, 5 p. (1974/75)
147. J.L. Nicolas, On highly composite numbers, in *Ramanujan Revisited*, ed. by G. Andrews, et al. (Academic Press, San Diego, 1988), pp. 215–244
148. J.L. Nicolas, I.Z. Rusza, A. Sarkozy, Partition function (with an appendix by J.-P. Serre). J. Number Theory **73**, 292–317 (1998)
149. D. Niebur, A formula for Ramanujan's τ-function. Ill. J. Math. **19**, 448–449 (1975)
150. K. Ono, Parity of the partition function in arithmetic progressions. J. Reine Angew. Math. **472**, 1–15 (1996)
151. K. Ono, *The Web of Modularity: Arithmetic of the Coefficients of Modular Forms and q-Series*. CBMS Regional Conference Series in Mathematics, vol. 102 (Am. Math. Soc., Providence, 2004)
152. K. Ono, Unearthing the visions of a master, in *Harmonic Maass forms and Number Theory*. Current Developments in Mathematics, (2008), pp. 347–454
153. T.R. Parkin, D. Shanks, On the distribution of parity in the partition function. Math. Comp. **21**, 466–480 (1967)
154. H. Petersson, Theorie der automorphen formen beliebiger reeler Dimension und ihre Darstellung durch eine neue art Poincaréscher Reihen. Math. Ann. **103**, 346–369 (1930)
155. S.S. Pillai, On Waring's problem $g(6) = 73$. Proc. Indian Acad. Sci. **12A**, 30–40 (1940)
156. S.S. Pillai, *Collected Papers*, vol. 1, ed. by R. Balasubramanian, R. Thangadurai (Ramanujan Mathematical Society, India, 2010), p. xiii
157. H. Rademacher, On the expansion of the partition function in a series. Ann. of Math. **44**, 416–422 (1943)
158. S. Ramanujan, On the product $\prod_{n=0}^{\infty}[1 + (\frac{x}{a+nd})^3]$. J. Indian Math. Soc. **7**, 209–211 (1915)
159. S. Ramanujan, Some definite integrals. Messenger of Math. **44**, 10–18 (1915)
160. S. Ramanujan, Highly composite numbers. Proc. Lond. Math. Soc. **14**(2), 347–400 (1915)
161. S. Ramanujan, On certain arithmetical functions. Trans. Cambridge Philos. Soc. **22**, 159–184 (1916)

162. S. Ramanujan, On certain arithmetical functions. Trans. Camb. Phil. Soc. **22**, 159–184 (1916). See also *Collected Papers*, Number 18 (AMS–Chelsea, Providence, 1962), pp. 136–192
163. S. Ramanujan, Proof of certain identities in combinatory analysis. Proc. Camb. Philos. Soc. **19**, 214–216 (1919)
164. S. Ramanujan, Some properties of $p(n)$, the number of partitions of n. Proc. Camb. Philos. Soc. **19**, 207–210 (1919)
165. S. Ramanujan, Congruence properties of partitions. Math. Z. **9**, 147–153 (1921)
166. S. Ramanujan, Highly composite numbers, annotated and with a foreword by Jean-Louis Nicolas and Guy Robin. Ramanujan J. **1**(2), 119–153 (1997)
167. B. Ramakrishnan, B. Sahu, Rankin–Cohen brackets and van der Pol-type identities for the Ramanujan τ-function. Preprint (2007)
168. O. Ramaré, On Snirel'man's constant. Ann. Sc. Norm. Super. Pisa Cl. Sci. (4), **22**(4), 645–706 (1995)
169. R.A. Rankin, Contributions to the theory of Ramanujan's function $\tau(n)$ and similar arithmetical functions, II, the order of the Fourier coefficients of integral modular forms. Proc. Camb. Philos. Soc. **35**, 357–372 (1939)
170. R.A. Rankin, The construction of automorphic forms from the derivatives of a given form. J. Indian Math. Soc. **20**, 103–116 (1956)
171. R.A. Rankin, *Modular Forms and Functions* (Cambridge University Press, Cambridge, 1977)
172. K. Ribet, From the Taniyama–Shimura conjecture to Fermat's last theorem. Ann. Fac. Sci. Toulouse Ser. 5 **11**(1), 116–139 (1990)
173. T. Rivoal, La fonction zeta de Riemann prend une infinité de valeurs irrationelles aux entiers impairs. C. R. Acad. Sci. Paris Sér. I Math. **331**(4), 267–270 (2000)
174. G. Robin, Estimation de la fonction de Tchebycheff θ sur le k-ieme nombre premier et grandes valeurs de la fonction $\omega(n)$ nombre de diviseurs premiers de n. Acta Arith. **42**, 367–389 (1983)
175. L.J. Rogers, Second memoir on the expansion of certain infinite products. Proc. Lond. Math. Soc. **25**(1), 318–343 (1894)
176. P. Sarnak, Non-vanishing of L-functions on $\Re(s) = 1$, in *Contributions to Automorphic Forms, Geometry, and Number Theory* (Johns Hopkins University Press, Baltimore, 2004), pp. 719–732
177. I. Schur, Ein Beitrag zur additiven Zahlentheorie und zur Theorie der Kettenbruche. Berliner Sitzungsber. **23**, 301–321 (1917)
178. A. Selberg, Über einge arithmetische identitäten. Avh. Norske Vidensk. Akad. Oslo **1**(8), (1936), 23s
179. A. Selberg, Über die Fourierkoeffizienten elliptischer Modulformen negativer Dimension, Neuvième Congrès des Mathematiciens Scandinaves, Helsingfors, 1938 (1939), pp. 320–322
180. A. Selberg, On the estimation of Fourier coefficients of modular forms, in *Proc. Symp. Pure Math.*, vol. 8 (Amer. Math. Soc., Providence, 1965), pp. 1–15
181. A. Selberg, Reflections around the Ramanujan centenary, in *Collected Papers*, vol. 1 (Springer, Berlin, 1989)
182. J.-P. Serre, Zeta and L-functions, in *Arithmetic Algebraic Geometry*. Proc. Conf. Purdue University (Harper & Row, New York, 1963), pp. 82–92
183. J.-P. Serre, *A Course in Arithmetic*. Graduate Texts in Mathematics, vol. 7 (Springer, New York, 1973)
184. J.-P. Serre, Sur les répresentations modulaires de degré 2 de Gal($\overline{\mathbb{Q}}/\mathbb{Q}$). Duke Math. J. **54**, 179–230 (1987)
185. J.-P. Serre, *Abelian ℓ-Adic Representations and Elliptic Curves*. Research Notes in Mathematics, vol. 7 (AK Peters, Wellesley, 1998)
186. I.R. Shafarevich, On certain tendencies in the development of mathematics. Math. Intell. **3**(4), 182–184 (1980/81)

187. F. Shahidi, On certain L-functions. Am. J. Math. **103**, 297–355 (1981)
188. G. Shimura, On the holomorphy of certain Dirichlet series. Proc. Lond. Math. Soc. (3) **31**(1), 79–98 (1975)
189. G. Shimura, The special values of the zeta functions associated with cusp forms. Commun. Pure Appl. Math. **29**, 783–804 (1976)
190. G. Shimura, Differential operators, holomorphic projections, and singular forms. Duke Math. J. **76**, 141–173 (1994)
191. T. Shioda, On elliptic modular surfaces. J. Math. Soc. Jpn. **24**, 20–59 (1972)
192. M.V. Subbarao, Some remarks on the partition function. Am. Math. Mon. **73**, 851–854 (1966)
193. J. Tate, Algebraic cycles and poles of zeta functions, in *Arithmetic Algebraic Geometry*, ed. by F.G. Schilling (Harper & Row, New York, 1965), pp. 93–110
194. R. Taylor, Automorphy of some ℓ-adic lifts of automorphic mod ℓ representations, II. Publ. Math. IHES **108**(1), 183–239 (2008)
195. P.L. Tchebycheff, Lettre de M. le professeur Tchebycheff à M. Fuss sur un nouveau théorème relatif aux nombres premiers dans la forme $4n+1$ et $4n+3$. Bull. Cl. Phys.-Math. Acad. St. Petersburg **11**, 208 (1853)
196. P. Turan, On a theorem of Hardy and Ramanujan. J. Lond. Math. Soc. **9**, 274–276 (1934)
197. R.C. Vaughan, *The Hardy–Littlewood Method*, 2nd. edn. Cambridge Tracts in Mathematics (Cambridge University Press, Cambridge, 1997)
198. A. Walfisz, *Weylsche Exponential Summen in der Neueren Zahlentheorie* (VEB Deutscher Verlag der Wissenschaften, Berlin, 1963)
199. G.N. Watson, Ramanujan's vermutung über zerfällungsanzahlen. J. Reine Angew. Math. **179**, 97–128 (1938)
200. A. Weil, *Dirichlet Series and Automorphic Forms*. Springer Lecture Notes, vol. 189, (Springer, Berlin, 1971)
201. A. Weil, Two lectures on number theory, past and present. Enseign. Math. **20**, 87–110 (1974)
202. A. Wieferich, Beweis des Satzes, das sich eine jede ganze Zahl als Summe von höchstens neun positiven Kuben darstellen lässt. Math. Ann. **66**(1), 95–101 (1909)
203. S. Wigert, Sur l'ordre de grandeur du nombre de diviseurs d'un entire. Ark. Mat. **3**(18), 1–9 (1907)
204. A. Wiles, Modular elliptic curves and Fermat's last theorem. Ann. of Math. **141**(3), 443–551 (1995)
205. H. Yoshida, An analogue of the Sato–Tate conjecture. Invent. Math. **19**, 261–277 (1973)
206. D. Zagier, Ramanujan's mock theta functions and their applications, (d'après Zwegers and Bringmann-Ono). Sem. Bourbaki **60**(986) (2007)
207. D. Zagier, Elliptic Modular Forms and Their Applications, in *The 1–2–3 of Modular Forms*. Universitext (Springer, Berlin, 2008), pp. 1–103

Index

M.R. Murty, V.K. Murty, *The Mathematical Legacy of Srinivasa Ramanujan*,
DOI 10.1007/978-81-322-0770-2, © Springer India 2013